UNCHARTED

THE PIRATE & HER PRINCESS
BOOK ONE

ALLI TEMPLE

Copyright © 2021 by Alli Temple
Uncharted
All rights reserved.
eBook ISBN 978-1-7772451-1-5
Paperback ISBN 978-1-7772451-3-9

No part of this book may be reproduced in any form or by any electronic or mechanical means, including information storage and retrieval systems, without written permission from the author, except for the use of brief quotations in a book review.

This is a work of fiction. Names, characters, places, and incidents are a product of the author's imagination or are used fictitiously. Any resemblance to actual events, places, or persons, living or dead, is entirely coincidental.

Cover Design: Cate Ashwood Designs
Editing: Manuela Velasco & Adam Mongoya, Tessera Editorial
Proofreading: D. Ann Williams, Tessera Editorial & Anastasia Voll, Voll Content Marketing & Editing

Content warnings

This book contains violence, largely of a piratical nature. For more details, visit the content warning page for Uncharted.

For Ana.
You believe in the magic in me, this book, and everywhere in between.

―――――

For news on future releases, join the A-List, my monthly newsletter.

PART I

THE PRINCE

1

I met the chaperone three blocks from the first checkpoint. She seemed familiar, but chaperones were all meant to be similar, so it could have been my imagination. They were shadows to protect—or to give the appearance of protecting—their lady as she went about business in the city. Never heard and barely seen. They were all older ladies with upright bearings and gray hair barely visible under a black veil, which melded seamlessly with the strict black cloaks and dresses they always wore, regardless of the time of year.

I'd heard that it was a position many women of a certain age and standing sought. The positions weren't paid, so protecting a young woman from the moral quagmires she would inevitably face when she left the house was considered a suitable way for women—even those further up the social classes—to give back to society.

My new companion was unsmiling as she dipped into her curtsy and said, "My lady."

I nodded but didn't reply, not even offering an introduction. If she'd been my personal chaperone, she would already know my name—and anyway, a decent servant would never use their mistress's name in public, or so I'd heard. Once we were underway, she trailed after me at the required two-and-a-half paces.

If the soldiers at the checkpoints located between Redmere City districts ever noticed that I had a different chaperone every time we passed through their station, they never mentioned it. More likely they were even poorer at their jobs than city gossip said, but it was to be expected, as most of them hadn't had a decent meal since the turn of the year.

"What's your destination?" a guard at the second checkpoint asked. He was young, younger than me. His face was too thin, his eyes too big. He'd be dead by winter.

"I'm going to the dressmaker's on Ruby Street."

He sneered. "Shouldn't she be coming to you? A grand lady like you shouldn't be alone in this type of neighborhood."

Firstly, I wasn't a grand lady. A grand lady's boots wouldn't swallow mud in Redmere's dismal streets the way mine did. Secondly, I'd been in worse neighborhoods. And thirdly, "I'm not alone. My brother has sent a chaperone with me." I didn't gesture toward her. Grand ladies didn't acknowledge servants, and despite my boots, I had a role to play.

The soldier narrowed his eyes as he glanced over my shoulder. "You were here earlier."

My breath fluttered in the tight cage of my corset, but I suppressed any signs of nervousness. If he recognized the chaperone as having been through with someone else that day, there would be additional questions that neither of us could answer.

"Oh for mercy's sake, Fin," an older soldier growled. "They all look the same. Let the lady pass."

The young man stiffened and, for a moment, looked like he might refuse, but the older guard took a step forward with a creak of leather. My interrogator stepped to one side, eyes dropping to the ground as he bowed.

"My lady."

I didn't reply. I could have reported them both to the City Guard for questioning my morality when I clearly had a chaperone present, and they would have been flogged for their impertinence. But a flogging was inhumane and would weaken them so they'd be dead by the end of summer instead of winter. I didn't know if things in the city would have changed by winter, but this small mercy would give us both a chance to find out.

We continued through the third checkpoint and made two turns on dark, stinking roads to Ruby Street. This part of the city was quiet. Tall, narrow buildings lined both sides of the muddy road. Smudged, hungry faces peeked out the windows at me. The prince's taxes on farms had become so severe that it had driven people into the city, searching for respite and other ways to earn a living. But there was only so much work to be had, particularly with a population so poor they couldn't afford to buy anything but the food we no longer had enough farmers to grow. People got poorer and hungrier in a continuous cycle, and the prince did nothing to stop it. The streets grew more dangerous. People disappeared if they were unwise enough to venture out after the sun went down. Sometimes their bodies were found, stripped of what few possessions they had. Others were never seen again.

Here I was, pretending I had nothing on my mind other than the fit of a new dress. By the time we reached the shop, my boots were truly soaked through.

As I reached for the door, it swung open. I nearly collided with a young woman with bright red hair that slipped out from a poorly fastened veil.

"Oh, my lady!" She bobbed a curtsy as she gripped my sleeve to steady herself. "I'm so sorry."

"Step back from Her Grace." The chaperone was very good at her job. It was a shame I couldn't ask for her again. Not everyone I'd met on these missions was as good at the charade as she was.

"Of course." The redheaded girl was still bobbing. "Of course. I'm sorry. My lady. I mean, Your Grace."

I kept my eyes fixed on the shop door. When the street was quiet again, the chaperone stepped past me to open it.

"Lady Georgina!" The dressmaker was ready for me.

I'd heard it said this dressmaker was the best in Redmere City. She was from somewhere else, though I'd never worked up the courage to ask where. Her skin was a tawny gold, noticeably darker than nearly anyone else's in Redmere. Living and economic conditions being what they were, the city wasn't exactly a draw for craftsmen and tradespeople from abroad, but the dressmaker's creations were so fine and in demand that I had no doubt she could make a life for herself here. And she'd found other ways to keep herself busy, though I wasn't supposed to know about that.

Under normal circumstances, I would have never had an opportunity to find out about the quality of her work. Dresses like hers were meant for private parties held behind closed doors, where the color and the cut couldn't be seen by the general public. We never held parties like that at home because none of Jeremy's friends were the sort to venture so far into our neighborhood. Even if I knew anyone who held parties like that, we couldn't afford a dress like the ones made in this shop.

Still, she greeted me like an old friend. "Lady Georgina, so good to see you again. Your last dress was acceptable?"

As if anyone needed more than one dress. I heard that, among the prince's inner circle, most of Redmere's morality laws were either flouted or ignored altogether. But despite Jeremy's best efforts at social climbing, we would never rise that high.

I gave her the indulgent smile that would have been expected. "Oh, yes. Perfectly lovely. I received so many compliments."

In fact, the dress had been disassembled and no doubt given to families who might sell the fabric and use the money to keep themselves alive for a few weeks longer, but we were all playing our parts.

"Excellent. I'm so pleased you've come back. This way. You will be delighted with our newest creation."

We played this charade every time I came, even though the shop was always empty. The chaperone stayed by the door and would alert us quietly if anyone entered while I was being fitted.

"I see you have a new assistant," I said as the dressmaker led me into a small room with mirrors mounted on each of the walls. A young woman waited inside. She held a dress made of so many yards of heavy fabric that she, herself so small and so thin, nearly disappeared behind it.

"Oh, yes. The last one got married, poor girl. But Celia here, her family is too poor to worry about finding her a husband, aren't they, dear? Now let's get you undressed and see if this new gown fits."

The dressmaker and her assistant helped me out of my layers of clothing. The restrictions on what a lady—especially a noble lady, even a relatively obscure one like myself—could wear in public were as effective in limiting our freedom as the rest of Redmere's laws combined. The heavy overcloak. The buttons that reached from my wrist to my elbow. The collar that ensured a lady remained graceful and modest at all times, but with the heavy gray veil meant we couldn't turn our heads farther than an inch or two in any direction. Then, the undergarments. I dreaded the stiff restriction of the corset every morning.

By comparison, the dressmaker and her assistant were relatively unencumbered. No overcloak since they were inside. The dressmaker had pinned her veil back so it would stay out of her face while she worked, while her assistant only had her hair tied up in a black scarf. No doubt she had a veil to wear when she was outside, but they were too heavy for someone who spent their day hunched over their work.

"Oh, dear," the dressmaker clucked. "You've torn the hem of this underskirt. Celia will repair it for you while we finish this fitting."

The underskirt was more than torn. It was stained from the black mud in the streets and was more patches than original fabric, but the assistant gathered it up and carried it off without a word.

Those that stayed in the country and worked the land were given a certain amount of freedom. In the city, the most women could hope for would be to quietly work for their husband, mending fishing nets or mixing healing powders. A dressmaker's apprentice—even if the dressmaker wasn't Redmerian by birth—must have seemed like a dream. Had she known what this dressmaker's true business was though, Celia might have reconsidered.

It took nearly as long to get me into the new dress as it had to get me out of my traveling clothes. I never understood why we insisted with this part of the performance since we had no spectators. It wasn't as though I would ever wear the new dress, but the dressmaker always insisted. She said the City Guard had never inspected her shop, so it was only a matter of time before they raided the entire place.

As she slipped layers of skirts over my hips and cinched and pulled the corset to her liking, I pictured a different dress.

"What are you wearing?" The little girl—if she is a little girl under all that mud—glares at me suspiciously. Her hair is long and probably brown, although it is hard to say, and she wears pants, even though my last tutor said that girls could be flogged for wearing pants now.

"It's my new dress," I say, spinning in a circle so she can see the way the skirt puffs out when I move. The sleeves are too tight, and I cannot get my arms over my head the way I would like to, but the new tutor said that little girls who want to be elegant ladies when they grow up never have any need to lift their hands over their heads.

The muddy girl sniffs, wiping her nose with the back of her hand. We are standing in the stable yard at my father's house. It is summer and has been hot for days. I do not know where she has found so much mud, but I hope she will show me.

"You can't climb trees in a dress like that," she says.

I stop spinning, enjoying how the world keeps going round and round for a little longer. "I've never climbed a tree before."

Her eyes go wide. "You haven't?"

I shake my head. She goes back to eyeing me like I am from another world. "What's your name?"

I straighten and recite the names as the tutor has taught me. "Georgina Elizabeth Millicent Cressida Wright."

She giggles. "That's a funny name. I'll call you George. My name is Lou. My brother and I were catching frogs. Do you want to see them?"

After that, we are inseparable. Climbing trees, catching frogs, terrorizing the household staff with our made-up games, and reading stories smuggled from a trunk of my mother's old things. Lou loves the tales of pirates and sea monsters. I love the ones about dragons and lost princesses. When we are together, the rest of the world doesn't matter.

"Your brother is so kind to buy you something like this," the dressmaker said.

I coughed on a laugh. Jeremy's "kindness" was present in the wet squish of my toes inside my boots.

"There." The dressmaker smoothed down the skirt and stepped back. "What do you think?"

This was always my least favorite part; the dresses were beautiful, but they made me intensely uncomfortable. My day-to-day dresses were as restrictive and shapeless as possible. Plain colors, black or gray, with no embellishments. But the dress I'd been fitted with today was the kind worn in private. They were meant for when you wanted someone to look at you, particularly a man —and I had no desire for a man to look at me in that way.

This dress was dark, but metallic threads in the seams showed off tiny flashes of color against the material. The bodice was more fitted, revealing curves that a woman—regardless of whether she was a queen or a beggar—wasn't supposed to show in public, even if every inch of my skin was still covered from my throat to my toes. The exceptions were the sleeves, which fluttered away from my elbows. I'd heard they were meant to show off an elegant lady's wrists as she ate or took a drink from a crystal glass, but I found them drafty as cool air brushed over my bare arms—and, anyway, Jeremy had sold off our crystal years ago.

"You look like a queen," the dressmaker said.

I looked ridiculous. The fine fabric, so light it felt like it floated over my skin, would never survive the walk home. It clashed terribly with the drab heaviness of my veil. Even a dressmaker who could see my naked limbs would not be allowed to see my hair.

I glanced at her reflection in the mirror. Her brows were pinched in the center.

"Is something wrong?" I asked.

She opened her mouth to speak, but then her teeth clacked shut again, and she ran her hands over the flowing length of the sleeves. "It suits you. That's all."

The assistant returned. "I've finished." She held out the underskirt for the dressmaker's inspection. She took it, running her fingers over the seams and shaking her head.

"You'll need a new one of these. We can only repair it so many more times."

Her warning was perhaps the only true thing she said to me that day.

They helped me dress again. Underskirts. Overskirts. Collar. Buttons. So many buttons.

"I'm sorry I don't have a boy to carry the dress home for you," the dressmaker said as we emerged into the shop.

"My chaperone will carry it," I said carelessly, because that was what Lady Georgina would say.

She wrapped up her creation in paper, securing it tightly with rough hemp string. She used more of both than was strictly necessary, but we all knew that these materials were hard to come by among the poor and would be put to good use.

"Thank you, Lady Georgina. I've always appreciated your business," the dressmaker said as she passed the package to the chaperone.

"You'll send the bill to my brother," I said.

"Of course." Her tiny frown was back, the faintest tremor in her brows, but it wasn't my place to ask what was bothering her. She'd be paid, though not by Jeremy. If he ever knew how much money was spent on me in dresses here, his face would turn purple with rage, but this was just another secret to keep from him. I followed the chaperone out the door.

The young soldier at the second checkpoint wasn't there as we made our way through. I hoped he was all right. It didn't need to be me that reported him. Anyone who had overheard our conversation and felt it was improper could have alerted the City Guard. We'd been through here not two hours earlier, but justice could have been enacted that swiftly. The palace tolerated no deviations and no impropriety.

As if to prove that point, the final checkpoint was abuzz as we approached it.

"They're going to hang him!" a boy shouted, running through the small crowd waiting to pass the inspection.

Two soldiers in the dark green uniforms of the City Guard were loading a bound man into a wagon. He thrashed and struggled against them, but one smashed a heavy club on the man's spine, and he cried out as he fell into the wagon.

When they were satisfied he was secured, they mounted their horses. One of them turned toward us and spoke clearly to be heard over the twenty or so people who had gathered.

"This man is a criminal. He has perverted our laws and morals. Justice will be served."

"Justice will be served," we all said in reply, because that was what we were expected to do. I'd become very good at hiding over the years. I couldn't be arrested for the thoughts in my head or the desires in my heart, but others had been taken away for not spouting the lies the Guard wanted to hear quickly enough.

"It's not true!" the man shouted from the back of the wagon. "I've done nothing wrong!"

"That's what they all say," a man near my right shoulder muttered to no one in particular. "I heard they actually found him in bed with another man. No shame. No deniability. Disgusting." He spat on the ground.

Someone shushed him. I dipped my chin to hide the flush of my cheeks behind my veil. The wagon creaked forward, heavy wooden wheels kicking up mud as it lurched away. The man continued to call out his innocence, but the crowd had already turned from him by the time the crack echoed back to us. He'd been struck again, this time hard enough to compel his silence.

It wasn't always like this. At least, that was what the old women who sat on stoops and old men who hunched over cups of strong tea would tell you. They'd say that, in their youth, Redmere had still been poor, but people had been free to dress as they pleased and earn a living any way they could, even if women had usually raised the children while men had made most of the money.

Then, the king had come. He was a younger son, and he'd poisoned his brother to take the throne. He said the country needed change, a return to something he called "societal order." Under his rule, laws were passed to define classes and the appropriate roles of men and women, and for a while, it worked. People felt they had a purpose. But the king overreached, declaring war on neighboring kingdoms, costing Redmere in both gold and lives before he finally retreated to his palace.

To refill his coffers, the king taxed anything he could. He conscripted sailors into his navy and sent them to raid ships that came too close to Redmere's shores. Some were successful. Many were never heard from again. Without husbands under the king's so-called societal order, the women and their families at home starved.

There was a rebellion when I was small. The people of the city stormed the castle. It was even rumored that men from my father's estate went to help, though my father could never openly support them or we'd have lost everything. The siege went on for weeks before the king sent mercenaries into the streets and killed any rebels they found, along with too many innocent citizens.

The king had finally died last winter. His son, Prince Beverly, led the country now, waiting for the year of mourning to be over before he could officially take the crown. If the king's rule was cruel, Beverly's was merciless. The edicts we all followed grew by the day, with a population too depleted, hungry, and frightened to resist. The mercenaries never left. They now made up the City Guard commanded by the prince to enforce laws and maintain order by any means necessary. People adapted. Struggled. Starved. They turned on their neighbors, hoping to win favor with the Guard or even a scrap of food.

But the rebellion wasn't entirely dead. Now, before the prince officially became king, was the biggest opportunity we had to take back the country.

The checkpoint line moved slowly. With the Guard's presence lingering, the soldiers were suddenly motivated to new thoroughness. Questions were asked, bags and cargo inspected. I let my veil drop over my shoulders. With so little showing, I was nearly anonymous. Just another pale face in dark fabric. It was why I could move through the city the way I did, because few people would remember me. One more girl in too many layers of fabric.

"Lady," the soldier said as I arrived at the head of the line.

"That was quite the scene," I said, trying to sound bored. If the Guard was going to be in the area with more regularity, I would need to be careful. *More* careful.

"Going home?"

"Yes. My chaperone and I have just returned from the dressmaker's."

He glanced over my shoulder at the chaperone and motioned her forward.

"What's in the package?"

"A gown for my lady," the chaperone said.

He eyed us. "You walked to the dressmaker's?"

"My brother's carriage was in use."

"Open the package, please."

I stiffened. "Surely that's not necessary."

He flushed, and his gaze dropped, but he didn't step out of my way. "I'm sorry, lady. The Guard, you saw them. There's no saying if they'll come back. I need to be seen doing my job. Please. My family needs me to do this job."

It was rare to hear it said so plainly. No one wanted to work for the prince. A checkpoint soldier was little better than a spy as far as his neighbors went. At least the fishermen in the harbor and the shoemakers in the city could be said to work for themselves. There was no such separation for those that worked the checkpoints, but money—even a little—was money, and food was scarce.

"Be quick." I motioned to the chaperone, and she released the package to him. He used a blunt, rusty knife to open the string and, like it had been under pressure, the wrapping erupted, releasing a flurry of fabric.

A single piece of creamy white paper fell to the muddy ground, and my heart stopped. The chaperone smothered a cough beside me.

How could the dressmaker be so foolish? We had rules for a reason.

The guard bent and picked the paper up from the ground. He held it at arm's length, squinted, then turned to another guard. "Can you read?"

His colleague shook his head. The guard went to another man, who also said no.

"You." The guard pointed at a man in line behind me. "Can you read?"

"I—" The man stepped back, eyes wide, complexion going pale as he was singled out. "I can."

The guard thrust the paper at him. "What does this say?"

I shivered, despite how my skin was suddenly too hot in my clothes, as I stared at the single paper that was about to condemn me.

The man glanced at me, an apology for what was about to follow, before he examined the page. His voice was halting as he read. "To Lady Georgina. A dress for a queen."

The guard frowned. "That's all?"

The man nodded quickly and handed the paper back like it would burn. The guard squinted at it again, as if now that he'd heard its contents, he'd be able to read and verify what the man had said. Eventually, he sighed, gathered the paper and the dress back up, and handed the whole thing to the chaperone without bothering to wrap it again.

"Have a good day, lady." He bowed stiffly toward me.

The chaperone and I parted ways once we were out of sight of the last checkpoint, just in front of the print shop. We didn't say anything, because neither of us was rash enough to congratulate the other. The city was full of eyes. Instead, the chaperone dropped her curtsy, clutched the dress to her chest, and disappeared down an alley as I let myself into the print shop's front door.

"George, is that you?"

"Yes." I undid the laces of my cloak and sighed as the weight dropped from my shoulders. I longed to pull off the heavy veil. The pins were digging into my scalp. But that was a liberty I wouldn't be able to enjoy until I was safe at home.

"Any trouble?"

"The City Guard arrested a man." Almost anyone who was arrested in the city was charged with immoral behavior. Public drinking, swearing, making music of any kind, speaking with an unescorted woman. *Being* an unescorted woman. These were all considered immoral. "Found him in bed with another man."

Consorting with a member of the same sex was seen as especially depraved. I shuddered at the memory of the man's stricken face as they'd loaded him into the cart. I knew what it was like to want something you could be killed for, but I'd never acted on it. Of course, the fact I couldn't even leave my own home without an escort and had no friends who would call on me went a long way in keeping me safe from my own nature.

Niall appeared as I entered the back storeroom. "Well, that was foolish of him."

"They're going to hang him."

"They don't hang people for that anymore." Indeed, there were fewer public executions these days. I'd heard the prince found them messy, which I was sure he thought was the only reason to do away with them. "He'll go to prison for the rest of his life." Niall pursed his lips. They were thin and always tinged toward blue, like he was cold and could never warm up. "Did you get his name?"

"No," I said. "And I didn't recognize him."

"Shame. Imprisoning a man for what he does in the privacy of his bedroom is barbaric, but it makes a better pamphlet if we know his name." He led me to the back room. "Now help me with these levers."

The trapdoor was a marvel of engineering; it took three levers pulled to just the right point to open it. The City Guard had inspected Niall's shop nearly a dozen times over the years, almost as if they knew they were in the right place but couldn't find the proof they needed.

We descended into the dark spare room. If the Guard ever found it, we'd be hanged despite the prince's distaste for capital punishment. The second press stood in the middle of the room. Pages hung in the air from strings, their ink drying. The pamphlets shouted their bold and treacherous headlines.

Prince Beaverly Unfairly Persecutes the Poor
Daughters Sold into Marriage for Food
A Hundred More Men Lost at Sea. When Will it End?
Stop the Tyrant Beaverly

That last one was my favorite. Niall had it specially illustrated with a caricature of the prince. His face had been drawn overly large with two great teeth pressed over his front lip, while a broad, flat tail poked out from under his robes.

I ducked behind the hinged screen set up in one corner of the dim room and began to undress. "They inspected the dress today. There was a note inside."

"What?" Niall's voice reflected all the terror I'd felt in that moment.

"It was addressed to me. She said the dress was meant for a queen."

Niall growled. "I'll have someone speak with her. She knows the risk you're already taking. Adding to it is unnecessary."

"I'm fine." My trips to the dressmakers had never earned more suspicion than the occasional lecherous glance from a soldier who hadn't had the lust starved out of him yet. I could handle myself.

"George," Niall said sternly.

I sighed. "There's always risk. But I manage." I emerged from behind the screen, suitably covered in my gray dress again, and handed him the patched underskirt. "She said we need a new one. The material is so thin, the stitches won't hold."

To prove my point, he hooked a finger in the wide hem the dressmaker's assistant had sewn and pulled. The whole thing gave way with only a moment of resistance.

A dozen sheets of paper, each one carefully folded and hidden in the skirt, fluttered to the floor.

"Now, let's see. What news here is fit to print?" Niall asked as he bent to gather them. Once upon a time, he'd tried to hide these from me, saying that it was better if we each only knew the smallest piece of the part we played in Redmere's resistance. But one afternoon about a year in, I'd gone to the dressmaker's, and her assistant had been so diligent in hiding the papers in the underskirt that Niall had missed one, and I'd only found it when I'd returned home. I'd recognized the crown's seal at the top of the page before I'd even read the first word.

"Hmm." Niall scratched his chin as he read through the pages. "There's a new tax on corn growers. As if they had any money for the old tax. Count Snowham has been dispossessed of his lands seized by the prince. No doubt Snowham's wife said something unkind about the prince's new horse. Do you know the count, George?"

I shook my head, scanning the pages that Niall dropped onto his worktable. "Not unless my brother owes him money."

"None of this is very useful. One of the prince's fastest ships was lost. It ran afoul of pirates after Captain Cinder kidnapped Lord Parrington's wife. I'm sure Parrington's wife is very pretty, but that's the third ship to go down this summer. They'll have to start blaming the losses on sea monsters soon."

"There's no such thing as sea monsters," I said.

"Do you think the prince is ready to admit defeat then?" He grinned at me, and I laughed.

"That would require him to acknowledge he'd been beaten by a woman."

There were many pirates who roamed the seas around Redmere—some former subjects, others from further afield—but Captain Cinder was the fiercest of them all. On her ship, the *Crimson Siren*, she prowled the ocean, killed men mercilessly, and dragged away their wives to parts unknown. Her legend was the sort of thing people used to frighten their children into obedience. *Eat your dinner or Captain Cinder will come for you while you're sleeping. Listen to your father or he'll sell you to Captain Cinder.*

The prince had called her an abomination to Redmerian morals and made it his mission to hunt her down. In the last few years since Cinder's legend had first reached our shores, hundreds of sailors had gone to the bottom of the ocean in pursuit of her. Still more, both simple fishing vessels and ships loaded for trade, had sunk for daring to trespass in her domain.

My best friend, Lou, had been lost at sea eight years ago. As girls, we'd read stories from books we'd hidden from my tutors, tales of daring pirates who braved storms and wicked kings to find buried treasure. But Lou's first voyage had been her last, and for years, the idea of her body trapped at the bottom of the ocean had tormented me.

I shivered. Niall, unaware of the dark turn my thoughts had taken, squinted at a new page. His breath quickened. "Oh. Oh, this is interesting."

"What is it?" I stood on my toes, trying to read over his shoulder.

"The prince is getting married." He sighed. "Poor girl. I didn't think any man in Redmere hated his daughter enough that he'd want her to be queen. We'll have to do something about that."

"We will?"

He waved me off as he read aloud. "Prince Beverly of Redmere is pleased to announce his betrothal to the future queen of Redmere. The engagement will be formally proclaimed at the Duchess of Capra's birthday celebration, with the marriage to be performed seven days later."

"That quickly?" I had no idea when the duchess's birthday was, but normally a couple had to wait two months from the date the engagement was announced. Officially, this was to give them a chance to get to know each other, but Jeremy had said once that it was so the bride's father had time to pay off the groom's debtors to avoid any unpleasantness at the wedding.

"You can do these things when you're the prince," Niall said seriously. He chittered through his teeth, mocking the rodent-like man in his caricatures.

"But who is it?"

"The prince asks that all citizens of Redmere welcome his new bride with open arms. Please join in celebrating the elevation of Lady Georgina Eliza . . ." His voice faltered.

"What?" My insides grew cold with every syllable.

Niall's eyes were glazed as he dragged his attention from the paper that now shook between his hands. "Lady Georgina Elizabeth Millicent Cressida Wright, granddaughter to the Duke of Bearford."

The secret room beneath the print shop grew quiet as we stared at each other. Niall swallowed hard and spoke first. "George, I'm so sorry."

I laughed, because what else was I supposed to do? "No. You're joking. It's a terrible one, but you must be joking."

"I'm not. It's your name." Niall crumpled the paper in his fist. "George. You're going to be the queen."

2

"You can't marry the prince," he said.

I snorted. "I know that."

"If he found out about . . ." He motioned toward the papers I'd brought.

"I know." That was only the beginning. A prince's wife would need to bear heirs, which would mean sharing a bed with the prince, and—well, sharing a bed with any man was not something I aspired to do.

"Do you think he knows already? About you? About us?" Niall asked.

How could he? You didn't marry a woman who was smuggling news from the palace. We'd always been so careful.

Over the years, I'd pieced together that the shop had a network of messengers and runners to distribute its less-than-legal wares while Niall had functioned as the bespectacled and unthreatening shopkeeper upstairs. It was illegal to speak openly against the prince and the City Guard, and Niall rarely left his shop, but he'd set the type and inked the rollers on pamphlets that called the prince a coward and a tyrant. I'd smuggled palace intelligence from the dressmaker's shop to his. If any of us were ever discovered, we would all pay for our treason.

When I launched myself at Niall, he opened his arms and held me tight.

"I'm sorry," I said.

"For what?"

"We'll be strangers, you and I. From today forward, we've never met."

Niall pushed me back, just far enough that we could see each other. I studied his face, trying to remember every last detail. The brown hair, the green eyes, the crooked tooth he tried to hide when he smiled.

"You've meant so much to me. I've learned so much. I'm sorry it has to end."

I'd met Niall in the most unlikely way. He'd been beaten and bleeding and hiding in our stables. I'd just had another fight with Jeremy and was looking for a place to escape.

When I'd helped Niall limp back to his shop, I couldn't have imagined how my life was about to change. I'd insisted on calling a doctor. Niall had protested, but the cut over his eye wouldn't stop bleeding; when he'd bled through a fourth bandage, he'd relented. But I'd seen the silent plea in his eyes when the doctor had asked what had happened to him. I'd stepped in, smoothly lying that we were husband and wife out for a walk when a thief had tried to rob us. Niall had heroically protected me and earned a beating in reward.

It only took one lie to sweep me up into all this. It had been thrilling to have some power after being subject to the whims of the men around me for so long.

Now, those adventures were over. In Redmere, a woman couldn't refuse the man her family chose for her as a husband—and I could only assume this was my grandfather's doing, since it was his name in the official proclamation. At best, she would be shunned and made homeless. At worst . . .

I couldn't imagine what the consequences would be to refuse a prince, even one as horrible as Beverly.

"Goodbye." I brushed my fingers above his eyebrow, arched more sharply than the other after the doctor's stitches.

"Goodbye?" Niall's other brow rose to meet its partner.

"What other choice is there? It's over for me."

Niall snorted. "You can't marry him. No matter what you think, he'll find out about what we've done here eventually, and I can't—I won't let him hurt you. You can't marry him."

"What else can I do?"

He smiled crookedly. "You have to leave."

My pulse pounded. "I don't have anywhere to go." I had no money in my name, no friends outside the city. I didn't even have a horse of my own in Jeremy's stables.

"Do you think printing is the only thing I do?" He put a hand on my shoulder. "You're not as friendless as you think. I can get you out of here."

"How?"

He shook his head and tsked. "We don't ask questions. You know the rules."

I trusted Niall more than I had anyone since Lou.

"I'll come back tomorrow," I said.

"What? No. We have to get you out tonight."

I shook my head. "I have to go home first."

"Home? George, that's not your home."

It wasn't. Had never been so. Not since the day Jeremy's carriage had rolled up at the school and he'd told me to get in without even looking at me.

But it was where my bracelet was.

I stomp up to my room with all the twelve-year-old fury I can muster and slam the door. Not that there is anyone to come after me and tell me to stop behaving like a child. My father is gone, away on business that somehow never makes us money and only seems to make him sadder and thinner. Even the tutor is gone since I will be leaving for school next week. It is only me in the house, with the servants who make sure I get fed a few times a day and otherwise do not speak to me.

She is gone. The wagon that will carry Lou to the city has disap-

peared up the road. I watched her from the gate, trying to be brave as she got smaller and smaller, but once she was out of sight, I suddenly felt lonelier than I ever had in my entire life.

I cry into my pillow for a while. I read a book last year—most of it anyway, until the tutor found it and took it away from me—where a girl loses the boy she loves when he is kidnapped by a dragon, and she cries just like this, inconsolable into her pillow.

Except it turns out that when no one comes to tell you that everything will be all right and to stop crying, weeping gets a little boring after a while.

I burrow under the blankets, my hands stuffed under my pillow, and that is when I find it, wrapped in a little bit of plain fabric—the thin metal circle and the letter.

"Georgie,

If my father finds I spent all the money I was supposed to use on food for the journey to Redmere City, he'll most likely beat me, so I can't give this to you in person. The tinsmith in town made it. I want you to wear it and think of me. I will come back for you. We will be together.

Your best friend,

Lou"

I wear the bracelet every day, hiding it under the sleeve of my school uniform. I never take it off. When word comes that Lou's ship has been lost and she has drowned, the bracelet is the only thing that keeps me anchored to the world as grief drags me to the bottom of the ocean.

"I'll be back tomorrow before the sun comes up. I promise." I kissed his cheek, even though that small gesture was considered illegal if anyone saw. Once, Niall had asked me to marry him. We both knew it was impossible. Redmerian law said a woman couldn't choose a husband on her own. Besides, Niall was too good a man to have a wife who didn't love him the way he deserved.

He didn't look happy, but he hugged me once more. "Please be careful."

I squeezed his shoulder. "Jeremy's staying with friends. If it weren't for the curfews, I'd come back tonight." During the day, the print shop was close enough that I could go from the house to the shop with little chance of being stopped. Once the sun was down though, a lady couldn't be outdoors without her husband, brother, or father. But the moment a shaft of light peered over the horizon in the morning, I would be back here.

THE LANTERN that glowed above the front door should have been my first indication of trouble, but I was so busy reeling from the prospect of my future that I didn't notice.

Queen? Who thought I would make a good queen? There were fishwives who would be better choices.

Not that my grandfather would know that. I hadn't seen him in fifteen years. My mother's family was one of the oldest and most well regarded in Redmere, and they'd never approved when my mother had married my father—an obscure country count with no standing at court. My grandmother was a cousin of the king's, and his estate was said to be the largest among the dukes. Perhaps he thought to salvage what he could from a decades-old love match after all. A princess in the family would be quite the achievement.

I opened the door and stepped inside, throwing off my cloak and handing it to Ashley, our doorman. "I'll be taking dinner in my room."

"Your brother wants to see you."

"What?"

He sneered. He was an older man with patchy hair in a sickly brownish yellow that always looked like it was molting. Ashley didn't think much of women in general and me specifically.

"Your brother is in the dining room."

I went still. Jeremy had left the day before to "visit friends." What that actually meant was that he would be losing huge sums of money gambling. He'd won, but mostly lost, several fortunes over the years, including his own, even though gambling was forbidden. But if you knew where to look or who to ask—and Jeremy did—you could find a game of cards or a weekend party in a house with heavy shutters. His most recent announcement that he was going out was the reason Niall and I had planned to send me to the dressmaker's today.

I glanced at Ashley, who still held my things. I could snatch them back, run out into the street, and take my chances with the City Guard patrols that came out at dusk to ensure curfews were being observed. It wasn't far to the print shop, but there was no guarantee I wouldn't be seen or that Jeremy wouldn't send Ashley after me. I couldn't lead them to Niall.

I lifted my chin and said, "Thank you, Ashley." His lip curled as he bowed, but he didn't say anything else as he departed.

I walked toward the dining room, also well-lit. Jeremy made himself comfortable when he gave no thought for others.

A floorboard creaked under my foot, and he said, "Georgina."

There were days I was sure my brother had forgotten I lived in this house. Weeks when I was certain he didn't even remember my name. And yet today, of all days, he knew the sound of my footsteps.

Jeremy sat at one end of the table. He wore a high-collared shirt and a heavy coat with jet buttons. The law required only that a man's throat and wrists be covered, but Jeremy had never been one for simplicity.

"You called?"

"Don't just stand there. Sit. We're having dinner."

We were? We never had dinner. Ever. Not even on the first night, when I'd carried all my worldly possessions to my new bedroom myself because my brother had lost all his money and let the household servants go the week before.

I gathered my skirts and came to the table, pulling out the chair at the far end opposite him.

"No." He drummed his fingers on the table. "Here. Sit next to me. Sister."

The last word made me go cold. I forced myself to calm as I

moved around the room. Once, it had been elegant, a perfect place for our father to entertain guests when he'd been in the city. Now, closer inspection of the fine furnishing showed the wood was chipped and the upholstery on the seats was frayed.

I sat, folding my hands on the table like the demure Redmerian lady Jeremy expected me to be. Lady Georgina. She was modest and obedient and simply grateful her brother was here to look out for her. He glared at me like he knew exactly what I was doing.

A servant came forward to arrange place settings for us, as if it hadn't been certain that dinner was being served until that very moment. She set a heavy candelabrum on the table, and the heat of the dozen or so lit candles made me flinch.

"We must be celebrating something," I said. "Did you win at your party?"

"In a manner of speaking." His smug smile made my stomach curdle.

We didn't say anything else until food was set down in front of us. Jeremy wouldn't go to the expense of serving several courses. Instead, while the plates were elaborate, trimmed in gold, the meal they contained was nothing more than boiled vegetables and poached fish. Poultry was expensive and reserved for the rare moment Jeremy might have a guest, while other meats like beef were out of reach for our table.

When he did finally speak, he didn't mince words.

"I've arranged a marriage for you."

My heart squeezed as I forced myself to stay calm. "Oh?"

"To the prince."

I giggled. I couldn't help it. The idea was so ridiculous, I had to laugh, or else I would burst into tears right here.

Jeremy eyed me curiously. "That's all you have to say?"

I took a big mouthful of fish and chewed in an exaggerated manner before saying, "Thank you, brother." Gravy leaked out of the corner of my mouth and dribbled down my chin.

He leaned back in his chair and threw his napkin on the table. "Don't be disgusting, Georgina."

Georgina, Georgina. I'd heard that name more today than I'd heard it in the last month. Why was she suddenly so popular? What made her more interesting than me?

"My name is George."

He scowled. "That's a child's nickname. You're going to be queen. No one's going to take you seriously if you insist on being called George."

That would be what he was worried about: how others would react.

He and I had relatively little history together. Jeremy was fifteen years older, a son from my father's first marriage, and already off into the world by the time I was born. We had very little common ground, but one thing I knew for sure—Jeremy was a snob. While the money in his possession was as thin as the runny gravy that circled my dinner, Jeremy would always make every effort for the appearance of wealth and respectability. It was why he never had guests anymore. Too busy to entertain at home, he'd say. Too in demand. In truth, the house was a ruin that Jeremy was embarrassed to show. He would be afraid that I would embarrass him too.

My smug glee evaporated as his words settled in my head. "Wait. You did this?"

His smile was as friendly as a snake's. "Surprised? I know you don't think much of me, but I have connections. I'm told the prince is very excited to meet you. There aren't many eligible duke's granddaughters looking for a husband, you know." Because the prince had dispossessed most of the dukes in an effort to maintain control of the kingdom. "It's nice to know your grandfather's name is still good for something. The prince was very impressed when he heard who you were." Jeremy's chin wobbled as he chewed.

Impossible. I pushed my dinner around my plate with my fork. "I'm sure he was."

Jeremy was staring at me. I tried for my sweetest smile, then stopped suddenly, because I'd never smiled at my brother before.

"You're not very surprised at all, are you?" he asked.

"What?" I choked on a piece of fish. In all the shock of the day, in all the plans that were busy writing and rewriting themselves in my head, I'd forgotten that Jeremy didn't know that this wasn't the first time I was hearing about this. "No, I am," I said very seriously. "So surprised. I'm overwhelmed, in fact. Speechless."

He eyed me for a moment longer before returning to his meal. "We are invited for noon tomorrow. We will meet the prince and his court for luncheon."

I had to hold back another snort. No one called it "luncheon" unless they were trying to sound impressive.

Jeremy continued as if he didn't notice me struggling for control. "Afterward, I will return to the house."

Of course he would leave me there. He was very pleased to have elevated an obscure half-sister to the rank of princess, but once I was safely deposited at the palace, he would be only too happy to be rid of me.

I hated my brother. For six years I'd tried, if not to win his approval, then to at least not inconvenience him. And what had it gotten me? A marriage to the most reviled man in the kingdom without so much as a few whispered words of brotherly encouragement.

"It must be a relief," I said before I could stop myself, "to finally have me out of your house. Brother."

Be nice, be nice, be nice. A voice chanted it over in my head. The time between me and the gift of never seeing this horrible man again could be measured in hours. But my temper was boiling, and when my "brother" glanced up with his flat serpent's eyes, it was too late.

"It is." Jeremy's smile was cruel. "You've been a burden since the first time I saw your name in our father's will."

"If I was such a burden, it's a wonder you bothered to take me in at all."

He snorted. "The will was very clear that I was to take responsibility for you."

I gripped my fork like a weapon. I'd heard all this before—how he was my guardian, how he couldn't marry me off without my mother's family's blessing. He hurled all of that at me before as if it were my fault, but now, the way he said it held an element that I hadn't heard before.

"Or else?"

"What?"

"If you hadn't come to get me at school? If you hadn't taken me in and given me a home"—if it could be called that—"what would have happened?"

His smile turned cruel, and even without knowing the answer, the venom inside me seethed. Deep inside, I'd managed to convince myself that although he certainly didn't love me as a brother should, he'd cared for my future enough that he'd given me a place to live. Our shared lineage had been enough for him to give me a roof, clothes, and food.

"Tell me." My jaw ached.

"He would have disinherited me. All of it. The house. The money. Gone. Because of you." He spat the last words out, but the spittle that landed on my fish didn't matter because my appetite was gone.

I had the good sense not to point out that he'd nearly lost all of it by now. The house was his by reputation only, with the deed and most of the valuable possessions inside mortgaged. Jeremy might not think I knew, but I did. What else was there to do during the endless days when he was "out with friends" but snoop? Over the years, I'd seen it all. The ledgers, the promissory notes, the letters from debt collectors.

Jeremy's face turned red. "You think you're so high and mighty, don't you? Just because your mother should have been a duchess?"

My mother had died when I was born, and my father had never recovered. A love match, people had whispered where I'd grown up in the country. In those days, the laws weren't so strict, and while relations with my mother's family were strained, there had been nothing they could do to stop the wedding. That had changed in the intervening years. Beverly and his father were not disposed to letting women make choices in their lives. It wasn't long after my parents were married that the laws were changed. By the time I was born, there were no more love matches.

I stilled. "Did you see my grandparents?" He would have needed to get their blessing.

Jeremy snorted. "The old man died this spring. Your uncle is the head of the family now."

If I'd had a pistol, I'd have shot him right there, consequences be damned. For his coldheartedness, I would kill him. The rage inside me was terrifying.

Instead, I folded my hands in my lap.

"I'm tired, brother. I'm going to bed." In mere hours, I would be free of all of this. He'd always underestimated me, and it would never occur to him that I had help to escape. He'd be angry to find I was gone, but I trusted that Niall would have me far away from the city by then.

"Where did you go today?"

My head bobbed up. "I'm sorry?"

"You weren't home when I returned. Where were you?"

"I went to the print shop." I smiled sweetly. It had always rankled Jeremy that I worked with Niall. I'd seen the sour look on his face when I'd come back after a day at the shop with ink under my nails and stains on my skirt. But Niall paid me. Not much, but enough that I never needed to ask Jeremy for money, and that meant he was willing to look the other way on the indecency of a sister who worked to earn a living.

"The print shop?" His smile mirrored mine, and it made my stomach quiver.

"Yes."

"Will he manage when you're gone, do you think?"

I shrugged, choosing my words carefully. "I expect so."

"He wasn't worried?"

"About what?" I pushed my chair back from the table.

"That once you're settled at the palace, you won't betray them all? That you won't run to your husband and tell him exactly what it is that happens at that shop?"

For a moment, the room went dark, as if all twelve candles in the candelabrum had been blown out. Slowly, my vision swam back into focus, only to settle on the smug expression on Jeremy's miserable face.

"Oh yes, I know," he cooed. "I've always known. Since the day you found the printer beaten in the stables."

"How?" I was too dumbfounded to contradict him. He'd always underestimated me, but in this, I'd underestimated him.

The predator's smile widened, showing a line of yellowed teeth. "Who do you think had him beaten?"

Fish and bile rose in my throat.

Jeremy cocked his head. "You thought you were being so clever, didn't you, sister? You think I don't know what you and your friends have been up to all this time?"

A single tear slipped down my cheek. I slapped a hand to my face to hide it, but it was too late.

"Why?" I asked. It could have been a question for so many things. Why hadn't he done anything to stop me? Why did he think he could marry his traitor sister to the future king?

Jeremy chose the most immediate question. "Because it wouldn't have made a difference. Men like the prince, like me—we want to win. We know what it takes. You could have printed whatever you wanted, told whatever lies you felt you needed to. It doesn't matter. In the two years that you've been playing rebellion, has it made any difference?"

I pressed my lips together to force my chin to stop trembling. Niall. All of it. We'd only ever been fooling ourselves.

"I was happy to let you do it." Jeremy examined his nails. "It kept you out of my way. But it stops now. Do you hear me?" His voice cracked off the walls, and I nodded unwillingly. He smiled in response. "Good. Because I expect you to fall in line. Do what is right for our family. And if you think you can escape, if you think there is a rescue coming, let me assure you there is not. If you make one move outside of what is expected between now and the time the prince slips a ring on your finger, remember that I will still know exactly who your friends are and what"—he punched out the *t* between his teeth—"they are up to. And I will not hesitate to do my duty as a loyal subject of the prince and tell him everything. Justice will be served."

My whole body was tight and trembling. I'd misjudged him terribly. Where I'd only ever seen the playboy and the faded society gem, a cunning manipulator had stepped into place.

Later, after he'd dismissed me with a simple "Good night, sister," I fled to my room, biting back tears of frustration. He'd used me like a cat played with a mouse and I hadn't seen it until it was too late. With trembling fingers, I pulled away the pins that held my veil in place. My scalp ached, along with the rest of me. I let my hair fall down my back. Many women kept their hair short. What was the point of leaving it long when it was covered all the time? But I had so little that was mine. My hair was my one point of defiance, even though there was no law that said it had to be cut. Even if I was the only one who saw it, I knew what it looked like beneath the heavy cloth. I knew who I was, even if no one else ever noticed me.

But that was all about to change.

I lay awake in bed. The moon tracked a slow path outside my bedroom window, counting the minutes and hours. When would Niall know I wasn't coming? When would he realize I'd been wrong, and now, I was trapped? I prayed he had the sense not to come here.

When I finally slept, I dreamed of Lou, just as I'd done for years. She stood on the bow of a great wooden ship at the bottom of the ocean, hair billowing in weedy strands. Her arms were outstretched, reaching, as if she were waiting to carry me away.

3

A servant came in the morning with an armload of clothes I'd never seen before.

"Your brother had these made for you."

More like he'd begged them off friends' mistresses. For all his aspirations of being accepted into the upper echelons of polite society, I knew some of his friends hadn't subscribed to the same practices behind closed doors. These dresses hadn't been made. They were from women who were even less socially accepted than I was. I was proven right when the first two dresses didn't come close to fitting. The first could have held two of me. The second didn't go over my hips.

"This is impossible. I'll wear the gray one."

"My lady." Her eyes were wide. "You can't. Your brother was very specific."

The dress that finally fit was velvet, black with the barest hint of red. There must have been a hundred silver buttons that went from my chin to toes. The weight of it was enormous, increased by a train behind it and billowing sleeves that draped from my shoulders to the floor before gathering over my forearms in another neat line of silver buttons. The buttons would have been scandalous, deemed excessive in the way they drew the eye, but it would all be hidden under my cloak, as was proper. My feet had been pinched into leather boots with fine heels and yet more buttons up my calves that were as confining as the ones on my arms. She even produced a new veil in the same mahogany velvet. It immediately pulled on my hair, dragging my head backward as she pinned it to my scalp.

At the last moment, I slid Lou's bracelet on my wrist. The bracelet had been made for a child, and I had to force it over my hand, but it meant too much to leave behind.

I gave the maid a thin smile. "A keepsake."

Her eyes were watery as she kissed my cheek. "You're too good for him." I didn't know if she meant my brother or the prince.

As I teetered down the stairs in narrow boots and endless skirts, Jeremy waited impatiently by the door. At no point did he offer to help me, even when my heel snagged in my train and I gripped blindly at the banister. If I fell and broke my neck, the prince would need a new wife, and then where would Jeremy be?

He'd probably stuff my body into the carriage and try to convince everyone at the palace that I was simply sleeping.

As I approached the door, Jeremy was already walking outside, stepping into a carriage he must have rented for the occasion. I hesitated when I reached it, and the ancient footman leaping to my attention kept us from an endless waiting game as I tried to get into the carriage without any assistance.

"We're going to be late," Jeremy muttered as the door closed. The multitude of fabric that filled the small space between us threatened to suffocate me.

The carriage pulled away from the house with a wild jolt that had me bracing against the sides of the box. Jeremy's lips curled. I turned away, even though the curtains were drawn.

The palace stood in the heart of the chaos and gloom of Redmere City. Buildings were pressed so close together that the roads had narrowed and were, in some cases, impassable by anything wider than a rider on a horse. As a result, we had to take a long and winding route toward what would be my new home.

The journey was exhausting, the carriage stuffy. I wouldn't give Jeremy the satisfaction of asking for a window to be opened. Sweat trickled down my spine and pooled in the dip of my pelvis. The tight sleeves and high collar choked me.

I hadn't been able to return to Niall, but I would soon be free of my brother. I would find a way to send word to the print shop and alert Niall that Jeremy knew everything, leaving nothing for him to hold over me. Nothing to threaten me with but my own life, and by then, I would be queen, and he would be an impoverished minor noble with no reputation to speak of.

I would be queen.

Jeremy's gaze snapped to me as a small laugh escaped from between my lips. It was part amusement and part delirium. I followed up with a snort for good measure, and his face darkened.

In all of this, I'd only focused on the immediacy of being married to a prince I already hated. But someday soon, they would crown him king. When they did . . .

Beneath my sweat-soaked skin, hope—tiny, silly hope—flared to life.

I would be the most powerful woman in Redmere. Surely that had to count for something. Surely there would be ways to make a difference, and not just by smuggling palace documents through the city in my skirts. What did queens do with their days?

I wished, for the first time in a long time, that my mother was still alive to tell me how fine ladies spent their time now that I was about to become the finest lady of them all. They'd tried to teach us in school, but their teaching had been focused on the pretty skills needed to catch a husband and maintain a home, and I hadn't been there very long. When my father died, Jeremy had refused to pay for my education, instead bringing me to the city to learn what I could by myself.

At last, the carriage rolled to a halt. I waited, listening to the muffled sounds of the driver giving someone my name. He used all of it, every single syllable.

The carriage lurched forward, but it only traveled a few minutes longer before shuddering to a halt once more. The creaking vehicle fell silent, and I held my breath. Even Jeremy seemed uncertain what to do next.

When the carriage door was pulled open, I expected to see the same elderly driver who had helped me in. Instead, a much younger man, dressed in a black-and-silver uniform that matched the pennants flapping above the palace towers, stepped back from the door and bowed.

Jeremy was the first to move, pushing past me without so much as a "good morning" to the new footman or a backward glance at me as he adjusted the lapels of his coat.

The footman appeared unfazed. He held a black-gloved hand out to me.

"My lady."

My stomach tightened. Panic squeezed at my lungs while my heart battered at my ribs like a trapped animal.

My lady.

I was no lady. I was nobody.

My clothing made it impossible to reach more than a few inches away from my body. The footman must have been used to these problems of fashion, because he reached into the carriage, gently took my hand, and carefully led me out, ensuring my boots were clear. I climbed out of the carriage to the cobbled courtyard below.

The world tipped and faded, but I did not faint. The sun beat down, baking me inside the ridiculous costume.

Jeremy took my hand—much more firmly than the footman had—and led me up to the wide stairs of the palace. It was only then that I noticed the party of men and women standing there, watching our approach. They were posed like the ridiculous classical tableaux I'd been forced to enact in school. Each held themselves stiffly, their spines and limbs arched. The few women there were dressed modestly, but hints of color at their cuffs and hems spoke of elegance beneath their cloaks and veils.

Jeremy puffed out his chest and strode toward them like a warrior returning home from a great victory. I struggled to keep up, my feet catching between the steps and my skirts. I tripped, and something tore, and still Jeremy continued his ascent.

When we were only a step below the group from the palace, Jeremy halted, and I nearly fell again. I was roasting in my clothes. If we didn't get inside very soon, I would faint.

It was a struggle, but I scanned the crowd, trying to find the prince's face. It seemed impossible that he wouldn't be front and center, and yet the man who led the welcoming party was too old to be my soon-to-be husband. He had to be at least forty if he were a day and—

A sharp elbow in my ribs brought my attention back, and Jeremy cleared his throat. He was bent at the waist in a deep bow and waiting for me to do the same.

I'd been taught to curtsy at school but hadn't bothered to use the skill in years. Coupled with the impossible shoes, heavy skirts, and the swimming feeling behind my eyes, my execution would have left me with an hour of remedial study. As it was, once I'd wobbled to an appropriately low point, Jeremy spoke.

"May I present my sister, Lady Georgina Elizabeth Millicent Cressida Wright, eldest granddaughter of Hector, Duke of Bearford, Earl of the Eastern Isles, Viscount of . . ." His words bubbled in my ears as if he were underwater.

The sensation of my hand being taken brought me back around, and I started when I found myself face-to-face with the older man who had been on the stair closest to us. He had what the schoolteachers would have called "elegant manners." He bent low over my hand but didn't kiss it because that wasn't done.

"My lady," he said. "We are so glad you have arrived."

The way he said it made it sound as if I'd been traveling for days instead of bumping along in a rented carriage for the last hour.

"Thank you . . ." I hesitated. There should be a title there. "My lord"? "Sir"?

He grinned at my discomfort, but unlike Jeremy, his smile didn't speak of having the upper hand. "I am Count Crawford, the prince's cousin. I regret to inform you that the prince was called away this morning."

"He's not here?" Jeremy snapped with all the horror of a disappointed child. Despite myself, despite everything, I was unable to stop the roll of my eyes in response and then flushed when I caught Crawford's grin. He was handsome, although his neatly trimmed beard wasn't fashionable in Redmere anymore. His hair was slicked back and tied at the nape of his neck, exposing a single small diamond pierced through his ear. It was a daring look that would have earned him countless whispered comments and sidelong glances in the streets of the city, but I supposed a prince's cousin could wear what he liked.

The count straightened, but he kept my hand tucked in his. For no reason other than desperation, it made me feel less alone.

His smile was flawless as he turned his attention to Jeremy. "Regrettably, His Highness had some . . . difficulty . . . at the naval yard that required his immediate attention." He squeezed my hand. "I know he was very much looking forward to meeting you, but what is a few hours' delay when you have the rest of your lives to get acquainted?"

The safe feeling vanished. My clothes resumed their efforts to strangle me.

"A few hours," Jeremy muttered.

"His Highness asked me to thank you very much for the safe delivery of his bride. He is indebted to the gift you have bestowed on him."

My temper rolled. I was no gift, no possession. I was a living, breathing human being, not a chest of jewels.

Jeremy was mollified by the count's words. His shoulders relaxed, and the pucker of his mouth gaped a few times before curling into a smile. "Of course. Of course. The honor is all ours."

The courtyard fell into silence. The count and his entourage faced Jeremy, like in the games Lou and I had played with the village children when we were small. *Red Rose, Purple Clover, we call Jeremy over.*

Except the invitation never came.

Eventually, not even Jeremy could ignore the silent tension forming in the gap between himself and the palace representatives.

"Well. That's done. I trust you will take care of my sister." As if he'd ever done so himself. "Georgina. Be a good girl." As if I were a child.

Crawford was watching me from the corner of his eye. He winked, lightning quick, and brought my arm toward him so it was clasped against his body, a silent signal to Jeremy whose side I was on now.

My brother bowed once more and turned his back on me.

THE GROUP who had assembled to greet me outside—no more than eight people, once I was able to think long enough to count them—was nothing compared to the crowd gathered in the palace. There must have been five times that many, mostly men dressed in formal black coats and stiffened collars or the severe grays and greens worn by magistrates and officers of the City Guard. The wives stood the traditional pace and a half behind their husbands' shoulders. None of the women spoke to me.

I could still barely breathe, and at no point did anyone offer to remove my cloak. Instead, Crawford, who never let go of my hand, led me down the line of people, introducing each one individually. It was a blur. Lord So and So. The Viscount of Somewhere. Lord Someone, Chief Magistrate of the Court of the

Flying Pig. Each of them bowed, and I replied with a curtsy, managing better than I had on the steps.

I had no idea how many people I'd spoken to or what I'd said to most of them, but then, suddenly, they were all gone except for one girl in a dark gray dress.

"Ah, here we are," Crawford said.

I didn't recognize her at first, but she knew me. Her eyes widened as she inhaled sharply, and then—

It was one strand of red hair peeking out her veil that gave her away. She'd been outside the dressmaker's shop the day before.

She gathered herself before I could react and curtsied low. "My name is Rosie, my lady. I'm so glad to meet you," she said, addressing a space somewhere around my knees.

"She will be your lady's maid," Crawford said as if he hadn't noticed anything wrong.

"My what?" I hadn't meant to say it out loud, and certainly not to sound as surprised as I did, but it was too late. The girl squeaked, and Crawford grinned while he patted my hand.

"Yes, your brother did say you were used to doing things on your own. But a princess must have a maid, and a queen...well..."

A maid. What was I going to do with a maid? I was bringing so few clothes with me. My maid would have the simplest, most redundant job in the whole country.

My nose had been itching for the last few minutes, and without someone to help me out of the heavy layers I wore, I couldn't do anything about it.

Did a lady's maid's duties not extend to scratching her mistress's nose?

I snorted at that thought, then finally laughed outright when Rosie's eyes widened again. Her eyebrows would disappear into her veil along with her hair if they went any farther. We had so much to talk about.

I bit my lip to calm myself. "I'm very pleased to meet you too."

Crawford let go of my arm, but the fabric of the dress still stuck to my skin where he'd held me.

"I'll leave you to become acquainted. She'll show you to your rooms. I'll send someone to collect you when Beverly returns."

So many thoughts went through my head at once. They were, in no particular order: No one would collect me, because I wasn't a misplaced shawl. Crawford had called the prince "Beverly" with no title and no formality. Finally, "Beverly" would be here sooner or later, and now I knew there was at least one person in this castle who might already know I was a traitor, so how long would it take before he knew too?

Rosie led me down hallways and up more sets of stairs than I'd ever climbed in my life. I'd sweated through my clothes—again—and my legs shook by the time she opened a door.

"This is yours."

The room was the grandest thing I'd ever seen. The bed was so tall I'd have to climb to get into it, and the sprawling window showed an uninterrupted view of the glittering sea beyond the harbor. It would have been a dream, but it came with conditions. It would be mine as long as I lied about everything I'd ever been or done.

"What do you think?" Rosie bobbed up and down on the balls of her feet expectantly.

"What are you doing here?" I asked, unable to stop myself.

Her eyes darted around the room, and then she hissed, "What are you doing here?"

"I'm marrying the prince. What were you doing at the dressmaker's?"

"Making sure your wardrobe was finished."

My wardrobe? She didn't even know me.

"Is that all you were doing?" Would it be better or worse if she said no? If she was there as a customer, then she might be trustworthy—safe in her ignorance. She might know why I was there, and she might also be with the resistance. But she could just as soon tell others what she knew and how I was involved if it meant saving herself.

She put her hands on her hips. "What else would there be?"

We stared. She spoke like the common people of the city, but the spark in her eye said she knew more than poverty and despair.

"Are you a spy?" I whispered so softly I barely heard it myself.

She smiled sweetly, with no indication that I'd said anything odd. "I am the personal maid to the future queen of Redmere."

This was exhausting. I couldn't be looking for monsters in every corner. Until I had reason to suspect she would betray me, I would trust her . . . a little.

I flopped down onto a fussy-looking green couch. "Is Rosie your real name?"

"I don't understand."

"Are you Rosie, or are you Rosemary, or Rosalie, or some other kind of Rose?"

She bit her lip, and it made her look incredibly young. She couldn't be a spy. "It's just Rosie, my lady. Rosie Delaney."

"Well, Rosie." I lifted a foot and let it drop heavily on the table in front of the couch. She looked aghast, and I grinned. She'd probably never seen a princess put her feet on the table before. I flexed my ankle. "You will call me George. Nothing else. Is that clear?"

"George?" Rosie's nose wrinkled, but she caught herself, going back to gnawing on her lip and curtsying. "Of course."

"Good." Hopefully the command would stick. Someone needed to know what my name was. "Now help me get these boots off."

Regardless of her true profession, Rosie was good at following directions. She had both boots undone and off before I even had the laces of my cloak open.

"Your cloak is very severe," Rosie said as she turned her attention to the fastenings at my collar.

"Thank you?"

"My grandmother wore one just like it."

I sighed. "My brother picked it out for me."

Rosie was very talkative and kept up a steady stream of chatter while she worked. Her father was a merchant and owned a shipping company by the harbor. She had nine brothers and sisters. She was the eldest girl. Her aunt was a cook in the kitchens and that was how she'd come to work in the palace as a household maid.

"I never thought I'd ever be a personal maid to a princess. But then Count Crawford himself told me I'd been chosen for the position." Rosie smiled shyly. "I hope we'll be friends. I mean, you could never really be friends with a maid, but close to it, possibly. If you think you might—"

I closed my eyes, letting her words wash over me. Occasionally I would murmur a yes or no, but I couldn't drum up the energy to say anything else. It had been a very long time since I'd had a friendly conversation with someone. Even Niall, who had been my friend, kept our talks professional and short in order to keep us safe.

"There you go." The front of the cloak was pushed open, and I surged for breath.

"I'd never leave the palace again if it meant I didn't have to wear that damn thing."

She giggled. "You don't speak like a princess."

I eyed her. "How many princesses have you known?"

"Well, none. But—oh, George!" Her eyes were wide again.

"What?"

"Your dress!"

"What about it?"

"It's beautiful!"

It was?

I must have spoken out loud, because Rosie emphatically said, "Oh, yes!" and rushed forward, letting her fingers smooth over the shimmering velvet of my sleeve.

"If you can get all the buttons undone, you can have it."

Rosie stared up at me. "Really?"

"Isn't that how princesses are? They wear each dress only once."

She snorted. "Where did they find you?"

Perhaps she was a spy after all.

I scrunched my toes, the knuckles popping after being confined for so long. "What about the boots? Would you like those as well?"

Rosie wrinkled her nose. "They're very nice."

"But?"

She grinned. "My grandmother was very fond of that style too." I smiled, my chest warming around new trust. Whoever she was, she wouldn't betray me.

A servant came shortly after with a tray of food. It contained fruits and cheeses but also cured meats that were a luxury in Jeremy's house.

"Is the prince back yet?" I asked.

The servant bowed and left without saying anything.

"Oh, he wouldn't know." Rosie hovered over the tray, eyeing it hungrily.

"He won't?"

"No! He's not even a footman. Just a kitchen boy they dressed up to impress you. He won't know where the prince is." She grabbed a cube of cheese and popped it into her mouth. She really was nothing like Jeremy's servants. A grand lady would be appalled that a maid would dare to eat first, but I didn't care. I hated for the food to go to waste, and I had no appetite.

"But where's the prince?" I asked, and Rosie froze midchew.

"I'm not supposed to know," she said, swallowing hard.

"Supposed to?"

She busied herself filling a plate with cheese and fruit, glancing at me nervously.

"Rosie?" I prompted. If she was the person who had brought

the papers to the dressmaker's shop, then there were many things she wasn't supposed to know.

Rosie brought the plate to me, settling onto the couch. She also carried a large white napkin the size of a sail. I felt ridiculous as Rosie spread it over me, but it did cover me from the bodice of my dress to my knees.

"There was a . . . problem. At the harbor." Rosie whispered it, as if someone might be listening, and perhaps they were.

"At the harbor?"

"The prince's fleet was attacked. By pirates." Her mouth made a little O.

I sat up straighter. "Captain Cinder?" In everything that had happened, I'd forgotten about the news of the ship that had been lost.

"Five ships were sent out. Only one returned this morning with her captain and a few crewmen left to tell the tale."

"It was only one ship that was lost." I stuttered as I realized that information wasn't common knowledge yet. "Or so I've heard."

"That's what they want you to think." Her eyes flashed, and my heart sped up. She hadn't admitted that she was carrying documents to the dressmaker's, but she hadn't denied what I'd said either.

"What they want me to think?" I asked.

She leaned in closer. "I heard Lord Parrington's wife disappeared. Parrington is very wealthy. He owns half the farmland south of the Kirble River. Anyway, suddenly, his wife was gone, and he kicked up such a fuss that the prince had no choice but to send ships out searching for her."

"The prince sent those crews to die. No one escapes Captain Cinder." I dropped my head to rest on Rosie's shoulder despite the fact we'd only known each other for an hour.

"But that's why they're only saying one ship was lost. The prince would never admit to going to all that trouble to find one nobleman's wife, even a very rich one." Rosie sighed. "It's romantic, isn't it?"

"Being murdered by pirates?"

She patted my knee. "No. Captain Cinder. Imagine all that freedom. Going where you want. Doing what you want."

"Including murdering innocent sailors."

She shrugged. "They shouldn't go after her then."

"They don't have a choice!" I sat up, my moment of ease evaporated. "There's no other way for them to earn a living, and if they refuse their orders, they'll be hanged. What about the trade ships attacked by pirates when they mean no harm?"

"Shhh." Her eyes rounded as she pressed a hand to my mouth.

"Don't shush me! How many has he—"

"Princess!" Her voice was sharp, and I suddenly remembered where I was. He might walk through that door at any minute. This wasn't Niall's shop or Jeremy's house. I was in the palace. I was going to marry the prince and would be expected to act like a princess.

I asked, "What do we do now?"

Rosie stretched her arms over her head until her spine popped, and then she settled down, arms crossed over her chest and eyes closed. "Now we wait for the prince to send for you."

We waited a long time. And then longer. The sun went down. Another tray of more food than I could possibly eat was delivered. Rosie and I nibbled at it, but the longer we waited, the more strained our conversation became because there were so many things I couldn't tell her.

My eyes grew heavy, and the pull of the veil had left me with a headache. Rosie was asleep next to me on the little sofa, head tipped back and mouth open as she snored softly, but she stood the instant the soft tap sounded at the door. She wiped at her lips and stumbled across the room before she caught herself and straightened, smoothing her hands over her dress. Her veil was askew, and strands of red curls were sticking out like a wild halo.

When she was presentable, she opened the door. A hushed conversation followed.

"Well?" I asked when the messenger had departed.

She pursed her lips, and my stomach knotted as I waited for the news, but finally, she said, "He's not coming."

4

I spent another sleepless night staring at the ceiling. Once word had come that the prince wasn't able to meet his future bride today, there had been nothing left for Rosie and I to do but release me from the ridiculous dress and get ready for bed. Rosie had curtsied once I was dressed in a plain nightshirt.

"Good night, George."

A quiet tremor of panic had fluttered in my chest as her hand went to pull the door open.

"Wait."

She did. "Yes?"

I licked my lips and told myself I was being silly. But the space of the room felt too big, and the wind whistled oddly around the tower. Despite everything, my courage failed me. Beverly lurked —at the edge of my consciousness or just outside the door.

"Stay here tonight?"

She had, curled up in a ball of red hair and wrinkled underclothes, on the far side of the big bed in a room that wasn't really mine. Like I'd needed a nurse to stay with me. I hadn't needed comfort like that in years. Not since those first days after learning that Lou had died.

I am sick for days after word comes about Lou. The doctors who are called to the school cannot find anything wrong with me, but I cannot eat without being ill, and I cannot sleep without having terrible dreams of a ghostly Lou who comes up from the bottom of the ocean to drag me down with her. I wake up screaming—waking up the other girls in the dormitory—and cannot settle.

They start letting me spend the nights in the infirmary, where I will at least not disturb anyone else. When that does not help me, the nurse gives me some sort of foul-smelling tonic to help me sleep. Except it does not help either, because I sleep so deeply that I cannot wake from my dreams and instead have to drown over and over, night after night.

My isolation only worsens the longer I am sick and frightened. When my father dies and the money for my education runs out, the headmistress says I cannot stay, and I am relieved. She says I am going to live with a brother I have never met, and I do not care.

It is years before I sleep through the night on my own.

I gave up on sleep before the sun rose. I settled myself by the window instead, watching the sky slowly turn from black to gray to blue and sending glittering lights over the sea. Slowly, I turned the bracelet on my wrist, thinking of Lou, far away and lost to me forever.

"George?" Rosie's voice drifted sleepily from across the room. She was sitting up in bed, rubbing at her eyes.

"Go back to sleep. It's still early," I said, before moving to one of the small sofas that faced an empty fireplace.

A rustling came behind me, followed by a hiss, as Rosie's bare feet hit the cool floor.

"How long have you been awake?"

"Not long." I flinched as Rosie leaned over my shoulder, one hand on me as if it were nothing to touch me. How long had it been since anyone touched me in any informal way? Niall, for all his kindness, was always typically Redmerian in his restraint, and Jeremy could barely look at me, much less offer me any kind of brotherly affection.

"What's that?" Rosie asked, her hair brushing my cheek.

For a second, I nearly covered the bracelet. It was an old habit, running the smooth metal through my fingers, feeling as it went from cool to warm with the heat of my skin. No one had ever asked about it before. It was old and tarnished and, over time, had become something almost secret, so plain as to be invisible.

I slid it over my wrist, wincing where it pinched against the skin and knobby bones. "When I was very small, I had a best friend named Lou. We grew up together. Lou's father was my father's stable master. My mother died when I was born, and in Lou's family there were twelve other siblings to look after, so we were left to grow up on our own, running wild over the estate until someone would come call us and send us home to bed."

Rosie's fingers were in my hair, and the gentle care of it was something I could get used to, despite the strangeness of my surroundings.

"My father never got over my mother's death. He let the estate go to ruin and fell deeper and deeper into debt. Money became so tight that Lou's family was struggling to put food on the table, and so Lou was enlisted in the navy."

"A girl at sea?" Rosie asked with awe in her voice.

"They dressed her up as a boy. Cut her hair. I don't think her family had worried to the point when she would be found out. They needed her wages to put food on their table."

"I've always wanted to go sailing in a big ship on the sea."

I couldn't join her laughter. Not with what came next. "Lou drowned."

"What?" Rosie's hands slipped in my hair.

"Her ship was attacked by pirates. The vessel sank, and the whole crew drowned."

"Oh, George." Rosie sounded on the verge of tears.

"It's all right. It was a long time ago." It didn't hurt, not like it had then.

"How old were you?" Rosie asked.

"I was twelve."

Rosie came to stand in front of me. "You're mine now." Her

chin tipped up determinedly. "I may just be a maid, but I'll be the best maid and friend you've ever had."

I laughed. My list of maids was a list of one, and the list of confidantes I'd had was nearly as short.

"Yes, I think you will." I tried to smile. My insides felt hollowed out and raw, and terror still simmered, waiting to boil over, but I would move past this. I had no other options.

Then, the sun was up, and still he didn't send for me. The one benefit of Jeremy's relative indifference to me for all those years was that it gave me a moderate amount of freedom. Waiting for the prince's leisure in this room, no matter how grand, felt like being caged.

"Would you like a tour of the castle?" Rosie asked. "I know all the best secret passages."

I grinned but then glanced at the black-and-red dress from the day before. It would take more than a few dusty secret passages to convince me to put it back on.

Rosie must have guessed the direction of my thoughts, because she laughed and said, "Come with me." She crooked a finger at me before walking to the door at the far end of the room and then through it.

It shouldn't have been surprising that on the other side of the door was a dressing room. What was surprising was for it to be full of more clothes—dresses, shoes, and jewels—than any one person could wear in a lifetime.

"But where . . ." I stared. There were more colors, more fabrics, than I'd ever seen before.

"He had them made for you."

"Who?"

"The prince. I told you, I went to make sure your clothes were being delivered the day before yesterday."

I swallowed down my awe. The prince had them made for me. The money spent on the contents of this room would feed a family in the city for generations.

How long had the prince known I was coming?

"What am I supposed to wear?" What in this room would hide the look of "traitor" the first time he saw me?

She produced a simple, gray dress that wasn't all that different in style from the ones I'd worn in Jeremy's house. The fabric was finer, the stitches were smaller, but it didn't have the suffocating weight of the dress from the day before. The veil, too, was subtly better made than my old one had been, but it felt familiar on my head.

That was until Rosie opened a wooden box on the table and stepped aside. "What do you think?"

Inside the box was a riot of shimmering brooches and other jewels. I shook my head. "I couldn't. It's not appropriate."

Rosie scoffed. "Not appropriate? They're fit for a queen, and you're the future queen."

"I can't."

"He'll expect you to look the part." She pulled out a shining starburst of silvery diamonds and bright sapphires.

"That?" I snorted. "I'll fall over if you pin that on me."

"Not on the dress, silly." Rosie fumbled with my veil, pulling at the hair underneath as she added the odd weight of the pin to the band above my forehead.

"There." She stepped back to admire her handiwork.

I barely recognized the woman in the mirror. She was a stiffer, tenser version of me, tied up and strapped down. The veil was lopsided now, sending little strands of lightning pain over my head and down the back of my neck.

"It's immodest."

Rosie snorted. "Just wait."

"What?" A woman in the city could be sentenced to six months of hard labor if a man said her clothing was too ostentatious.

"You'll see. If you dress too severely, they won't respect you."

"Who?"

She frowned. "Didn't they tell you anything?"

"About what? I only found out about this whole marriage yesterday."

She placed a hand on the wall to steady herself. "Yesterday?"

"How long have you known?"

"They announced you were coming two months ago."

"Two . . . two months?" How could I have underestimated Jeremy and his machinations so much?

My hands fluttered over my dress and then froze at the crispness of the elaborate skirts under my palms.

A dress for a queen.

The dressmaker's words, read in the halting voice of the man who'd stood in line behind me at the checkpoint. At the time, nothing more than a compliment from a craftswoman to a patron.

Had everyone known? The whole city had conspired, and no one had thought to warn me until I had nowhere to run.

I couldn't breathe. The corset, the dress, the room, the stone of the tower—they were all pressing down on me. I couldn't—I clawed at my waist and the slick fabric that encased me.

Rosie was there. She shushed and murmured like the nurse had done when I'd woken up at school convinced that Lou's ghost had been in my room. "George. George. Listen. You need to breathe."

I shook my head as my vision swam. "I can't. I can't—he'll know. He'll look right at me, and he'll know what I've done. They'll all die. Everyone. My friends, the chaperones. All of you. Because of me."

Pain sparked on the side of my arm, and I yelped, skittering away. The pain was small, but it gave me something to focus on, leeching away the crushing weight on my chest.

Rosie held another diamond brooch in her hand, the pin of it poking out from between her fingers.

"Did you just stab me?" I asked, horrified.

"I needed your attention." She dropped the brooch and led me back out to the main room. She smoothed her hands over my arms, rubbing the spot where she'd pricked me. "I am so sorry this has happened to you. No one else would want to be in your position, I know. But he doesn't know about what you've been doing. He wouldn't have brought you to the palace if he did. I've been going to the dressmaker's for years. If he knew what we were doing, I would have been killed a very long time ago."

I considered her red hair, her loose dress. "How old are you?"

"Twenty-two." She touched the brooch in my hair, the gesture almost motherly, and I wondered how she'd seemed so young the day before. She was older than I was. "I know this is difficult and frightening. But trust me when I say you look like a princess. We'll figure out the rest as we go."

I felt like a fraud.

Lou's bracelet was tight on my wrist, and I tucked it neatly inside the plain, gray sleeve. It gave me a quiet tension on which to ground myself. I brought my hands forward, gently clasping the tips of my fingers the way I'd seen the ladies on the stairs do when I'd arrived.

"I'm ready," I said.

Rosie led the way. As we crossed through the great hall and into parts of the palace I didn't know, Rosie pointed out rooms where historic events had happened or where scandals had erupted. As we progressed, a growing line of servants trailed after us.

"What do they want?" I whispered.

Rosie glanced over her shoulder mid-narrative and giggled. "They want to feed you breakfast."

"I don't understand."

"Breakfast is served wherever the lady of the household wishes," the servant at the head of the little group said.

I turned back to Rosie. "Is there somewhere outside we could eat?"

The garden Rosie took us to was like a dream, at once wild and controlled. Great vines climbed over the walls, and hedges had been trimmed to create small alcoves with stone benches, where people seeking a little privacy could sit and find shelter. It reminded me of gardens at my father's, though those had been smaller and less well-tended as the years went on.

"This is the festival garden," Rosie said, still leading the way. "It was built over four hundred years ago by King Roland the Slobberer."

I laughed. "That's not what he was called."

"It was. We can look it up in the library after we eat."

Like this was where we were supposed to be all along, a small table was set up in the center of the garden next to an elaborate floral sculpture of horses running over an invisible plain. As we were seated, a dozen servants appeared, carrying baskets of fresh breads, cut fruit, and pots of sweet tea.

"How are we going to finish all this?" I sighed.

Rosie shrugged. She helped herself to slices of a pink-fleshed fruit with black seeds and then slathered green jam on crusty white bread. "They don't know what you like. Once they do, they'll offer less."

I couldn't bring myself to ask what would happen to the plates I rejected. I didn't delude myself into thinking that they were distributed to the poor. We'd know if the palace was handing out kitchen scraps. There would be throngs lining up for them. There were not.

Perhaps I could change that someday.

Everything offered to me was delicious, and even if I was forced into a lonely existence where Prince Beverly acknowledged my presence as rarely as Jeremy had, at least there were breakfasts like this with Rosie to look forward to.

Just as my unseen husband-to-be's name flitted across my mind, a commotion spread among the servants. In an orderly rush, they disappeared.

Prince Beverly, ruler and tyrant of Redmere, stood at the far side of the garden.

My pulse throbbed, pounding against Lou's bracelet around my wrist.

He didn't move, like a hunter assessing its prey.

"My lady?" Rosie asked, speaking more formally than before.

I straightened my spine. I would have to face him sooner or later, and probably every day for the rest of my life, unless I could find a way to escape without endangering Niall—and now Rosie. No sense in delaying this meeting.

"Stay where you are," I said to Rosie.

Unexpectedly, the prince also obeyed my command.

We stared at each other with only the steady trickle of a small, constructed waterfall against one garden wall to interrupt us.

I rose, fighting the urge to cross my arms protectively over my chest. I needed to learn to deal with this man if I was going to survive here.

The silence stretched.

I waited. For what, I wasn't sure, but I would know it when I saw it.

He bowed, bent at the waist until his torso was parallel to the ground. Then, he stayed there.

Behind me, Rosie gasped.

I lifted my chin. A lady would have curtsied, but he'd kept me waiting, and I wouldn't cower before him. "Good morning, Your Highness."

He straightened as slowly as he'd bowed. His mouth was twisted at one corner in a quiet smile. Then, as if he'd received some invisible signal, he launched into motion, covering the distance between us in quick steps. Just as suddenly, he dropped to one knee, head lowered as he took my hand.

"Lady Georgina," he said, eyes to the ground. "I came to apologize. It is unspeakably rude of me to have left you waiting and unwelcomed. I am embarrassed as a man and a prince for the reception you have received. Please accept my sincerest apologies. If you would like for me to send for your brother to take you home again, know that I will do so immediately."

A short, high-pitched sound squeaked behind me, which might have been the chirp of a bird or my maid choking back her surprise. Either way, I kept my attention on the man kneeling in front of me. Real distress swirled in his eyes as he looked up at me.

Was this the fearsome Prince of Redmere?

"Your Highness," I said.

"Lady Georgina, I—"

"My name"—I was pleased that my voice stayed steady—"is George."

His eyes flickered, but he nodded before I could understand what emotion the glimmer meant. "George." His hand was still in mine. "It suits you."

I started to speak, but he held up a palm and rose. "I have to apologize again for how poorly this has started between us. It is unthinkable that you should arrive without me to greet you." He ran his free hand over the back of his neck. "There was some trouble with the fleet. It was more than a bit of trouble. A disaster, and no way to salvage it. Good men lost, and that is my fault for sending them out to sea. When I returned to the palace last night, Crawford told me that I was in no shape to meet you but I . . . you . . ." His eyes swept up and down in a way that made me blush and bury my hands in my skirt, despite my best intentions to remain firm. "I beg you to forgive me. This is not how our marriage will be. You will never be an afterthought. My father loved my mother, and I wanted . . . I hoped . . ." He looked away, biting his lip the same way I did when I was uncomfortable.

The garden fell silent again. The penitent man in front of me was so at odds with the caricature I'd grown to know in the print shop. His father had loved his mother? Did he plan to love me? He'd be very disappointed to find out a man's love wasn't to my taste, or that I kept expecting him to sprout two great teeth. Prince Beaverly. I was supposed to hate him.

If he saw my hesitation, he didn't understand the reason for it. He reached inside his coat and pulled out a small velvet pouch, unwinding the laces as he spoke. "I see you found the jewels I left for you in your room." My fingers brushed the starburst Rosie had pinned to my veil, and he smiled. "It looks very pretty on you. Not gaudy and overdone like so many of the other women in the court wear. Would you please do me the honor of wearing this"—a small pool of jewels tumbled out into his hand—"as a symbol of how much I admire you and apologize for everything I have done to offend and upset you so very early in our relationship?"

He stood there with a fortune in his palm. Whole families could live for a year on what he was offering me, all because he hadn't been able to meet me yesterday.

Gingerly, I plucked at a stone and lifted it. The small string of diamonds and sapphires trailed after it. Before I could say anything, he took the bracelet from between my fingers, opened the clasp, and clipped it around my wrist. I flinched under his touch, but he only smiled and held my arm out so the jewels glinted in the sunlight. Lou's bracelet was still hidden beneath my sleeve, and it seemed to tighten in warning.

The prince brushed his fingers over my pulse, and my heart fluttered like a frantic bird, like it knew we needed to escape. He leaned forward, and for a horrible second, I thought he might kiss me, even though such things were forbidden among unmarried people.

"You are beautiful. I could not have asked for a brighter jewel," he said instead, keeping the barest space between us. His nearness made me uncomfortable, but I couldn't back away. If I did, I'd be giving up ground to this man for the rest of my life.

"Thank you, Your Highness."

"So you forgive me?"

"Yes, Your Highness." What else was I supposed to say?

"Beverly." He clasped both my hands in his.

"Beverly." My lips felt clumsy around the name, and the intimacy made my stomach sour. Yet despite the awkwardness, this man was not the monster I'd expected to marry.

The prince suggested a tour of the city. Still uncertain of how a refusal would be received, I didn't point out that I'd lived here for years.

The prince led me to a small courtyard where Count Crawford waited with a carriage. The count arched an eyebrow and pressed his lips together in a mocking pout as we approached.

"Did you forgive him already? I hope you at least made him grovel."

"There was groveling." Prince Beverly grinned. "My Lady George drives a hard bargain."

I didn't like the way he said my name or the way he referred to me as "his." A servant approached us, leading a tall, black horse that tossed its head and pawed at the ground. The prince waved a dismissal.

"Not today."

The count's eyebrow hadn't lost its arch. "You're not riding?"

"That would be ungentlemanly. What sort of fiancé would I be to leave Lady George to ride in the carriage alone after I'd only just apologized for not being present yesterday?"

Rosie hovered at the palace door. Could I ask that she come with us? She wasn't a chaperone, but neither of these men had any legal right to take me anywhere in public either. But the prince made the laws, so who would tell him he couldn't accompany me through the city? The carriage door was open, the prince and Crawford waiting expectantly, and so I turned my back on Rosie and stepped quietly inside.

The carriage was so ornate it might as well have been a palace all on its own. It was so different from the awful, uncomfortable ride with Jeremy the day before, not least of all because yesterday I had anonymity in the dark, rickety old contraption he'd rented. Today, I was very aware of every turned head and wide eye as we passed.

The smell of the ocean, which was always present in Redmere City, grew stronger, mixing with tar and dead fish as we approached the harbor.

We passed the long wharfs and the men selling their catch to the few people who could afford it, then we crossed under a high archway and into another wide cobbled courtyard like the one at the palace. Although the building in front of us was grand, it was substantially smaller. Uniformed officers armed with rifles stood at attention by the door, as did another pair at the gateway we'd just crossed.

"Where are we?" I asked as we pulled to a halt.

"The admiralty," Beverly answered on a long sigh. "This won't take long. Some unfinished business from yesterday. Crawford, stay with the lady and see that she has everything she needs." His voice had lost some of the soft solicitousness he'd shown in the garden.

Crawford inclined his head. "Of course."

The prince stepped down from the carriage, striding past the guards without a look at them or me.

The carriage fell into silence. I should have brought Rosie with me after all. At least then there would be conversation. The smell of salt and slime was overwhelming. I plucked nervously at my sleeves.

"Oh." Crawford smiled. "I see you didn't let him off so easily after all."

My gaze followed his until it landed on the bracelet that twinkled silvery-white and blue on my wrist. I tugged my sleeve back down to cover it.

Crawford chuckled. "It was his mother's. She was such an elegant lady. Did you ever meet her?"

"She died before I was born," I said sweetly. She would have been appalled to see me as a child, with my hair down and my face streaked with mud, a wild thing too far from the city to be worth noticing by the crown and its laws.

A sound echoed outside the carriage. A child crying. It had been going on for a while, but in all the strangeness surrounding me, I hadn't registered it until now. It grew louder, and other wails joined it, throwing it out of tune.

Beyond the gate we'd entered, a crowd milled about.

"Your Highness!" a woman called.

"Please!" another said.

I sat back in my seat, suddenly nervous that they would see me.

"Who are they?"

"Widows." Crawford smoothed his mustache. "Or they will be once the navy releases the official list of the dead."

There had to be fifty people at the gate, not including children, and they were all women. They were dressed in black with their hair bound up in ragged scarves and tattered veils.

"All widows?"

Crawford sighed the same way the prince had when they'd arrived. "Just the most desperate ones, I suppose. The rest know to wait. There's no hurrying the admiralty. But it isn't anything you need to worry about."

"But—"

"The prince will deal with it."

A boy, no older than eight or nine, broke through the crowd and was small enough that he slipped past the guards at the gate to run across the courtyard. A woman screamed, and the boy raised his arm, even as he ran. Soldiers rushed toward him but couldn't reach him before the thing in his hand was launched forward.

It hit the carriage with a flat thump. Pieces of rotting garbage broke over the edge of the window and landed in my lap.

"Guards!" Crawford lurched forward. "My lady, are you all right?"

Of course I was. The count should have been far more concerned about the boy, because at that moment, four fully grown men seized him. The boy cried out as he disappeared under a barrage of uniforms and the butt of a rifle.

"Stop!" I was moving before I knew it. Behind me, the count called out, but I ignored him as I hopped down from the carriage. The boy struggled, caught by the collar of his coat.

"Let me go!" He got a solid kick at the guard's shin before he could react, and the boy was rewarded for his trouble with a harsh shake and a slap across the face.

"Stop!" I strode across the stones, practically at a run, as the boy struggled again.

"Filthy brat!" The guard lifted his hand, and I leaped, grabbing hold of his thick wrist and pulling him off balance before he could hit the child again. He must not have seen me coming at all, because he tilted and cursed, and the boy slipped free of his grasp. He might have made a run for it, but there were three other guards to take up the work of their colleague. One kicked out savagely and caught the boy's ankles, sending him sprawling to the ground.

"No!" I reached for him then yelped as a hand caught my veil and pulled me back. "Let go of me!"

"Stop!" The voice rang out over the mounting chaos, and everyone froze. The count stalked toward us. His face was red, his eyes so narrow, they were nothing more than black slits.

"Your Worship!" the guard who still had his hand in my hair said. "These two were—"

"Unhand the lady."

"But sir, she—" Whatever the guard was going to say was cut off by the count's fist against his jaw. He yelped, and he let me go. I tumbled to the ground.

"That lady is your future queen."

"But—"

I ignored the sound of fist and skin connecting again and scrambled to the boy who now lay curled on the ground. I put a hand on his shoulder. He jerked, but then he rolled, staring tearily up at me.

"Are you all right?" I asked. He nodded, and I pulled him upright into a hug.

"My Lady George." The count was still fussing behind me. "I'm sure we can find someone who will deal with the boy. If you would just—"

"Is your mother here?" I asked the boy. He nodded into my neck. "Should we go find her?" He detached himself but clung to my hand. Without a look behind me at the count's reaction, we walked toward the crowd at the gate, now larger with gawkers no doubt drawn by the commotion. Women and children pressed against the guards, who were struggling to hold them back. As I approached, the boy let go of my hand and ran into the arms of a woman who gathered him up and sobbed.

"Thank you! Thank you so much!" she said to me.

I stayed on the opposite side of the guards, but I smiled. "No harm done. No reason to hurt him."

"I couldn't have borne it if they'd taken him away. We've lost so much already."

"Your husband?" There were so many strained faces in front of me. So many women, some even younger than I was, some old and shrunken by age and starvation.

"And my brother. Please." The woman reached out despite the guards and grabbed at my skirt. "Please. You have to help us. You have to tell them. We'll starve if they don't—"

"Get back!" The count stepped between us.

"Please!" The woman's voice rose, and the crowd behind her picked up the sound, echoing it in a collective moan.

"I don't know what I can—" I tried to say, but the noise was growing, people pressing in. The guards struggled to hold them back, and more soldiers came to join in holding back the human tide coming through the gate.

A hand gripped my shoulder, gentler than the one that had pulled my veil. I turned to fight off whoever was there, but it was Crawford. His grip was firm, but his eyes were wide and sympathetic.

"We can't help them. Not like this," he said. I opened my mouth to protest, but he shook his head. "You'll only stir them up more. Please, my lady. Not like this."

I glanced over my shoulder. The boy and his mother had

vanished, but the crowd was swelling. Angry voices rose, ignoring the guards' orders to stand down.

A familiar flash of glasses in the sun caught my attention, and for a moment, my heart stopped. But then I looked back, and whatever I'd seen must have been a trick of the light. Where I thought I'd spotted Niall, looming tall and lanky at the edge of the crowd, there were now only unfamiliar faces.

I followed Crawford back to the carriage. The horses were dancing nervously in place. I ignored the count's offered hand, instead hitching my skirts up and climbing back into the carriage on my own. As soon as he joined me, the door was slammed shut, and the carriage lurched forward.

"You're a fool," Crawford said.

"They were hurting that boy! I couldn't let them." I adjusted my veil. The hair beneath it had come loose, and I wouldn't be able to fix it without taking it off completely, which was something I couldn't do until we returned to the palace.

"When you're queen, you can save as many little boys as you like. But what you did was pointless at best and dangerous at worst. If the prince—"

"What would the prince do? Would he have stepped aside and let the guards beat that child?"

Crawford swallowed. The carriage jolted to a halt. We were still within the grounds of the admiralty office, but the sound coming from the gate was farther away.

I fidgeted in my seat. What had I been expected to do? Sit in this ridiculous contraption and look the other way?

"What do the women want?"

He shifted, brushing at a fleck of dirt on his coat. "Their husband's pensions."

"And?"

He gritted his teeth, but finally, he spoke. "And the admiralty won't pay it out until it can be proven that the men are actually dead."

I inhaled sharply. The only thing I could think of was Lou, whose body had never been brought home.

"But that might never happen."

The count nodded. "If no bodies are found, and if the men don't return, then after a year—"

"A year? What are they supposed to live on for a year? What good is their grief if there's no way to pay for food for a year?"

He set his jaw. I was overstepping what he expected from a gentle lady, but whatever my heritage was, I was no princess.

The carriage jostled as a door was opened, and like a gust of fresh air, Prince Beverly climbed in.

"Ridiculous. A bunch of old fools who still think my father is in charge. Driver!" he bellowed. I stared out the window as the carriage rolled forward once more.

"How was the meeting, Your Highness?" Crawford asked mildly.

"Oh, don't call me that. You know I hate it when you're formal," the prince growled. "They wouldn't listen. They're insisting on sending more ships out. I said it wasn't safe. I said their own incompetence had sunk my best ships, but will they listen?"

The carriage rolled out a separate gate from the one we'd come through. This one was smaller, and there was no sign of the stricken women who had been waiting at the other one.

The prince leaned forward and patted my hand. "I hope that wasn't too boring for you. If it were up to me, we wouldn't have gone there at all, but the navy can barely function without my attention. I promise you, this afternoon will be much more enjoyable."

I tucked my hand into my sleeve and continued to stare out the window.

I was a fool. Crawford had that part right, although his reasoning was flawed. It wasn't my fault. The last few days had been surreal chaos, and all I could do was fight not to drown. But the two men in front of me would be disappointed if they expected me to step into line and not speak out when someone was being hurt. My days in the print shop were over, but that didn't mean I couldn't make changes.

"Why is your hair exposed? And what happened to your dress?" The prince's brows were drawn together. I followed his gaze. My dress was dark with mud just above my knees. I rubbed at it but only succeeded in smearing it.

"There was an incident," Crawford said.

The prince's attention snapped to him. "An incident? How long was I gone for? What sort of incident?" His steely eyes swung back to me. "Did you leave the carriage?"

I bit back the retort that no, I'd just managed to find mud inside his immaculate carriage. Instead, I said, "The guards were assaulting a boy."

"After he assaulted you!" Crawford said.

"After he what?" Beverly's voice rose.

"A bit of garbage does not make an assault." I stared pointedly at the count.

"Garbage?" the prince asked.

"The child slipped into the courtyard from the crowd. He threw—" The count explained, but Beverly cut him off, still speaking to me.

"And you intervened?"

"They were hurting him!" This was what I'd feared when Jeremy had sneered that I would be leaving his house. This was what I'd imagined when I'd cried in Niall's arms. This spoiled, self-centered prince who couldn't see why the incident in the courtyard was anything but a personal inconvenience.

As if to prove my point, Beverly slumped back in his seat. "This is perfect. How could you be so thoughtless? We'll be late now."

My fury stumbled. "Late?"

Beverly muttered something to himself. I waited, but he didn't say anything further.

Finally, the count spoke. "It's my mother's birthday. She's also the prince's aunt. There is an evening planned in her honor at the summer gardens. We were going to have lunch with her first as a private gathering to welcome you into the family. Did no one tell you?"

"No." My face flamed in embarrassment, even though I wasn't responsible for my ignorance.

"Well, it doesn't matter now." The prince glared at my stained skirts.

"It's not as if I fell on purpose. They were hurting—"

"Yes, a poor, unfortunate child who had only attacked the carriage."

"There was no attack! There was one desperate child!"

"Any such act of defiance against the crown is punishable by death." His tone was flat as he said it. It wasn't a threat, just a statement of fact.

Too far, George, too far. I took a long breath, staring at my husband-to-be. Could I do this? Truly? Would it be better to infuriate him to the point where he took my head now? He'd said he would.

Don't be stupid. I'd only known him for a day. Too soon to give up. There had to be a way to survive.

I mirrored him and slumped back in my seat. "It doesn't matter. They'll be dead within the year anyway."

He scoffed. "Now you're being dramatic."

"Crawford told me."

Beside the prince, Crawford blanched. "I did?"

"You said they were the poorest. The most desperate. Without their widow's pensions, those women and their children will starve."

Beverly laughed. "Don't be silly. There is more grain in the fields this summer than there has been in a decade."

"And how will they pay for it? What good is grain if there's no way to buy it?"

The carriage fell silent. The two men stared, and I stared right back. Wretched Prince Beaverly would know the kind of woman he was going to marry.

At last, the prince sighed. "What exactly are you asking for?"

"I've been served more food in the last day than those women will see in their households for the next month. Surely something can be done."

He sighed. "This is what you want?"

"It's what anyone would want."

He watched me for a minute longer, and I kept my shoulders square and my chin level. Never mind my muddy dress or my twisted veil. We would be equals.

"Crawford," Beverly said.

"Yes, Your Highness?"

The prince's eyes never left me the whole time he spoke. "Send a message to the admiralty. Tell them the palace grain stores will be made available to any of the families whose men are currently missing at sea."

"Sir—"

"It is a wedding gift from the Lady George and myself to our people. Until the matter of the missing is resolved, none of them will be allowed to go hungry."

Heat poured over my ears and down the back of my neck. I'd won.

"It will be done," Crawford said.

Could it be that simple?

Beverly leaned across the carriage and gently clasped my hand. His expression had gone soft, like it had been in the garden that morning.

"Will that do?" he asked.

I studied him, adrenaline still fizzing in my veins. It was so hard to read him. Maybe with time I would learn. But today, I didn't truly know if I'd won or lost.

"Yes." I wouldn't thank him. Not when what we'd just agreed on would affect so few families. There were so many more who would still struggle.

"Can we carry on with our day now?" He traced a finger over

the sparkling bracelet on my wrist. "Please, George. I would like us very much to be friends."

I wanted to be angry at him. Wanted to list all of his offenses against his people. But antagonizing him more wouldn't produce the right results over the long term. I had time. Niall had always said we needed to be strategic in our resistance. There was time for me to change him and Redmere, too.

"Yes, Your Highness."

"Beverly." He grinned an earnest smile that had me blushing despite myself. I couldn't help it, particularly when I caught sight of the spark of approval in Crawford's eye as he watched us silently.

"Beverly," I said.

"George and Beverly." He laughed. "We'll be quite the pair."

5

We returned to the palace because my muddy dress was unacceptable for my role. The prince said we would cancel the lunch.

"My aunt is a bit of a snob anyway." He grinned, and Crawford laughed softly beside him.

A rider had been sent ahead of us, and Rosie was pacing anxiously in the hall as I entered. She was a flurry of activity. When we returned to my room, I was stripped out of my dress with such force that I nearly fell.

"Take off your boots." Rosie tossed the muddy dress in the corner. "The laundress is not going to be pleased about that skirt at all."

"My boots?"

"George." Rosie's eyes were wide, and she heaved. "You can't wear those boots to meet a duchess. If I'd known that was where he was taking you when you left the garden this morning, I would have insisted on putting you in something finer."

"You won't even let me choose my shoes?"

"Those ridiculous boots you wore yesterday say you can't be trusted."

Rosie called for lunch—more endless trays, and I resolved to speak to someone in the kitchen as soon as possible—then began the arduous task of dressing me to meet a duchess. My heart fluttered. The announcement we'd read at Niall's said my engagement would be formally announced at the duchess's birthday, and then Beverly and I would be married in a week.

When I was dressed again, the prince and I rode out in the carriage together. The count had gone on ahead.

"He hates riding in these things," Beverly said. He'd also taken advantage of the return to the castle to change his clothes. That morning, he'd been dressed in a severe black coat, nearly military in its cut, but he'd replaced that now with one that was dark blue, trimmed in black fur. It was the opposite of the dress Rosie had put me in, which was the color of pewter and trimmed at the neck and cuffs in white fur like a rabbit's, though I suspected it was made from something far more wild than the commonplace rabbits that had lived around my father's house and fed us on more than one evening. The sleeves flared from the elbows like the gown I'd worn at the dressmaker's shop, and I found myself unconsciously tugging at the hems, trying to keep my wrists covered.

"Do you not like the dress?" he asked as I pulled on the sleeve yet again.

"It was very . . . thoughtful."

"Yes, well, I heard that your brother wasn't able to provide you with an acceptable wardrobe, so it was my pleasure to do so. In private, like tonight, a little frivolity is acceptable, don't you think?"

Acceptable for whom? For him and his friends? Even the dressmaker wouldn't make a dress like this. The pewter fabric shone a little too brightly, and the fur was too white and would draw attention. No woman I'd ever seen would wear a dress like this unless they had a prince on their arm to shield them. What a privilege he offered. Freedom, as long as I was willing to accept his gifts and fine words.

Many people would have been more than willing to make the trade.

I forced myself to hold still as Beverly reached for my hand, tangling our fingers together. Then, as if the touch were not enough, he sat on my side of the carriage so we were pressed together from knee to shoulder. "What man wouldn't want to look after his wife? You're going to be very popular tonight," Beverly said, stroking a thumb over my knuckles. He wore a heavy gold ring encrusted in rubies on his heart finger, and the metal warmed against my skin.

"Will there be very many people?" I asked, trying to think of some conversation topic that wouldn't be loaded with half-answers and winks that made me squirm.

"A few hundred, I should think." He said it casually, then laughed when I gaped at him.

"A few hundred?"

He kissed my knuckles, and I was too shocked at what he'd said to pull my hand away.

"They'll all want a glimpse of you, the future queen, of course, but you'll only be expected to speak to a handful of them. I'll stay with you the whole time." He squeezed my hand, bringing it to his chest. "George, please don't think that what happened yesterday is any indication of how it'll be for us. We'll be there together, and I'll protect you."

I bit my lip. There were so many questions. Why would I need protecting? How would it be for us? If there were a few hundred people who were well-connected enough to be invited to a duchess's birthday celebration, what had possessed him to choose me as a wife?

Without any warning, Beverly kissed me.

I'd never kissed anyone before. It was wetter than I'd thought it would be. His lips were smooth and soft, and his breath brushed warmly over my skin before he pulled away, giving me a crooked grin and stroking a thumb along my jaw. My skin prickled, but otherwise, I felt nothing. Could he gauge my reaction—

or lack thereof—just by touching me? What would he do if he knew?

"That was very forward of me," he said.

I licked my lips. Nervous laughter threatened to bubble out of my throat, but laughing at a prince after he'd kissed me seemed like the worst thing I could do. My fingers skimmed over my dress, which was suddenly scratchy and uncomfortable.

"Did I overstep?" he asked. My heart thudded in my chest. I was so confused. A few hours ago, we'd been arguing over starving children and his responsibility to look after them, and now we were dressed like royalty—we *were* royalty!—and kissing in carriages.

"George?" His hand was back in mine, and I started at the sensation. "Look at me. Did I upset you?"

Helplessly, I shook my head.

"Did you like kissing me?"

Had I? The mechanics of kissing had been more pleasurable than I might have expected, but there was no rush of desire, no surge of warm feelings, unlike the way the heroines in the books Lou and I had read as girls had felt. I didn't feel that and never would, but admitting that would get me killed almost as quickly as admitting to treason.

My brain fluttered with a hundred, tiny, panicked thoughts. Niall saying they didn't hang people for that anymore. The soft press of the prince's thumb on my jaw, his fingers on my wrist as he offered me presents. Would he always be so gentle? There would be children—or at least the expectation of them—not too long in the future. What if I couldn't? Not just bear children. What if I couldn't bring myself to be with him the way I'd need to if he wanted an heir?

"I don't know," I said, feeling suddenly miserable.

He cocked his head to one side, smiling crookedly. I half expected him to pat my head and call me a good girl. Instead, he brought our hands to his chest.

"We'll be all right, you and I," he said. "You, George, are everything I could have hoped for."

If only he knew what I felt inside.

6

The sun was setting as we arrived at the summer gardens outside the city.

"My grandmother had it built," Beverly said as the carriage pulled around. "My grandfather was always off fighting one war or another, and she said she needed something to do. It's said she was always fond of gardening, but I don't think anyone imagined she would take her enthusiasm to this scale."

The carriage door opened, and Beverly stepped down. A footman appeared, but the prince waved him off. He helped me down himself and tucked my hand in the crook of his arm.

"You might want to build something like this once we're married." His tone was so conversational, and my head only continued to whirl.

"A garden?"

He shrugged. "Or whatever would please you. You will be a beautiful queen, and if it would make you happy, I would let you build a hundred gardens."

Or feed a hundred families? I didn't understand this man at all. His words were so thoughtful and thoughtless at the same time, but before I could say anything, he led me through the gate.

I'd imagined a welcoming committee as there had been when

I'd arrived at the palace. At least Crawford, ready to attend his prince or scold us for being late. But he wasn't there. Music played in the distance, but Beverly and I were alone.

"Where is everyone?"

Beverly chuckled. "They're all in the garden."

"They've started without you?"

His hip bumped playfully against mine before he took a step forward. "You're going to have to learn, my dear George, that it is the prerogative of royalty to arrive as they see fit and to always make an entrance." When I went to take my place a pace behind him, he held me firm, keeping me next to him instead. "No, George. Tonight, you stay at my side."

"But—"

He placed a finger beneath my chin so I had to look at him. "Another privilege of the station. The rules are ours to make."

The garden was an endless tangle of carefully constructed shrubbery. There were no offshoots, no forks in the road to confuse the traveler. It was simply a long and winding walk to the center so anticipation could build.

It wasn't empty. The labyrinth wound in a spiral, but after the first trip around the longest loop on the perimeter, a few scattered people appeared. Couples who gazed at each other, daring convention in the relative privacy from one curve to the next. The occasional chaperone stood a respectful distance aside, keeping a watchful eye on their lady. Their presence was a silent reminder we were still in Redmere, even if the ladies were dressed as I was in colors a shade too bright and with jewelry that no one would wear in public. Many stared as we went past, and I stared right back because I'd never seen so many women in one place, and certainly none who looked as at ease as they did. Along with the fine dresses and ornamentation, they laughed and smiled in a way you never saw in the city streets. Where did they live? Nowhere they'd have to pass the starving widows in the harbor on the way home. They couldn't face that and still be so carefree.

The path widened as we approached the center, which was good because many of the people we came across joined us as we made our way. By the time we reached our destination, a procession had formed with me at its head, still holding my place at Beverly's right hand.

The hedges opened up, welcoming us into a large, sunken amphitheater. Scores of people stood about. There were long tables heaped with food—roasted fowl, pretty cakes, and everything in between—and torches that lit stone stairs up the aisles where people might sit to watch a play, if plays were something still done in Redmere. Three men in vibrant costumes were doing a merry dance while others played sparkling flutes to the amusement of the people around them. I hadn't seen dancing like that since I'd left my father's house.

"It's quite something, isn't it?" Beverly spoke low in my ear.

"It's. . . " It was wrong. Why could the prince have this kind of entertainment while anyone who played a tune with a pair of wooden spoons risked being taken by the City Guard?

"Beverly!" Crawford's voice caught my attention as he strode through the crowd, and then I was distracted again as every head around us turned. There'd been lively chatter as we'd arrived, but as Crawford came to greet us, all activity stopped.

"Time for that entrance," Beverly said, and my eyes widened. I thought we'd already made our entrance with every person we'd passed on our way down here. But those people were only a fraction of the crowd gathered for the party.

Beverly stepped forward, lifting my hand to the level of our shoulders. My sleeve fell back, exposing both Beverly's diamond bracelet and Lou's plain silver one. I trembled but held my ground. Now wasn't the time for fainting, and whatever these people saw, it wasn't a traitor. I'd carried on a double life with Niall and the dressmaker. I could withstand these people and their scrutiny. Time for my entrance.

"My lords and ladies!" Beverly said, voice pitched to carry across the entire space. "Friends, all of you. I know many of you have worried for the state of our country, and possibly a few have even been worried for me." Beverly pushed out his lip and furrowed his brows in an exaggerated plea for sympathy, and a ripple of laughter went out over the crowd. "I ask you then, friends, to cease your worry and prepare to celebrate. I have found a bride, and I trust you will be as pleased with her as I am."

There were a few shocked gasps and more excited chatter as Beverly proceeded to recite a litany of my qualifications and credentials to be their future queen. My too-long list of names, followed by the names and titles of my ancestors.

"Ladies and gentlemen, I cannot tell you how proud I am to introduce the woman at my side. She is as kind as she is beautiful, and she will do us all proud as the queen of Redmere. Friends, we are all honored to be in the presence of"—he took a half step back so that I stood alone—"Princess Georgina!"

I shivered as the echo of Beverly's voice died and the silence thickened. Time expanded while hundreds of eyes examined me. I focused on my breaths—one, two—while my heart beat a rapid staccato in my chest.

Crawford knelt, his hand to his heart. He was followed by the people immediately around him. One by one, the entire crowd cascaded down until all of them, men and women, knelt where they were. Never mind their fine clothes, never mind whatever dirt might be beneath them on the paths and rows of the amphitheater.

"To Princess Georgina!" Crawford's voice carried across the space, and in one breath, the cry was echoed. It was followed by applause that started like rain and grew to a storm as everyone joined in.

My knees wobbled at the sight of it all, the idea that it was for me. A steadying hand gripped my elbow. The prince was there again, his mouth close to my ear as he said, "I hope you don't mind me using your proper name. I want to keep George for myself."

The applause and cheers continued, growing again as the

prince drew me near. On an invisible signal, a servant appeared, carrying a silver tray with two fine crystal glasses on it. My throat was parched, and I took one gratefully.

"To you," Beverly said as he lifted his drink toward me.

The crowd dissolved into its loose association again. Beverly wrapped my free hand around his arm once more and led me through the throng. He'd promised to stay near me, and he was true to his word. He'd also been right in that while every single person we passed stopped their conversation to look at us, I had to speak to very few of them. A duke here, an ambassador there, and we never received more than their congratulations before Beverly moved us on.

"Your Highness! Both Your Highnesses." A smiling older man with a round face stepped in front of us. I nearly tripped on the hem of my skirt, and the way Beverly went rigid next to me said he hadn't been expected to stop either.

"Lord Parrington," he said, smile bland.

"This is such a wonderful evening. Your Highness, Princess Georgina, so wonderful to meet you." Lord Parrington bowed deeply, and as he did, I suddenly remembered where I'd heard his name before. He was the man whose wife had been kidnapped by Captain Cinder.

"Lord Parrington," I said, then hesitated. Should I say something about his wife? The ships that had been lost? Instead, I managed a weak, "The pleasure is all mine."

A young woman was standing behind Parrington's shoulder. She appeared younger than I, and while she wore her veil, it was perched higher on her head so that the first inch of fine blonde hair was visible. While my elegant dress was done up to my chin, hers left her throat exposed. The look was daring, and I'd seen women arrested for less.

Beverly seemed to notice my attention had strayed because he said, "I see you've brought your daughter tonight."

Parrington beamed. "Yes, well. After the . . . er . . . situation with her mother, I thought . . ." But whatever he thought was cut off as Beverly cleared his throat. Parrington flushed and stammered to a halt.

"Your Highness." The young woman dropped into a graceful curtsy. Her voice was smooth like honey, and I couldn't tear my eyes away from the thin line of her scalp where her hair was parted or the gentle curve of her lips as she smiled at me. She was beautiful, like the princesses I'd imagined in storybooks. I shouldn't be staring the way I was, though she was dressed to invite the eye. Maybe her father had even brought her here to find her a rich husband. They couldn't have known their future queen would be just as intrigued.

Parrington was still uncomfortable and took his daughter's hand in his.

"If you'll excuse us. I've just seen someone I need to speak with," he said, and hurried them both away.

"The nerve of that man," Beverly muttered.

"They seemed charming," I said.

"But who could Parrington possibly see who was more important to speak with than you?" His eyes sparkled, and he continued us on our way.

We didn't get very far before we encountered the large man in red.

He stood out even before we were close to him. He was taller than the guests around him and dressed in a coat the color of dark rubies where most of the rest of the guests had chosen Redmerian grays and black. Where even the prince wore a collar buttoned to his chin, this man's jacket was fastened with laces, most of which were undone and hanging sloppily from his neck, showing off his throat and the white shirt he wore beneath.

The man was very drunk. Alcohol was not illegal in Redmere, but drinking too much of it was prohibited in many contexts. The party had been going for some time before we'd arrived, and while many guests spoke more animatedly than they might in normal conversation, this man stood with a crowd of other men, arguing loudly about who had the faster horse.

As our tiny entourage approached, the man laughed and leaned back, then his arms flailed. He was large and gathering some steam, and without any obvious attempt to stop himself, he tumbled directly into our path.

His glass, full to the brim with red wine, poured freely down the front of my dress. I stared in horror as the crimson stain spread from the white fur trim all the way down to my toes. Warm hands swiped futilely at my stomach, almost like they were trying to catch the wine before further damage could be done.

"My lady!" The drunk man pawed at me. "My lady, I'm so sorry! I'm so clumsy."

"What happened?" Count Crawford asked as he approached us.

"You fool!" Beverly was on the man in red in an instant, shoving him away.

His eyes bugged out as he stumbled back. "Your Highness! I'm so sorry."

Beverly wasn't moved by his apology. He grabbed the man by the collar of his coat and hauled him close despite his size.

"Yes. 'Your Highness.' I'm pleased to see you're not so drunk as to not recognize who I am. And, if you failed to pay attention, that lady"—he dragged the man around so he could stare at me with frightened eyes—"is my betrothed and your future queen."

"Please." Even though he was taller than the prince, the man's feet scrabbled as his fingers grabbed at Beverly's hands, desperately seeking release.

"Please? After you've insulted a princess?" Beverly's voice turned low and mean. "After you've embarrassed her on the very evening she's introduced to the entire kingdom?" He gave the man a shake. "You should be whipped for daring to touch her. In fact—" He shoved his prisoner toward Crawford, who grabbed hold of him and nodded solemnly.

My stomach turned. They couldn't flog a man over an accident like this.

"No." I rushed forward, grabbing the prince's elbow. "Please. You can't."

His shoulders tensed like he might shake me off. "He touched you. He insulted you. I should—"

"No." I stepped in front of him. Beverly's expression was murderous. My nerve nearly failed me, but I set my shoulders and planted my hands on his chest. "Please. Don't spoil a perfectly good evening."

"*He* has spoiled it for you."

"He hasn't. It's only a dress. Please." I closed the space between us, trying to find the same sense of intimacy we'd shared in the carriage. "Please. Beverly." I cringed inwardly at the use of his name, especially with so many people in earshot, but I needed his attention. "Not for a dress. Let him go."

His chest heaved under my palms as he continued to glare over my shoulder. His nostrils flared. I needed another way to placate him. He'd kissed me before. Could I kiss him now? It would cause a scandal, and I'd have to deal with the aftermath, but the immediate concern of the man in red would be forgotten.

The prince let out a long sigh. His hands covered mine, patting gently. The tension melted underneath my palms, and a few seconds later, he blinked. His gaze came back to me, and he smiled gently, wrapping my hand tightly against his chest.

"You want to spare this man?"

I tried to match his gaze, hoping he'd understand. Hoping I looked enchanted by his kindness to everyone watching instead of desperate to avoid his wrath. "You've given me so many other dresses. Why hurt him for this one?"

"It's your night. He should be punished for his insolence."

I glanced over my shoulder. The man was still caught firmly in Crawford's grasp, the velvet of his coat crushed in the count's fist, and his eyes were frightened.

"I'm sorry," he said, voice wavering.

I turned back to the prince. "There. You see? He has apologized. Let him go."

He stared at me, but then his expression softened further. He nodded at Crawford. "As the princess commands. We will not have him whipped. But see that he is escorted off the grounds."

A murmur of approval spread over the crowd, and the man in the red coat babbled his thanks as he was led, still not altogether gently, away. As he disappeared, the prince turned his attention back to me. He smiled and brought my hand to his mouth, kissing the knuckles. Excited whispers ignited around us.

"You are so brave," Beverly said. "And kind. Redmere will be so lucky to have you as queen."

Still aware of the people watching, my gaze dropped. I hadn't done anything particularly special. It *was* only a dress. But then I saw the great stain that trailed down the entire length of my gown and made a small, sad noise.

"We should go." Beverly drew me close to him.

"No." I fought disappointment that came from so many angles. The moment—that brief shining thing where I'd felt confident among all these people—was gone, and I didn't know how to find it again. Everyone was still watching me, but where I'd been a princess, I was now just a poor girl in a ruined dress.

"Yes. It's not fair to you to stay. We'll return to the palace." He snapped a finger, and like before, a servant appeared. This time, instead of a tray of wine, he carried a cloak, which Beverly fastened around my neck.

"There." He smiled, and I put on my bravest smile in return. "Still a princess."

"We don't have to go." With the cloak, the stain was hardly visible, though now I felt shabby in the plain gray.

He squeezed my hand. "The privilege of royalty extends not only to making an entrance but to taking our leave any time we choose. Come. There will be other parties."

But this one had barely started. I glanced over my shoulder, and a dozen or more heads snapped away from me, as if they had —and they undoubtedly had—been listening to every word being said.

"Take me back to the palace," I said.

———

THE RIDE HOME was less eventful than the trip to the gardens. After Beverly fretted a little longer over my dress and I assured him I was fine, we lapsed into silence, which didn't bother me in the least. I was exhausted. The carriage rolled through dark country roads, swaying gently, and I dozed as my mind reeled from everything that had happened.

By the time we'd arrived at the palace, I must have dropped off completely, because I started when Beverly set a hand on my shoulder.

"I don't mind carrying you," he said, wide smile visible even in the dark.

I forced myself to sit up straight. "I'm all right."

Servants opened the doors for us as we approached. Another privilege of royalty. Regardless of the time, there were always lights on in the great hall and servants ready to open the door. That privilege, however, did not appear to extend to my own personal servant, because Rosie was nowhere to be seen.

Beverly pressed a gentle kiss against my cheek. "Good night, George. You were perfect today."

My sleepy brain faltered, and all I could do was bob with a curtsy. "Thank you."

He laughed softly. "Sleep well. I have something special planned for tomorrow." His hand lingered in mine, but then he turned and left.

Despite the time and my fatigue, I was able to find my way back to my room, only getting turned around once. Rosie was asleep in a chair as I let myself in, but she sprang to attention as I closed the door, eyes wide and voice mournful at the state of my gown.

"Two dresses in one day!" she said as she undid the laces. "And the fur too! I don't think we'll be able to save this."

Today had been an adventure and definitely far more of a success than the previous one. The prince was . . . well, he was temperamental. Spoiled. But not a monster. I almost wished he was. Things had been simpler when I'd been prepared to hate him. Two days ago, I'd felt smart and brave doing what I could to help Niall and spread the truth about the prince and his actions. I felt outmatched in every way, and I wondered if I'd been making any difference at all.

I slept, but not gently. Ideas and strategies whirled through my mind. I should try to escape. I should sneak a letter to Niall. I could confide in Rosie and we could go together. I could stay and be the queen that Redmere needed so desperately. No more passing letters. Here, if I could find a place, I could be a real champion for the people. Beverly wasn't a monster. Perhaps he would listen to me like he had in the garden last night.

When the sun finally peeked through the windows, I climbed out of bed, careful not to disturb Rosie. A soft robe was draped over one of the arms of the sofa, and I pulled it on before hastily pinning my veil into place. I needed to find the prince. If nothing else, I wanted to make sure the man in red from the party last night had really been released. And I wanted to talk more about the families at the harbor. Feeding them was a kind gesture. Finding ways to help them and others like them, even after their pensions were paid, would be better.

But where to find the prince? I had no idea where he stayed when he was in the palace.

"Rosie." I shook her.

"Mm?" she muttered sleepily.

"Where are the prince's rooms?"

"What?" Rosie rolled toward me, rubbing at her eyes.

"I want to find the prince. Where would he be?"

"His rooms are past the gardens," she said, pushing up to her elbows. "But you want to see him now?"

"Yes." I felt like I'd been awake for hours. No reason to wait. He had me perpetually off-balance, and if the best I could manage was to catch him before he was dressed for the day, I'd have to be satisfied with it for now.

"I'll get you some clothes. Let me come with you."

"No, it's fine." I didn't need an escort or a guide. I wanted to meet the prince as an equal, not a child who needed to be supervised all the time.

I made my way from my room to the palace hall with no trouble at all and mentally patted myself on the back for my success. The trip to the garden was more difficult. Rosie had led the way there the day before, and she'd taken a number of side trips to show off various rooms and features of the palace. Whether that was the most direct route was hard to say, but I did my best, and passed rooms I knew and portraits hung on the wall that I recognized.

Somewhere, I must have missed a turn, because I found myself in a short hall with only one door. When I opened it, I wound up in a library. The walls were covered from the floor to the tops of the high ceilings with books. I'd never been a great reader other than the adventure stories Lou and I had read together. My tutors had tried to instill a love of literature, but I'd never found the stories and warnings of long-dead men particularly appealing. But surely here, where there must have been more books than there were people in the city, I would find something I would like.

Maybe Beverly liked to read? This was his library, after all. I hadn't yet given much thought to how the prince spent his time when he wasn't busy doing princely things. A man who liked to read couldn't be all bad.

From the far end of the room, voices filtered through a door that had been left ajar. It was early, but apparently, I was not the only person awake in the palace.

As I drew closer to the door, the voices became more distinct. I recognized Beverly's first and then the count's soon after. My pulse picked up. I paused long enough to make sure I wasn't interrupting. They were mid-conversation, and while I doubted they would mind my arrival, I'd wait if they were discussing something important.

It did seem that they were.

"Don't be so arrogant," Crawford said. "You cannot risk a land war for the sake of a few miles of trade route."

"But we need to establish trade with Yagrad. All we have left that anyone wants to buy is fish and wool, neither of which earn nearly enough money."

"We can simply go around the Oarian border and cross into Yagrad from the south. It's only a few miles."

I didn't know where these places were. I'd never been on a journey longer than the trip from my father's house to school, and then from school to the city. Neither had taken more than a few days.

"A few miles? It's half a mountain range. It would take weeks to go around!" Beverly sounded irritated.

"Better than paying the tariffs in Oaria to go through."

"We can't afford them anyway." He sighed. "If only we could go by sea."

"You know that's not an option. Not with pirates roaming the coasts."

"Yes, the pirates. What a nuisance. They've cost me as much as—"

A fly buzzed passed my ear, then made lazy circles around my head, distracting me so I didn't hear the end of his sentence. I tried to swat it away. The fly was persistent, and it took a few tries, but eventually it flew off. By the time I'd turned my attention back to the men in the other room, their conversation had moved on.

"I'm going back to the admiralty this morning. They're insisting on searching for the dead. Don't they know we can't afford to pay out all those pensions?"

I shrank back, hiding behind the open door as my scalp prickled.

"Will you be taking the princess with you again?"

Beverly laughed. "Of course."

"She did very well yesterday."

"She was perfect."

I flushed under their praise. It was vanity that kept me where I was, and that vanity was what saved my life.

"She is utterly perfect," the prince said again. "I didn't think you could do it, but you managed it."

"I do enjoy my work."

His work?

"Yes, but how you found such a beautiful, softhearted innocent is beyond me."

"The city is full of pretty, young women."

"But one with a titled family too? Who also has no family at all? No one to interfere as I mold her. How many of those can there possibly be?"

"I believe only one, sir."

My heart fluttered with fear.

"Oh, don't 'sir' me," Beverly said. "You're insufferable when you're being smug."

"She did very well with the widows yesterday. They responded to her almost immediately."

"It's the eyes. Those big, pleading eyes when she's upset. Who could say no to those?" Both men laughed, and I went cold.

"She is a bit more . . . spirited than her brother let on," the count said.

Beverly laughed again. "Yes! She does have a head on her, doesn't she? But that makes it all the more effective, don't you think? Next time, I'll make sure we have our little disagreements more publicly instead of in the carriage. It'll make it more convincing. The softhearted queen cannot bear the dastardly king's indifference to the suffering of his people. Look how in love they are. See how he has a change of heart because his beautiful wife asks it of him. They'll be in love with her by the end of the summer, and by extension, they'll love me in time for the coronation this winter." He clapped his hands, and I started at the sound. I bumped into the bookshelf, and it creaked. The count and Beverly didn't appear to hear me, because the prince continued.

"Yes. Perfect. Everything I could have hoped for when I asked you to find me a wife. Her temper just makes the game more interesting. If you'd brought me some innocent maiden, one who could be brought to head with a few mean words, there would've been no fun in that at all."

"It will make your endgame a little more difficult to pull off," the count said cautiously, but the prince only laughed.

"Nonsense. It just means we play a longer match. Give her time to build up her legend with the people. Queen Georgina, patron saint of the oppressed common folk of Redmere. We'll name a charity or two after her, have her present some flowers from time to time. The longer the people are with her, the less they'll notice what we're doing behind the scenes." He laughed again. "Maybe I'll even get an heir or two off of her. She's pretty enough. That would be no hardship. She has the sweetest mouth, did I tell you?"

My skin crawled, and my stomach heaved.

"So far as that?" the count asked.

"It wasn't part of the original plan, but you truly have brought me a treasure, Crawford. Why not take advantage?"

"And then?" Crawford said.

"And then." Beverly's voice was casual, but his next words spiraled my fear into panic. "When the moment is right, the saint will become a martyr."

7

How the prince and Crawford didn't hear me as I stumbled out of the library was a mystery, because I did it with all the grace and stealth of an intoxicated cow. If they'd found me, there would have been no hiding what I knew.

But their conversation continued as if they'd been discussing the weather.

"We'll tell the admiralty there will be no more searches," the prince said.

"We haven't really got the sailors to crew a full complement of ships anyway." I could picture the count staring out the window for all the interest his voice held.

Beverly sighed. "The whole situation with Parrington's wife has been absurd. No man should love his wife that much. We really weren't ready to send out that many men. Not this month. Did I tell you he was at the party last night? Practically threw his daughter at me even though Georgina was right there."

My feet and legs threatened to give way, my vision wavered, and my chest ached as I wound unseeingly through the castle's spiraling staircases and hallways. Even the servants had vanished, so no one was around to see my distress.

A martyr.

I would need to leave. Rosie would have to come with me too. If the prince had no compunction around killing me, then he'd absolutely not hesitate to find out what Rosie knew if I suddenly disappeared.

A sob threatened to burst free.

He was going to kill me.

I didn't want to die. Not anytime soon. Not for him and his plans.

Rosie was still asleep where I'd left her. Her hair was mussed and fell over her face. She was the picture of dreamy obliviousness.

A tear rolled down my cheek, and I wiped it away roughly. Now was not the time to fall apart. I would outsmart him. He was ruthless, but he underestimated me. I had time. He didn't mean to kill me today, and he didn't know that I'd heard him.

Wordlessly, I slipped into bed next to Rosie, who frowned in her sleep, but then simply rolled over and settled again. I stared at the ceiling, desperately trying to get my racing mind to follow Rosie's example. I couldn't panic. A rash decision would be disastrous.

My chin trembled. A plan. Such an absurd thought. What sort of plan would that be? Would I rally the men of the prince's army who were loyal to me? Lead the people in a carefully orchestrated rebellion?

I made the only choice I could.

Jeremy knew. The prince will kill me. If you really are more than a printer, I need your help.

The ink was barely dried as Rosie stirred. I had no idea if it was usual for a princess's maid to share a bed with her mistress, but I was hardly a princess, and Rosie's presence was the only thing keeping me from crumbling into total despair.

"What's wrong?" Rosie asked.

I blinked. I must have looked awful. "I have a headache." My voice was a croak, but it was too soon to upset Rosie. Until I knew what we were going to do, sharing what I'd learned this morning was risky. The more people who knew it, the greater the chance the prince or the count might find out.

Rosie clambered out of bed. "I'll get you some tea."

"I need . . ." My voice wavered. "Do you know the . . . the printer? Niall?"

She shook her head, and I couldn't hear any dishonesty when she said, "No. Why?"

It figured that she wouldn't. Safer if we each only knew one link in the chain. And Rosie's link was—"I need you to take a note to the dressmaker."

She froze in place, eyes wide. "Why?"

I couldn't tell her. Sending her out with my note was enough. "Nothing. Just a thank you for all her dedication. The dresses are perfect."

Rosie nodded slowly. "I'll have someone—"

"No!" The word came out more sharply than I meant. "I would appreciate it if you took it yourself." I had no idea how the dressmaker would get the note to Niall. That step had been my responsibility.

A knock sounded at the door.

I must have made a sound, because Rosie spun, eyes widening.

"George?"

It was him. He'd come for me after all. Toyed with me until my little mouse heart was ready to burst on its own.

I crumpled up the note and tossed it into the fire, waiting until it smoked and lit before I turned back to Rosie. "Answer it." I would find a way to face him.

Rosie went to the door and opened it. Instead of Beverly bursting through and dragging me off to his dungeons or to the main square to be publicly denounced, a quiet conversation followed between Rosie and whoever was on the other side of the door. With no more fuss than that, the person left again, and Rosie shut us in.

"Who was that?"

"The prince is going to the harbor again. He asked for your company, but I told the messenger you were unwell."

No. *No, no, no.* The room spun.

"I need to get dressed."

"You do not."

"I'm fine." I couldn't hide from Beverly. The longer I avoided him, the more sure he'd be that something was wrong.

"You aren't!"

I rounded on her, glaring, and was sorry for a moment when she stepped back. She was the only person in the whole world I trusted at the moment.

"Please. I don't want to stay cooped up here all day." I forced a smile as I stumbled toward the dressing room. "I'll be fine."

We argued, but she helped me dress. "You really don't look well," she muttered as she did the buttons at my throat.

"It's a headache. It won't kill me." Unlike the prince, if he ever knew that I'd heard him. He said he was playing a long game. I closed my eyes and ignored his comment about an heir. The memory of his mouth on mine the previous day made me shiver.

"You see?" Rosie spun me. "You're sick. This is ridiculous."

I shook my head, miserable again. "It's nothing. I didn't sleep well. There's so much to get used to. Help me pin my veil into place."

She stared, fingers drumming on her hips, then disappeared into the dressing room again. I paced while she was gone. I didn't know when the prince would be leaving, but I didn't want to be left alone here. Perversely, now that I knew he meant to kill me, I didn't want him to be out of my sight.

Rosie dressed quickly and emerged with two heavy cloaks over one arm.

"What are you doing?" I asked, sick horror twisting in my stomach.

"I'm going with you."

"What?"

She buttoned me into one of the cloaks and pinned my veil in place. "A princess shouldn't travel unescorted. I allowed it yesterday because His Highness was so romantic in the festival garden. But it's not done, even with princes. And you're ill. You need someone to attend you." She slung the second cloak over her shoulder with a flair that I would have appreciated if I weren't trying to choke down a fresh round of tears at her dedication.

"That's not necessary." It was hopeless, but I had to try one last time.

"It absolutely is. You should have a whole army of maids to attend you, not just me. But since I am what you have, you aren't going anywhere without me."

As I followed Rosie down the hall, her last words rang in my head. A whole army of maids. That was how it was supposed to be, wasn't it? All I had was her. Was keeping me isolated and friendless part of Beverly's plan? With fewer maids, there would be fewer people who would notice if something was wrong and offer opinions as the prince manipulated me into whatever scheme he dreamed of next.

What if Rosie was a spy after all? Not with Niall, but a spy for the prince? Her kindness could be a façade; our encounter in front of the dressmaker's a matter of chance. She might have been placed to feed information on my behavior and any uncomfortable questions I might ask the prince.

I couldn't think like that. If I believed that even Rosie was against me, I'd lose all hope.

Beverly and Crawford were nearly out the door as we finally arrived.

"Wait!" I hurried past Rosie. The men paused.

"George." The prince smiled, and his gentle surprise was almost worse than if he'd shown me the face of his true plan. "I was told you were unwell."

"I'm fine." My smile was so tense, my face felt like it might crack. "Nothing a little fresh air and sunshine won't resolve."

"And the aroma of the wharf?" He ran his hands down my

shoulders. I forced myself not to shrink back. I could do this. The long game. I would find a way to survive and ultimately to escape. My note to Niall was gone, but I could write another one. Even princesses must need to have something printed from time to time. I would find a way to contact him that didn't risk Rosie and the dressmaker along the way.

"Nothing better." I glanced over my shoulder, toward where Rosie hung back. "My maid will attend me."

Beverly scowled, but whatever he saw in Rosie gave him no pause because he took my elbow and walked me out the door.

"It's just as well that she comes too," he said. "I hate to leave you alone, but I'd much rather ride. Fresh air and sunshine, as you said."

My nerves fluttered, but I focused on walking in a straight line. A carriage was brought around. The footman held the door open, and I didn't flinch as Beverly took my hand and helped me up.

When the door closed firmly again with Rosie and me stowed safely inside, I exhaled.

Rosie clucked. "You should be in bed."

I leaned out the window, watching as the palace gates rolled by. At this moment in time, it was better to be anywhere but in the palace.

I'd never been betrayed before. I'd been abused, forgotten, left behind, and abandoned, but never outright lied to. Not when it mattered—except for the day Lou had promised to come back and then never had, but that was incomparable.

The scene at the harbor was much the same as it had been the day before. Guards at the main gate let us through while women and children pressed themselves against the bars.

The problem with realizing you'd been betrayed was that it made you question everything else. Had all of it been a lie? Had the prince sent anyone to open the grain stores? Were the people at the gate even who he said they were? What if they'd been planted there to gain my sympathy? What if the entire scene with the boy the day before had been staged? There had never been any risk to him, and, like a fool, I'd waded into the fray and played right into his hands.

The carriage door swung open, and he was there again, smile sparkling in the bright sun.

He held out his hand. "I told you I had a surprise for you," he said as he led me across the courtyard. I expected to go into the building, but instead, he brought me to the center, where the cobblestones met in something that looked like a compass star. A number of gray-haired men in severe uniforms and standing upright had formed a line, and they bowed as we approached. My heart thundered. They must have been there for a completely innocuous reason, but to me, they looked like a firing line.

"My Lady Georgina," Beverly said grandly. "May I present to you the admirals of the Redmerian Navy."

More bowing. I sweated nervously as I inclined my head at each. The prince said these were good men after a fashion, who were insisting on looking for survivors from the ships that had been lost. They had influence. Maybe I could ally myself with—

"I have an announcement," the prince said before dipping his lips to my ear so that only I could hear what he said next. "I think you'll be very pleased with me, George."

I was not. I would never be.

I smiled at him as if he hung the sun. It must have satisfied him, because he lifted a hand and called to the guards they'd passed.

"Open the gate!"

After a brief hesitation, the gates were pulled open with a great groan of metal. For a second, silence filled the courtyard. The women and children stared, wide-eyed, and stayed where they were.

"Go to them." Beverly nudged me forward. "Invite them in."

Like the guards, I hesitated, but couldn't see how his request was anything other than what it seemed. I glanced at Rosie, who stood near the carriage. Her face was bland as she stared at something out on the water.

I didn't see the boy from the day before or his mother, but the faces of the people gathered were the same. Hungry. Frightened. Mistrustful.

If I couldn't save myself, what hope did I have of helping these people?

I couldn't stop the wobble in my voice as I said, "The prince would like to speak with you. All of you. Please. Come in."

My stomach knotted. These people needed me, which was what the prince had counted on. He would prey on my isolation and sympathy to turn me into a figurehead while he worked behind me to destroy livelihoods and grow his own power.

I wouldn't let him. I didn't know how yet, but I wouldn't.

I didn't get the chance.

A flash to my left caught my attention, but I didn't even hear the boom before an invisible hand caught me squarely about the waist and pulled me off my feet, hurling me to the stones.

Or, rather than a hand, the force of the blast as the stone wall of the naval yard was blown in with a deafening explosion.

Rocks and chaos filled the space. Children screamed and men shouted. My chin connected with someone's boot, and I tasted blood in my mouth. My ears rang, and no matter which way I positioned myself, I couldn't find up.

Soldiers ran in every direction. The world was a cloud of dust, and smoke billowed through the gaping hole that had once been a wall.

The prince was across the courtyard, shouting at someone. He seemed completely unconcerned with the welfare of his bride-to-be. If I ran now, I could disappear before anyone noticed.

Rough hands grabbed me, hauling me to my feet. My veil snagged on something and pulled free, ripping out what felt like whole clumps of hair. But I had no time to dwell on that because strong arms dragged me toward the opening in the wall.

No. No, no. That was the wrong way. That way led to the wharf. I needed to get into the city, where I knew the streets and the places to hide. If I could make it to the print shop, Niall would help me, and I would do my best to get away before Beverly's men came for us and put Niall and everyone else he knew at risk.

But I was going the wrong way!

I kicked and struggled, digging my nails into the arms that held me tight.

"No need for that," a man's deep voice said in my ear, gritty as if he'd been shouting. He sounded amused, and it only made me struggle more.

Another man I couldn't see laughed and said, "The princess is a fighter!" in a deep accent I didn't recognize.

"Let go of me!" My words were shrill as I put all my weight into escaping. We were nearly to the wall. Behind us, shots rang out, and I shouted, even though a mountain of a man was between me and whoever was shooting. I tried to turn to see my captor's face, to look over his shoulder to see if the prince had noticed what was happening to me. Whether it was a better fate to hope he rescued me or to take my chances with these men was unclear.

Another shot echoed over the courtyard, and the man holding me grunted. I squeaked as he tripped. If he fell carrying me like this, I'd be crushed. When he stumbled again, I struggled, desperately trying to get free before he fell.

A new hand grabbed for me, and I was pulled from the iron arms as he toppled forward. I still had no chance to escape, because the man who had me now was running, pulling me along so fast that I would also fall if I tried to slow long enough to fight him off.

"Let me go!"

This new man's head was covered in a black cowl, and he

didn't turn back as he moved toward the docks. My corset dug into my ribs and hips, making it hard to breathe. I beat at the man's hand on my arm, but the cloak Rosie dressed me in was voluminous, and each of my blows was hampered as bunches of fabric were caught between my fist and his hand.

Rosie.

What had happened to Rosie? She'd been farther from the blast than I'd been, but in everything that had happened, what had become of her?

"Stop!" We were beyond the wall and into the bustling harbor, where everything was also chaos. Men rushed in the direction from which we'd just come. None of them seemed at all concerned about the man in the cloak abducting a princess.

I had to get back and find out what had happened to Rosie.

We passed a long table with a dozen fish on it abandoned in the excitement, some half-gutted and others staring lifelessly at the sky. One still had a knife embedded in its fishy host, and I reached desperately, catching it by its handle. I nearly lost it, slippery as it was, but I gritted my teeth, tightening my fingers around the hilt.

I slashed out desperately. He cursed, and I was surprised at the line of red that welled up on the back of the hand still tight around my wrist. I cried out as I slashed again, this time catching his forearm where his cloak had been pulled up.

"For God's sake, George, stop!" He turned to me, and the brief glimpse of his face—the long nose, the flash of his glasses under the hood—stopped my heart. I gaped, tripped, and nearly stabbed myself with the fish knife as I fell, instead catching my cheek against the hard edge of the wooden table.

Niall was on me in a second, but I couldn't have run away even if I'd tried.

Niall.

I went to speak, but all that came out were small, whimpering gasps.

His thumb wiped at my cheek. The pain mixed with relief at the sight of him, bringing tears to my eyes.

"Niall?" I wheezed.

"Yes. Silly girl. Did you think I'd abandon you?"

I didn't have the air to cry, but I wished I did.

"We have to go," he said. "They're waiting."

We were up again, but this time, I ran with him. His hand was on my elbow, guiding me through the people. The gesture was so like what the prince had done over the last few days, but where Beverly's hand on my arm had been about control, Niall's was only about support.

Shots sounded behind us, spurring us on. The crowd was thinning.

At the end of the wharf, a ship loomed.

"Almost there," Niall said.

Two men were running toward us. I couldn't see them clearly, but their clothes weren't from Redmere. Their pants billowed, and one wore a hat with a bright red feather that waved as they hurried toward us.

Another shot echoed over the water.

For the second time in the span of minutes, I was knocked to the ground.

The vibration of footsteps on the wooden boards of the pier rattled through my chest. I tried to push myself up, but Niall had flattened himself against me.

"Niall," I hissed. "The soldiers are coming."

He groaned and planted a hand to the left of my head. His hand and the cuff of his shirt were soaked in blood.

Heavy leather boots appeared in my line of sight, and Niall's weight was pulled off me.

"Take her," he gasped, and I was unceremoniously heaved over one man's shoulder. The other brought Niall to his feet. His cloak was open, and the front of his shirt was covered in red.

"Niall!" I called, but the man who carried me was running down the end of the pier toward the ship.

The man carrying Niall struggled. They were mismatched, and Niall's rescuer was too short for the task. Behind them, the soldiers closed in.

"Niall!"

A soldier brought up his gun, aimed, and fired. Niall and the other man collapsed. Which of them had been shot was unclear, and it didn't matter, because the soldiers were on them both a moment later.

I closed my eyes. This wasn't right. I'd needed an escape, but not at the expense of Niall's life.

There were more hands, grabbing, pulling. My clothes—the heavy cloak, the corset—weighed a hundred pounds, dragging me down even as I was lifted up the rope ladder on the side of the ship.

Salt—from my tears or something else, I didn't know—stung my cheek where I'd cut it. Wood groaned, and bullets flew overhead, and all I could do was crouch and tremble. I went to wipe my face with my sleeve, but instead could only stare at the streaks of red smeared over my clothes. Blood. My blood, Niall's blood. I didn't know. It didn't matter.

A hand on my shoulder pulled me along the deck. I nearly bit it. I was so tired of being manhandled, of being shoved around, and of being directed for someone else's agenda.

Rosie's face swam into view, and for a second, I only felt cool relief. Then, another face joined her. A woman with brown hair and cool eyes. Her scowl was fierce, but held a sadness I recognized.

Lou. Beautiful Lou.

Dead Lou, who had left me behind even when she promised she would come back for me. Maybe she finally had?

So I must be dead as well.

At this point, that was fine.

PART II

THE PIRATE

8

Unsurprisingly, the accommodations of the bowels of a ship were about as pleasant as the bowels of anything. The small, barred cell where I'd been taken was rank with mold, dead fish, and unwashed bodies. Despite the tranquil picture a ship moored in the harbor painted, the interior of a ship making its escape from the same harbor was a noisy place full of creaks and groans, of boards grinding together, and the occasional squeak from a rat that couldn't be seen in the suffocating gloom.

With nothing else to do, I fumbled my way out of my cloak, finding the ties in the dark and loosening them so I could breathe. I had no way to remove my corset with the dress Rosie had laced me into that morning.

To think, only a few hours ago, my greatest worry was that my fiancé might murder me at some point in the future. The immediacy of being kidnapped from under his nose suddenly muted the shock I'd felt in the library that morning.

Somewhere in the dark, a foot scuffed on a board, followed by a soft curse.

"Hello?" I asked.

"George?"

I straightened. "Rosie?"

"Where are you?" Rosie's voice was clearer now, closer.

"I'm here." I groped forward blindly. I'd been in this place for what felt like hours, but my eyes had barely found any light to adjust. I winced as my hand landed in a puddle of something cold, but then my fingers brushed against the bars of the cell. Shortly after, a warm hand closed over mine.

"Oh, I found you." The relief in her voice was as warm as her skin. "Are you all right?"

"So much better now that I can hear a friendly voice. How did you get here?"

Rosie snorted gently. "I wasn't going to let them take you without me. I saw the tall one pulling you along the dock, and I knew what they were trying to do, even though you were putting up a good fight. No one ever notices servants anyway, so it didn't take much to climb aboard in all the confusion, and I'm very good at making myself unobtrusive when I want to."

I laughed, grateful for the release of nervous energy. I tightened my grip on the bars. "What happens next?"

"There don't seem to be very many of them. No more than thirty or forty. If I can find a way to unlock your cell, we might be able to escape."

Forty pirates. "You're not suggesting we fight our way out, are you?"

"No. But if we stay close to shore, we could jump once it's dark and swim for it."

"Swim?"

"Can't you swim?"

I sighed. "Not well, and certainly not in the dark."

"You float the same whether the sun's out or not."

We stayed like that for a long time. The damp encroached, worming its way into my flesh. I wrapped my cloak around me to fight the chill. The gentle tremors in Rosie's hand said she felt it too, but with the bars between us, we could only huddle against the cold metal, searching for places where we might touch and warm each other.

We dozed. We talked. The cold ate into my bones. My eyelids grew heavier.

A voice hummed tunelessly far away. A flickering light followed. It could only be a lantern, but after hours of inky black, it might as well have been a bonfire. My hand was cramped around the cell bar, and Rosie's must have been as well, because she didn't let go of me, only sluggishly pushing herself closer to the metal and farther from the approaching light. We had nowhere to go, and the owner of the lantern was definitely coming for us.

He was tall, big enough that only his chest was illuminated by the lantern in his hand. He had to hunch not to hit his head on the low-slung timbers, but he moved with a confidence that said he knew how to navigate the space. He loomed over us, holding the lantern higher. Wild shadows careened off the walls, making his eyes look like sunken pits.

He grinned. "I was told we had a princess. I didn't know there would be two of you."

"Stay away from us," I said through chattering teeth.

The giant laughed, a big, rumbling sound that echoed in the small space. "I would. It doesn't smell so fresh down here." His nose wrinkled in the bobbing light. "But orders are orders. The captain is ready to see you."

Ready. Despite everything, my temper winked to life. "My maid and I are not presentable to see your captain."

"Oh, I don't think the captain cares what you wear." He glanced down at Rosie. "She'll be very interested to see that there are two of you now."

My growing nerve shriveled.

She.

"Your captain is a woman?"

His teeth were bigger than my fingernails, and he showed every one of them as he smiled.

"Cinder," Rosie whispered.

"Very good, little miss." He stepped forward. Rosie pressed

herself back, spreading her arms wide, as if she might protect me from his approach. The giant chuckled. "I like you."

"You stay away from her," I growled.

"I would, but she's in my way. The captain wants to see you." He pulled a heavy ring of keys off his belt and took another step toward us. We knotted our fingers together.

The giant set the lantern to one side and scooped Rosie around the waist as if she weighed nothing. One minute, she was squeezed against the bars, and the next, she was tucked behind one of the giant's massive legs, staring in mute shock back at the place where she'd been.

"Princesses never pick the right guard dogs. Need something bigger." The giant chuckled as he bent to unlatch the cell. My legs were stiff, and I struggled to my feet, but the giant waited patiently. My foot snagged in the hem of my long dress, and something tore. I pitched forward and gasped when the big man caught me.

"Easy there, lady. Can't have you smash your pretty nose before we get you above deck." He was still grinning, but the expression had moved from carnivorous to kind. I had the conflicting thoughts that I could burrow against his body and find some warmth and that my hair was uncovered and he shouldn't see me like this. The big man seemed indifferent to both these ideas, because he spun me around, turning me in the direction he'd come. Rosie was there, and we wrapped our hands together.

"Come along then," the giant said pleasantly, as if we were about to embark on a tour.

We were deep in the ship's guts. There were several ladders and levels to climb and hatches so narrow, I couldn't understand how the big man fit through them. If the goal was to get me so thoroughly lost that I had no chance of ever escaping, then the plan was a successful one.

Quite abruptly, the giant man opened a door, and Rosie and I stumbled into the sunlight. The salt air was crisp, replacing the dank musk from the cell, but that was the only improvement.

"You're very pretty, lady." There was a cackling laugh from behind us. I whirled with Rosie clinging to my arm. A bald, whip-thin man with a scraggly beard leered at us. Where the giant man had too many teeth, this man hardly had any.

"I've never seen a real princess before." His breath stank of rot. I recoiled, pushing Rosie behind me.

"Janos!"

The pirate slunk away like a street dog as a woman dressed from head to toe in black approached us.

Cinder.

I'd stopped believing in stories meant to frighten small children a long time ago, but no one in Redmere would ignore the tales of Captain Cinder. How many ships had been sunk, how many lives lost, because of this one woman?

The captain stood before me. Her skin was brown, undoubtedly dark from birth, but darker after so many years on the open sea. Her eyes were bright copper. Her smile was cruel.

"You've caused quite the stir, Your Highness." Her accent was unexpected, rich and pointed, hard around the consonants.

"I . . ." My mind was blank. "I wasn't expecting you to—"

"Janos!" the woman snapped. The thin pirate still lurked at the edge of our little group. When she called his name, he lurched to her side, knocking his thumb against his forehead in a small salute.

"Yes?"

"How many men did we lose in our efforts to procure our new guest?" She put a hand on her hip, and my throat tightened further. Captain Cinder wore a loose shirt tucked into wide-legged trousers and cinched with a heavy belt. Though she was covered from ankle to shoulder, I'd never seen a woman wear anything so revealing before.

Janos wheezed a laugh through his gummy grin. "Three men lost."

"Three. What was our aim?"

He stepped toward me, eyes twitching in their sockets, and this time, the captain didn't stop him. He curled a finger around a strand of my hair as I shrank away.

"To catch a prize."

The captain's face was implacable. "And did we catch her?"

Janos laughed and sniffed at me like he might be trying to decide if I might be good to eat. "With a sweet morsel on the side." With lightning speed, he reached around me, snagging Rosie by a handful of her hair. She screamed, and I lunged for her, but the pirate dragged her forward and tossed her to the deck. A small crowd had gathered, and a few of them laughed. The captain glanced at them, eyes amused.

"A stowaway." She squatted, tipping Rosie's chin up. I started forward, and the giant's hand clamped on my shoulder, fingers digging into my arm.

"I wouldn't. The captain has plans for you," he said softly in my ear. I struggled, but his grip was a vise.

"We don't allow stowaways on board this ship," the captain said to Rosie. "We went to Redmere City for one woman, not two."

"I go where my mistress goes."

The captain tsked. "That is a loyalty that will get you killed. Princess"—she flicked her gaze to me—"do you know how much food a person eats at sea?"

I waited, but the silence grew. "I do not."

The captain turned back to Rosie, and her smile was like a serpent about to strike. "Too much. Throw the stowaway overboard."

"No!" I said, but it was drowned out as a cheer when up. Men descended to the deck, rushing toward us. I threw all my weight forward, and the grasp on my arm slipped. I stumbled, and Rosie was already moving, reaching for me. We grabbed for each other to keep upright. I spun, moving Rosie behind me, pushing her toward the ship's rail and away from the encroaching sailors.

My eyes swung to Captain Cinder's. "You can't do this. She's innocent!"

Cinder shook her head. "This is my ship. Everyone on it is here at my pleasure and leaves when I say. Your companion here wasn't invited. Would you rather she starve to death? There's no food for her."

"I'll share what you give me." I glanced around us nervously. Janos was closest to me, and another man, with black hair and a vicious scar that trailed from his hairline to his nose, stood behind him. He reached for us, and I skirted away, tripping over ropes and pulleys and the uneven footing of the wooden deck.

"It doesn't work like that," Cinder said. "It's in my best interest to keep you fed and well taken care of. I have plans for you. But the girl? She is of no value to me."

Rosie whimpered. I pulled her close. "You can't! Please." I wasn't above begging. "You can't kill Rosie. She's very small. You'll hardly notice she's here."

"She can stay with me," the scarred man said. "I'll find a way for her to earn her keep."

"You're disgusting," I spat.

"You'd do better not to antagonize my men," Captain Cinder said flatly. "We're wasting time." She took a step forward, pushing through the crowd, forcing me to retreat further.

"You can't do this! I am the future queen of Redmere, and I won't allow it!"

Cinder puffed out her chest. "You won't? Out here, you are nobody. What are you going to do? Run to your prince and ask him to intervene?" Her gaze was unwavering. This was happening. Rosie was going to drown, and I couldn't do anything about it. Rosie's face was so pale even her freckles had disappeared. She was crying softly.

"You cannot take her," I said through gritted teeth.

Cinder snapped her fingers. "Ender!"

The giant man moved silently through the crowd. Behind me, Rosie sniffled and buried her face in my shoulder. My mind raced as Ender approached. I thought of the way he'd lifted Rosie like she weighed nothing. How easy it would be for him to take her from me and toss her over the side like trash.

I took another step back, and something rolled under my foot, nearly causing me to fall. It was a long wooden pole, smaller around than my arm, and on one end was a curved hook. I dove for it, swinging it wildly as it came up. I nearly caught Ender across his middle, and he danced back.

"Stay away from her!" My voice rose desperately. "You will not touch her. Any of you." I stepped back again, away from the gathered men and the gleam in Captain Cinder's eye. Rosie moved with me, and I kept the hook between us and Ender the whole time.

"This princess has some spark!" Janos laughed.

"Don't call me that."

"My lady," Ender said, hands raised, palms out. "Put the hook down."

"Get away from us!" I swung the hook again, but I was clumsy, and Ender grabbed it. He yanked, and it slipped from my grasp. Rosie stumbled behind me but didn't let go, and she righted herself before we could go down.

"Please." My throat was tight, and a fat, traitorous tear rolled down my cheek. "Please don't take her."

"Why do you care?" Cinder asked.

"She's my friend." My only one now that Niall was gone. For a second, I was back on the wharf, his weight on me. His blood was no doubt still on my clothes.

Rosie grunted, and our retreat came to an abrupt halt. I risked a glance behind me to find us pinned against one of the cannons on the deck. We could go no farther, and taking the time to climb over it would only result in our capture.

"Your friend?" Cinder came forward, moving past Ender until she was only a foot away again. "And what would you do for your friend?"

Given that she was my only friend in the whole world, now that Niall was dead? "Anything."

Captain Cinder's lip curled. "Anything?"

I couldn't stop the quivering of my chin, but I nodded.

She tilted her head. "I've already told you I can't afford to feed you both. Would you starve instead of her?"

I nodded again. "Yes."

"I only have bunk space for one of you. Would you let her sleep in a cabin while you slept with the rats in the hold?"

"Yes."

"My men spend many lonely nights at sea. If one of them wanted to spend the night with her, would you take her place?"

I trembled at what Captain Cinder was suggesting. My hands were fists at my sides, fingernails digging deep into my palms. "I'd tear his arms off first."

Janos tipped his head back to roar with laughter. "I don't think he'd need his arms for what she means!"

Captain Cinder and I were nearly nose to nose. "And if I said the only way to end this was for one of you to be at the bottom of the ocean by sundown, who would it be?"

Ever since the day I'd received the letter telling me of Lou's death, I'd been afraid of the sea. So deep, so big. It took what it wanted and never let it go. Now, the only options were for it to claim either me or Rosie.

It had been too late to save Lou. But I could still help Rosie.

Our chests were nearly touching. I leaned forward to deliver my response directly to Cinder's ear so there would be no misunderstanding.

"I'd do my best to take you with me so you could never hurt another person again, and I would drag you all the way down to be sure the task was done."

I'd never wanted to hurt another human being before. Not even Jeremy with his carelessness and manipulation, or Beverly with his lies and scheming. But the woman in front of me had been responsible for the deaths of so many people at home. If the last thing I ever did was take her to the bottom of the ocean, at least Lou was down there to welcome me.

Cinder gave me a thin smile, but she did not move.

Behind her, someone applauded. In the open silence of the ocean, and without a word spoken by anyone there, the noise was loud, echoing out across the waves.

The spell of the moment was broken, and I stumbled back until Rosie was wrapped around my waist again. We both stared.

The crowd dispersed, and even Captain Cinder fell away. A single figure stepped forward. I hadn't noticed this sailor before. Altogether, he was unremarkable. He wore loose clothes and a wide hat that shadowed his eyes. His feet were bare and his steps assured as he walked toward us. With each step, the crew faded away, like frost melting in sunshine.

"Well done," the stranger said. He pulled the hat from his head, revealing brown hair kept in fine braids down his back. "Really." He pulled the shirt off too, revealing a smaller, more fitted one that did nothing to hide the swells and curves of breasts beneath. I could hardly tear my eyes away from her in terrified fascination. As she advanced, the sailors at her sides cast their gazes downward and knocked their thumbs to their foreheads in salute.

"That was a spectacular performance, Highness." With every word, her voice rose to a woman's more usual pitch. The clip of her vowels was all too familiar, sounds I heard every day in Redmere.

"Who are you?" I asked.

"Oh, I think you know." She passed Captain Cinder—or whoever she was—who also dipped the brim of her hat, though her gaze stayed on me. It was still full of mocking self-assurance, like she already knew the outcome of a horrible practical joke but —yes—I knew it too.

"Cinder."

"Very good, Highness. Right on cue. And?"

The ship rolled on the waves, and for a second, the sun was in my eyes.

"And?" I held a hand up to shade my face, trying to stay focused as Captain Cinder—the *real* Captain Cinder—approached.

She tsked. "Come on, princess. I thought you'd do better than this."

The ship righted itself again, the sun disappearing behind a sail. Bright splotches swam in my vision for a moment. Then, as they cleared, the true face of Captain Cinder loomed before me. Brown hair faded in the sun, muddy brown eyes. A tattoo of an octopus wrapping its tentacles around her throat, caressing her skin, while a purple stone that shone like the sun on the waves winked from one earlobe. She was beautiful. Deadly. A greater predator than even the prince.

But it was the scar that caught my attention. Her lip was scarred on the right side, and it made my heart skip in a way that nothing else had. Not like it had at my brother's announcement that I would marry the prince, at Beverly's casual statement that he would murder me when I was no longer useful, at the Impostor Cinder's attempt to drown Rosie.

The scar could easily have been dismissed as a minor and unfortunate side effect of the seafaring life. A lucky miss in a sword fight, or a swinging rope in the rain.

But I knew.

Oh God, I knew that scar.

I shook my head. "No."

The scar twisted as the lips below it stretched into a smile. "Go on."

The little cut had looked so much bigger on a smaller face. It bled like a fountain that morning so many years ago.

Rosie's arm tightened around me, but it did nothing to ease the shaking.

"You can't be."

Captain Cinder ran her tongue over her teeth. "I am. Say it."

Having been cooped up in the house for too many days in a row, Lou and I sneak into the kitchen on a cold winter morning and steal the cook's largest pan. It is round and made of iron, with handles on either side that we hold between us. We run out the back door and up the snow-covered hill that faces the rear of the house. The pan is heavy because it is so large that a little girl can fit inside if she tucks herself tightly together.

I am the first to go, and the ride is exhilarating. Cold air blasts through my hair, leaving it to trail in long streaks behind me.

Next, we tuck Lou into the makeshift sled. I use all of the muscles in my childish body to heave her over the edge of the hill, and her laughter trails after her, all the way down the hill.

The pan veers toward the right. It is a gentle thing at first, then more noticeable, particularly as Lou does not slow down, her laughter still cascading across the snow, oblivious of how the game is turning. I am already running down the hill, calling out after her as Lou careens away from the kitchen door—before coming to an abrupt halt as the pan collides with the tree stump that Cook uses to chop wood for the kitchen fire.

Lou's little body is catapulted through the air, arms and legs flopping like a rag doll, but she hits the ground on the other side of the stump.

"No." On the deck of the *Crimson Siren*, Captain Cinder's fabled ship, I shook my head, desperately trying to deny the truth that stood smiling calmly before me.

"No!" I slip in the snow and crawl to the spot where Lou lies. The blood is bright red, nearly glowing on the snow.

Captain Cinder's smile grew, showing off a line of straight white teeth, except for one in gold in the space directly below the scar on her lip.

Lou sits up, swaying dazedly in the snow. Fat child's tears roll down her face, mixing with the blood that flows from her nose and where her lip has torn.

"George," she says—or tries to say, because it comes out a garbled

mess. She turns to the snow and spits, sending out blood and one perfect, creamy tooth.

I stared at the golden tooth in the pirate captain's mouth, and then my gaze followed the line of the scar upward, until I was staring into the eyes of my oldest friend.

"Welcome aboard," Captain Cinder said.

My face was wet with tears, and I shook so hard, I would have pitched over the rail and into the ocean if Rosie weren't still holding onto me.

"It's all right. It's all right. Don't cry." I mop at her face with my sleeve. "It's all right, Lou."

On the deck of the ship, air took a long time coming in. But when it finally did, it ripped the name right out of my throat.

"Lucinda."

9

I'd never fainted before, but then again, the list of things I'd never done shrunk by the hour. The world had stretched and wheeled in a tight spiral, and the next thing I knew, I was lying on a lumpy cot that smelled distinctly of sweat and dead mice. The odor made my throat clench.

Across the narrow space, a hunched man with only two tiny wisps of hair on his head grinned at me. His skin was the color of amber, and his forehead was bound in a greasy, blue kerchief, which he tugged at in a mocking version of the salute the sailors had all given Captain—

The stretching feeling threatened to come back, and I focused on breathing slowly as a whirlpool of emotions threatened to pull me under.

Captain Cinder. Lucinda.

Lou.

She was alive. She was here.

And she was the pirate who haunted children's dreams.

The old man's face came into view. "Are you feeling woozy again there, lady?"

Woozy was the least of it. I wanted to cry, scream, dance, laugh, and vomit all at once, and so I did none of it.

"Where is she?"

"Who?"

I scrambled up to sit but had to stop there as my vision swam. "How long was I unconscious?"

His face was kind, his smile gappy, as he patted my hand. "Not long. No need to worry. They carried you down here, laid you out, and I was just preparing a salve for that cut on your cheek when you woke."

I ran a finger over my face, feeling the tender spot where the skin had split during my kidnapping from Redmere. In everything that had happened since, I'd nearly forgotten about it. It seemed urgent to consider now as the man approached with a clay pot and a rag that was only slightly less soiled than the one wrapped around his forehead.

I squirmed, trying to create more space between us. "You're a physician?"

"I am. Doctor Selim Sarkiss, at your service."

I eyed him. "Really?"

He pouted, but his grip was strong as he helped me stay upright. I was wearing only the fine silk undershirt and underskirt that Rosie had dressed me in that morning. My corset and gown had vanished.

I went to cover myself, but too much of me was exposed for my hands to reach. "Where are my clothes?" My loose hair brushed over my bare shoulders, and I wanted nothing more than for a hole in the deck beneath me to appear and swallow me up.

He laughed. "I needed to make sure the blood on the dress wasn't yours. Wouldn't do to have you impale yourself when the captain's gone to all the trouble to fetch you." The man dabbed his cloth into the little pot, and I watched him suspiciously.

"Are you really a physician?"

"I was a ship's surgeon in the Vestrian navy until I joined up with the captain." He was having trouble getting the appropriate amount of whatever potion was in the pot onto his rag.

"But why would you do that?" Cinder had terrorized Redmere for years, but she must have been just as vicious with other nearby countries like Vestria. How could someone who had served their country then decide to join the woman who hurt so many?

"I got shot in the head."

"What?" My outrage turned to confusion.

He cackled, a wet sucking sound, and slid the kerchief from his head. An ugly scar, nearly four inches long, ran above his ear. "It was a while ago. Didn't kill me, as you can see. But"—he lifted his hands and they shook violently—"I wasn't much good for a needle and thread or not shredding a man's guts while digging a ball out after that. The navy didn't have much use for me anymore."

"And there was nothing else to do but become a pirate?" Out of everything that had happened, it was an inane detail to focus on, but it was safer than contemplating the woman who . . . The world shifted again as Lou's slow approach replayed in my mind's eye, and I turned my head away from the doctor.

He didn't seem affected by my shock. "I'm too old to take up farming or learn a trade. And I missed the sea. When we go out on long runs, the captain lets me bring a lad as an assistant. I do the diagnosing and the medicating. He does the stitching. I don't suppose you have much skill with a needle and thread?"

I choked as he pressed the dirty cloth with the mixture from his pot against my skin. His hands were steady enough for that. The fumes from the salve went straight to my brain, and I coughed and spluttered while the doctor laughed hysterically.

"What is that?" I asked, wiping at my face with my sleeve.

"It'll keep your wound clean."

And burn my skin off at the same time.

He returned the pot to a cabinet on the wall. The shelves all had high lips, no doubt to keep delicate containers in place when the waves grew too rough.

"Selim!" The woman in black strolled through the door of the cabin. Her appearance made my heart skip, because if she was here, then it was only a matter of time before—before—

"You certainly know how to make a scene, Highness." The woman's flat expression said she wasn't impressed.

Neither was I. The last time I'd been face-to-face with this woman, she'd been threatening to throw Rosie overboard.

A new fear roared to life.

"Where is my maid?"

The woman sneered. "Your maid, Highness? I thought she was your friend."

"Where is she?" I felt incredibly exposed, perched on this narrow bed in the center of the room, wearing nothing but my underthings.

The woman who wasn't Captain Cinder advanced. Her copper eyes flicked back and forth as she studied my face, and I held perfectly still, meeting her gaze. I may have been the swooning maiden, but now that I was upright again, I would not back down.

The woman laughed softly. "Your friend is alive. I'll take you to the cabin where you'll be staying during your . . ." She looked me up and down. "Your voyage with us."

In the months after Lou had died—but she hadn't died, had she?—I'd dreamed of escaping everyone and everything and sailing away to worlds unknown. The way this person said "voyage" did not make it sound like the exciting adventure I'd imagined.

Lou. Lou wasn't dead.

"I want to see her."

A fine eyebrow arched. "Excuse me?"

"Lou. The captain. I want to see her."

"You don't issue orders around here, Highness. The captain will call for you when she's ready."

"You've taken me from my home," I said, trying to find the serpentine tones the prince liked to use when bringing someone over to his way of doing things. "The least you can do is grant me an audience with your captain."

"Princess."

"No. This is not up for negotiation. I will see your captain now."

She didn't look pleased, but finally, she said, "Wait here," then spun and disappeared as suddenly as she'd arrived.

Wait here. As opposed to what? Wander the decks where dozens of leering pirates would see me like this? Stumble about with my hair and limbs exposed until I encountered the ghost of my dead best friend?

"Maro's all right." The doctor had retreated to a safe distance, but he stepped forward again.

"Maro? That's her name?"

"First mate. They—" The doctor chuckled. "They weren't too pleased that—"

"They?"

"Maro's people don't separate men from women. They are people, each of them."

"Does she . . . do they do that often?"

"Do what?" He busied himself putting away his pots.

"Pretend to be each other? Maro, the captain, and Lou, a sailor."

He laughed. "Hardly. Captain's very proud. Wouldn't let just anyone pretend to be her. But she and Maro . . . They've been together a long time." He leaned in conspiratorially. "Sometimes you hear rumors that they—"

"Selim." Maro reappeared at the door, a bundle in their arms. "Perhaps you could give Her Highness some privacy to dress herself?"

The doctor gave me a knowing smile, although I didn't understand what secret he thought we'd shared. He hurried out, bringing one shaking thumb to the scar by his ear as he passed Maro in the door. When he was gone, they tossed a heap of cloth on the bed.

"I trust you can manage without your maid?"

I lifted the long trousers. "I can't wear this." I needed as many of my wits about me as I could when I met Lou, and struggling with unfamiliar clothes—no matter the novelty—wouldn't put me on the best footing.

They shook their head. "Not my problem."

"It's immodest. I would prefer to wear a skirt."

"I would have preferred that we'd left you where we'd found you, but we can't all have what we want, Highness."

I bit my lip and laid the shirt they'd brought on the narrow cot. It had an open neck, and the sleeves didn't look like they'd reach to my elbows. Maybe I was a coward, but now that I was free of Redmere—though that freedom was nebulous at best—I longed for the anonymity I'd felt moving through its streets in my heavy clothes.

"I'll need something to cover my hair."

Maro sighed heavily, but I glared at them, fists clenched in the heavy fabric that they'd brought, so much rougher than the fine things Rosie had dressed me in for the last few days.

Finally, they said, "Get dressed. I'll be right back."

The shirt was blue and cut with a neck so wide, you could see my collarbones clearly as I pulled it over my head. It was embellished with silver buttons along the collar and down the sides. The sleeves did reach my elbows, but only barely. To think I'd felt exposed in a dress that showed my wrists.

The trousers were easy enough to step into and do up but so loose that even when I pulled the drawstring at the waist, they still fell to the floor. Maro, or whoever had picked out these clothes for me, had apparently anticipated this, because I'd been left a wide, heavy belt made of leather, similar to the one Maro themself wore. It was so long I had to wrap it around myself twice, but once it was on, the trousers stayed in place.

I was very aware of the split seams that left my legs free and made a different shape than my skirts ever had. I'd wondered, from time to time, what it would be like to wear pants. The answer was that it was freeing and disorienting all at once.

Silver caught my eye, and I glanced down at the bracelet on my wrist. Lou's bracelet. A token I'd worn to show what I'd lost.

Now she was here. Would she laugh at my sentimentality?

Self-conscious, I slipped it off. I was struggling with where to hide it on my person when Maro reappeared and tossed a bright scrap of green silk toward me. It fluttered in the air until I caught it. I could have used Rosie's help to pin my hair up, but in the end, I looped it through the bracelet's ring before tucking the whole thing under the scarf and tying it securely at my nape, leaving the tails of the scarf to trail down my neck. It was not entirely unlike the way the working women in Redmere did their hair, so it would suit just fine.

As armored as I could possibly be, I turned to Maro, who was waiting impatiently by the door. "This way, Highness. The captain is looking forward to seeing you."

I am in my room, watching a squirrel determined to make a nest between a pair of branches that are too wide set for the purpose, when the bedroom door opens with a bang. Lou's face is a mask of fury as she slams the door shut again.

"What?" I rise from my seat at the window.

"We're running away," she says. Her hair is unbrushed and stands out in uneven clumps that look not unlike the squirrel's nest.

"What?"

"Take only what you can carry. We're leaving now." Lou doesn't wait. She flings open the wardrobe and starts hurling things to the floor.

I hurry to her, collecting clothes as I go. "What? Lou, what are you talking about? What's happened?"

Lou glares, but her eyes are shining with tears. "I'm leaving. I want you to come with me, Georgie, but if you don't want to, that's fine. I'll go alone."

"Go?" Normally I am the one who comes to Lou when things are bad, when my father is drunk or too long absent from home. Lou's family is a warm spot in the middle of my life, although they do not

have much to share, so I only tread on their hospitality when absolutely necessary.

"Yes. Go!" Lou whirls. "They don't want me here anymore, but that doesn't mean they can just send me away. I choose." She thumps her slender chest. Where my body has already started to soften and curve into a woman's, Lou's is still straight and rail thin.

I fall back. Something is wrong. Lou has a temper, but she never acts impulsively. To storm into my room and announce we are leaving is completely out of character.

"Lou." I place my hand on her shoulder, and she shudders in reply. "What happened?"

The shuddering that grows while the silence stretches is worse than Lou's fury. She rarely cries. Not unless there is real pain.

I stroke her hair, smoothing out the lumps and swirls. I've always envied Lou's hair, soft and wavy and a light brown that glints in the sun, while mine is fine and too dark to be really pretty. When my breasts started to grow and Lou bemoaned her lack of development, I told her I would gladly trade my breasts for her hair.

"What happened?" I ask one more time, and finally, Lou turns, flinging herself into my arms with great heaving sobs.

"They're sending me away!"

"To school?" I will be leaving for school in a month. Perhaps my father has found a way to send Lou with me. That isn't so bad. We will be together. Nothing to be so upset about.

Lou's eyes are stormy as she pulls away, swiping at her nose with the back of her hand. "

"Father says I'm going to sea."

Sea? "On a boat?" I am too dumbfounded to say anything cleverer.

"They're sending me to the navy. He said that since you're leaving, it's time to earn my keep. I'm supposed to pretend to be a boy so they can enlist me."

I stare. "But you're too young to work."

Lou sniffs. "They sent my brothers away when they were both ten."

"But they're boys. You're a girl. You can't—"

"There's no money. They only let me stay this long because of you."

So this is my fault. If I were not leaving, then neither would Lou.

I pull myself together with all the bearing of the lady I might be someday. Bravely, I put my hands on Lou's shoulders, staring deep into the eyes of my best friend in the whole world.

"I'll fix this," I say. "We'll always be together."

Lou. We were going to see Lou. She was here. She was alive. How was she alive? How was she a pirate?

Why had she never told me?

"Highness?" Maro said. I realized I'd stopped following them on the deck as I tried to weave answers from nothing but spindly questions.

"Sorry."

Lou. *Lou, Lou, Lou, Lou, Lou.* It played over and over in my head. She wasn't dead. She was alive, and she was here, and we would be together after all this time, like I'd promised. I was elated and afraid. The rushing anticipation, coupled with the rocking of the ship, left me weaving behind Maro like I was drunk.

We climbed a short set of steps before Maro pulled open a door and stood aside like they wanted me to go in.

"Wait." I went to smooth down the front of my dress but found the rough fabric and heavy leather of my borrowed clothes instead. A pointed cough brought my attention ahead of me to Maro's narrowed gaze.

"After you, Your Highness."

Lou. I took a deep breath. We were going to see Lou. I had nothing to be afraid of.

The cabin was darker, but my eyes adjusted quickly. At the far end of the space was a long set of windows that must have stretched the width of the ship. As I grew accustomed to the space, I gasped. This was no moldy cell. No foul-smelling infirmary. This was . . . grand. A stateroom. A heavy, wooden desk sat by the windows, the sort that had lived in my father's study. To the other side, two low, plush settees were arranged around an ornate table. The floors, instead of the worn wood that was everywhere else on the ship, were covered in rich carpets in so many varied colors.

It was . . . It was elegant. Prince Beaverly—may he rot—would have been impressed.

"You can go."

I didn't see her at first. She stood in the far corner, beyond the furniture and opulence. In the shadows.

"Captain." Maro stood next to me. "We don't know—"

"You can go." Lou's voice—*Lou's voice!*—made me shiver. In all the years she'd been gone, I'd imagined what she would look like if she were still alive, but I'd never once given any thought to how her voice would have changed. In my mind, her voice, the girl's voice of my memories, had stayed the same.

It hadn't. It was . . . I struggled for words and wished she'd speak again. But the cabin filled with silence as she and Maro engaged in some wordless disagreement before the first mate finally snapped to attention and bowed deeply at the waist. "As you wish, Captain."

They shut the door firmly behind them, and I was left with Lou, alone.

"You're dead." It needed to be said.

Her laugh was a low sound, almost husky, like a man's. I was pleased she found my comment amusing. "Not dead."

"They said you drowned." I took a step forward.

"More like a very long swim. You wanted to see me, Highness?"

I nearly snorted, but it got caught in a sob, and it bubbled out as a sloppy cough instead. "I'm not a princess, Lou." Her name on my tongue was the sweetest thing I'd ever tasted. The smile won out over the tears.

Lou moved from where she'd appeared. The braids in her hair were gathered over one shoulder, the beads and other shiny bits woven into the ends clicking as she walked. Her clothes made my breath catch. She'd changed out of her sailor's garb, and if Maro's clothes—and the clothes I now wore—were indecent by

Redmerian standards, Lou's would have had her shot on sight. Her trousers were made of what looked like layers of sheer orange fabric gathered at her ankles and waist. Her top consisted of a long swath of fabric that had been wrapped and knotted around her torso and shoulders so it covered her breasts and not much else. Even her navel was exposed. The tattooed octopus was centered on her chest and still wound its way around her throat, tentacles waving as she spoke or swallowed. She wore a draping type of coat —if it could be called a coat. It was made of the same sheer fabric, except in a purple so dark it was only visible when it caught the light. The wide sleeves billowed as she walked, and the fabric masked the color of her skin while still showing off her shape.

Twelve-year-old Lou would have been so pleased to learn her curves had softened with time.

My adult self could barely look away. Like this, she was everything I'd never been allowed to want. She would have been beautiful in rags. Now, she was dressed like a goddess out of a storybook. I'd dreamed of this moment on the nights when I didn't dream of her reaching out to me from her watery grave, and she was more perfect than I could ever have imagined.

She folded herself onto one of the seats opposite me.

"Sit, princess."

The name should have been a warning, even if her unfamiliar clothes and voice weren't. The straight line of her mouth when mine curved up so high I thought my cheeks might split should have told me something was wrong. But my fascination with her appearance and joy at her resurrection were overwhelming. I swam in so much relief after so many lonely years.

I sat. "Where have you been?"

She cocked her head to one side. "Do you know where we are now?"

I shook my head. "Still near Redmere, I imagine."

"Redmere." She glanced over her shoulder to the windows that overlooked the sea. "Is that the border of your experience?"

"What do you mean?"

Lou's eyes flicked up and down, like she was evaluating me. My excitement was tinged with nervousness now. Something was wrong. She wasn't happy. Not in the way I was happy. Lou had always been more restrained of the two of us, but her silence now felt sinister.

The belt around my waist grew suddenly tight and dug into my lowest ribs. I shifted, trying to find a comfortable space.

"Where are we going?"

"You don't need to know that just yet, princess."

"I'm not a princess."

"Not for lack of trying, though?" The question was flat and emotionless, and yet it made my breath and my pulse quicken. Where was the reunion? The happy tears? I promised her we'd be together again and now could finally make good on that promise, and she didn't seem to care in the slightest.

"Trying?"

"Isn't it what every girl dreams of? To find yourself on the arm of a prince with everyone watching you?"

I shook my head. The wheeling sensation I'd first felt when Lou had appeared threatened to return. "I don't understand. I didn't want it."

She clucked her tongue. "Oh, I'm sure."

"He was going to kill me."

"Whatever for, Highness?"

My mouth dropped open. My supposed sins were all I'd been able to think about for days, and now she wanted me to admit them to her when I could hardly believe she was a real person. I looked her up and down, then again. I couldn't take my eyes off of her. She was so beautiful. But I couldn't bring myself to tell her so.

"I was a spy," I said instead. "Part of the resistance that formed after the rebellion."

She snorted. "You? A spy?"

I tugged at the too-short sleeves of my shirt, trying to find somewhere to hide in a room that was entirely Lou's.

"We were helping. Trying to stop the prince. There was a dressmaker. She would hide information from the palace in my skirts and—"

"So you were a courier then," Lou said with a dismissive wave of her hand.

"No. I—"

"Running hidden messages through the streets. A very cozy little life. Do you think all rebellions are as bloodless as passing secret notes to schoolmates? You get to play spy while the people around you take all the risk until you can move on to a new adventure. Or betray them to your fiancé."

"Play spy? Betray?" I couldn't hide the shock in my voice. "I was—"

She pouted. "Oh yes, I suppose it was very exciting. A break from the boredom of your life. But as the future queen of Redmere—"

"It wasn't a game," I said as I clenched my fists. "Every time I went out to pick up messages, the City Guard might have discovered what I was doing."

She tilted her head, eyeing me, and in that moment, all the familiarity was gone. The scar, the freckle on her left cheek. They were the only features I recognized. Everything else, from the sharp angle of her jaw to the chilly emptiness in her eyes, was foreign.

"You were never in any real danger. Not if that's all they would let you do. I'm sorry to tell you the truth, Highness." She picked at her nails. "Despite the rather spectacular production it took to get you out of Redmere, I don't want you getting ideas about your importance on this ship for the short time you're with me."

Everything about this conversation left me feeling as if I were on the losing end of a footrace with no hope of catching up. It was ten times worse than the prince's games, because Lou didn't seem to want anything from me, while I wanted everything from her.

"I'm not staying?"

She laughed, a low chuckle full of derision. "Of course not. What would I do with a princess? Royalty doesn't do well on a ship like this. Always making demands. Clean bedding, fresh food. You acquiesce to one request, and suddenly, you're treated like a servant and lose all credibility with the crew. I can't have that, now can I?"

"So you'll ransom me? Send me back to the prince?"

Her amusement hardened to a steely flicker. "I wouldn't give you back to that bastard if he offered me a whole country, and not that foul, starving one you call home either."

"It's your home too," I said, but even as I spoke, I had the sinking feeling I was making a mistake.

She continued as if I hadn't even spoken. "And anyway, I've already been paid for you. My instructions are to deliver you to safety."

"But Lou—"

Her narrowed gaze on me sent a chill up my spine. "You will call me 'Captain,' Your Highness."

My anger skidded to a halt. Captain. I'd been so taken by the sudden reappearance of my friend that I'd failed to consider this other element. I glanced around the cabin again, taking in the rich furnishings, the thick carpet. I studied Lou, with her strange clothes and the hard set of her mouth.

Cinder.

"The ships," I said softly.

"Excuse me?"

"Four ships lost, only a few men returned." The women at the gates with their hollow eyes and starving children.

"Their fault for tempting pirate-infested waters. We're not the sort who can be trusted," she said with a bored flick of her wrist.

"They were your people, Lou."

"My only people are the crew on this ship. I have no connection to Redmere."

Not even me? The moment of hurt was quickly doused by the horror of realization.

Stay off the beach. Captain Cinder kidnapped two girls here last week. We'll never hear from them again.

Captain Cinder was seen by a fisherman. She's on the hunt for men to take to the deeps.

She'd haunted Redmere for years, was whispered about when the sun had gone down or when a child had vanished and was never seen again.

What had she done with them? Any of them?

I knew.

"You're a murderer."

The one gold tooth flashed wickedly. "I'm a survivor. The sooner you understand that, Highness, the easier this trip will be for both of us."

I stood, nearly stumbling over the sofa in my haste to get away from her and the atrocities she'd committed. "You can't!"

She pouted, all wide eyes and exaggerated lips. "Can't what, Highness?"

I thrust my hands in my hair, squeezing in frustration. "Stop calling me that!"

She pulled herself to standing slowly, like a snake uncoiling in the sun. "You don't know what I can and can't do, Highness. You don't know me at all, despite what you might think."

"But—"

She rose in a cascade of shimmering fabric and winking beads. "We're done. You asked for this audience, but clearly, we have nothing more to talk about. We will not speak again until we've reached our destination. Ender!"

"Lou, wait."

"Captain?" The giant opened the cabin door, as if he'd been waiting.

"Escort the princess to her cabin."

"This way, princess." The giant gripped my elbow, and the contact was like lightning.

I whirled, snarling at him. I was so tired of being led around like a dog on a leash.

"Get your hands off me."

He stepped back, big palms out. "Of course, Your Highness."

"Don't call me that." No one would ever call me that again. The title should never have been mine in the first place. Even now, only hours away from the prince and the palace, I was ashamed that I'd ever thought I could make a place for myself there.

"Princess." The name came from behind me. I froze. "You are a guest of the *Crimson Siren*. You are here at my leisure, do you understand?" Her voice. Without her face to ground me, I would never have known it was Lou speaking to me. The last of the joy gave way to the tears at the edges of my eyes since I'd entered this stateroom.

I nodded stiffly. I wouldn't turn. She didn't get to see me cry. I'd already done my mourning for Lou. Captain Cinder deserved none of my tears.

"Good. Then you will do as my crew says. I promise you are safe here, and if anyone makes you feel unsafe, you have only to let Maro know. But a ship runs on order and discipline. I won't have you disrupt that. Do you understand?"

"Yes, Captain." I stared at the open door.

"Thank you. Ender."

The giant gave her a jovial salute. As he reached for me, he remembered himself and stood by the door. "After you, Highness."

I left without a backward glance. It might be better if I never saw her again. It would hurt less.

10

The wind wrapped around me like a sinister lover as I marched away from Lou's cabin. The little strip of land in the distance was getting smaller and thinner with every minute, and around us was blue. So much blue.

I was free. Free from Redmere, from the prince and my brother—and yet, I felt completely unmoored.

"This way, Highness." The giant's voice was gentle, and the sun streaked over his ruddy skin like firelight. I froze.

"You."

He might have grinned. His red beard was so thick that I couldn't even see his lips, only the twitching of hair that might have been a smile.

"Hello, princess."

He was the man in the red coat at the party. The loud, drunk one who had ruined my dress.

"What are you doing here?"

"It's my home."

"But you . . ." I squinted. It was him, wasn't it? It was so hard to tell without the velvet and the ridiculous hat. "You were at the party."

His beard wriggled as he laughed delightedly. "And a fine

party it was! I don't get to go to such a fun evening or eat such delicious food very often. Or meet such pretty ladies." He smacked his lips together, eyes twinkling. Despite everything, despite whoever that creature with Lou's face in the other room had been, I wanted to laugh with him.

"Do you always pour your drink down the front of a lady's dress?"

What was visible of Ender's cheeks under the hair turned pink, and he glanced away. "Ah, well. That was poorly executed."

"You didn't mean to ruin my dress, then?"

"Ender! Are you changing professions now? Going to try your hand at being a maid?" A wicked laugh rolled from above us. Ender glared upward, and I followed, shielding my eyes from the sun. Overhead, men were climbing over ropes and moving among the sails.

"Janos!" This came from Maro, behind us at the ship's big wheel. "That's enough!"

A dark snicker rolled down from the rigging, but Janos didn't say anything else.

Ender resumed walking and our conversation as if we hadn't been interrupted. "Oh, I'd meant to do it."

"Ruin my dress?" I followed, ignoring the shivery feeling between my shoulder blades that Janos, Maro, or possibly even Lou was watching me.

He shrugged his big shoulders. "I didn't give the dress much thought, though you did look very pretty in it, princess. But it would have been easier to grab you then. We'd thought maybe you'd disappear for a moment to clean up so I could snatch you, and the *Siren* could slip away in the dark."

"Grab me?" If he'd tried to drag me away from the party, I would have kicked up a fight.

A very cozy little life. Lou's words, her taunt that I'd only been playing the role of a spy when others took all the risk, came back to me. A cold shiver in my chest whispered that she might have spoken the truth, and I squashed it down.

Ender glanced over his shoulder at me, and his grin was sheepish. "The plan was good, only I didn't expect the prince to be quite so upset. It was just a dress, after all."

The prince. He'd made quite a show of it. The attentive fiancé, devoted future husband, ready to defend his lady's honor . . . until he decided to murder her.

"You should have taken me then." Before I'd overheard his plan. When I still believed that people could change.

Ender laughed, oblivious to my turmoil. "It would have been easier. That explosion caused quite a mess."

We came to a narrow entryway and a narrower staircase at the front of the ship. Ender had to turn sideways to get through. He continued his pleasant narration of the finer points of kidnapping a would-be princess as we descended.

We paused at a door at the bottom of the stairs. Ender pulled a key from his pocket and twisted it in the lock. A high-pitched shout rang out as he opened the door, followed by Ender's deeper, louder one, which was the only warning I had before he ducked and a shoe collided with my face.

"Get out of here, you bastard!" the woman's voice shouted.

"Easy there!" Ender took a step back.

"Where is the princess?"

"Rosie?" I asked.

The space fell silent. Then, "My lady?"

I pushed past Ender, skirting under his armpit, which was so high up that I hardly had to duck at all. On the other side of him, in the cabin, was Rosie. As I made my way inside, her eyes widened, and she threw herself at me.

"George!"

Relief washed over me. "Are you all right?"

"Fine." She glared over my shoulder. "Except some people don't know how to treat a guest."

"I only locked the door because you attacked the doctor."

"I didn't attack him." She stepped between me and Ender like a ferocious mother bear, even though she didn't even come up to

Ender's clavicles. Despite it, she poked him in the chest. "He wouldn't tell me where the princess was, and I said he couldn't leave until he changed his mind about that."

"You didn't!" I said.

"She did. Threatened to tie him to one of the bunks." Ender's eyes sparkled with amusement.

Rosie turned back to me, running her hands over my arms. "Are you all right? They didn't hurt you?" She took in my appearance and spun back to Ender. "So you're willing to let her out of her ruined dress, but I'm forced to stay in mine?" Her sleeve was torn at the shoulder, and one of the laces on the front had snapped, leaving her bodice open enough to show the undershirt beneath. Somewhere, she'd lost her veil, and her hair, even cut short like it was, formed a halo of orange fire around her head that only made her look more fearsome.

"I'm sorry, little miss." Ender dropped his head in a shame that nearly had me laughing again. "I'll see to it right away." He glanced nervously between us. "If I leave the door unlocked, you promise not to cause any problems? The captain said you're not to be treated as prisoners, but I can't let you loose if you're going to cause trouble for the crew."

"Trouble?" Rosie started for him again. "I'll give you trouble, you overgrown—"

I grabbed her wrist. "We'll be fine. Thank you, Ender."

He was eyeing Rosie like she might produce a knife and stab him at any moment, but he smiled when he glanced at me. He knocked his thumb to his forehead. "I'll be back soon, lady."

When he was gone, Rosie hugged me again. "Are you all right?"

I pulled her tighter so she couldn't see my face. It was nearly impossible to say how I was after everything that had happened. "We're fine. We'll be fine." We would be. We had to be.

"Is it—" She pulled me over to one of the low bunks against a wall. "Is it really—the captain. Is it really her?"

"So it would seem."

"She's your friend, the one you told me about?"

"Yes." No. That friend might be dead after all.

Rosie's eyes rounded. "Your best friend is Captain Cinder."

If I ever returned to Redmere, the prince would have more than enough ammunition to have me killed, and "best friends with Captain Cinder" would undoubtedly be at the top of my list of crimes. I'd never be able to prove I wasn't a traitor with that around my neck.

Best friends with a murderer. A monster that haunted children's dreams and killed hundreds of innocent men.

I was a traitor, regardless of what Lou might think of me. No, I'd never plotted to kill the prince or betray him to his enemies, but every trip from the dressmaker's to the print shop would have been enough to hang me.

Had it been enough, though? Had we changed anything? Niall was dead, and I was gone. Would anyone in Redmere notice? My eyes stung at the thought of Niall's empty shop. What would happen to his body? His family? I'd never met them, but he must have had one, and now their son had been involved in the attack on the harbor. He shouldn't have taken the risk. Not for me. There would be no more pamphlets, no more caricatures—but now I wasn't so sure those had ever made any difference. With Lou's presence emanating from elsewhere in the ship mingled with the lore of Captain Cinder, the world was suddenly a much bigger and more confusing place than it had been a few days ago.

The door burst open again, making us both jump. Ender loomed because his size meant he could hardly do anything else. He turned his head away, one hand over his eyes as he thrust out a new bundle of clothes, as if Rosie might start undressing right there. Her grin was sly as she took them from him.

"Thank you, sir," she said primly. Ender spread his fingers to peek at us and, convinced our modesty was intact, dropped his hand. He glanced again at Rosie and blushed furiously.

"I brought the princess's underthings too. If you—if you need anything else, little miss, you just let me know. Name's Ender."

Rosie gazed up at him through her lashes. "You're very kind, Ender."

The giant man continued to blush and stumbled over his feet as he reached for the door, giving us an apologetic smile before he closed us in. There was no click of a lock as he departed.

Rosie giggled. I gaped. "What was that?"

She grinned as she unlaced her dress. "He *was* very kind!"

"So you decided to flirt with him?"

She was tangled in a shirt with sleeves that fell below her knees. "We need friends here if we're going to survive. They already tried to throw me overboard once."

"They're not going to throw you overboard," I said fiercely, pulling the shirt down for her.

Her head popped out through the sagging neck of the thing, practically open to her shoulders. She pulled the laces as tight as they would go, bunching the fabric, and still her cleavage was visible.

"They're pirates. Who knows what they'll do?" She rolled up the shirtsleeves until her hands were free. Her trousers somehow fit her, and I would have to ask Ender later how he'd found them when mine were only upright through the grace of my belt.

"We're safe," I said as she sat down next to me. "Lou said we were safe."

"You believe her?" She pulled a stray thread from the side of my shirt.

"I . . ." I didn't know what to believe anymore. I put an arm around Rosie's shoulders. "We'll stay safe together."

———

We remained in our cabin for most of that first day. The air was stuffy, and the rocking sensation without any windows or points of reference to steady ourselves was unnerving, but neither of us got sick. There was even sunlight funneled in from the deck above us through prismatic glass mounted into the ceiling.

As the light began to fade, Ender returned to bring us a meal of something salty and over-seasoned in tin bowls. Rosie flirted outrageously with him until his ears were pink under his shaggy hair and he couldn't meet her gaze. She ate her meal with a smug smile, then had half of mine as well. I didn't have much of an appetite, and the strongly-flavored fish stew didn't appeal to me.

No one bothered us again. We curled up on our narrow bunks and tried to sleep. The mattresses were thin and felt even thinner after the plush luxury of my room at the palace, which made me feel guilty after what Lou had said. Rosie didn't seem to mind the beds. She was asleep in minutes and snored so loudly, it could be heard over the continual groans of the ship and the shushing of waves.

Every time I closed my eyes, I saw Niall's blood on the wharf, and I'd wake up crying. Or I'd fall more deeply asleep and dream of Lou. It was the same dream it always was, with Lou deep at the bottom of the ocean—except where before, it had been my friend at twelve years old in her smart uniform like the day she'd left, it was this new Lou. The ties and straps of her orange garment wafted out from her like an elegant octopus, while tentacles from an unseen creature slid over her shoulders and around her waist. Her arms reached for me like she was the *Crimson Siren* come alive, and every time I was close enough to touch her, I would wake, sitting upright with a shock, my heart pounding.

We couldn't stay. Lou had made it clear my presence was an inconvenience. She'd been paid already for whatever she was contracted to do with me, so her obligations had been met. I would go see her and ask that Rosie and I be let off as soon as possible. The prince would no doubt be in pursuit, but he'd known me for two days. Only he and the count really knew what I looked like, and there had to be a way to disguise my appearance. Even dressed as I was, surely most of the prince's men would overlook me when they searched for an abducted Redmerian princess.

The glass in the ceiling glowed again when I finally gave up on sleep. Dawn. I'd tossed and turned all night. Dressing was simple since I'd slept in my borrowed shirt. I slipped into the too-large pants and wound the belt around my waist. My hair was a tangle, but I reached for the green scarf to tie it up again. Lou's silver bracelet clattered to the floor, still caught up in the material from the night before. I held it in my palm. If I'd been outside, I might have been tempted to throw it overboard; even in the confines of the cabin, I couldn't bring myself to wear it. It reminded me too much of the dichotomy of the Lou in my memories and the one on this ship. Instead, I slipped it under my pillow and made my way up the narrow ladder to the deck.

My solution was risky, but staying here was too painful.

The sun was barely over the horizon, burning orange in the distance. The sea and sky were a mottled purple, like a new bruise. At the far edge of the sky, the last remaining stars sparkled. A few figures were hunched against the railing or the mast, but they didn't appear to see me or care that I was about.

As it turned out, Lou was already occupied. I hesitated. The last time I'd hung behind open doors listening to others' conversations, I'd learned my fiancé planned to kill me, but Maro's clipped accented consonants made me pause.

"She's not worth it, Cinder. You can't put us all at risk like this, even if she is a princess."

"The prince won't take this lightly. She's not another nobleman's unhappy wife. We can't just drop her at the next port and send her on her way."

My heart rattled in my chest at her words. That was what I was about to ask for. But if I requested it, maybe she would grant the request anyway. Maro clearly wouldn't be disappointed to see me go. If I could bring them onto my side, even briefly, Rosie and I could find a way to get off this ship.

But Lou continued. "The only way to get her to safety is through Kiril, and to do that, we have to go to Andel's. I don't like it any more than you do, but make the preparations. We're heading to Beldridge."

"Captain." Maro's voice had lost some of its anger. "Talk to me. There's more you haven't said."

I hated the compassion in their voice. Hated that Lou didn't throw it back like she had with me. Did I disgust her that much? Bore her? Or was it more to do with who Maro was to her? The doctor had hinted that their connection might be more than that of colleagues . . . if pirates could have colleagues.

I shuddered at the idea of them together, of Lou touching anyone with kindness or desire when she had none to give me. The jealousy was childish. She and Maro fit together, cut from the same cloth. But once, Lou and I had been peas in the same pod. This new Lou was too hard. She'd suit Maro nicely, and I didn't like that one bit.

While I mused, the cabin had fallen into silence, as if they were having another of those wordless arguments I'd witnessed the day before.

At length, Maro said, "As you wish, Captain." I could picture them giving another formal bow, acknowledging that Lou's authority was absolute.

Footsteps sounded inside the cabin, most likely Maro leaving. I stumbled backward, but the distance between the cabin and the hatch I'd emerged from was too great, too exposed. Instead, I ducked behind one of the heavy cannons lining the deck, relying on its dark shape in the poor light to hide me. Maro's footsteps approached, and I closed my eyes, sending up a silent prayer that they would walk past.

The footsteps turned, followed by the creak of hinges and the sound of feet descending a ladder.

The ship fell silent again.

I let out a long breath. Time to face Lou once more. Hopefully, for the last time.

"Good morning, princess."

A man leered down at me where I was still crouched by the cannon. He'd crept up on me silently and was pleased with himself. He'd been among the men present when Maro had threatened to throw Rosie overboard. His missing teeth and sour breath were distinctive.

Janos.

I stood, brushing invisible dirt from my clothes. "Good morning."

He cocked his head to one side. "Out by yourself, Highness?"

"I'm just on my way to see the captain." I went to step past him, but he followed, staying in front of me to keep my back to the rail.

"It's early for a fine lady such as yourself to be out and about."

"Yes, well... if you'll excuse me."

When I went to push by him again, he grabbed my arm. I tried to pull away, but his grip tightened, fingers pressing into my skin.

"I've never met a princess before."

My body tensed, but I tried my best to play the part and show him I was weak. "You've seen a princess now. Let go of me."

His fingers were like iron, and he would leave bruises where he held me. "You must be used to very fine men paying attention to you, aren't you?" He stepped closer. His breath was hot and rank, like old meat left in the sun too long. It made my stomach roil, and I turned my head away, even as he pressed me against the rail.

"Let me go," I hissed, but he only laughed.

"Not until I have had a chance to look at you." His voice was soft but carried a threat beneath it as he gripped my other arm.

"You've looked," I said, fighting to stay calm.

He slid a grimy hand over my scarf, pushing it back to let my hair fall free. "You're very pretty, Highness. Your hair is so soft. So clean. Do men tell you that?"

I shook my head and closed my eyes, fighting traitorous tears.

His finger brushed along my jaw. "So pretty. Skin like silk. I want to see what's so special about you. You must be worth a lot of money to someone. I want to see why. Try for myself."

When his lips touched my throat, my confident quiet broke completely. This was too far, too much. Lou had said I would be safe. I screamed and pushed at him. He laughed again and tightened his arms around me.

"No need to be like that, Highness. I won't hurt you."

I had no room to fight him, no space for me to kick him. His scalp was completely bald, so I didn't even have any hair to pull. I did the best I could and raked my nails over his head, gouging. He shouted and recoiled, letting go long enough to swing his hand back for a slap. I cried out and brought my hands up to ward him off.

A pistol was pressed to his temple. The click of the hammer was loud in the silence of dawn.

"Janos. You will let go of the lady." Maro's tone was hard, and the man stepped back immediately. The pistol stayed firmly in place.

"The princess. She was . . . she was unwell. Fainted again. I was just—"

"You're not supposed to be on watch," they said.

Janos swallowed. "No, but I—"

"Where's Klav?"

"He's—" The whites of Janos's eyes were visible as he glanced vainly at the gun pressed to his head.

"Anything wrong?" It was Ender, lumbering out of the shadows as if he'd been conjured from them. My heart slowed a little at his appearance.

"Ender," Maro snapped. "Find Klav. Get the captain."

"Right away." He disappeared as quickly as he'd come.

"Are you all right?"

It took me a moment to recognize that their question was for me.

"Yes." I was ashamed at how much my voice shook.

"What were you doing up here?" They still held the pistol at Janos, but their eyes narrowed in my direction.

"I—" I cleared my throat. "I couldn't sleep."

Their lips tightened, and they went to say something else, but a commotion broke out behind us. Lou strode down the deck.

Her eyes were full of murder, and her heavy, black coat, so different from the floating purple one she'd worn the day before, billowed behind her like an avenging demon. Ender followed behind her, dragging a scarred sailor—Klav, I supposed—by one arm.

"What's going on?" She looked right at me, but it took me so long to find the words that Maro spoke before I could.

"Janos attacked the princess."

"What?" She spun toward Janos, who flinched back in a way he hadn't when Maro's pistol had made its appearance.

"I didn't, Captain. I was only trying to—"

"Who was on watch?" Lou asked Maro.

"Klav. But he wasn't at his post when I found Janos and Her Highness."

I wished they'd stop talking about me like I wasn't here, but Lou's attention was already on the man in Ender's grasp.

"Where were you?"

Ender thrust Klav forward, and he stumbled, falling to one knee. "Captain. I thought I heard—"

Casually, slowly, almost as if she didn't know she was doing it, Lou took one step forward to set her boot on the back of Klav's hand where he'd planted it on the deck. He choked and tried to pull back, but she kept him firmly in place.

"If you want to have any bones left for the doctor to set back into place, choose your words carefully," Lou said.

Klav whimpered but held still. "I didn't—I thought—I saw the lady, and—" Lou, impatient with his progress, pressed down harder. He yelped. "Janos said! He said if I saw her, I should—"

"You shut your mouth!" Janos shouted. "You shit for brains, you keep your mouth shut."

Lou turned on him like a snake choosing a mouse. "What did you do, Janos?"

Janos set his jaw and narrowed his eyes.

Her gaze traveled back to me. "What did he do?"

I took them all in. Ender still in shadow. Klav on his knees and cradling his hand. Maro with a gun trained on one of their own crew. Janos glaring defiantly at his captain. Lou staring at me with cold eyes I didn't recognize.

Overwhelmed, I shook my head.

Lou's lips puckered like she'd bitten something bitter, but she turned to Maro. "Flog them both."

The order was followed by a curt acknowledgment from Maro and protests from Klav and Janos, but they were dragged away. Suddenly, it was just Lou and I on the deck. Her eyes skimmed over me, resting on my bare arms where red marks from Janos's fingers were showing. Reflexively, I covered myself, uncomfortable under her scrutiny. My hand went to my hair, but the scarf was gone.

"You shouldn't be up here." Lou's voice was flat. Tears prickled in the corner of my eyes, and not from the wind. All I wanted from her was comfort. A gentle question to make sure I was all right. Instead, I got accusation, so I flung it back at her too. "You said I'd be safe." It was my fault for believing her when she was a liar and a killer.

"I'll take you back to your cabin." She reached for me, but the brush of her fingers on my skin was enough to make me think of Janos's crushing grip, of the prince's slithery hand on my back.

I recoiled. "It's fine. I know the way."

I didn't need anything from her.

I COULDN'T HIDE the bruises from Rosie for long. They were a livid purple that stood out from my skin, even in the irregular cabin light. She clucked and cursed, and when Ender appeared to check on us, she threw another shoe at him.

"What was that for?" he asked, looking offended.

She pointed an accusing finger into his chest. That she had to stand on her toes to do it didn't seem to bother her in the slightest. "You were supposed to keep her safe."

It was absurd that he should tremble in front of her, but he did. "Little miss, I—"

"Look what happened!" She flung a hand in my direction, and I had to fight not to cover my arms again. We'd torn my underskirt into strips so I could tie my hair up again, but I still felt far too exposed. Rosie had decided to forgo a kerchief entirely, red curls flying in every direction, and I admired her bravery. I'd dreamed so many times about losing the weight of my veil, but I still craved the security the anonymity gave me.

Ender sighed. "I'm sorry, little miss. The men involved are being dealt with."

"I should hope so," she said.

"The captain will flog them at sundown today. She's requested you both be there."

I rushed to stand beside Rosie. "What?"

"It's discipline," he said. "The whole crew will be there. You should be as well. The captain asked me to inform you."

"Inform us!" I shuddered. "Take me to the captain."

Ender took a step back. "I can't. She's occupied at the moment."

"Occupied?" The nerve. "We're on a ship. She hasn't exactly gone into town on business."

Ender's lips quirked up beneath his beard, and the idea that he might be laughing at me was enough to make my blood boil. "You've had a fright, princess," he said slowly.

"I'm not a princess," I said. "Why won't anyone believe me? I never wanted to marry him. I'd rather see him dead at the end of a long rope and his kingdom broken up into pieces."

Rosie clapped happily beside me, and Ender's eyebrows rose, but he nodded approvingly.

"That's good, prince—" He caught his tongue between his teeth and grinned. "Lady. You'll need that strength."

"For what?"

"For the flogging." Ender nodded sympathetically when I shuddered. "It's a hard thing to see. But if you don't come, they'll think you're soft. Mercy isn't rewarded in a place like this."

"Mercy is the only thing that matters." If the prince had shown any mercy to his people, even a single grain of food or a single coin to spend, it would have seemed like the greatest gift.

He shook his head sadly. "Think about the life you want for you and the little miss to have while you're with us."

I glanced at Rosie, who folded her arms. "We can manage just fine," she said.

"I don't doubt you can," Ender said, "but you're still expected to be there." He knocked a thumb against his forehead and excused himself.

I huffed and paced the tiny length of the cabin when we were alone again. "I don't suppose we can still swim for it."

Rosie shook her head sadly. "Even in the daylight, it's too far."

I rolled my eyes. "Very funny."

"But you said in the cell that it was too dark, and—"

"Yes, yes." I held up a hand and stared up at the ceiling, listening to the ship's crew moving above us. "She can't flog them. It's barbaric."

"But he attacked you."

"He didn't hurt me. Not much."

"But the next one might."

That brought me up short. Rosie pressed her lips thin as she watched me, and finally, I slumped down next to her on her bunk. She patted my hand, and I dropped my head to her shoulder. Here was the comfort I'd craved with Lou.

"I'm afraid," I said.

"So am I."

"We're going to escape. The next port, the next ship to go by . . . When the opportunity presents itself, we're getting away from here."

"And the flogging?" she asked.

I couldn't bear the idea of going but couldn't discount the

chance that, short of barricading ourselves in here, either Maro or Lou herself would likely come to march us up onto the deck.

"We'll go," I said.

Let Lou think she'd won until we had a chance to be free of her.

11

Rosie and I were brought to Maro on the quarterdeck as the sun went down. Ender and another crew member led Janos and Klav, wrists bound and shirts removed. They tied them so their torsos were each draped over the side of a cannon, naked backs exposed to the sky. At a salute from Ender, Maro stepped forward and listed off the charges. When they said my name, the tension in the small, assembled crowd shifted palpably.

"Does anyone here have any evidence why these two men should not receive their punishment as prescribed by Captain Cinder?" Maro asked.

The crew was silent. The waves crashed, and the heavy canvas of the sails flapped in the wind. A few angry glares were sent my way as if I'd somehow brought this upon the two sailors, but no one said anything to contradict Maro's words.

On some unspoken signal, the captain's cabin door opened, and Lou emerged. She was dressed in simple black sailor's clothes, her hair tied back and buried under a black kerchief. We were dressed more or less the same, she and I, but in contrast to my white scarf and silver-buttoned shirt, Lou was all shadow. In her hand she carried a thick-handled whip with a single length of leather. The sight of her like that made my stomach twist.

She stopped below us and looked up at Maro. "Have the charges and the sentence been read?"

Maro snapped to attention. "Yes, Captain!"

"Does anyone here dispute the facts as they have been read by the first mate?"

Silence.

Lou glanced back up at me, and I shuddered at the emptiness in her eyes. "Your Highness. Will you beg for mercy for your attackers?"

Mercy is never rewarded out here.

I should have asked her to stop. But this twisted Lou-monster and her crew expected me to be weak and soft, and the prince had proven that weakness could be used against me.

When I said nothing, she smirked and turned back to the crew. "The lady is pitiless."

Someone laughed among the crew, but the sound was cut off almost immediately.

With no further ceremony, Lou strode toward the two men awaiting their punishment.

The flogging was brutal. The hiss of the whip as it sailed through the air. The grunts, and later cries, of the men on the cannons. Lou's heaving breaths that became more labored with each swing. I lost track after the tenth lash.

As she started on the second man and the first welts rose up on his skin, my stomach heaved, knowing what would come. I stumbled to the ship's railing to retch. Bile caught in the wind, blowing away from my lips. I wiped my mouth with the back of my hand and waited for the feeling to pass, but the whole time I could feel their eyes on me, waiting, judging. When I was confident it was over, I wordlessly took my place next to Rosie again. She was pale, but she wrapped her fingers around mine, and we stayed where we were.

Finally, the deck fell silent again. I exhaled and let go of Rosie's hand. The ship rocked under my feet, and the wind carried the metallic scent of blood to my nose.

"That was well done, Highness," Maro said softly. I glared at them. I didn't need their approval, nor anyone else's on this ship.

Ender and the sailor who had brought the two prisoners went to the cannons and began the grim task of untying the limp forms. I allowed myself a single glance to make sure Janos and Klav were still alive. Janos screamed when they straightened him up. Klav was silent but staggered on his own feet as the doctor led them away.

The whip was still clutched in Lou's fist. Her kerchief had come loose, exposing the tight coil of her hair underneath. She turned slowly, almost as if she were asleep, and took two staggering steps of her own before she caught herself.

When she glanced up at us, my heart stopped.

On a day late in the fall, we find a litter of kittens in the stables. There are six of them, little white and gray bundles of fur and tiny mews. We never see their mother, and we are barely more than babies ourselves.

First, we name them. Smudge, Snowball, Smokey, Shadow, Starlight, and Stormy. Good mothers name their children so they know they are loved. That's what Lou says.

Next, we set about keeping the kittens warm and fed. Lou steals two blankets from the small room where the grooms store saddles and harnesses, and she makes a cozy kitten nest in the corner of the stall. I go to the kitchens and beg for a bowl of milk.

We play with them all afternoon. Smudge dies first, although at the time we think she is sleeping. Lou says we will have to stay up all night, taking turns feeding the babies. We try, but our little bodies let us down. My eyes hang low, and my limbs grow heavy. The kittens make tiny squeaking noises, and I know I need to stay awake to look after them, but it is so hard.

Lou wakes first, or maybe she struggled all night while I slept, desperately trying to keep the five remaining souls alive and failing. Either way, it is the sound of quiet crying that wakes me. Lou is huddled in the corner, her back curved away, head bowed between her shoulders.

"Lou?" I rub a sleepy hand over my eyes.

"Go away."

"What?"

"Go away!"

Still fuzzy-headed, I crawl over the straw. Lou's soft sobs grow louder as I approach, her spine drawing into a tighter C.

"Lou?" I kneel behind her and place one hand on her shoulder.

Lou whirls, hair wild, eyes red and wide. "Leave me alone! Get away from them!"

In the straw between her knees are six, unmoving, furry bodies.

"What happened?" I lean forward, only to be pushed roughly back.

"Don't touch them! Stay away!"

My tears spill over. "What happened to the kittens?"

Lou's expression is a mask of horror and pain. Her face crumples as though the bones beneath her skin are falling to dust. "I couldn't help them." Her ragged voice makes me cry harder. "They needed me to take care of them, and I couldn't help them!"

Lou's face was etched in stone. A pitiless mask, as if everything that had just happened left her with no more feeling than the mindless pulse of the waves against the hull. I'd expected the desperate plea of the child trying to save her furry charges. Instead, she might as well have been a corpse.

For hours after, I couldn't shake the memory of her face. My friend was gone.

DESPITE THE COOL breeze on the deck, the air inside our cabin was stifling. Even with the thin blankets we'd been provided, I was too warm. I threw mine off in disgust, staring into the dark as the *Crimson Siren* creaked and rolled around us.

"Rosie," I said.

"Yes?" The reply came so quickly, I knew she couldn't have been asleep either.

"Were you a maid or a spy first?"

"What do mean?"

I couldn't see her, but I sat up anyway. "I mean, are you really a maid, or are you actually a spy who became a maid to infiltrate the palace?"

The cabin went so quiet, for a moment I thought she wouldn't answer. I don't know if I could have taken that. No one was who I thought they were. But the silence ended with a rustle of bedding and bare feet on the floor, and she groped her way onto the mattress next to me.

"I told you my father ran a shipping company," she said.

"Yes," I said, trying not to be impatient.

"What I didn't tell you was that seven years ago, he killed himself because the prince ruined him."

I gasped. "How?"

"The crown commandeered three of my father's ships—which is to say, all of them. My father had some of the fastest civilian vessels in Redmere. The navy said they needed them after two of theirs had been lost to pirates."

To Cinder. Rosie didn't have to say it.

"What happened?"

"They were sent to trade in Yagrad, but they were lost less than two days from Redmere. A storm took down two and toppled the mast on the third. She limped back into port six months later. Most of her crew had starved to death.

"The crown was supposed to compensate my father for his losses, but when the money came, it was only a fraction of what the ships were worth. He had employees to pay, suppliers demanding their share, and ships to refurbish, and he had no money to do it with." She laid her head on my shoulder. "He hung himself, and my mother was forced to sell our house to pay off his debts."

"Oh, Rosie." I didn't know what else to say. She'd been such a bright, cheerful spot in all this chaos, and she'd spoken about her family with such love. I hadn't thought to question any of it.

"I was angry. I needed work. My aunt got me a position at the palace, but my brother . . . he'd started frequenting these meetings where they . . . talked about certain things."

And passed out pamphlets where the tyrant of Redmere stared out at Rosie's brother with great buck teeth and rodent eyes.

"I'd been at the palace for a few years when he brought me to meet some friends of his. They were looking for someone they could trust, someone who could leave the palace without attracting any notice. I got sent out on errands by the kitchen, so it was easy enough for me to slip away. All I had to do was take the letters."

"The letters?" I asked.

She shrugged. "Or whatever they were. I can read, but not very well. Someone would leave them under the mat where I slept, and I would carry them out into the city."

"And take them to the dressmaker?"

"Sometimes," she said. "There were a few others. An apothecary. A cooper. None of them were too far from the palace because I couldn't be gone too long without arousing suspicion."

"How old were you?" I asked, trying to keep track of the details.

"Fourteen, almost fifteen, when I started."

At fourteen and fifteen, I was still stumbling through the end of my school days, hoping for some fantastical rescue that would take me away from Jeremy and bring me back to Lou. Rosie had carried so many years of secrets.

"Were you afraid?" I asked.

"Not really. We'd already lost everything. If I could find a way to hurt the prince even a little, it made it better. My father didn't deserve what happened to him."

I wrapped an arm around her. "You're so brave."

She laughed. "You were going to marry the prince."

"I didn't have much of a choice."

She burrowed against my shoulder and yawned again. "There's always a choice. I could have killed myself like my father did. Or I could have turned my brother in and earned a little favor at the palace. I chose to help in what small way I could."

Lou had insinuated I hadn't done enough, that others had carried the risk. But what I'd done wasn't any different from Rosie, and she seemed very brave to me.

"When we get out of here," I said, "we're going to go back to Redmere."

"To the palace?"

Perhaps not there. Even if I hadn't lived at the palace very long, if Rosie snuck me in as a new maid, someone would be bound to notice my resemblance to the missing princess. But there had to be more ways to help. Rosie's brother would know. I could get lost in the city where the prince or Jeremy would never think to look. Hide in plain sight as a dressmaker's assistant. Or start a new print shop and pick up where Niall's work had been cut short.

If I could be free of Captain Cinder, I could go home and be the princess Redmere truly needed.

12

Of course, escaping a pirate ship was easier said than done.

We woke the morning after the flogging, and the *Crimson Siren* was quiet for once. No groaning rigging. Only the gentle sound of water lapping at the hull.

"George?" Rosie asked.

"Yes?" I kept my eyes closed, not ready to face the world yet.

She sighed heavily. "Should we go outside?"

For all my brave words about escape the night before, the idea of going up on the deck and facing Lou, Maro, and the crew made me want to curl up in the dark cocoon of the cabin and stay there forever.

A knock sounded on the door.

"Good morning, ladies." Ender's voice rumbled from behind the panels.

"What do you want?" Rosie growled as she strode to the door and opened it.

"Good morning, little miss." Ender grinned. "Petru's in a mood. I've been sent to fetch you for breakfast if you want it."

"Petru?"

"Our cook. He says no more bedside service. If you want to eat, you're to come to the mess."

The cause of the ship's relative silence became apparent as we emerged onto the deck. We weren't moving. A steady breeze blew over my face as I faced ahead, but the sails hung and flapped in the wind instead of straining tautly with it.

A small cluster of crewmen were gathered along the rail, and only then did I notice the other ship to our left. It was a much smaller vessel, with only one mast and a few sails furled tightly against it.

"What's going on?"

A man cried out, and Klav's scarred face appeared in the group by the rail. He was being helped over the side and down the ladder.

"We're lightening our crew," Ender said, eyes narrowed.

"What?"

"Janos and Klav will be no use to us the way they are right now. We came upon an obliging fisherman about an hour ago. He's agreed to carry them to the nearest port."

I watched as Janos was helped over the rail next. He moved stiffly, and I shuddered at the thought of his muscles straining under the wounds from the day before as he made his way to the longboat below.

"Just like that? You happened to find someone willing to take on two hurt men?"

Ender shrugged. "Most likely he was relieved we weren't going to sink him. The captain will pay him handsomely, of course."

"Oh, of course." I scoffed. "Cleaning up her handiwork. If she hadn't flogged them, she wouldn't have had to go to the trouble and expense."

"Would you rather we keep them on board?"

I opened my mouth to retort, but the wind carried a new waft of tar and saltwater toward me, and with it came the memory of Janos's sour breath on my neck.

At the very core, I was still angry with Lou. But I wouldn't be sorry to see him go, regardless of what had happened to him afterward.

I stared at the small ship beside us for a moment longer. Now would be the time to run. My lighter clothes had that advantage. No one would be expecting me to chance the escape. I could be over the rail and halfway down the ladder before anyone caught up to me.

But I had no way of communicating any of that to Rosie, and the small fishing vessel was undoubtedly slower than the *Siren*. Even if I were to convince the new captain to set sail, we'd be caught again in no time, and I couldn't put him at risk. Lou had been charitable enough to spare him in exchange for Janos and Klav's passage. She might not go that far once he'd stolen her prized captive.

A gentle breeze blew across the deck, and my stomach turned at the rotting stench that wafted toward us.

"What's that?" Rosie asked, covering her nose and mouth. She looked a little green around the edges.

Ender wrinkled his nose. "Cephyr guts."

"What?" I asked.

Rosie laughed. "But cephyrs aren't real."

"They're rare," Ender said with a shrug. "But not imaginary like most people say. You catch one, she'll have enough oil in her to keep a whole city's lamps burning for years." He belched. "As long as you can stomach the stench long enough to get her to shore for processing. Worth it, though. The fangs make for good ivory if you can get to them."

We peered over the side at the boat below us. The vessel was larger than I'd first imagined. It sat lower in the water, but that was apparently because her hold was open and overflowing with slimy tentacles as big around as my torso.

The smell made my eyes water. "That's a cephyr?" We did hear stories at home about ships lost to one of the legendary creatures, but no one knew anyone who had ever seen an actual cephyr up close . . . presumably because she ate them.

"A small one."

I didn't regret seeing Klav and Janos go, but I did have some sympathy for their traveling conditions if the reek was that strong from up here.

"Now," Ender said with a smile. "Time for breakfast."

Rosie made a gagging noise, and I wondered whether either of us would be able to stomach it.

The "mess," as Ender called it, was in the center of the ship, a level below our cabin. The tables were heavy boards strung between thick ropes suspended from the ceiling. Ten or so men were hunched around two of the tables, and a few heads turned as we entered. Steely eyes glared at me, and Rosie plucked at the hem of my shirt as she followed, but Ender continued a cheerful stream of conversation. The rest of the sailors returned to their cups and bowls without incident.

We took a small table near one end of the room. The mess was dark and smelled of too many meals cooked in close quarters. Oil lanterns hung from the ceilings, casting wheeling shadows. Rosie and I hesitated, staring at the low stools around the table. Sitting facing the rest of the crew felt like opening us up to their silent judgment, and sitting with our backs to them meant we would imagine it instead, which wouldn't be any better.

We huddled on the far side of the table, and I smiled tightly whenever eyes glanced our way. Ender went to the scowling cook, Petru, and returned shortly after with three tin plates containing the same salted fish stew that seemed to be the primary source of nourishment aboard the *Crimson Siren*. Rosie sighed forlornly next to me as Ender set the plates down.

"Don't let Petru hear you like that, little miss." Ender took the stool opposite. His wide body had the added benefit of blocking most of the pirates from my view.

Rosie scooped a large serving of her meal and put it in her mouth, clasping the heavy spoon between her teeth and grinning wildly.

Ender chuckled. "Well done."

My appetite hadn't returned after our encounter with the cephyr. Instead, I eyed the sailors who were watching us. Their scrutiny was a heavy thing. We would never find a means to get away if Rosie and I were being watched all the time.

"Ender," I said.

"Yes, lady?"

"Could I trouble you for a glass of water?"

Rosie raised an eyebrow at my exaggerated politeness, but Ender only shook his head. "I wouldn't recommend the water to drink here, lady. It sits so long in barrels it goes stagnant, and that's if a mouse doesn't fall into it."

I wrinkled my nose, and he pushed up from his seat. "But there's ale to be had if that'll suit you."

I'd had the ale on board. It tasted not unlike swamp water. I didn't want to imagine what the actual water tasted like.

"Ale is fine," I said sweetly. "Thank you so much, Ender."

"What are you doing?" Rosie hissed as soon as he was gone.

"I need you to find a reason to stay in the kitchens," I said to her quickly.

"What?"

"This looks to be where the sailors are when they aren't on deck. We need to know more about them if we're going to escape. Who's friendly? Who drinks too much? Who falls asleep on his watch and won't notice when we steal a longboat?"

"We're going to steal a longboat?" Rosie's eyes widened.

I hadn't worked that part out yet. But the key to successfully making my way between the print shop and the dressmaker's had always been to know which soldiers worked at which checkpoints and which streets the City Guard patrolled most heavily so I could avoid them. Right now, aside from a few, the *Crimson Siren* was crewed by a nameless, faceless horde. We needed to know their routines and their weaknesses better.

Rosie's face lit up. "It's a good thing we're already spies," she whispered.

"Exactly."

She winked. "Leave it to me."

Ender returned shortly with three mugs of ale, which I thanked him for profusely. The tips of his ears turned pink, then brighter still when Rosie smiled at him.

We ate in silence for a long while, until the salt from the stew burned my tongue.

Rosie pushed her bowl away with disgust. "Is this all you eat here?" she said, perhaps a bit louder than necessary. "I can't feel my lips anymore."

"Do you have a complaint with my cooking, m'lady?" Petru stomped over to our table, wiping a ladle with his stained apron.

She glared at him. "Do you even soak the fish before you cook it?"

He snorted. "In case you hadn't noticed, good water is a premium in a place like this. I'm not wasting it to make my cooking acceptable to a princess like you."

Ender cleared his throat softly and pointed a meaty finger in my direction. "This one's the princess."

Rosie scoffed and pushed back from her stool, making the table swing wildly. "That's ridiculous. If they're drinking ale, what do you need the water for? Come with me." She stalked away, leaving Petru to curse and trail after her. Ender and I stared wordlessly as Rosie, without so much as an invitation, pulled an apron off a hook by the small iron stove and wrapped it around her waist. Petru shouted and swore, but she grabbed a knife and pointed it meaningfully in his direction, and he blustered for a moment before falling silent.

The look on Ender's face was a mixture of fear and awe. I hid my smile behind my mug.

"The captain won't like it if she hurts herself," Ender said, still not dragging his eyes away. Rosie moved pots and scraps around with a lot of bluster and commotion. The rest of the men in the mess were watching her as well.

"Lou will like it less if the cook gets in the way and she has to stab him, I think."

That brought Ender's attention back around, and his beard trembled with a muffled laugh. "No loss there. It's a miracle no one's died from Petru's cooking yet as it is."

With Rosie suitably entrenched, I turned my attention back to finding out what I could about the others around us. "Have you been with L—with the captain for long?"

He poked a spoon at his stew with distaste, as if Rosie's sudden revolt had given him permission to admit how inedible it really was. "A few years. Three since last summer, I suppose."

"Where did you live before that?"

He hunched down into his seat. "I'd rather not say."

"Why not?"

"I—wife, sisters, brother, parents. We were run off our land, and they got sick. My family died. I—I went a bit wild with it all. Killed the landlord and ran away."

My breath caught. The soft misery in his eyes was so at odds with the violence of his words. "So you joined the crew here?" Grief was an awful thing. The death of his landlord might have been justified. But signing on with pirates? I didn't know if I could rationalize that.

"Not right away. I traveled. Worked where people would hire me. Someone always needs a big man for something, whether it's building a barn or guarding a wagon. I'd never thought of going to sea, until . . ." He glanced nervously around, and I leaned in closer.

"Until?"

"There was a festival. For someone like me, there's usually contests. Feats of strength. It's a good way to earn some coin and usually get a dry place to sleep for a night or two. I did well, won the wrestling bouts, and nearly won the heavy toss too. Then, I'd had a bit too much to drink in the tavern to celebrate myself and nearly lost it all when two lads who were handy with a knife got hold of me outside. But this woman appeared. She had them both running with their tails between their legs with just a few words. Then, she offered me a gold coin the size of my eye, right there in the mud. Said there was more of that if I'd come with her."

"Was it Lou?"

He nodded. "I knew a woman like her didn't get gold like that through respectable means, but I was a long way from home and spent more nights sleeping by the side of the road than I did in a bed."

That was enough? He'd sold his conscience for a mattress and a few gold coins?

Ender shifted uncomfortably, like he could hear my silent judgment. "She's a good captain. Fair. You do as you're told and don't cross her, she'll leave you to yourself."

Until she flayed the skin from your back, called you a coward without knowing anything about your life for the last eight years, and murdered her own countrymen with no remorse.

I crossed my arms over my chest. "We'll have to agree to disagree when it comes to Lou."

Ender stirred his spoon through his congealing stew. "I heard you knew the captain from before. That's why you call her L— what you do?"

Call me captain. Was her authority so absolute that her crew was afraid to say her name?

Except me. I grinned. "Lucinda and I were children together." I watched him closely as I said her name, trying to judge how far his loyalty or his fear went.

Ender glanced nervously around him, as if the person in question would leap out from nowhere if he dared to be disrespectful. "What was she like?"

I pictured the Lou of my childhood. Wild. Fierce. Braver than I, but heartbreakingly tender with those weaker than her.

Like the kittens.

"Shorter," I said.

Ender laughed, making his beard tremble and his eyes dance.

A volley of vicious swearing cut through the air behind us. Rosie had cleared off all of Petru's cooking, and she was hauling a bucket of water to the table, over which she promptly poured its contents. Petru shouted, and Rosie flung a cloth at him and told him to start scrubbing.

The awe was back on Ender's face.

Above us, a whistle sounded. The people in the mess all lurched to their feet as if they were loaded on springs, Ender included.

"What—" I started, but Ender already had his back to me.

"Change of watch. Little miss, are you coming?" He knocked a salute to Rosie as he passed.

"Clearly, I'm needed here." She glanced up. "Unless you need me, George?"

"I think you should stay," I said, and she gave me a smart wink.

"I'll take you back to your cabin then," Ender said to me.

"Actually, I'd like to see the first mate, if you don't mind."

He frowned. "Maro?"

"Yes, please."

"Oh, I don't know. Is there something I could help you with instead?"

It would be easier, but going through Ender wouldn't get me what I wanted in the long run.

"No. It has to be Maro. If you don't mind."

We made our way back outside. The fishing ship was gone, and the crew was once again abuzz with activity. Maro was at the wheel, but Lou was nowhere to be seen. The door to her cabin was closed, and I stared at it for a long moment as if it would eventually become invisible and reveal the occupant inside.

How many others had she dragged into this life? Ender. The doctor. They could have had safe, respectable lives on land, and instead they'd chosen piracy and the life of an outlaw. What was it about Lou that tempted men into this existence?

Ender led me up to the quarterdeck and knocked a salute to Maro. "I've brought the princess."

Maro's eyes were on me as they said, "So I can see."

Ender cleared his throat. "She'd like a word."

They barely acknowledged him. "Where's her friend, the maid?"

"She's commandeered the mess."

This caught Maro's attention. "Excuse me?"

He gave them his jovial grin. "Told Petru his cooking wasn't fit to eat and took control of the whole operation. Last I saw, she was scrubbing his worktable."

Maro wrinkled their nose. "Probably the first time it's been cleaned in years." They nodded as if something had been decided, then laughed to themself. "Leave her there. Petru's knives are too dull for her to be any real risk."

"I'll be needing something to do as well," I said.

Their laughter died. "Excuse me?"

"I can't spend all my time sitting in my cabin waiting for my prince to come."

They snorted. "I'd like to see him try."

I ignored the comment. "I need work. I'm used to being out of the house and busy."

"Yes." Maro smiled. "The captain said you were some sort of messenger in your home city."

More feigned ignorance, though that second comment cut more deeply. "The captain also said I'm not a prisoner here."

"Yes, but—"

"You've made it clear I'm not an honored guest. Rosie is in the kitchen, and I'd like to be useful as well." With Rosie down below and me working among the crew on some menial task, we'd gain a better sense of who these people were and how we could outsmart them when the time came.

Maro eyed me, clearly looking for subterfuge. They were smart, and very likely, I'd still be commanded back to my cabin, leaving Rosie to do all the work on her own.

But to my surprise, they asked, "Can you cook too?"

I tried not to sound apologetic as I said, "No."

"Sew?"

They were testing me. Mocking me.

"Do you have much need for a seamstress at sea?"

"If you can sew a dress, you can repair a sail, princess." Maro gestured toward two men who sat on the deck, a wide white expanse of a canvas between them. They worked a wicked curved needle in and out of the heavy fabric.

"I'm sure I could figure it out."

Their gaze slid to the ship below us. "Ender."

"Yes?"

"The deck is looking slippery."

Ender stiffened, and the small gesture made my heart patter. But all he said was, "Of course."

"Have the princess swab the deck instead. Let her show us what her spine is made of."

Ender looked unhappy, but he gave a quick salute and led me back down to the main deck. It was only when he picked up a wooden bucket with a long rope tied to its handle that I realized my plan had worked. We would find a way to get off this ship, I knew it.

He threw the bucket overboard, then pulled the rope up again when water sloshed over the top. "We have to swab the deck at least once a day," he said, "so the wood stays watertight and doesn't become slippery." He tipped the bucket over, pouring water across the boards at our feet.

I failed to see how adding more water kept the deck watertight, but I nodded. "I can do that."

He gave me an apologetic smile, and then nudged a gray stone the size and shape of a brick toward me. "Then we scrub."

"With that?"

"Stone keeps the wood smooth."

Maro meant to literally test my spine. Swabbing was brutal, back-breaking work. Pour the water, kneel, and grind the stone back and forth against the deck. The stone wasn't as heavy as it looked, but it was wide in my hands, making my knuckles cramp as I worked.

As I reached the far end of the ship for the first time, I sat back on my heels, wiping my brow. I was soaked from my feet to my hips. Several sailors were watching me. My shoulders ached, and I'd have blisters by the end of the next pass. I had the ridiculous thought that I'd never be able to do this work in my corset and cloak.

The scrap of cloth wrapped around my hair had come loose. I glanced around me as I fumbled for the knot. My fingers were wrinkled from the water and my joints ached, so the task was a challenge, but finally, it came undone and my hair tumbled loose.

Maro strode by and glanced down at me. "Had enough, Highness?"

"Not at all." I struggled to get my hair done up again and finally admitted defeat, letting it fall down my back while I tied the cloth around my brow to keep it pulled back. I stood and groaned as muscles popped and protested. I tossed the bucket over the side and hauled it back up, even though my arms shook with the effort.

"If you've changed your mind about the chores . . . " Maro said.

"I'm fine," I said, pouring the bucket perilously close to their toes, but they only smirked.

"Find some cloth to bind your hands too. You still won't be able to move them tomorrow, but at least they won't bleed." They carried on down the deck before I could question or thank them.

Swabbing the deck certainly gave me the opportunity to find myself among the crew. But if I'd hoped for a chance to speak to them and see if there were others who might be useful to me, I was out of luck. The sailors gave me a wide berth, and their conversations were always brief and businesslike, so there wasn't much to listen in on. Any time I tried to watch them, I'd lose track of the stone and pinch my fingertips.

By the end of the day, I was so sore and tired, I could barely hold my head up when I joined Ender in the mess. The mood around us was merry, and the reason for it became obvious when

Rosie set down two steaming bowls of fish stew in front of us. At first glance, they looked the same as what we'd tried to eat that morning, but one bite showed us the difference. The burning tang of the salt was gone, and while the peas and carrots couldn't be called flavorful, they were at least edible. Before, they'd been dry and tasteless, even in the broth.

"You've done well, little miss," Ender said. Rosie gave him a wink and went back to her stew pot with a sway of her hips that had him watching the whole way. A number of other sailors called out to her as she went by, and she favored them all with a wink and a smile.

"Do you know someone named Kiril?" I asked.

Ender's attention snapped to me like a shot, and in fact, all of the merriment around us ceased in an instant. The whole space went silent, as if all the occupants were holding their collective breath.

Ender cleared his throat and moved to sit beside me. "Where did you hear of him?" His voice was strained.

I blundered on, too tired to reverse course smoothly. "I—I heard someone say the name. Who is he? Are we going to see him?" It was Lou I'd heard say his name, but I couldn't admit to eavesdropping on the captain.

He glared at the people around us, and ten heads ducked away.

"No one goes to see Kiril. You don't just call on the brokers."

"The what?"

"The brokers," he said, voice barely above a whisper. "They . . . he . . . Kiril is the . . ." He cleared his throat. "You shouldn't ask about him."

The mood had shifted, and in spite of my aching body and tired head, I knew it was my fault. Fear had filled the room over the course of a few questions. It was evident in the uneasy glances around us and the hunch of so many shoulders.

The crew finished their meal and left without much more than a quiet salute to Rosie. Whoever this Kiril person was, they were afraid of him, and we were on our way to him. Lou had said we had no choice. That he was my only chance to get away from the prince.

Whoever he was, I suddenly had no desire to reach him. I would need to get Rosie and I off the ship as soon as possible.

13

I swabbed the deck for three days. Every time I thought I was done, I was greeted with the reality that the task would need to be repeated the next morning. I was the most tired on the first night. I hurt the most on the third. Maro's tip about the rags on my hands was somewhat helpful; blisters still formed, and they stung in the salt water when they cracked, but they didn't bleed.

No sign of an opportunity for escape. The men steered clear of me. Rosie had better luck making friends in the mess, but we were still in an empty ocean with no sign of land. Even if we launched a longboat as I'd said, we couldn't float aimlessly hoping for rescue or row in whatever direction struck our fancy. I'd have to ask Rosie if there was a way to sneak food from the kitchen. If it did come to a longboat, we would need provisions if we were going to survive.

On the fourth day, I nearly dropped the bucket and its rope overboard. Ender had to catch it, and he eyed me carefully. "Are you all right, princess?"

"I'm fine." A knot had formed in the space between my shoulder blades, but my muscles didn't ache nearly as much as they had the day before. I'd like to think I was growing stronger, but the possibility was strong that I was simply numb.

Ender set the bucket down and motioned me to follow him. I did, watching the way each crewman carefully looked away as we passed. Still spooked about the ghostly Kiril?

"Apologies for the interruption," he said as we approached Maro at the wheel. "I'd like to reassign the princess's tasks."

I stretched my shoulders and did my best to ignore how he talked about me like I wasn't there, as well as the desire to remind them once and for all that I wasn't a princess.

Maro eyed me. "Had enough?"

I dropped my arms and squared my posture. "Not at all."

"Change of scenery might be nice," Ender said. "The fixtures are looking a bit dull."

"The fixtures." Maro's expression became pinched.

"Yes. Would do the crew some good to bring a bit of sparkle, don't you think?"

Maro glanced between us. "What do you say, lady?"

"Show me what to do." I'd upset something among the crew with my question about Kiril, and I wouldn't win their favor back by playing the grand lady now.

A ship had a lot of brass, and I soon became very aware of it all—from the bell that hung at the bottom of the stairs, to the quarterdeck, to the fittings on the great winch for the anchor. All of it had a mottled, greenish tinge that could only be removed with thorough rubbing and a fragrant paste Ender said was made from flour, salt, and a sour fruit called a lemon. The work was less painful than scrubbing the decks but infinitely more tedious.

A pirate I didn't know approached as I was scrubbing at a lantern. The patina on the brass was so old it had gone from green to black, and the lantern's small door had a bad habit of pinching my fingers as I went.

"You'll need to do the caps next, Highness," the pirate said, brushing a thumb over his eyebrow.

"The what?"

"The lady's got her hands full with the lantern, as you can see," Ender said, puffing himself up importantly. Though he'd been happy enough to leave me to my wet work with the bucket, today he seemed to have designated himself my personal chaperone and supervisor.

"I'm nearly done," I said, scrubbing hard and almost pinching my finger again. Doubtful the old thing would ever get back to its original gleam, but the shine was slowly returning.

"Then all that's left after that is the caps." The pirate grinned.

"What are those?" I asked Ender. He grimaced, looked upward, then glanced over his shoulder to where Maro and another man were conversing on the upper deck.

"She wants to do a good job, Ender." The pirate cackled. "Don't you, Highness? Going to impress the captain? Make a good little wife for someone someday, you will."

The mention of a wife made me bristle. The last man who wanted me to be a good little wife had also wanted to murder me.

"Show me," I said to Ender.

He frowned. "I don't think—"

"Have you done it before?" I asked, growing impatient.

"Yes."

"Then?"

He scowled at the other man, who was doing an excited little dance, hopping from foot to foot. "It's your back if this gets to the captain. She wants the lady kept safe."

"Why would it not be safe?" I said.

Ender stared at me, then sighed and pointed overhead. "Because the caps are at the end of each of the yard arms on the mast."

My eyes flew up, and I nearly blinded myself in the sun. "The yard arms?"

"Well, you've got your mast here," the other pirate said, holding one arm upright between us. "And then the yards, here, they run across to hold the sails, and the yard arms, well, they—"

"That's enough, Berix," Ender said. "The lady gets the idea."

I stared above me again. It was a long way to the first yard that carried the heavy sails perpendicular to the masts.

"There are brass caps on the end of each?" I asked. From this distance, it was nearly impossible to see them, but something sparkled in the sun as the ship rocked.

"The *Siren* was a Vestrian frigate. The yards are capped with a brass likeness of the Vestrian king. Wouldn't want the face of fellow royalty turning green, now would you?" Berix laughed again, delighting in his own joke.

"You don't have to," Ender said, nervous. "The captain won't—"

"I don't care about the captain." I'd hardly seen her in days except for a brief glimpse as she strode from the cabin to Maro at the quarterdeck, with no acknowledgment to me. "Show me how to get up there."

"Of course, of course." Berix ducked and bowed, extending an arm toward the heavy rope ladders that scaled the sides of the ship and up into the sky. "Rigging is this way. All you have to do is climb."

With two rags tucked into my belt and the pot of paste snug inside my shirt, I started upward. Berix whooped, and Ender grumbled, but their voices fell away quickly, replaced with surf and wind.

The first few feet were easy, even with my tired limbs. The steps in the rope rigging were wide and relatively stable. As I went higher, it became more challenging. First, my arms burned. Then, the ladder wobbled. Where the rigging had been fastened to the railing below at two points, up top it was only fastened at one, making a large triangle. As I reached the apex, the ladder twisted and weaved with my progress.

I pressed my forehead to the tar-stained rope but quickly realized my mistake as the world rocked around me. The rolling as the *Siren* cut through the waves was apparent on the decks, but with every rung I climbed, the ship swung farther and farther, like the weighted end of a pendulum.

When I risked a glance down, Ender and Berix had been joined by others. All their faces were turned to watch me climb.

Another ten feet above me was a small mezzanine with the first yard above it, and new rigging continued from there. The mast had two more yards above the one I'd nearly reached. Glancing over my shoulder, I counted two more masts—the first with three yards as well, the last with only two.

I climbed farther, and my whole body shook. I considered whether it would be better to begin with the nearest yard and start polishing there, or if I should climb to the very top and get the worst of the swaying over with.

"What are you doing?" a raspy voice over my right shoulder asked. I yelped in surprise at the astonished-looking sailor splayed out above me over the yard.

"I've been sent to polish the caps."

The pirate gave a wicked smile. "Well, come on over then, you can polish my cap any day!"

Up it was.

The rigging above the first yard narrowed. When I'd started, three or four people could have climbed abreast without any interference from their neighbors. Now, the ladder had only room for one. The farther I climbed, the quieter everything became. The waves were replaced with only the hiss of wind. The horizon continued to tilt wildly from side to side.

When I'd used the guise of doing chores onboard to get closer to the crew, this was not at all what I'd envisioned.

At the second yard, the first thing I saw looking down was the churning water, dark blue and foaming. Next were the people on the deck. Most, if not all, of the crew had gathered. Rosie was there, arms waving wildly. Ender stood beside her.

My legs quivered under the strain of keeping my body against the rigging as the whole boat tipped toward the sea and back again, but I wouldn't fall. I might not have earned the crew's respect, but I had their attention now.

The ropes slung underneath the second yard were nearly within my grasp when I slipped. One second I was climbing, and the next, my foot had stepped into air. I cried out, hands grappling while the rope cut into my skin. A rough sting burned my thigh. I'd stepped *through* the hole in the ladder with my leg dangling out the other side, bare skin exposed where my pant leg had been pushed up to my calf. Shaking, I righted myself and continued on.

The wind whipped tears from my eyes as I reached the yard. The first step onto the ropes was even more terrifying than the climb had been. Where the ladders had been strung tight, the ropes under the yard sagged beneath my weight. I flung my torso over the yard, feeling the little tin of paste press against my chest. Whether either of the cloths were still safe in my belt was anyone's guess, but I couldn't let go long enough to find out.

Slowly, as the wind swirled around my ears and tugged at my scarf and my hair, I made my way toward the end. The ship wheeled in all four directions now, but I was nearly there. Two feet, possibly three, and I could reach around to the end of the yard. The wind howled in my ears and made the sails flap with a booming sound that had me biting my lip to keep from crying.

Tentatively, I slid one hand down the last few inches and around the end. I groped blindly for the cool surface of the brass cap there.

Nothing but smooth wood greeted my trembling fingers.

I gritted my teeth and leaned out as far as I dared until the tip of the yard was visible.

Empty. Metal studs kept the ropes and fittings from falling off the end, but beyond that, it was blank.

No king.

Laughter from the sailor on the yard below wafted its way up on a breeze. I risked a glance to the deck beyond him. They were all there, the whole crew, their faces turned to see my stupid pride on display. My options were to climb down and face their laughter or let myself go and hope the ocean took me instead of the hard wood below.

The climb down took forever. My arms and legs trembled to

the point of weakness. The pot of brass paste tumbled out of my shirt, and I couldn't bring myself to care.

Gradually, the rocking decreased, and the wind subsided. The pirate on the lower yard laughed and tipped an imaginary hat to me as I passed him, but I simply glared in reply.

The last twelve feet were the worst. By then, my limbs had convinced me that it would be fine to let go and plummet into the sea. The wind died, making room for the endless rush of waves once again. With every step, I expected it to be joined by the chorus of laughter. Poor, spoiled princess. Sweet, unworldly, and gullible.

When my feet touched solid wood, my knees buckled, and I would have finally tumbled to the deck if Rosie hadn't been there to hold me. I tensed for the crew's amusement.

Instead, the air around me filled with thunderous applause and cheering.

"George! That was . . . I was so scared! That was incredible. Was it as high as it looked?" Rosie asked breathlessly. I smiled weakly and patted her on the back. She danced in a circle, which didn't help settle the churning in my stomach.

A solid hand clapped my shoulder, and Rosie pulled away to let Ender enfold me in a tight hug as well. "That was well done, lady. I don't think any of us thought you'd make it to the second spar!" The big man's tight embrace went a long way in grounding me, reeling in the dreadful spinning in my head and leaving only ragged adrenaline.

Then, Ender stumbled backward. I went to call out but was shocked into silence as Lou's fist connected with his solid cheek. He hit the deck like an old tree in a thunderstorm, and Lou towered over him, despite his size.

"What the hell do you think you're doing?" Her face was a mask of ferocious fury.

I thought she might flog him. Beat him until he didn't get up again. The anger on her face was like a furnace that would burn for days.

So I did the only thing I could think to do. I pushed her.

"Stop!"

Lou nearly toppled over Ender's prone body before she spun, rage turned toward me. "This is not your concern, princess."

"It is! It is definitely my concern. Ender didn't climb that ladder, I did."

She sneered at me. "Are you going to beg me to spare him?"

I swallowed hard. Kindness and mercy were not weaknesses, no matter what they all thought.

"I made the choice to climb the ladder. I knew it was a joke, and I did it anyway." I had, even if I hadn't wanted to admit it. "If you have issue with my actions, take it up with me, not Ender."

The emotion in her eyes flickered, but before I could think too hard on it, she had my arm in a grip like iron. "Is that what you want, Your Highness? To feel the consequences of your actions? Allow me to show you."

14

Lou dragged me down the deck toward her cabin and flung open the door. I stumbled toward the nearest sofa. It tipped, and I nearly went over. I only had a second to gather myself before she was in my face, eyes flashing, spittle flying from her lips.

"What in hell's name were you doing up there?"

My voice croaked. "I—"

I should have known the question was a rhetorical one. "I didn't think you could possibly be that stupid. What possessed you to—"

"But Ender said—"

"Ender?" She reared back. "I am doing everything in my power to keep you safe, and you deliberately endanger yourself by—"

"You?" I couldn't help the cracked way the word came out of my throat. I was still shaking, and fire boiled under my skin as my temper flared, fueled by all the nervous tension of my climb. "You're not doing anything! You won't speak to me, won't acknowledge my presence. You're just waiting sell me off to some monster your entire crew is afraid of."

"What? That's absurd—"

"Who's Kiril? Why does everyone look at me like I've invoked a demon when I say his name?"

"You shouldn't be poking your nose where it doesn't belong, princess."

"Stop calling me that!" I lunged to my feet so we stood face-to-face, chest to chest. It turned out I was an inch or so taller than Lou. I pulled myself straighter, and she must have known what I was doing, because she grinned widely, the one gold tooth flashing in a film of spit and sunlight.

"Have you grown a backbone, Highness?"

"You have no right to laugh at me. You're a murderer and a liar. I'm—"

"Oh, I know exactly what you are." She didn't yield a scrap of space between us. We were both breathing hard, and fabric brushed softly against my middle as she inhaled. Her nearness, the flecks of silver in her eyes, the dark mole in front of her left ear—they were stirring something alongside the temper, and I needed to move away before it grew too hot.

"Ender said—"

"Ender said you could polish the caps on the yards." For once, Lou sounded weary.

"How did you—"

"It's an old trick." She stepped back. Her distance brought relief. "A practical joke for new sailors."

More silence. More cautious study. The laces on her shirt were partially undone, and a flush of red spread beneath her collarbones before it disappeared under the octopus and the rough fabric.

"I'll go back to my cabin." I might have developed some measure of comfort among the crew, but her scrutiny was still too much. Too painful.

"Wait here." Without another word, she spun and left me alone in the cabin.

I paced because I couldn't find a comfortable spot on the sofa. My body ached from my adventure up the mast, and I was still fuming at Lou's anger. The room was as grand as it had been the first time I'd entered it. The furniture was ornate, the rugs finely made. A painting hung on one wall of two ships engaged in combat, flashes from cannons captured in a moment of eruption. Did they remind Lou of her glorious victories? Of the ships vanquished and the lives lost?

The door swung open, and a riot of silk fell through the opening.

"Here," Lou said, plucking at the fabric on the floor. "You can fix this."

"A dress?" My hands ran reflexively over my borrowed clothes. I wasn't used to them, but I'd stopped tugging on the short sleeves to try and hide more of my arms beneath them. I had to admit, they'd been better suited for the last few days of drudgery than my old clothes.

I nudged at the pile of stiff material on the floor with one toe as if it might spring to life and attack me.

"I assume you know how to sew. That must have been something you were taught."

I lifted the fabric. It was heavier than I expected, layers upon layers of skirting and a corset sewn into the bodice. The dress was a mess. It had more torn seams than ones intact. The hem was a ruin of dangling.

"I can't wear this. I'm fine in the clothes I have."

"It's not for you."

"Who's it for?"

Her eyes narrowed in irritation. "Can you fix it or not?"

She'd ignored me for days, and now she wanted me to fix a dress?

I folded my arms over my chest. "I'm not feeling particularly helpful," I said. "I'll go back to swabbing the decks in the morning."

Her laugh was a dark thing. "Don't consider this a request. You have no leverage here."

"Where are we going?" I snapped.

"What?"

I pulled the fabric toward me. "You said you couldn't be bothered to maintain a royal guest on board your ship, and yet I'm still here with no indication of how long I'll be onboard. So, where are we going? Tell me that much and I'll fix your dress."

She eyed me, her jaw tight. I held the dress in front of myself, pinched between two fingers like it was personally offensive.

"I'm taking you to Kiril. He's a . . ." She swallowed. "Business associate. He'll be able to get you away from the prince."

"You care that much?" I laughed. Whoever he was, he was more than a business associate. The fear that had permeated the crew at the mention of his name wasn't as obvious with Lou, but I could hear the crackle in her voice she'd had as a child whenever she was frightened.

"No, but the people who paid me for your passage do, and it was a lot of money."

"Which people?" I would need to find them when I went back to Redmere.

She held up a finger, her bravado returned. "One question, Highness. That's all you asked for."

I glared, but I wouldn't be able to push her much further. "And this Kiril person has a fondness for dresses?"

I'd have been arrested in Redmere for suggesting a man might wear something like this, but Lou's mouth curled with wry humor before she said, "No, we're making a stop first. I have to see a man about a stone."

"What sort of stone?"

"Enough." The word was clipped. "You will fix the dress. I'll get you whatever you need to make it wearable."

"Fine," I said, turning toward the door with the silk bundled under one arm.

"Where are you going?"

"To my cabin. Have Ender send scissors, needles and thread, and a lantern."

"Oh, no." Lou grinned as she blocked the door. "You'll do the work here."

"What?" I couldn't hide the alarm in my voice.

"The light is better here," she said, then ducked her head and muttered something that sounded like, "And I can keep an eye on you."

I smirked and gathered up the dress again. "I'll need needle and thread. Scissors."

She gave me a little bow. "As you wish, Highness."

———

Our truce, if it could be called that, was an uneasy one. Lou's cabin, which had once seemed so elaborate, was suddenly confining when I spent more than a few minutes in it, and Lou had ample time to spend with me. Or maybe she really didn't trust me not to go scrambling up the mast again.

The dress was a disaster and gave me a reason to avoid conversation. Decades out of date, Rosie had said when she saw it. No way to salvage it unless the whole thing was taken apart. She tried to help, but in just a few days, she'd made herself indispensable in the mess and couldn't spend more than ten minutes with me before she was sent down below again.

Whenever I was in Lou's cabin, she was there too, scouring maps and having hushed conversations with Maro in a language I didn't know. I did have the opportunity to witness a few violent arguments, however.

"No!" Maro pounded on the desk and, when Lou didn't react, threw a cup across the room, knocking one of the paintings off the wall. "This is suicide. We need another way."

Lou's gaze caught mine, and I glanced down quickly, focusing on my work.

"We'll be there in two more days, and this is the best plan we've had."

"We are not cat burglars."

"No." Another glance at me as I watched from under my lashes. "The goal here is not to blend in. He's notoriously unfaithful. We only need to catch his attention and get him alone."

"Is this Kiril?" I asked. I couldn't help myself. I hadn't spoken to anyone all day.

The cabin fell into silence. When I looked up again, Maro was glaring at Lou with horrified eyes while Lou vibrated with tension.

"You told her?" Maro asked.

Lou scowled at them. "Only what she needed to know."

"It's not Kiril, and you should be glad for that." Maro snarled at me. "But Rickard Andel—"

"Has something we need," Lou said.

"What's that?"

Something silent passed between Lou and Maro before she said, "A ruby."

Maro sighed but didn't say anything else.

"A ruby?" I asked, nonplussed.

Lou rolled her eyes. "I suppose you've seen many jewels in your life, but this one is particularly large and notable."

"So you plan to steal it?" She couldn't just buy it. That would be too simple and too civilized.

"She thinks she's going to pop it into her cleavage and walk out the front door," Maro grumbled.

I flushed at the mention of Lou's cleavage, even though it was well hidden behind a plain shirt today. One of them chuckled at my discomfort. When I glanced up, Maro's smile was dark, while Lou watched me intently.

"In Redmere, I'd hide letters from the palace in my underskirt," I said.

"We aren't likely to have time for needlework, Highness," Lou said.

I swallowed. The idea of helping her made my stomach sour, but if it meant facilitating the end of this voyage, I might be willing to do it.

"I could sew a pocket into this dress. In the lining."

Lou eyed me, as if she were trying to see the depth of my deception. I rolled my eyes and jabbed my scissors in her direction. "The sooner we get that ruby, the sooner Rosie and I can be on our way." And the more Lou thought I was compliant and helpful, the less she'd worry about me trying to escape.

Another silent glance between the two of them. This one made my heart drop.

"What?" I asked. "What is it?"

Maro sneered at Lou. "You might as well tell her, since you're in such a forthcoming mood."

"Tell me what?"

Lou flattened both palms on her desk. "We won't be able to send the maid with you. Even with the ruby, it won't be enough for passage for two."

I flung the dress to the floor. "Excuse me?"

"I told you we should have drowned her," Maro said lazily.

"We'll leave her in Beldridge Landing when we stop to see Andel."

"No." I stamped a foot in outrage. "No, you will not!"

Lou sighed wearily. "Calm yourself, Highness, you'll make yourself ill."

I hadn't even known Lou was alive for more than the last week, and already, I was so tired of her patronization. But in this case, I would use it to my advantage. Lady Georgina, ready once again to play the spoiled society girl.

"You can't leave her behind. She's my friend!"

Her calm cracked ever so slightly, making something inside me quiver. "Would you rather I kept her here? Forced her to work in the mess for the rest of her life? Are you that selfish? She's a stowaway who never should have been aboard this ship. I'm offering her a chance at freedom."

"You can't take her from me!" My voice cracked rather convincingly.

"Why not?" Lou looked amused. "What do you need a maid

here for? What will you ever need a maid for again? Let her go. No one is looking for her. Let her have a decent life where she can find one."

Let her off this ship so she could go home to the family who loved her and the resistance that needed us both. With any luck, I would find a way to go with her.

Pressing on with my act, I stepped over the dress, kicking it behind me. "You can finish this yourself," I said—though it was very nearly finished anyway—already formulating strategies in my head.

We had two days until we reached our next destination.

Then, Rosie and I would run.

15

I tried to contain my turmoil but only got as far as rolling over in my narrow cot for the fortieth time before Rosie gave an aggrieved sigh. "What's wrong?"

"It's almost time," I said.

"For what?"

"In two days, we're stopping somewhere. It'll be our best chance to get away."

"Escape?"

"Lou is already planning to leave you there. I just have to find a way to join you."

"And how do you propose we'll do that?"

"We'll see when we get there." If I was lucky, more than Lou and Maro would go ashore. Fewer sailors on the ship meant fewer eyes to see me slip away. I might need a disguise. And Ender liked Rosie well enough. Maybe I could convince him to take her to me once Maro and Lou were gone. Maybe he would even come with us. He didn't need to stay on this ship and live the pirate's life. "But I'll find a way to come with you. Wherever they take you, I'll come find you. If I can get that far, we'll figure out our next step together."

Rosie sighed in the dark. "It's a shame we didn't know we were going to be kidnapped."

I laughed, feeling a little better for it. "It's not the sort of thing one plans for."

"No, but if I'd known, I'd have packed a few things. Maybe a few of those jewels, the brooches, and some earrings. I could have traded it for a place on a fast ship to Redmere."

I rolled onto my side. "They were from Beverly. I don't want anything to do with them."

"They're only jewelry. I don't see how they bear any responsibility for who bought them."

"He was going to have me murdered. I don't want his gifts, now or ever."

She was silent for so long that the dark pressed in on me. Finally, words came, though her voice sounded very small. "He was going to kill you?"

I snorted. "Well, I don't think he was going to do it on his own. Beverly doesn't strike me as someone who would dirty his own hands if he could have someone else do it for him." But then, the realization gripped me. "Oh my goodness. I never told you, did I?"

She sniffled in the dark. "I think I would remember something like that."

The cabin floorboards were worn under my bare feet when I shuffled across the small space between our cots. I found her hip and gave it a gentle shove, waiting until she'd stopped moving before I crawled in next to her and pulled her close. "I'm so sorry. I heard him speaking with Crawford in the library the morning we were kidnapped. I—in everything that happened after, it slipped my mind to tell you."

"Slipped your mind?" she wailed. "How can something like that slip your mind?"

"Would you like the complete list of distractions that have occurred since that morning?"

She hiccupped on a watery laugh. "It has been a bit much."

I held her tight, humming and rocking the way my mother might have, the way Lou and I did when we were small and alone.

We arrived in Beldridge Landing two days later, and Ender collected us in the afternoon.

"The captain is ready." His voice was subdued, his eyes downcast.

"You don't like this any more than I do," I said, looking for my opportunity. He glanced between us, but when he might have said something, he only turned back to the open door and waited.

Under other circumstances, I would have been excited for my first glimpse of our destination. The town was very impressive. The houses on the waterfront were tall and built so closely together, it was impossible to tell where one ended and the next began. But unlike dreary Redmere City, they were all painted the same creamy white, reflecting the sun back at us so brightly that I had to shade my eyes with one hand.

Not to mention the people. The wharf was full of sailors moving to and from the longboats tied up to the pier, while twenty or so tall ships were moored in the harbor. Vendors wheeled carts and shouted to passersby. Women in vibrant colors strolled among them, and the sight of them made me flush. Some of them wore dresses with no backs at all, just strips of fabric tied around their necks. Others wore skirts that were slit open in the front so that one could glimpse an ankle or even a calf with each step. None of them had any sort of sleeve to speak of. Many protected themselves from the blazing sun overhead with bright umbrellas painted to match whatever they'd chosen to wear that day. A few wore veils to cover their bare necks and shoulders, but these were made of light fabric that floated in the breeze, as opposed to the drab heaviness I was used to at home.

"You'll need to pick your jaw off the deck if you don't want to trip over it."

I flinched at Lou's voice behind me, but it was only when I turned around that my jaw really did drop to the floor.

She was wearing the dress I'd repaired. The creamy white of the silk made her tanned skin glow.

If we'd been children, I'd have said she was beautiful.

I was sorry I'd never get that chance.

"You've done a fine job altering it." She ran her hands over her shoulders, where the wide fabric held the dress up but did nothing to cover her arms or even most of her chest.

"Why do you even have it?" I grumbled.

Lou gave me a grim smile. "It belonged to a friend of Maro's."

"Wouldn't she want it back?" The dye on the silk was very fine, the colors swirling like water.

"She tried to cut Maro's throat in their sleep. Maro wasn't feeling very charitable after that."

"I'm not the forgiving sort," Maro said, coming up beside her. They wore the same sort of gown, with the same deep neckline and wide skirt, but theirs was black, giving them the appearance of a menacing shadow at Lou's side.

"I'm sure she'll understand." Lou's smile turned amused.

I didn't ask what had happened to the dress's former owner.

At the edge of cream silk below Lou's collarbone, a black tentacle waved from her skin. I struggled to take my eyes off it.

Lou was oblivious to my gaze and instead cleared her throat. "All right. Ender."

The giant stepped forward. "Captain."

"We'll be going ashore with the maid. If we're not back by two bells after sundown, leave without us."

She didn't mention why they wouldn't return, and the casual way she said it made me ache. Despite it all, I still grieved for my lost friend, even while she stood in front of me.

"Yes, Captain."

Lou glanced at me, shifting uncomfortably. "Say your goodbyes, Highness."

I'd considered many options for finding a way off the ship. I didn't know how long Lou would be gone, and there was no indication that other sailors would be allowed to go ashore. I didn't like my chances of being able to slip away with no one noticing, so I decided to go for the direct approach instead.

I'd never been much for playacting. Too serious as a child, too alone as an adult. Lou had always been the one with the flair for the dramatic, but I did my best.

"Please. Please don't take her away." I stepped in front of Rosie the way I had on our first day.

Lou sighed impatiently. "This has been explained. There's no negotiation."

I shook my head. "Then let me go with her. Please. Just to say goodbye. Let me stay with her as long as possible."

"We're wasting time," Maro growled behind her.

My only choice was to put on the full show.

I burst into tears.

We lie together in my bed the night before Lou is sent away. Her hair has been cut short, and somehow, it makes her eyes look huge in her face, even in the shadowed moonlight of my bedroom.

"Let's run away," I say.

She shakes her head and reaches to tuck a strand of hair behind my ear. "It's too late. If I don't arrive in the city, I'll be reported as a deserter. They'll arrest my parents if they can't find me."

This is my fault. I should have run away when she had asked me to, before plans had been made, before my father had bought me new dresses for school and Lou had spent weeks learning to speak with her voice lowered so people would assume she was a boy.

"I'm sorry," I say. My throat is tight and my eyes burn.

Lou's hands tighten in my nightgown. "No. Don't cry. Georgie, you can't."

"Why not?" My voice breaks, and tears spill over.

"Because if you cry, I'll cry too, and then we'll never get to sleep."

"I don't want to sleep," I say furiously. "If we sleep, think of all those hours we'll never get back. This is the last time—"

"Shh." She tangles her fingers with mine, and her voice is raw when she says, "Not the last time."

"It is," I say, hysteria bubbling under my words. "It is. Something terrible will happen. I can feel it." I am overcome, but it does not matter because she is crying too. We are wrapped around each other so tightly that we are one sobbing mass of skin and bones and the soft cotton of our nightshirts.

"Please," I say into her neck. "Please don't leave me."

"Please," I said through my tears. "Please let me go."

"Princess—"

But I wouldn't let her continue. "Just for the day. Wherever you're going, let me stay with her for today. We won't cause any trouble, I promise. I just . . ." I took in a big heaving breath. "I don't want to be alone. I'm so frightened. She's my only friend, and . . ."

"Captain," Maro said, eyes narrowed.

I clasped Lou's hand in mine, and the contact made us both start. I dropped to my knees, clutching at the skirts I'd labored over so painstakingly. "Please. Whenever you've done what you came to do, I'll come back with you, I promise. Just today."

Lou scowled at me. My face must have looked a wreck. I'd done my best to tie my hair back, but after so much time without hot water or a mirror, it had become hopelessly tangled and stuck out at odd angles from my makeshift scarf.

"We're likely to be in a hurry. We won't exactly be able to stop off and collect you."

"Ender can get me," I said, gesturing frantically toward him. He looked distinctly uncomfortable, as men often did when women cried, but he nodded.

"Please." I dropped my head to the deck. "Let me go with her for a few more hours." My throat was raw, and my words were hoarse. I hated that I had to crumble in front of Lou like this, but it was the best plan I had.

"This is ridiculous," Maro said. My hands tightened around the hem of Lou's dress, holding firm even when she turned away.

I waited, counting long seconds, until finally, she said, "Ender."

"Yes, Captain?"

"Lower the longboat. You'll accompany the princess. If you lose sight of her for even an instant, I will take your eyes out, do you understand?"

I risked one more glance at Ender. He gave me the faintest twist of a smile before he knocked his thumb to his forehead. "Yes, Captain."

The trip from the *Siren* to the waterfront was short. The sun was hot on my skin. The sights around us of the boats and sailors, the collections of barrels and crates that lined each side, made me falter for a moment. The last time I'd been in a place like this, things had exploded around my head before I was pulled toward an unknown ship.

Rosie and I looped our trembling hands.

"Stay close to me," I said.

"Keep up!" Lou called from the head of our party. She and Maro strode ahead of us like light and dark horses leading the charge. Rosie and I must have looked incredibly shabby in comparison, but we followed with Ender at our backs.

We'd only taken two or three steps down the busy harborside road when there was a bloodcurdling shriek. It was hard to see what was happening at first, but then a girl—no, a woman—broke through and hurtled toward us. She was petite, but everyone in her path hurried out of her way.

"Captain!" she cried.

"What's going on?" I asked.

"Here we go," Maro growled.

The woman leaped into the air, wrapping her legs around Lou's waist and her arms around Lou's neck. For a moment, I thought the stranger was attacking her, but then my concern turned to shock as I realized she was . . .

"Ahem." Maro cleared their throat pointedly.

The strange woman was kissing Lou. Rather passionately.

In public.

Rosie gasped, but I couldn't look away from the tight grip of the woman's fingers in Lou's hair or the satisfied purr Lou made as the woman brought her lips away for just a second.

"Pull yourself together," Maro said. It wasn't clear if they were speaking to me or to Lou. Around us, people came and went, as if nothing out of the ordinary was happening.

"Captain!" they snapped. Finally, the strange woman let go of Lou, setting her feet on the ground. She winked at us.

"Plenty to go around." She looked me up and down. "You're not really my type, but—"

"Davina." Lou beamed at us as she slipped an arm around the woman's waist and pulled her close. "You remember Maro. And this is . . ." She faltered. "Cressida. And Rosie. You know Ender."

My gaze shot to Lou's at the use of my middle name. In the whole time we'd been aboard the ship, she'd never once called me by my given name.

"Pleased to meet you." Davina gave me her hand, and when I took it, she shook it vigorously as I was about to curtsy.

"The pleasure is mine." My response sounded stilted.

"Why didn't you tell me you were coming?" Davina asked, taking both of Lou's hands in hers. The expression on her face could only be called adoration. "The last time you were here, you left so suddenly, I didn't think we'd ever see you again."

Lou was scanning the crowd. "Oh, you know. New business. Suddenly, Beldridge is looking appealing again."

"There's something here for everyone." She waggled her eyebrows and pulled her bottom lip between her teeth. Her gaze flicked to me again, and I did my best—and failed—not to stare. Her dress reminded me of the orange thing Lou had worn the first day I'd been to her cabin. Her body was draped in silks that hid the barest of essentials and nothing else before swirling around her hips and ankles. Her skin was a rich brown, darker than the tiled roofs on some of the buildings around us. A loop of gold was pierced through her nose while another dangled a string of tiny, tinkling bells from one earlobe. Her smile was warm and inviting, and even I could tell what she was offering.

Lou watched me with a knowing smile that made me wish for my old veil to hide my blush. She said, "We need your help, Davi."

"Of course! This way."

Lou hurried with her, and the rest of us trailed after them.

"She seems very . . . friendly," Rosie said.

Maro glanced at us from the corner of their eye. "Cinder has friends like that everywhere."

"Really?" I tried to sound disinterested.

"Does it make you uncomfortable seeing two women like that? I know it's . . . not done where you're from."

I shook my head, speechless. If only Maro knew. I was uncomfortable, but not for the reasons they would expect. What I felt wasn't disgust. It was longing. Even if Lou would never look at me like that, I could only hope someone did someday, even if I'd made up my mind to go back to Redmere, where the odds of finding a woman who would admit to feeling the way I did were slim.

Ahead of us, Lou and Davina were walking with their arms around each other's waists. The crowds of people—so many people, of ethnicities and origins I couldn't even guess—moved around them like water around stones. I held my breath as a tall man in a dark coat approached, even as Lou pressed her nose into Davina's hair and said something that had them both laughing, but the man continued on as if nothing they were doing was out of the ordinary. I couldn't control my stare, waiting for him to realize his mistake and call them out, but he kept walking.

My eyes met Maro's again. "Not everywhere is the same as your home," they said.

My spine stiffened. "I know that."

Davina's hand was on the small of Lou's back, while Lou's arm moved over Davina's shoulders.

I couldn't even begin to name the riot of feelings that leaped in my chest. Too many things, all at once. Joy, grief, curiosity . . . To see Lou like that—the soft touches, the quiet words in Davi's ear, in *another woman's* ear . . . How could she have found a place where she could be like this in public when I'd been left behind to hide my fear in Redmere?

I shut the questions away. I was leaving. Lou was lost, and I would never find the answers I was looking for. But knowing there were places like this and actually seeing them . . . What else was out in the world?

Davi took us through busy streets to a building that faced a corner of a bustling thoroughfare. A sign above the door said the name of the establishment was The Captain's Peg. A fearsome pirate painted onto the weathered wood, with a flowing cape and a wooden leg, leered at us. He looked nothing like the pirates of my acquaintance but much more like the illustrated pirates on the pamphlets circulated in Redmere.

The inside of The Captain's Peg felt cobbled together without a central idea for what the finished product would look like. The furniture was varied—curved and square, ornate and plain. There were low sofas like on the ship and high-backed chairs like we'd had at Jeremy's house, but arranged here and there around tables or empty space as if there had been a great many people here recently who had all suddenly vanished.

"Bit early for the usual suspects," Davi said as Maro closed the door behind us. "Most everyone is still asleep."

"It's after noon," I blurted. Three heads turned to look at me.

"Cressida is Redmerian. She has a very diligent work ethic," Lou said as she sat down on one of the sofas, spreading out her limbs the way she did in her own cabin.

Davi whistled. "A long way from home."

"Her father found her in the dairy with two of the milkmaids." Lou traced small circles in the deep green velvet of the upholstery, nails leaving curving trails in their wake. She grinned at me, and small sparks slithered over my breasts and down my stomach. If only that was what had happened. I would have enjoyed the scandalized look on Lou's face when I told her.

"Shocking." Davi gasped, but her tongue was pinched firmly between her teeth as she grinned at me. "You'll fit in here nicely."

Her certainty made my stomach turn with uneasiness.

"Captain," Maro said with their eyebrows raised. "We have *business*."

Lou's gaze swung lazily from me to Maro. The loss of it was a relief; I could breathe again.

"Sounds serious," Davi said.

"We're here for the ruby," Lou said.

Davi's eyes went wide. "Really?"

Maro sighed heavily. "No subtlety at all. This is a disaster."

"We don't have much time." Lou glanced at where Rosie and I were still huddled by the door. "We need help. The smaller of the two ladies here needs a new life. Make the arrangements." She pressed a small purse into Davi's hand.

Davi considered us. "And the Lady Cressida?"

Her use of the honorific bothered me. How could she know? I'd come in my stained ship's clothes. Compared to me, Lou and Maro were the ones who looked like nobility—albeit wildly underdressed nobility.

Lou gave me a lazy smile, her one gold tooth flashing, and the sight of it made me quiver. "She has a little ways longer to go. She's only here to say her goodbyes, and then Ender will take her back to the *Siren*."

"Are you sure?" Davi looked me up and down. "A face like hers and breasts like those? She'd do well here."

My mouth dropped open, but my anger was for Lou. "You're leaving Rosie here? With her?"

Lou's eyes went flat. "You've pushed my charity enough for one day. Don't judge others for what they do to survive."

"It's not so bad." Davi sank down, draping herself in Lou's lap. "You might find you enjoy it. Many of my girls do with the right company." She ran a hand over Lou's stomach and up her ribs, alongside one of Lou's breasts. My mouth went dry at the intimately familiar gesture.

"Oh, that's it." Maro stormed passed me and hauled Davi off Lou, dragging her away by her elbow.

Davi hissed and spit at her like a cat. "Let go of me!"

Maro released her, and she stumbled backward until she caught the edge of a table. She glared at Maro, who was already turning back to Lou.

"Let's get on with this." They tugged at the shoulder of their dress. "This material itches my skin, and chatting isn't going to get us out of here and to safety any sooner."

"There's a party today. Guests should have arrived by now." Davi sounded bored, and she chewed absently on a fingernail.

Lou spread her hands over her skirt. "I figured as much. He's always entertaining when he's not working."

"Hunting, more like," Maro said.

Davi gestured to a hallway that led farther into the building. "You know the way. Rear door is easiest."

Lou and Maro stood in a rustle of skirts. Lou nodded once at Rosie and stared pointedly at me before moving on to Ender. "Take the prin—take Cressida back to the *Siren* no later than sundown."

"Yes, Captain."

Then, she and Maro were gone.

The room fell into silence. With any luck, I would never see Lou again.

16

We spent the waning afternoon in The Captain's Peg. Patrons entered from time to time, and a few of them gave Rosie and me a hopeful once-over that ended abruptly when Ender stepped forward with a glare. By and large though, they were greeted enthusiastically by Davi's employees, both male and female.

The sounds that filtered down from the upper floor of the building were enough to make me want to vanish into the uneven cushions of Davi's sofas. A lifetime in Redmere hadn't left me completely naive. I knew what sort of business this was. But to hear it so clearly was a completely different thing than the way it was whispered about at home.

As the shadows grew on the street outside, I yawned and asked, "Would it be too much trouble to have a bath? I'm more salt than skin now."

Ender glanced at the fading sun. "We should get back to the *Siren*."

Davi waved him off. "I know what it's like on that ship. Let the woman bathe." She gave me an obliging smile. "I'll show you to the bathing room. It's usually quiet this time of day."

"Perfect." I beamed at her, then held a hand out for Rosie. We followed Davi as she led us down the same hall Lou and Maro had exited through earlier.

Ender trailed after us, and as Davi pushed open a door, he said, "Captain's orders were to—"

"Yes, yes." Davi waved a hand. "You're a man of your word. Look." She pushed the door open wider. "Whatever your captain is worried about, we'll be fine. Give her a few minutes to wash the tangles out of her hair, and then you can have her back. See? No windows, no other entrances or exits. We won't go anywhere."

My heart sank at her words. The simplest solution would have been to convince her to let Rosie and I sneak out a window and take our chances in the streets, but we would find another way.

The bathing room consisted of a large, round tub big enough for several people to fit in at one time. It currently had one occupant, who sat with her head tipped back against the edge. As we entered, she opened her eyes and gave us a slow smile.

"Hello." She arched, pressing the tips of her breasts out of the water. My eyes widened.

"Oh, stop!" Davi snapped. "Irjana, get dressed. They're friends, not customers!"

The girl rolled her eyes and took her time retreating, as if she wanted Davi to know she was doing it of her own accord. She wrapped herself in a silk robe that barely covered her thighs and clung to her wet skin. The swell of her bottom was visible as she disappeared the way she'd come. I didn't realize I was staring until Davi laughed.

"Like what you see? I've heard your people don't"—Davi grinned—"*approve* of relations between women. Or between men."

I thought of the man that day at the checkpoint before my life had been turned upside down, calling to us that he was innocent. About Maro, whose people didn't feel the need to distinguish between genders. About Lou's breath on my face as we'd yelled at each other after I'd climbed the mast. I couldn't want her, but I'd never wanted anything else.

"Irjana wouldn't be a good start for you," Davi continued when I didn't say anything. "But I have other girls who would be gentle, if that's something you would like?" Her knowing gaze left me feeling far too exposed, and when I turned away, I was met with a questioning glance from Rosie.

I nearly plunged myself into the tub with all my clothes on.

The three of us found ourselves submerged in the water together. Davi grinned at both of us with patient amusement, while Rosie had also her knees pulled up to her chest self-consciously.

"So, a new life?" Davi asked. "You must have run into some trouble."

"I'm going back to Redmere," Rosie said at the same time I said, "I'm going with her."

Davi gave me a pout. "Oh, I don't think Captain Cinder will like that. She seemed very clear you were to return to the *Siren*."

I scowled. "And what Cinder wants, she gets?"

"Generally." She turned to Rosie. "Back to Redmere? What's the point of having the captain take you away from there if you plan to go back?"

"Having the . . . We were kidnapped," Rosie said.

Davi's laugh was a high, trilling thing. "Kidnapped?"

"She's a pirate," I said. "It's what they do."

Her smile vanished as she glanced between our equally serious faces. "You mean you aren't one of Cinder's women?"

I pulled my knees tighter to my chest, ignoring the memories of the sinuous mermaid on Lou's arm or of her lips on Davi's. "I don't know what you mean."

"You mean she didn't save you?"

"Save me?" Hardly. "No, she . . ." But hadn't she? In a storybook, Lou might have been the heroine, charging in to save the princess from the wicked prince.

Or she would be the villain. She was manipulative, a liar, and a murderer.

But the longer I spent on board the *Siren* with men like Ender, who had done terrible things but were still kind, the less I was sure who the villains were. Even Lou, who was cruel and hard, hadn't done anything particularly villainous in the time we'd been on the ship. The flogging had been brutal, but the men involved had hardly been singled out unfairly.

The prince. He was a villain. I had no doubt of that.

"I'm not supposed to exist," Davi said as she reached for a bar of soap and a soft cloth. "In Sevnan, where I come from, my mother's people are seen as inferior. Uncivilized. But my father fell in love with her anyway. Children like me are a crime and to be taken away so the shame of our existence wouldn't be seen. But my parents hid me from my father's family."

My chest burned at the thought of parents who loved their daughter so much, they would protect her like that.

Davi's face turned sad. "Except he died, and then, my mother did too. I tried to survive on my own, and for a while I did, but . . . they tolerated me in Sevnan because of the services a woman like me offers, but it couldn't last. So I paid a man a lot of money, and he got me away."

"You paid a man?" I asked.

"Oh, yes. I'd heard from one of the girls I worked with about a man who helped women like me. For the right price, of course. But if you were in a situation and had no means to escape on your own, he'd arrange for your passage and take you to a new life."

I blinked, struggling to follow. Davi watched me before placing her soap and rag on the side of the tub. She dropped her head underwater, disappearing except for a slow trail of bubbles.

I glanced at Rosie. Her mouth was slightly open, eyes wide.

When Davi reemerged, I'd hardly let her clear the water from her face before I asked, "How did you escape?"

"He brought me to the captain, of course! She already had two other women onboard. Was there no one else with you?"

"No."

Davi frowned. "She usually has a few. It's a busy line of work, if you know what I mean."

"Piracy?"

Her laughter tinkled like the bells in her ear. "No, silly. Saving women in need of a new life."

I thought of all the women at the wharf, the starving widows who would be dead by winter if no one helped them. They all needed a new life, but Lou had come for *me*. Had blown through a wall to get to me. But what if it wasn't because it was *me*? What if it truly was about the money?

I glanced around us, thinking of the naked woman who had been in the water when we'd walked in. "Is that how it works then?"

"How?"

"Does the captain bring you . . ." The question faded in my throat, and I had to try again. "Is that where you find your . . . colleagues?"

"A few," Davi said, and my heart sank.

"Oh." The idea that Lou would promise escape to women like Davi and then leave them here to earn their keep so far from home made my stomach turn.

Davi didn't seem nearly as upset. "She's never brought me anyone who didn't want to be here though. I couldn't take on everyone she picks up. I'd flood my own market. And I let all my girls choose their customers. We get enough business here, we can be particular. Compared to the places a lot of them are coming from, having the right to say no is all the freedom they want or can manage. They get regular meals, regular pay, and they never have to be afraid of a man again."

If I were still in Redmere, the prince and I would have been married. He might even have killed me by now. If Lou hadn't come, I would have been afraid of what he might do every day we were together.

Pieces were coming apart in my head. The anger, the fear. The whispers.

Watch out or Captain Cinder will steal your daughters.

But what if those daughters wanted to be stolen?

She's not another nobleman's unhappy wife. Lou had said that the first morning I'd listened in on her and Maro.

I felt myself slip underwater to the haven Lou had always kept for me in my dreams, where she'd held her arms open and waited for me to sink down to find her.

What if we hadn't been kidnapped at all? What if we'd been rescued?

I pushed back up to the surface, gasping for air.

What if I never saw Lou again?

But the pieces still didn't fit together fully. Maybe she'd saved Davi and other women like her, but there was still the question of the lost ships, of the men who left Redmere City and were never heard from again. For every wife or daughter who went missing, whole crews had disappeared too, and they had for years. She was responsible for their deaths.

When we were clean, Davi helped us into soft robes fortunately a little longer than the one Irjana had worn. Rosie helped me brush my hair out but left it uncovered so it could dry.

Davi opened the door to the bathing room, and immediately, Ender pushed his way in.

"Stay where you are." His face had a hard set to it, at odds with his usual affable demeanor.

"What is it?" Davi asked.

"Unwanted visitor."

My heart fluttered. Everything about Ender's posture was alert.

"Who is it?" I asked.

His scowl was like a thundercloud. "It's Count Crawford."

17

The room wavered for a second. The count. Crawford was here? How had he found us?

"Is the prince here too?" I asked.

"What prince?" For once, Davi looked worried.

Ender shook his head. "I only saw the count. He'd walked in the door, but I ducked down the hall before I could see if anyone else came in with him. He might recognize me."

The count had certainly had a chance to get a good look at him the night of the party. Ender had gone out of his way to make an impression. But I hadn't recognized him right away on the ship, and maybe the count wouldn't either.

"What is going on?" Davi pursed her lips.

Rosie, Ender, and I shot glances at each other, before I finally said, "The count is my former fiancé's cousin. He's looking for me. He's seen the *Siren* in the harbor and knows we're here."

"You were engaged to a prince?" Davi asked. Her eyes widened. "*The* prince? Beverly of Redmere?"

"Rosie and I were spies at the palace. If he finds us, we'll be executed. Please, you have to help us."

Silence hung in the room like humidity. Outside the door, I

could hear a man's voice. He was still a little way up the hall, but the long vowels of his aristocratic accent were noticeable.

"Get in the tub," Davi said.

"What?" Rosie asked.

"Get in the tub." She pointed at it with an imperious finger. "If he wants to have a look around, I don't have a good place to hide you, and he may have stationed guards at the doors in case you try to sneak out."

"Then what do we do?" Rosie asked.

Davi rolled her eyes. "What do you think?"

Ender blushed. Rosie squeaked. My feet were frozen to the floor. I stared at the door. Any minute now, the prince might come through. He'd take me back, drag me through the streets of Redmere, and brand me for the traitor I was.

"George." Rosie tugged on my sleeve. "Come on."

We slipped out of our robes and back into the tub. Ender averted his gaze, and Davi urged us on with rushed whispers. Ender pulled off his shirt, but his hands stuttered at the waistband of his pants.

"For God's sake, hurry," Davi hissed. "I have to go play the gracious hostess or he'll know something is wrong."

In the end, Ender joined us in the water, pants and all. He was so big, the water pushed dangerously to the lip of the tub.

We sat motionless, each of us unsure what to do with our limbs.

"You'll have to sell it better than that," Davi said, then slipped out to the hall.

I'm not sure we were convincing. The voices in the hall grew louder, and Davi's mixed with them, high and indignant.

"I run a perfectly legal and respectable establishment, sir!" she said. "I hope you can understand that my customers expect discretion."

"Out of my way." Crawford's words were clear. Ender put his arm around me and pulled me close to him. I buried my face his chest, turning my back to the door and ignoring how our skin felt pressed against each other. I'd never been so close to another human being in my life.

"Up you get, little miss," he said, depositing Rosie onto his lap with a splash and a squeak.

"Oh my goodness," she said.

"Now laugh," Ender hissed.

"What?" I asked.

"Laugh!"

The door swung open. Rosie let out a high giggle that sounded faintly deranged. I kept my face averted and did the same.

"What's all this then?" Ender bellowed. The vibration of his words rattled my teeth where my cheek was pressed against him.

"Out! Get out!" Rosie shrieked, splashing and cursing. I hoped my posture looked more like I was trying to hide my nudity than hide my face.

"I'm so sorry, sir." Davi's voice was all professional courtesy. "The gentleman is looking for—"

"I don't care if he's looking for his mother. I paid to have a little privacy with my girls here, and you're interrupting me. Now leave." Ender's arm around me was like a vise. I couldn't have moved if I wanted to, but it gave away a wariness his words didn't portray. If the count pressed the issue, Ender would leap into action.

"Terribly sorry." Even with Ender glowering at him, Crawford's manners were still impeccable.

The door shut behind us.

Slowly, Ender's grip on me loosened. I counted to thirty and listened as the footsteps went back up the hall before I unwound myself. Ender and Rosie had twin expressions of fearful anticipation.

Another thirty seconds before Ender blew out a long breath, pressing a gentle kiss to the side of Rosie's head. "Hope I didn't importune your virtue too much, ladies. Especially yours, little miss. Been a while since I had a pretty girl in my lap like that."

Rosie snorted. "You should have seen the count's face, George. I made sure he saw both my nipples. After that, he couldn't look at any of our faces."

She probably meant for her words to be funny. None of us laughed.

We sat in the tub, silently listening to the sounds around us. Periodically, a shriek of protest would sound, indicating that the count had disturbed another of Davi's guests. Footsteps echoed on the floorboards overhead. My fingertips wrinkled, and the water cooled to a tepid room temperature.

We all jumped when Davi pushed the door open. "He's gone," she said. "But you were right. He's seen the ship in the harbor. He knows you're here."

"And the prince?" I asked.

She shrugged. "I don't know."

"We have to alert the captain," Ender said.

"Leave. The three of you." Davi gave us an apologetic smile. "I'm sorry, but I have my livelihood to think of. Your friend seemed very determined. I can't risk that he'll come back and find any of you here."

"I'll take you back to the ship," Ender said. "Then, I'll go find the captain."

"You won't get very far," Davi said. "The party she's gone to, they're very particular about their guests. You won't fit the bill. Too big. Too hairy. If anyone sees you, they'll sound the alarm, and then Cinder and Maro will be in even worse trouble."

"I'll go," I said. "They'll let me in."

"Princess," Ender said. "I don't think that's a very good idea. The count could still be—"

"He won't recognize me," I said with more confidence than I felt. "He's looking for a Redmerian lady. Not—" I glanced down at my naked breasts still submerged in the water.

"If the idea is to not attract attention while you look for the captain, I'd suggest you put on a little more than you are now," Davi said. "But not those rags you came in here wearing either."

"I don't like this," Ender said. "The captain said—"

"She'll understand." I wasn't sure of that, and she *had* threatened to blind Ender if he lost sight of me, but after Davi's earlier revelations, I wasn't very sure about anything when it came to Lou. Was the legend of Captain Cinder real or some sort of facade she'd adopted? "We don't have time to waste. You need to keep Rosie safe and warn the crew. Whatever Lou is doing, we'll need to leave quickly as soon as she's done."

Ender looked unhappy, but Rosie wrapped herself around his arm. "We should do as she says."

"I spent two years hiding in plain sight in Redmere. I can make it to a party and back without attracting any notice."

Ender needed a few more moments of cajoling, but soon he and Rosie—in dry clothes supplied by Davi—were making their way out the front door. Ender bellowed like a drunken sailor on leave, and Rosie giggled as she gazed up at him adoringly, the gauzy dress Davi had given her billowing out behind her in a cloudy train.

"Now." Davi turned to me. "You'll need a little more work."

"I'd prefer not to waste time." The thought of dressing me up like a doll after the endless wardrobe and sparkling jewelry the prince had tried to buy my affection with made me uneasy.

Davi grinned slyly. "Highness, in my line of work, you become very skilled at making someone look put-together without much effort."

"Really?"

"Of course. What's the point in spending hours painting your face just to have someone kiss it off in the first five minutes?"

She was handy with her powders and paints, I would give her that much. I barely had time to cough from the chalky, white dust she'd puffed onto my cheeks before she'd moved on to smear something bright red and sticky on my lips.

My hair was still wet, but she pinned trailing ribbons and sparkling tassels into it.

"There." She pushed me toward a mirror at one side of the room.

I tilted my head to find my reflection, and the result was a shock. My skin was pale white, my lips bright red, my cheeks a fierce pink, and my eyes outlined in dark black.

I looked like an exotic animal and a child's poorly drawn portrait of myself all at once.

The dress she produced was less elaborate than the one Lou had worn, but the neck was cut so wide, the sides of my breasts were visible as the V plunged halfway to my navel. As I ran my hands over the stiff fabric, I wished I'd asked Ender to find Lou after all, but I had no time for regrets. I followed Davi silently through the back door and out into the street.

"I can take you as far as his gate."

"Do you know his house? You won't come with me?"

She shook her head. "The last time I was invited to one of Rickard Andel's parties, there was an . . . incident between me and his wife. I've been permanently uninvited. If I show my face indoors, I'll cause more distraction than good. I'm sorry, princess."

"I'm not a princess," I said on reflex. "You called me 'Lady' before, but I'm not even sure I'm that."

"You're something," she said. "Brave. Kind. All the princesses in the storybooks were brave and kind."

As we walked, we were gathered by a growing number of people all headed in the same direction. They seemed like vibrant, cheerful birds, all dressed in bright colors and loose-fitting clothing. None of them carried themselves with the fear that painted everyone in Redmere, even though everything about the public behavior in Beldridge Landing would have been criminal at home. As if to further prove the point, two men passed us, wrapped in each other's arms. They kissed like they were the only people in the world.

What would it be like to live in a place like this? To have grown up in a place like this, without the continual fear of your neighbors turning on you for the sake of a loaf of bread or a few coins?

Our destination became evident once we rounded the last turn. The house was brightly lit, and people spilled out of the front door and onto the street.

A man leaped in front of us, spewing liquid that immediately burst into flames. I shrieked and jumped back. Only Davi's hand on my arm kept me from falling completely. She laughed and cooed as the man bowed and danced around us. The scent of the fluid the man had expelled before he'd set it on fire clung to my dress and hair.

"Steady on. We're almost there," she said between clenched teeth.

She led me around to a side entrance in a garden wall. "Andel showed me this door. It's how I get my girls in while his wife is away. Up the stairs and right leads to the back garden, where the party will be by this time of the evening. Left is a hall with private offices and smaller rooms for guests. If Cinder and Maro are after the ruby, I'd start there first."

I kissed Davi's cheek. "Thank you."

"I'm sorry I couldn't do more," she said. "I owe Cinder everything. When you're no longer wanted by a vicious tyrant, feel free to come back for a visit."

I waited until she'd disappeared into the dark before I pushed the door open.

I'd expected the palace's twisting hallways or one of the unlit ones at Jeremy's house, but this was bright and welcoming. Torches in the walls shone a yellow-gold color along the plaster walls, and the floor was covered in a smooth stone that reflected the flickering light toward the ceiling.

No one was in sight, and the shoes Davi had lent me were soft and made no sound. If it weren't for the rustle of my skirt on the floor, I might have thought I was in a dream.

Well, if it weren't for that or the way my pulse pounded so hard in my throat, it made swallowing difficult.

Turn left, she'd said. When I came to the junction, I risked a glance to the right. The party she'd mentioned was clearly visible in an ornate ballroom. A crowd of men and women were gathered. Music played, and they laughed and drank from silver cups.

To my left was a long hall that seemed endless. More than a dozen doors lined it, and my nerve nearly failed me.

How was I going to find Lou in all this? What if she'd already been and gone? She could be halfway back to the ship and not even know I was here.

I should leave. No one had seen me. I could go back through Davi's secret door and rush to the harbor. I could even take my chances and try to disappear into the city, or find another ship or a wagon that could take me away from here.

But then I would never see Rosie again. I would never find out who Lou truly was—whether she was the pirate of my homeland's nightmares or the savior that Davi spoke of so ardently.

I pushed open the first door. The room was a daintily appointed sitting room. It was also empty.

I moved on to the next. Another sitting room, equally as nice as the first, although more masculine in its color and decorations. Also unoccupied. The next was a small room, much plainer, as if it wasn't meant for guests. The fourth—

"What are you doing here?"

I froze with my hand on the doorknob. Relief and fear warred for prominence as I turned.

Lou stood in the doorway across from me. Her face was still as ice.

"Lou, I—"

"You're supposed to be back at the ship." Every syllable was an accusation.

"Yes, I was, but Ender—"

"What about him?"

Her questions came so quickly, I struggled to hold onto my thoughts. "I was looking for you."

"And you decided you'd go up and down the hall slamming

doors until someone came to see what the commotion was? For God's sake, princess, have some common sense." In a flurry of angry curses and furious silk, she yanked me across the hall and into the room she'd been in.

"You have three seconds to explain yourself or I'll have you whipped when we—"

"The prince is here," I blurted.

Her threat cut short. "The prince?"

"Or Crawford. His cousin. He was at the brothel. I think they're searching the city for us."

More cursing. "But what are you doing *here*? You're supposed to be with Ender."

"I came to find you and Maro so we could get away."

Lou rolled her eyes. "You can't be here." She pushed me toward the back of the room, and it was only as I stumbled that my eyes lifted from her face to our surroundings.

"Where are we?" I asked.

This room was different from all the others I'd seen. Wooden carvings were mounted on the walls, mostly of women with their arms clasped about their chests, their backs arched, and their faces turned up to an unseen sky. Some were dressed, and others bare-breasted. Some had been painted in vibrant colors, and others in the same sun- and salt-stained wood as the deck of the *Crimson Siren*.

Between the figureheads were wood and glass cases that contained a variety of items. Swords. Pistols. Medals. Belts. There were even feathers and worn hats with a variety of embellishments.

I couldn't help myself from asking, "What is all this?"

"I'll tell you if you don't get us all killed," Lou snarled. She pulled one of the heavy curtains away from the window. "Get behind this. If you so much as sneeze, I will stab you myself."

Hardly the beatific saint of Davi's stories.

"But Count Crawford—"

"Yes, yes, I heard you. Now go." She pushed me backward.

The air behind the curtains was stuffy and warm. I parted them the tiniest fraction to gulp in the fresher air of the room. Lou had her hands on her waist, and she took a long breath. Calm rippled down her spine like water. The effect of it was spectacular, almost as if she'd slipped on a new set of clothes. She squared her shoulders and tipped up her chin. As if this strange room was hers to command, she pulled the chair back from the desk that stood to one side and slipped into it. She smoothed her skirts out and then leaned back on one elbow, the picture of perfect, powerful ease.

Somewhere, a clock ticked away the seconds, one by one.

We didn't have to wait long before the sound of laughter echoed up the hallway. Lou tossed her hair back, her beaded braids clattering.

The door burst open, and the laughter suddenly grew even louder, which was fortunate, because I couldn't help my gasp.

A couple, tangled in each other's arms and clearly intoxicated, tumbled into the room and closed the door.

"Oh, Ricky," the woman said.

The man laughed, a deep throaty sound, and buried his face in her breasts. She tipped her head back, echoing his laughter.

It was Maro.

The delight on their face was so foreign, I barely recognized them—but the black dress, black hair, and the glance they threw at Lou were unmistakable.

Maro started, gasping theatrically, throwing the man in their arms away from them. "Oh my goodness. I didn't know anyone would be in here."

The man stumbled away still grinning, but it faded as his gaze landed on Lou, lounging behind the desk.

His transformation was as dramatic as Lou and Maro's had been. One moment he was the picture of inebriated passion, and the next, his eyes had gone flat like a lizard's, and the color vanished from his face.

"Cinder." His voice was dry like paper.

I couldn't see Lou's face, but from the tone of her voice, I could picture her cold smile as she said, "Hello, Ricky."

He was older, perhaps fifty. Without any discomfort, he straightened his clothes and cleared his throat. He wore a longish coat and a black shirt unbuttoned nearly halfway down his chest, framing a heavy, red stone about the size of a large egg that hung from a chain around his neck.

His gaze moved to Maro, and his smile was ugly. "You must be the pet assassin."

Maro's sneer said they'd like to stab him for calling them a pet anything, but Lou lifted a palm from the desk and they stilled.

"You know why we're here, Ricky," Lou said.

"Kiril."

"You've had a good run. Better than most."

"I'd heard you left his service. Something must have gone horribly wrong if you're here for me. Trying to buy back his favor?"

"This doesn't have to be bloody," Lou said. "If you get down on your knees, Maro will snap your neck. They're very good at what they do, and it'll be quick and painless."

My blood went cold. I couldn't tear my eyes off the ruby around his neck. It pulsed in the light like it had its own heartbeat. Lou had said she needed the stone. She hadn't said anything about killing someone.

He pursed his lips, as if he were considering her offer. "This feels like rather a lot of work to go through if you only meant to break my neck." He smiled, teeth flashing like a predator's. "I think you want it bloody."

"I'm not like you," she said. "I've never enjoyed my work."

"Not even a little?" he taunted. "You've never seen the fear and panic in a man's eyes and taken some small joy in knowing you had that much power over him? Never watched a ship go down and marveled at your ability to control the fate of so many people?"

"Captain," Maro said impatiently. They lurked behind Ricky.

He was a full head taller than they were, and I suspected that was the only thing that kept them from killing him outright.

Lou's hands balled into fists on the desk. "On your knees."

The room fell silent, the three of them locked in a terrible standoff.

Slowly, unbelievably, he dropped onto one knee, then the other.

"As you say, Cinder," he said, "it's been a good run."

Maro stepped toward him, taking his head between their hands.

In a movement that had to be practiced, he rolled forward, arms locking around Maro behind him. They cried out, tumbling over his shoulder and sprawling on their back. Maro tried to recover, but he was on top of them in a second, fists flying, connecting with their face and sides in a hail of blows.

Lou was on her feet in a moment, coming around the desk. He leaped up as well while Maro curled up on themself.

"Two against one?" he said, breathing hard. "Hardly seems fair."

"When have you ever believed in a fair fight?" Lou circled him, arms wide.

He lunged, and she went with him, but she wasn't fast enough. He grabbed one of the swords that hung from the wall, swinging it wildly. Lou danced back, reaching blindly behind her until she also found a blade.

I'd only ever read about sword fights in storybooks. I'd imagined them to be light, graceful things, two opponents dancing on nimble feet, their blades moving in crisp movements.

Lou and Andel's fight was nothing like that. They swiped at each other, dodging and deflecting blows. They were both breathing hard within a minute as they moved around furniture, tripping over footstools and getting caught with the desk between them.

He smiled, brandishing his sword. "It's nice to see some fight from you. So often these days, a man sees my face and surrenders before we even get aboard his ship."

Lou's gold tooth flashed. "I'm worth ten of those men."

"You are. And I'll enjoy killing you ten times more."

The sword sliced through the air but locked with Lou's at the hilt. Hatred flickered in her eyes for the briefest second. He leaped back but came in again as she collected herself, using the hilt rather than the blade once more. His fist connected with Lou's jaw, and she stumbled back. Her own sword caught in the chair she'd been sitting in and clattered out of her hand.

"Captain," Maro grumbled from where they were slowly rising, "stop playing and kill him."

"I'm trying," Lou said through clenched teeth. She reached for the closest weapon at hand, an iron poker arranged by the fireplace.

She'd barely had time to grasp it before he renewed his attack. He brought his sword down, blade glinting, and Lou raised the poker to fend it off. Sparks flew as metal hit metal, and the sword glanced away. Lou lashed out, swinging her makeshift weapon, but he was comfortable with the sword in his hand and danced back before attacking again, even more viciously than before.

He thrust forward, backing Lou toward the fireplace. She swung, but with his next attack, the sword bit into her arm beneath the elbow, and she hissed. The poker fell from her hand.

He laughed darkly, pressing his advantage. Lou's shoes slipped in the ash, and she put a hand out to catch herself on the hearth. My heart pounded so hard in my chest I thought I might be sick.

Lou ducked as he brought his sword down again. The blade sank into the heavy wood of the mantel, and Lou, crouched beneath it, threw her uninjured arm up. A cloud of ash flew from her hand and into Andel's eyes. He cursed and fell back, leaving the sword wedged over Lou's head as he scrubbed at his face.

I expected her to grab the sword, but instead, she reached over the mantel to pull a tarnished ship's bell off its hook on the wall. I'd polished one just like that on the *Siren* and knew it was heavier than it appeared. Blood dripped down Lou's arm as she gripped it by its thick rope and swung.

If he saw it coming, it was already too late. The bell arced through the air and collided with his skull with a muffled crunch and a deadened chime. He cried out and tumbled toward the window, and I pressed back, hands over my mouth. He gripped the curtains, and for a moment, our gazes locked. Brass flashed behind him, followed by a second crunch. He fell where he stood, taking the curtains with him. Lou's face was a mask of calm as she brought the bell down on him again and again. His leg twitched, and blood splattered on her skirt and the carpet. By the time she was done, the chime was demented and its crack was wet.

The room was silent except for Lou's heavy breathing. Maro leaned against one of the glass cases across the room, arms over their chest. Blood trickled from their lip, and one side of their face was swelling badly, but they looked completely unfazed by the atrocity that had just occurred in front of them.

Lou stared down at the unmoving body at her feet before she leaned over it and gripped the red stone around its neck. With a sharp yank, the chain pulled free, but not before it forced the neck to arch and dragged the ruined face to one side, leaving a red streak in its wake.

When her gaze lifted and our eyes met, the mask was cracked. Her eyes were wide, her mouth open as she gasped for air, and she shuddered.

"You shouldn't have seen that." Her voice was so soft, I wasn't sure if she was speaking to me or the corpse on the floor.

"A bell?" Maro asked from across the room. "You could have grabbed another sword from every second cabinet in this room, and you chose to bludgeon him to death with a bell?"

"It has a certain flair, don't you think?" Lou asked, something flickering in her eyes before she forced a smile to her lips and turned back to the first mate.

"What's she doing here?" Maro's gaze was on me, and they looked as angry as Lou had when she'd found me in the hallway.

Lou slipped the glinting ruby from its chain and dropped it down the front of her dress. "The prince's cousin is here."

"What?"

"We have to leave. He'll be watching the harbor."

"You're only mentioning this now?" Maro snapped.

"It didn't seem like the right time before. Princess." Lou gripped my shoulders. "Princess!"

"Yes?" My voice wobbled. I couldn't look away from the body on the ground. The smell, the blood, it was seeping inside me. I would need a lifetime in Davi's washtub to be clean again.

"Do exactly as I say. We have to go quickly. No time for sneaking through the shadows. You have to pull yourself together, do you understand?"

"You killed him." I couldn't stop my hand from shaking as I pointed at the oozing corpse.

"No one will mourn him. Princess. Listen to me." She shook me hard. "George!"

My name caught my attention. "What?"

She put an arm around my waist, pulling me tight against her. Blood sparkled like tiny rubies on her chest. "They'll be watching for a pirate and a princess. They may not know to look for three of us. We have to make them think we're something other than we are. Do you understand?"

"I'm not a princess." My lips felt numb, and I shivered.

"She's in shock," Maro said.

"Get on the other side of her. Help me keep her upright. If anyone asks, she's had too much to drink."

They half carried, half dragged me out of the room, away from the ruined body on the floor.

PART III

THE PRINCESS

18

We went out the front door as if nothing was wrong. Noises from the party outside echoed behind me, but no one stopped us.

"Good night!" Lou called cheerily as we stepped outside. A few people replied with well wishes behind us, but we kept moving.

I glanced up at Maro. Their swollen lip and cheek were closest to me. "Your face," I said.

"Shut your mouth," Maro hissed, but as soon as we were out of range of the torches that lit the house's front, their face fell into shadow. No one noticed.

We made our way back the way Davi had brought me. Once or twice, Lou would mutter something like "Two guards ahead of us," and Maro would let go of me, slipping into the dark.

"You killed him," I said, my voice barely above a whisper.

"He would have killed me." Lou's voice was hard.

"You killed them all." So many men sent to the deep. "Why?"

She pulled me into her, burying my face in her chest. She smelled of sweat and blood, and I wanted to vomit.

"Please," she said. I thought she might have kissed my hair in the way Ender had kissed Rosie before. "Please, George. I need you to be strong a little longer."

Another set of arms were around me. Maro was back. We continued on. Maro and Lou took up a merry song I'd heard a few of the men sing on the ship late in the evening when the work was done. I tried to join them, but my voice sounded rusty and hoarse to my own ears. I staggered between them, letting anyone who passed think I was drunk. Three revelers on their way home after a raucous party.

Ender was waiting with Berix at the wharf. They sat in the longboat, wrapped in heavy cloaks that, in the poor evening light, made them look like a pile of oilcloth. Maro and Lou helped me down the ladder as the two sailors unfolded themselves and set their oars.

"Is she all right?" Ender asked.

"Bit too much to drink," Lou said, loud enough to be heard by anyone who might be listening. I was still leaning against her. Her skin felt so hot, I thought it might burn me. I pushed back, tipping off the wooden bench into the bottom of the boat. Water seeped through my skirts, and it chilled me instantly. I shivered so hard, my teeth chattered until I bit my tongue and tasted blood.

That was the last straw. I lurched to the side and vomited. My body clenched and spasmed.

"That's it." Lou's voice was no doubt supposed to be soothing, as was her palm on my back caressing in slow circles, but it all felt grotesque. "You'll be fine soon enough."

I didn't think I would. I'd never be able to wipe away the sight and sound of that man's skull caving in.

They helped me climb the ladder to the *Siren*. My feet kept getting trapped in my borrowed dress. I was still unsteady as strong hands lifted me over the rail and onto the deck.

"Get ready to depart," Lou said. Her voice was so calm, I hated it. How could she be so unaffected? "Take the princess to my cabin."

"I'm fine," I said, but the words felt uneven in my mouth.

"You're not. Take her to my cabin."

Gentle but firm hands—whose, I didn't know—led me away, and I didn't fight them.

Once I was in Lou's cabin, I couldn't breathe. The usual ship smells of tar and mold mixed with the blood and vomit, and the world spun around me. I paced, sucking in big breaths of air. I cried, and when I wiped my tears away, my hands came back smeared in a chalky white paste that reminded me I was still wearing Davi's makeup.

I searched the cabin for a way to wash my face, hiccupping on sobs as I went, but found nothing until I came to the door in the back. When I pulled it open, I found a smaller chamber that held a single bed. For a moment, all I wanted to do was lie in it, pull the quilt over my head, and forget the world. But I wouldn't be able to find comfort in Lou's bed.

A pitcher and bowl sat on a narrow chest of drawers opposite the bed, and when I lifted the pitcher, water sloshed inside.

My hands shook as I scrubbed my face longer than I needed to. I shuddered and wept. No matter how many times I rinsed my skin, I couldn't shake the idea it was coated in a thin film of blood and gore.

The ship swayed under my feet. Whatever Lou had done, we were underway.

When the water in the bowl was a cloudy gray, I stumbled to the outer cabin. I paced. I sat on one of the low sofas, but that only brought back the memories of the first time I'd been with Lou in here. Her disdain, her lack of compassion.

She'd shown me who she was, time and time again. I'd been so naive to believe Davi's fairy tale. Whatever she'd hoped to achieve by telling it to me had been lost in the crack of a man's skull under a bell.

Lou entered the cabin—maybe hours later, maybe minutes. I was working myself into a lather, pacing in tight circles.

Her face was flat, perhaps tired, but mostly resigned. "Highness," she said.

With a shriek, I crossed the space between us in three steps.

I slapped her. I'd never slapped anyone in my life, but so help me, in that moment it was the only thing I could think to do.

"You're a monster!" I said.

Her hand was on her cheek, her eyes and mouth rounded with shock, but it fell away quickly. Her only reaction was the same infuriating blankness, and all she said was, "Yes."

"You didn't have to. Not like that. Why would you kill someone that way?"

"Does it matter how I killed him?" She rubbed her jaw, showing me the bandage around her forearm. It was tied at one end, and blood seeped through it.

"'We need the ruby,' you said. You made it sound like a trip to the jewelers."

"Princess, you're clearly upset. Would you—"

"My name"—I shoved at her chest—"is George."

She pressed her lips together. "He wouldn't have given it to us. Is that what you thought was going to happen? Do you know what he is?"

"I don't care what he is. You took his gem to pay for my passage. You've made me culpable in his death!"

"He's a hunter. He hunts pirates. What you saw was his personal museum, full of trophies from the ships he's taken, the captains he's killed."

"Monsters, just like you," I spat.

"Yes."

"Liars."

"Yes."

"You knew you had to kill him from the moment you told me about him."

"Yes."

I pointed a finger at her. "You *wanted* to kill him."

"Yes." Her voice rose. "And all the men just like him. The ones who think it's a game. Sport. A way to pass time."

"Like you?" My lip curled.

The gold tooth flashed as she laughed. The sound was dark and throaty. "It's so simple for you, isn't it?"

I shook my head. Nothing was simple. Nothing had been simple since the moment Niall had read my name on that piece of paper.

Her smile was cruel, and I hated the monster that had consumed her. She continued. "You see the world so clearly. Good and evil. Black and white. People can be saved, risks avoided."

"You didn't have to cave his skull in!"

"Of course I did!" she snapped. "Because sometimes, risks can't be avoided. Sometimes, there's no other way but running right at the thing you fear the most."

"And bringing others with you?"

She swallowed, and her lashes fluttered. Perhaps the mask wasn't tied as firmly as I'd first thought.

"Have I tarnished you, princess?"

"Don't call me that!"

She brushed a hand over her bandage. "This is the life I lead. Your addition to it doesn't change that."

"You don't have to!" I wanted to touch her so badly. Clutch at her skirt like I had before and beg. "You don't. This life. The death, the lies. It doesn't need to be who you are. There's always a choice!"

The muscles of her jaw and her throat strained. "That is exactly why I had to kill him."

"So you could escape?"

"No. So you could."

"Stop! Stop avoiding my questions." I grabbed a cushion from one of her sofas and threw it across the cabin.

"Oh, that's good," she scoffed. "Very good, princess. Throw a tantrum and get it over with so we can move on."

"It's not a tantrum!" My hands balled into fists. "How could you? How could you do that? How can you live with it?"

"If I had the ruby, and you didn't know how I'd gotten it . . ." She spoke slowly, as if I were a child. She sounded like the prince, and I hated her for it. "Would you be this upset now?"

"Lou."

"If I'd come back here with the ruby in my hands and blood on my dress, you would have looked the other way and been grateful that I'd secured the means to buy your release."

"No, I—"

She pressed her advantage, stepping forward. "Don't pretend you wouldn't have. How many times have you passed a starving child in the street and turned your head the other way? How many times have you eaten at night knowing your neighbors haven't eaten that week?"

"That's not—"

"It's uncomfortable, isn't it, Georgie? Uncomfortable to know that your good fortune is because you're insulated from the people who truly struggle, who make the difficult decisions between life and death every day?"

Was she asking me to apologize? "I tried. The dressmaker's, I—"

She rounded on me. "When have you ever done the hard thing? When have you ever gone without? Fought for something? When, George? Was it when they engaged you to that monster? What choice did you make?"

"It was so fast, I—"

"Yes, yes, you were helpless. I know. What about before that? When you came to the city and saw the conditions there? Or further back?"

"Further back?" What did she know about my life before the prince?

Her calm was gone, and her eyes were burning fury. "When they said I'd been lost at sea, what did you do? Did you demand an inquiry? Did you send out people to search?"

"That's not fair, Lou. I was twelve." I stumbled back until I hit her desk, effectively trapping myself between solid wood and Lou's ire.

"So was I! Twelve years old, and I was sold to a pirate crew. I stabbed a man in the eye when I was thirteen. He had his hand up my shirt while the men around him laughed. I killed him a month later because losing his eye wasn't enough to deter him. Every day, every month after that—"

Her mask cracked in half, and what lay underneath was worse than watching a man die on his museum floor. The pain on her face so deep, it would drown me if I stayed too long.

"You were dead. They said you were dead!" I tried to backtrack, but the quicksand feeling sucked me down.

"But I wasn't! I was alive and suffering, and you did nothing! If what happens tonight disgusts you, if the monster I am today disturbs you, then know that your complacency is part of the reason we are where we are. You and me, Georgie. We'll always be connected, for better or worse."

Georgie. My name. My name on her lips. Such sweet pain, and with it came the dam of all the lost years, the grief and loneliness and the knowledge that I'd never loved anyone the way I loved Lou.

I raised my hand to slap her again, knowing I wouldn't get the chance. She grabbed my wrist to stop me, but I'd wanted the distraction, not the violence. There had been too much of that.

I kissed her.

The first time I realize I feel differently than my schoolmates is when I am fourteen. We are in class, and the painting mistress is attempting to coax a rendering of a bowl of plums out of each of us and onto our canvases. When she comes to mine, she leans over my shoulder. She smells of peppermint, and she laughs softly at my lumpy creation. The end of a paintbrush is pressed to her lips as she considers my work and, in that moment, I wonder what it would feel like to press my lips where the thin, wooden handle dimples her skin.

I cry myself to sleep that night because those thoughts are forbidden.

The only other person I'd ever kissed was the prince, except he'd kissed me and I didn't resist. That was a moment built on confusion, manipulation, and domination.

Kissing Lou was like diving into the ocean. The waves crashed down on me, stealing my breath—and it didn't matter, because her hand on my wrist disappeared before she was tunneling her fingers into my hair, pulling hard enough to sting. My hands were doing the same, desperate for something to hold on to as we fell to the sea floor below.

Her tongue was soft and then firm. Her skin was warm. I shivered when her teeth grazed my jaw, and an ache formed in my chest like my whole body was trying to constrict itself around my heart. She tasted of saltwater and sunshine. She was mine.

"Lou."

She pushed me back so roughly, I stumbled.

"That's enough." Her chest heaved.

"No, it isn't." I stepped forward, nearly tripping.

"Stop." She held out her hand. Her eyes were wild, her skin mottled with darkening spots of red.

"Why?" I wanted to sing that she'd finally let me in. I wanted to cry that she was putting me away just as quickly.

She shook her head and paced in front of her desk. "You need to leave, princess."

"I don't think so." If I left now, she'd never let me back in.

"Go!" she shouted. The word was as broken as her expression. I slumped down onto the sofa that she'd once occupied like a throne and crossed my arms.

"Tell me," I said.

"Get out, Georgie. I'll have Ender haul you out by your hair if you don't."

I glanced at the door. Someone would have heard her. Ender might be lurking just beyond, Rosie throwing herself between him and the latch, Maro sighing heavily behind them.

But she'd let me in. I'd seen the cracks, the hurt, and the pain, but also the need. She needed me the same way I needed her. There had been no one else for me since the day I'd met her, when we were too small to know what our bond would grow into.

"Say it," I said again, calm rushing over me like the tide.

"What? I don't know what you want me to say, George."

I crossed one leg over my knee and spread my arms over the back of the sofa the way she liked to do. I could see why she did it. The sense of power as I claimed more space was dizzying.

"Tell me that when you ripped me from the prince's arms, when you think of anyone touching me, you want it to be your hands on me and not theirs."

When I arched my spine in Davi's purple dress, her eyes moved over me uneasily. "You make your own choices, princess, not me." She walked toward me with slow, shuffling steps, as though her feet were betraying her.

"Tell me that you put yourself in that dress so that I, and not anyone else, could see your body."

"Be careful what you wish for, Georgie," she growled between clenched teeth.

But the dam had broken, and I couldn't stop the truth as it rushed out, swamping everything in its path. "I wish for you. I've only ever wished for you!"

She was on me in a second. Her mouth devoured my lips as her fingers tangled with mine, bringing them over my head. It was thrilling. In my dress, I felt more exposed than I'd ever been before. She licked over my throat, and she sucked on the skin under my jaw.

"Is this what you want me to say?" she asked as she spread her body over mine, fitting our legs around each other.

"Yes." I sighed as something inside me that had been broken a very long time ago knitted itself together.

"Do you want me to say that you've driven me to distraction from the moment Ender pulled you onboard?"

"Yes." All of it. Everything. I wanted to hear everything.

"That I loved you when we were twelve, and didn't know that what I felt wasn't how all friends felt about each other?"

"Did you?"

She drew a thumb over my lower lip, and her eyes were nearly black as I pressed my teeth against the nail.

"Do you need to hear me say that you are the most beautiful person I've ever seen? That I torture myself at night with thoughts of how pink and perfect you must be when you're naked?"

My face heated at the insinuation, and my breath caught as I realized that, yes, I very much needed to hear that.

She pressed her hands to my cheeks, sweeping her thumbs over my cheekbones. "Will knowing all that be enough when you leave me?"

I froze. The heat that had blossomed in my belly guttered and extinguished itself.

"What?"

The darkness in her eyes turned hard. "Do you need me to truly break your heart before you give in?" She pulled herself up to sit, leaving me breathless and cold. "Because I will, Georgie. God help me, I've tried everything else, but if I need to crush your heart like I crushed that man's face for you to finally understand why our chance was over the moment I went to sea, I'll do it."

I sat up as well, pulling my knees to my chest. The sofa was so small, I had no means of getting away from her, but the space opening up between us was growing with every breath.

"I don't understand."

Lou scrubbed at her face with her hands. "I know you don't. That's all I need to know to let you go."

I shook my head, and hot, frustrated tears pricked at the corners of my eyes. "You can't. You can't mean that."

"I've never lied to you." Her smile was grim. "There are many things I haven't told you, but not a single word that's come out of my mouth since you boarded this ship has been a lie."

"But you came for me." I reached for her arm, desperate to hold on to any part of the feeling that was fading from her cheeks and her eyes. "You rescued me."

She ran a hand over my hair, and the simple gesture held so much affection, I ached with it. But she said, "I didn't know it was you when we came to Redmere. I didn't know it was you we were coming for."

I gaped. "Who did you think it was?"

She patted my hand, once again making me feel like a child. I nearly clawed at her skin just to watch red welts form to make sure she was human.

"It doesn't work like that. Word came the prince had found a bride and she needed to be taken away from the city as soon as a ship could arrive. That's all we ever get. We know where to pick someone up; we know if we're going to have to force our way in."

I froze, letting her words settle. Regardless of what had passed between us and who she'd shown herself to be, a small part of me had always believed that Lou had come for me specifically. That she'd known I was trapped and had done everything she could to rescue me. "But Davi said—"

She froze. "What did Davi say?"

"That you saved her. That she needed to escape, and you came for her and took her away to somewhere she would be safe."

Lou's mouth twisted into a bitter smile. "Davi's resourceful. She would have saved herself eventually."

"But others. She said there were others. That you rescued them."

She shook her head. "I'm no saint, Georgie."

"So you would have come for anyone?" The newly healed part of me tugged at its stitches.

"We were only told there was an unwilling princess, and the resistance in Redmere was willing to pay an obscene amount of money to the person who could rip her from the embrace of her adoring prince. My contact had been preparing for months, gathering information. The only thing we didn't know was who the mystery princess was." She gathered my hand in hers, clutching it desperately. "Then, it was you, and you were here. On my ship. In my cabin. In my head. Do you know what you do to me?"

I shook my head, afraid to speak.

It was some small comfort that her eyes were wet when she brushed her lips over my knuckles. "You undo me, George. Utterly. Your face. Your determination. Your kind heart that reminds me how blackened mine has become."

"You're not—"

"I am. You've seen it."

The lash of a whip. The crunch of a man's skull.

"But you—"

"It's fine. I know what I am. It's why I never went back to Redmere. Why I never sent word I was alive. I'm not that girl anymore. She died a long time ago." She placed her palm to my chest. "But your heart is still good. I love how hard you fight for it. I'm so glad that one of us survived to be the woman we dreamed of being when we were small."

Tears spilled over my cheeks unchecked, but before I could protest again, she unfolded my curled fingers and kissed each one softly. "Go back to your cabin."

"No." I shook my head.

She kissed my hair. The gesture had no heat, no desire. It only offered comfort, and I hoped she'd found some, because I didn't. "I'm sorry for what I said before. You're not responsible for what happened to me. You couldn't have known. We were only children."

"Lou." I clung to her, but she pulled us both to stand and pushed me gently toward the cabin door.

"I'm tired, George, and this voyage isn't over yet. Please. I need some space to think." She turned and shuffled away.

I stayed where I was, trembling. All my earlier agitation had melted, leaving only bone-deep sadness in its place. If I left now, she'd spend all night building her defenses back up, and I'd never reach her again.

She put a hand on the wall as she reached the door that led to her bedchamber. Her whole body sagged.

"Sleep well, princess."

Didn't she know I hadn't slept well since the day she'd left me?

19

The ship was dark as I stumbled back to my cabin. None of the usual lamps were lit—all the better to slip away unnoticed from the harbor—and the crew was nothing more than silent shadows as they went about their work. No one acknowledged me as I crossed to the hatch near the front and descended to my cabin.

The taste of Lou's lips was still on my mouth, the burn of her fingers still on my skin. Still, I couldn't shake the broken look on her face, even as she'd told me that we had no hope.

I didn't know who she was. The old Lou had been lost years ago. But the one here now, the one on this ship, needed me. She was neither the monster nor the saint, and she needed me.

I was so caught up in my thoughts, I didn't notice the sounds coming from the cabin as I opened the door.

Rosie saw me before I saw her. She shrieked, and Ender banged his head on the bunk above them. He rolled to his feet, hands in front of him to ward off his attacker. He was a wall of muscle and matted, copper hair.

"Lady!" he said when he realized it was me. He used a big hand to pull Rosie behind him to shield her nakedness, while using the other one to cover his own as best he could—which wasn't very well.

I flushed, dropping my eyes to the floor. "I didn't mean to intrude."

"I'm sorry, lady. We didn't think—"

"What are you doing here?" Rosie asked, peeking out from behind Ender. "We thought you were with the captain."

"She . . ." She needed me, and she'd sent me away. Tears pricked my eyes, and my chin trembled, even as I caught my bottom lip between my teeth.

"It'll be my turn for the watch soon," Ender mumbled, scrambling into his pants, but it warmed my heart that he bent to kiss Rosie before leaving.

I closed the door behind him, giving Rosie a minute to get dressed.

"I suppose you knew he and I were . . ." The words were muffled as she pulled the shirt over her head.

"I'd hoped."

"And you don't . . . judge me for it?"

I could hardly judge her when my heart wished to be doing the same thing with Lou elsewhere. Instead, I sat next to her, running my fingers through my tangled hair.

"Are you happy?"

"That's a funny question." Rosie got on her knees behind me and worked out the snarls with her fingers.

"I don't mean are you planning to drag him back to land and give him a dozen children. But do you trust him not to hurt you while we're here?"

"Of course!"

"That's all I meant. We're far enough from home that I don't think the old rules apply anymore." If they ever really had. Redmere was a bubble away from the rest of the world. I ran a hand down my dress. My skin still raised gooseflesh as I thought of what would be done to me if I'd dared to wear something like this in the streets of Redmere City. But if we'd been able to stay in Beldridge Landing, we wouldn't have been given a second glance, even if I'd gone out with Lou's hand in mine.

Sometimes there's no other way but running right at the thing you fear the most.

Rosie braided my hair down my back. "So you told Lou that you love her, then?"

Of course she would know. She'd always been the cleverer of the two of us.

"I slapped her."

"You did?" Rosie scrambled to sit next to me.

"And *then* I kissed her."

She clapped her hands. "Tell me everything!"

I WOULD GET myself off this ship if only to have a good night's sleep. Rosie and I tried to squeeze together on her little cot, but I was restless and couldn't settle. I kept her awake until she eventually crawled out, grumbling, and slid into my bed.

Every time I closed my eyes, I saw Lou with the bell in her hand and death in her eyes. The pained regret on her face when the man lay dead and she realized I'd seen the whole thing. The women at the admiralty gates, pleading for their families and knowing it was hopeless, while I'd sat in an elaborate carriage and pretended I would have any impact on their fate if I could win the prince to my way of thinking.

When I did sleep, my dreams were full of Lou. Her sad eyes, her mouth on mine, her hands on my body, caressing in ways she hadn't in her cabin. I woke up in a cold sweat while Rosie snored gently across from me.

Lou hadn't known it was me. She would have come for anyone—and had come for many if Davi was to be believed. I'd heard Lou and Maro speaking about Lady Parrington that first morning. Lou said she'd been dealt with and I'd assumed she'd been killed, but maybe Lou had only meant they'd had to pass her on to someone like Davi sooner than expected so they could come back for me.

But then, she'd sunk four of the five ships that had come after her.

Were all those lives lost justified if it meant protecting one woman trying to escape her husband?

My emotions rocked with the sway of the ship, swinging between the ache in Lou's voice when she'd asked what I'd done when she'd been lost at sea and the businesslike way she'd explained how we would make our way back to the ship while a man's blood soaked into her skirt.

Slowly, the prism light overhead brightened. Gentle footsteps sounded on the deck. The *Siren* was rising for the day. Had Lou slept? If I went to her cabin, would she let me in? Would she sneer and call me *princess*? Would she kiss me again and call me by my name?

The sounds above my head shifted. A man shouted, and the feet went from gentle to urgent, running when no one ever ran onboard the *Siren*. The brass ship's bell, now gleaming thanks to my hard work, clanged with a repeated warning while orders were called, muffled in their words but not in their tone.

Even Rosie rolled over, rubbing at her eyes. "What's happening?" she asked blearily.

We were completely out of place in the gauzy dresses Davi had given us as we climbed up onto the deck, but our sailor's clothes had been left behind at The Captain's Peg. I was rapidly running out of strips of my old underskirt to keep my hair tied back as well.

More crew than usual gathered on the decks, and a nervous energy rippled over them.

Maro was at the wheel with Lou at their side. Lou was back in her dark captain's clothes, face set. For a moment, my steps faltered, afraid she might have reverted to her previous persona, taking the tiny flicker of our newfound relationship with it.

Nevertheless, I climbed the steps to the quarterdeck with

Rosie behind me. Lou's attention was behind the ship, a spyglass to her eye.

"What's going on?" I asked.

"Our attempts to slip away weren't completely successful," Maro said.

"Aha!" Lou's voice cracked the air, making me jump. "He's farther back than I would have thought. Maybe we did slip away, but he gave up on his search before daybreak and left the harbor."

"Yes, Captain. It's all an unfortunate coincidence." Maro's lips were pinched.

Lou gave them a lopsided grin. "You didn't used to be such a cynic."

"I've always been a cynic. It's you who has changed."

She tsked, but then her expression brightened even more as her eyes landed on mine. "Princess Georgina! Your fiancé has come for you."

My blood froze. "Beverly."

She motioned toward me. "Come see for yourself."

I took the glass with shaking hands and held it to my eye. I don't know what I expected. Beverly on the bow, staring right back at me? Even with the spyglass, I couldn't make out more than the dark shapes of men moving around on the decks.

But I could read the name, painted in dark letters behind the ornamental figurehead.

Perseverance.

"How far?" Lou asked.

"Four miles and gaining, ma'am," came the reply from another crew member.

"Yes, I can see they're gaining. Thank you."

"Yes, ma'am."

When I turned away from the *Perseverance*, Lou stood shoulder to shoulder with Maro. The two of them stared ahead, heads tilted together.

"What do you think?" Lou said.

"I suppose throwing her overboard isn't an option?"

Lou winked back at me. "They didn't mean that." The smile on her face was out of place after Captain Cinder's disdain or even her deep sadness last night, but I couldn't tell if the smile was meant for me or was fueled by the thrill of having the enemy in sight.

"Can we escape?" I asked.

"The *Perseverance* has more sail, and we're running downwind."

"I don't know what that means."

Lou's mouth quirked up on one side. "We can't evade her. Not without help."

"So what do we do?"

"Our best bet is to make a run for Piko Bank," Maro said.

"That's a thought. Better than running. You know how much I hate running. Let's see what she does."

What followed was a strange mix of tension and inactivity. We sailed on. The *Perseverance*, well, persevered. Slowly, the ship got closer, its details more distinct. The land ahead of us, too, took shape—tall, white cliffs dotted with dark trees along the top.

It was the slowest, least exciting chase I'd ever experienced. And yet, the entire crew had assembled, taken orders, and stood at the ready near the cannons that, so far, had only been used as a flogging post and something for me to trip over as I went up and down the decks with my bucket. Rosie found us functional clothes and went down to start her day in the mess, reappearing later with hard biscuits to hand out to the waiting men.

"This is all very exciting, isn't it?" she whispered to me as she joined us on the quarterdeck.

I shrugged. To be honest, I'd started to feel a little sleepy with my restless night and all the endless waiting.

"Petru says the *Perseverance* is one of the most sought-after prizes in the sea."

"Don't be silly. There's nothing on board that ship that a pirate would want," Lou said without looking at us. "It's all soldiers and ammunition. The guns we could get a price for, but we'd have to find room, and the *Siren*'s not built for storage."

"But what about all the people you've kidnapped?" I asked.

Lou's gaze flicked to mine, annoyance showing. "We've been out of the kidnapping business for several years, Georgie."

"What about the merchant ships you attacked?" Rosie gnawed on a biscuit.

Lou snorted. "You mustn't believe everything you hear. Kidnapping is impractical. Hostages are too much work." She gave me a wink but didn't clarify any further. "No pirate worth their sails takes on merchant ships unless they're full of gold. What do I want with a ship full of sheep and corn? One would have eaten the other by the time I got far enough away to sell it, and besides that, sheep stink."

There was something here. A piece I hadn't put together. Lou wasn't in the piracy business anymore if Davi was to be believed, but what about the men who disappeared? All the pamphlets from the dressmaker's about Captain Cinder prowling the trade routes for plum catches?

The *Perseverance* drew closer, inch by inch.

We are in the forest on our bellies, catching frogs near a spring. Their little green and black bodies are slimy, and we are wet to our elbows as we splash and run through the woods. Lou's eldest brother finds us, muddy and happy. We show him our prizes with glowing smiles.

"Do you know how to cook a frog?" he asks. We shake our heads. "It's a very special technique. You need to be patient."

We listen with rapt attention. A frog thrown into a pot of boiling water will jump out. A frog put in a pot of cool water will sit while the water is heated. It takes a long time, but by the time the water reaches a dangerous temperature, it is too late for the frog to escape.

The cliffs ahead of us were sharp and clearly defined by the time the *Perseverance* was close enough to make her attack.

The first boom of her cannon was so loud, I nearly dropped

to the deck. Rosie shouted, and we both flinched at the heavy splash behind us.

Lou laughed. "That's a pretty pathetic attempt at intimidation."

The *Perseverance* was near enough now that I could see the familiar dark colors of the uniforms worn by the men on the bow.

"Do you think he's on that ship?" Rosie asked.

"He must really love you if he is," Lou said. "I'd expect him to send men after you. I don't think he'd come himself. He is a prince, after all."

I checked through the spyglass again, and my heart stuttered at the familiar face, now close enough for me to see his perfectly groomed hair and neatly trimmed beard.

"I don't know if the prince is on board, but Crawford is."

My skin crawled at the sight of him, at the knowledge that he'd seen parts of me naked, even if only for a minute. He'd laughed when the prince had said he planned to kill me. He'd laughed when the prince said I was pretty enough to be a mother to his children. He'd been the first person I'd met at the palace, and so my brain had ascribed the role of ally to him, but he'd never been on my side.

Another shot from the *Perseverance*'s cannon cracked through the air, and the ball landed in the water to our right. I danced away from the splash.

"What are they trying to do?" Rosie asked.

The cannons boomed again with another roaring sound that shook the planks beneath my feet.

"They're trying to get us to turn." Maro's hands were firm on the *Siren*'s wheel. "If she can get us to turn, she'll either disable us or run us into the cliffs."

The cliffs loomed on my left. We couldn't land a ship there. It was an endless wall of stone and sand.

"At least they won't sink us out here. Who knows if the princess can swim?" Lou muttered.

"I can swim! You're the one who taught me how."

"And the sun's out," Rosie said, hopping back with a laugh when I elbowed her.

Lou gave us both a quizzical look before shaking her head. "They won't risk bringing us down before they have you."

The *Perseverance* was even closer now. Crawford was distinct in his military uniform with its high collar and precise ornamentation, as were the three other men gathered around the two cannons pointed directly at us from the bow. The boom as the first went off was deafening, and Rosie and I both fell to the deck, hands over our ears.

"Shouldn't we be firing back?" Rosie asked. We were fifty feet from the shore to our left, the wall of cliff overhead. Ahead of us, a long line of jagged rock stretched out into the ocean, and it would force us to turn one way or the other when we reached it. It had to be a few hundred yards away and was coming up faster than I'd like.

"We have to do something," I said. Nerves tightened my stomach.

"I agree." Lou didn't appear to be nearly as affected. Her tone was practically conversational.

"And?" I asked.

She frowned. "And what?"

"What are you going to do?"

"Oh, no." She shook her head. "This decision is yours."

I gaped, waiting for her to follow up with a comment about how princesses always needed to have the last word or get their way, but she pursed her lips and waited. Beside her, Maro's hands tightened on the wheel, but they didn't say anything either.

"I don't understand," I said finally.

"This decision is yours," Lou said simply.

"Mine?"

"Captain!" Maro said sharply.

But Lou's gaze was on me, completely ignoring the first mate. "I've put us in a position where we can best defend ourselves, so now, the choice is yours. They're coming for you. Say the word, and we'll open fire. If you want to go back, we'll run up a white flag and return you."

"But they'll kill you!"

She shrugged. "It would be bad form under a flag of truce. And we've escaped worse before."

Maro's knuckles blanched further, making me wonder if they really had.

"Do you want to go back?" Lou asked.

"No." The reply was automatic.

"Then you want us to fight. Excellent. Ender!"

"Yes, Captain!" Ender called from the deck below us.

"Prepare the guns!"

"No!" I said again. "Wait."

"Yes, Georgie?"

"Captain," Maro insisted, through clenched teeth.

But the use of my name made my protest die in my throat. Lou's gaze was calculating, but she wasn't trying to put distance between us anymore. In fact, her eyes bore right through me. She was speaking to me, not some image of a princess, and in doing so, she was showing me once and for all who she was.

Still, I hesitated. A ship like the *Perseverance* could have a few hundred men or more. Hundreds of souls that Lou had placed in my hand. "I—we—"

"Not everything is black and white, but this situation is relatively simple. We can't outrun them. In a moment, they'll be close enough to fire again, and this time, they won't miss. Hand-to-hand combat is messy, as you know."

I did. I'd seen it myself. "But . . ." I glanced behind us. Count Crawford was there, but so was his crew. I didn't know them, but I knew who they were. Husbands. Brothers and sons. Men whose families were relying on what the navy paid. Men whose children starved to death while they waited for pensions that never came.

I shook my head. "You can't ask me to do this."

Another cannon shot from the *Perseverance*—this one over our heads—broke a spar from the first mast. The ship bucked and rocked with the impact. The sound as the newly freed sail flapped uselessly in the wind made my stomach turn. I glanced over my shoulder. The sailors were partially obscured in a plume of smoke, but they were now so close, I could nearly make out the individual buttons on Crawford's coat.

Ahead of us, the spine of stone was closer, jagged gray with a rolling strip of white where the waves crashed against the rocks.

"Ender!" Maro called. "Secure that sail!"

"Right away!" Ender was already making his way toward the rigging.

"What?" Rosie lurched to her feet. "You can't."

"If it falls, it'll drag behind us and slow us down," Maro said as Ender started to climb.

"If he falls, he'll die!" Rosie said.

"Better him than all of us!" Maro snapped.

My head spun. Ender's life was disposable for the greater survival of the crew. How could I say that mine was any different? But with the *Perseverance* drawing ever closer, I knew what my answer would be.

Lou put a hand on my shoulder. The contact on my bare skin made me shiver. "Well?" she asked.

I shuddered as I said, "I hate you."

Her smile could almost be called kind. "You should."

The decision was impossible, but I also had no decision to make. "I can't go back. Not to the prince."

"No one deserves that. Don't think your survival doesn't matter."

I couldn't meet her eyes. I wanted to crumble into a thousand pieces and blow away like ash on the wind. Lou's crew at the cannons stood ready to rain fury down on sailors whose only crime was being powerless against a regime that was slowly killing them. These ones would be dead sooner rather than later, and it was my fault.

"We have to fight," I said.

Lou called to Maro. "Ready?"

"Yes, Captain."

I couldn't watch. I lifted my eyes to where Ender was still up in the rigging, clinging to the mast.

"Count it off," Lou said as she took a position at Maro's shoulder.

A countdown to their deaths.

"Ready! Prepare to come around!" Maro called. Acknowledgments were shouted, and feet sounded on the deck. The *Perseverance's* cannon boomed again, and Rosie surged in my arms, but the blast sailed wide of where Ender was perched.

"Now would be good," Lou muttered.

"Don't rush me," Maro said.

"Oh, I'm so sorry! Far be it from me to—"

"Three, two, one!" Maro shouted, and the ship careened, all the sails flapping. The men called out, and when I looked down again, they'd abandoned the cannons and were pulling ropes in tight. Overhead, Ender was holding firm to the mast.

The *Siren* rocked to one side, veering sharply toward the open ocean. My heart thundered in my ears as I understood what Maro had meant before about the risk in turning. The change in position brought the side of the *Perseverance* into full view, including the lines of cannons on three decks. I counted nearly fifty of them, and they were now pointing toward our exposed flank.

We were close enough that I could easily hear the commands on the other ship and plainly see the men at the ready, about to blow us to pieces. Despite Lou's reassurances that they wouldn't take down the *Siren* until they had me, the *Perseverance's* crew didn't seem to be as concerned with those details.

Then, a new sound, rougher and deeper than the cannons, filled the air. Nonetheless, I flinched away from it at the same time that Lou shouted, "Did it work?"

Even the ocean was silent, as if holding its breath, before the tension broke with the sound of cracking wood like a forest collapsing around us.

Maro clung to the wheel with Lou close beside them, but they were both turned toward the *Perseverance*. Behind us, something on the ship had changed. We could still hear the shouted orders, but the tone had changed from military precision to panic.

"It worked, it worked." Lou's voice rose with each word. "Maro, you genius, it worked!" She hooted and smacked the first mate on the shoulder while the crew of the *Siren* cheered.

"What worked?" I asked.

Behind us, the *Perseverance* rolled. For a moment it looked like she was turning to give pursuit, instead of opening fire, but then . . .

The ship had stopped.

On her decks, men were scrambling. The ship rolled again, followed by another deep crack, and I finally understood. Beneath the *Perseverance*, a dark shape, nearly black, lay under the water. Something solid. Something more determined than even the *Perseverance*.

And she'd run into it.

The *Siren*'s crew was delirious with celebration. Lou and Maro were wrapped in each other's arms, laughing and patting each other on the back.

"Did she hit that rock?" I said, stumbling to the rail.

"She did!" Too focused on her prize, she forgot to keep an eye on her surroundings in unfamiliar waters.

"But . . ." I gaped. "How could you know?"

"Because we've hit it before!" Maro laughed. "We'd commandeered a diplomatic vessel that drew more water than the *Siren*. She's somewhere right beneath our feet now. Spent a month at the base of those cliffs before someone scooped us up!"

I whirled back. The *Perseverance*'s hull exposed the open wound where she'd hit the ledge of stone. She'd been so intent on us that she hadn't seen the shoal until it was too late. The frog in the pot, now done and boiled.

Men plunged into the water while others clung to the rails. Lou and Maro continued to dance around in celebration, and I watched them in horror.

I hate you.

You should.

I had no doubt Lou's self-loathing was so deep that she would stop at nothing to make me see her the way she did.

My horror was knocked aside, just as I was when Ender appeared suddenly. He swept up Rosie where she'd been standing next to me and hoisted her into the air, laughing and dancing her around while she squealed. My heart was still pounding in my chest, and I longed for the giddy relief that was written so clearly on all their faces.

All I could hear was the cries of the sailors behind me as the *Perseverance* went down.

I ran. I hid in our cabin, hoping for peace and quiet to get my thoughts in order. All I was left with was a sense of isolation so profound, I might as well have been at the bottom of the ocean.

I'd hoped to return home. But how could I now? How could I look into the eyes of the widows who waited for news and tell them I would do everything I could to help when I had been the reason their loved ones would never come back?

20

No one came for me. Eventually, late in the afternoon, I wandered out to the deck, needing room to think.

Music and raucous singing filtered through the air from somewhere in the ship. No doubt the crew of the *Siren* was in the mess, celebrating their victory over the vicious *Perseverance* who was now at the bottom of the ocean, slumped against the great stone that had wrecked them.

The deck was mostly deserted. A few crewmen were at their posts on watch, but even Maro must have gone down to the celebration, because I didn't know the man at the ship's wheel.

No one asked me what I was doing as I started to climb. The wind was rising, but it didn't matter. I chose the mast with the ruined spar, knowing there would be no one there to see me. The sail had been removed, making the climb easier and giving the small platform at the top a sense of spaciousness.

I watched the sun set, and as the last light was on the verge of fading, Rosie appeared on the deck. She circled a few times before Ender came through a hatch and approached her. They talked for a moment, too far away for me to hear what they were saying. Then, the conversation ended abruptly when Ender pulled her to him, bending his head down to kiss her. He tucked her under his arm, and they disappeared back the way they'd come.

I was glad she could find an ally and a little comfort here.

The light disappeared. I stayed where I was. The wind whipped at me and raised goose bumps on my arms.

On deck, a whistle pierced the quiet. A changing of the watch. No one joined me on my perch. In the dark, I wasn't nearly as frightened as I'd been the last time I'd made the climb. With no real perspective of the rocking of the ship and the giant expanse of water below, I wasn't so afraid. It was safe up here. If I had a blanket, I could stay the night.

Time was hard to keep track of too. If I were a sailor, there might have been a way, but I was barely a princess. I was a penniless society girl that society didn't want. I couldn't say how long I'd been up there when the storm started. One moment, all was still and peaceful, and the next, a drop of water splattered on my skin. It was a big, fat raindrop, quickly followed by another, and then a third.

Then, a thousand rain drops fell at once.

The storm roared in across the ocean, churning and raging in an instant. The ship pitched and rolled. Before, where the dark had insulated me against the vastness, it was now disorienting. The wind whipped and sucked in every direction, plastering my clothes to my body while trying to tear them from me at the same time.

My little platform tilted and rocked, the boards growing slick in the rain. The ink black sky lit up with a long finger of lightning that raced to the waves below. The hair on my arms stood up as I gasped, and then I flinched when thunder rolled through the clouds overhead.

I needed to climb down.

The ship heaved, and the world reared wildly, making my feet slide out from under me. I couldn't see the edge of the platform, had no idea if I was close to it. I reached out, finding the mast in the next fork of lightning, and wrapped my arms around it as the ship bucked. I shut my eyes, fingers digging into the smooth wood, shrinking as more lightning lit up the inside of my eyelids. Thunder boomed on its heels.

My options were either being struck by lightning here or breaking my neck as I fell from the rigging. Or waiting until the *Siren* became fed up with my desperate clinging and flung me into the ocean herself.

The next flash was followed by the smell of burning wood and tar. My skin tingled, but I felt no pain. Not this mast then. I pressed my face to the solid surface and waited.

The shivering started when the thunder's growl drifted farther away. I was soaked, and the wind chilled the water against my body. The *Crimson Siren* thrashed, and my muscles ached from holding myself in place. My teeth chattered.

The night seemed endless.

A strong hand gripped my ankle. The shock of it was enough to rip my eyes open as I screamed.

The clouds were parting. The storm was now a distant growl. I had no idea how long I'd been up here, but the moon and a handful of stars had cut through the clouds, plainly lighting the fury on Lou's face.

"What are you doing? You could have been killed!"

"Go away." The words were garbled by my shivering.

Lou swore, but she climbed onto the platform and helped me to my feet.

"You're frozen through." Lou pushed my sodden hair from my face. Despite my lingering anger, I wanted to melt into her heat. "Can you climb?"

Climb? I could barely stand. It was too dark to see anything.

She sighed. "You have to get dry, and the only way to do that is to climb down. It's too rough to rig up a chair to lower you. You'd break a limb if you were lucky, or your head if you weren't. Georgie"—her hand on my cheek was so warm—"you have to climb."

The descent was slow. Lou went first, only going down far

enough that she could keep a hand on me while I lowered myself over the platform's edge. My legs wobbled, muscles threatening to give out as I let the ropes take my weight.

"Come on. That's the way." Lou's voice was soft, as was her hand on my calf, as I found a place for my foot and brought my arms down to grip the ladder. My shoulders burned, and every time the ship tilted so that gravity pulled me away from the rigging, only Lou's touch as she showed me where to set a foot kept me from falling to the sea.

The ship seemed deserted as we reached the deck. She brought me into her cabin and into the smaller room beyond.

"Take your clothes off," she said.

I trembled. "I'm fine."

"Oh, for God's sake." She reached for my belt.

"I can do that!"

"Then do it!" Lou went to a chest of drawers and pulled out a rough shirt. "You'll have pneumonia by the morning if you don't take that off."

I wanted nothing more than to get out of my sodden clothes, but I wasn't stripping in front of her. She may have saved me, but I was still angry at her endless manipulations.

She rolled her eyes and let the shirt drop to the floor. "Fine." She turned, and I worked quickly to get out of my clothes. "I don't know what you thought you were doing, climbing up there in a storm," Lou grumbled, but kept her back turned.

"It wasn't storming when I climbed up." The shirt fell to below my knees.

"And it didn't occur to you to climb back down when the lightning started?"

I bit my lip, then pulled the neck of the shirt closed when Lou glanced over her shoulder.

"Get into bed."

"What?"

"Get in." Lou pointed at the bed, which was covered with a thick quilt that looked heavenly.

"I can go back to my cabin." I didn't look forward to the walk across the open deck in only Lou's shirt, but it was the better option.

"You can't be trusted on your own. If you're going to act like a child, you need to be watched like one. Get into bed, Georgie."

Exhaustion and the chill won out. The shirt was doing nothing on its own to warm me. I backed slowly toward the bed, never taking my eyes off Lou, who I realized was also soaked. Her clothes clung to her, and her dark hair hung in stringy tendrils like seaweed on her shoulders.

I slid into the bed. The quilt was as divine as I'd imagined, and a second heavy blanket was hidden beneath it to smother some of my aches and pains. I burrowed down until the covers tickled my nose. When Lou reached for the laces at the collar of her wet shirt, I closed my eyes and rolled until I faced the wall. The sounds were different here than they were in the cabin I shared with Rosie, including the slide and thump as Lou opened and closed drawers.

I held my breath as she slid onto the mattress next to me. This was too much, too intimate. My emotions had left me raw, and the wind and rain had kept the wound open too long.

Her fingers trailed through my wet hair, tangling in the knots. "What am I going to do with you?"

The softness in her voice, the kindness I'd yearned for since I'd first seen her face, broke me open completely. I'd tried to be strong, tried to play her game and protect my heart at the same time, but I couldn't do it anymore.

She shushed and hummed as I cried. I pulled her arms around me, and she let me do it, her cheek resting on my shoulder.

"I killed them," I said.

"You had no other choice."

"There's always a choice," I said through my hiccups. "This whole situation. I could have chosen to run away. To not marry Beverly. But he was going to kill me, Lou. He was going to kill the only people I cared about. I know you don't think much of the work I was doing in Redmere, but I was trying to—"

"I know." She kissed the back of my shoulder. "I know. I'm so sorry. I was angry. I was scared. You were on my ship and I wanted to hate you. I needed to hate you and for you to hate me. I still do, but I'm sorry for what I said."

I should have been basking in her words, but all I could feel was grief. "Those sailors..."

"Shh... There's always a choice. But sometimes it's a choice about the pain you can live with. There's no shame in protecting yourself."

She'd said something similar on the deck earlier. My survival mattered. I wanted to ask if she meant my survival mattered to her or if it mattered to Rosie. Maybe Ender. I wanted to hear her say that and so many more things again, but the strain in my body was giving way to a heavy lethargy. It dragged me down into sleep faster than the waves would have dragged me to the bottom of the ocean.

―――

For all I had been half-frozen the night before, I woke up as if I were sleeping next to a roaring hearth. There were so many blankets on top of me, I could barely breathe, and a solid weight was pressed along my back. I gasped as I managed to get the covers away from my head. The air in the cabin was refreshingly cool against my skin. Then, as I rolled my head, I gasped again.

The weight behind me was Lou.

Who was awake and watching me.

"What are you doing?" I asked.

"Making sure you don't do anything dangerous, like climb the mast in a thunderstorm."

The day before came back to me, and a sick feeling lodged itself in my stomach. Lou had said we chose the pain we could live with, and this was one that would stay with me for a long time.

She didn't touch me but shifted so our bodies were curled together. Her breath was on my neck as she said, "Are you still thinking about the *Perseverance*?"

A lump formed in my throat as I nodded.

She said, "Drowning's not a bad way to go. It's relatively fast. Better than a painful, lingering death when the bits of the ship that lodge in your body after a cannon blast fester and kill you slowly from the infection."

"Lou." I choked.

"Shh." She touched me. Finally. Her hand slid over my waist as her chin hooked over my shoulder. "You didn't kill them. The prince did, by sending them out here and letting his ego and lust for power dictate his actions instead of knowing when he's beaten."

"Is that what this is for you?" I said. "A grudge match?"

"The prince, and his father before him, took me away from you because my parents couldn't feed me or themselves any other way. He took everything that mattered from me. I'll never stop making him pay for that."

I turned again so we were face-to-face. "Will you tell me about it? Please? I need to know what happened to you."

For a moment, I thought she wouldn't answer. Even when she finally opened her mouth, I expected a cutting remark or for her eyes to go flat as she told me not to be sentimental.

Instead, she told me the truth.

We have been at sea for two months when the pirates come. The captain is brave as he calls the men to their positions. My job is to bring water to keep the cannons cool. I run from gun to gun, but even with our firepower, we are unprepared when the second ship comes up behind us and pirates storm our decks.

Most of our crew is killed at the end of a sword or sent overboard. The captain is executed, despite his white flag of surrender.

The ship's boys are loaded onto a strange vessel and sent to crew ships across the ocean.

What follows is two years of terror and survival. Two years of fighting the sailors who see through my boy's disguise to the developing body beneath. I learn to fight, to kill, because I know the alternative will leave scars on my soul that will never heal. The men I kill are bad men. They want to hurt me because they think I am weak. I do not lose any sleep over their deaths.

I meet Kiril when I am fourteen.

"Kiril," I said. "He's the one who will help get me safe."

Lou's laugh was dark. "Kiril never helps anyone. But for the right price, he can do anything."

"What do you mean?"

She searched my face. I didn't know what she saw. I wasn't even sure what I would see the next time I looked into my own eyes. My painted face at Davi's had been the last reflection I'd seen, and that image had been such a long way from the frightened almost-princess who was uncomfortable even adorning her veil with jewels given to her by a prince.

"Kiril is what's known as a broker. Pirates, as a rule, are neither the most trustworthy nor the most trusting group of people. Without the brokers, the seas would be lawless, with crews double-crossing each other at every turn. We'd spend more time fighting each other than we would actually spend being pirates."

"Some people might argue that would be a good thing," I pointed out.

"People will always live at the fringes, Georgie. I'm not saying it's right, but whether through greed or desperation, someone will always be pushed into a life they never thought they'd lead."

I dropped my eyes. Lou squeezed my hand and continued, "No one knows how long the brokers have been in play, but their rules are simple. Pay them what they want, and they'll get you what you need. Any crew who crosses them meets a grisly end. If you need safe passage, you go to the brokers. If you have spoils to sell, a broker makes sure you get a fair price with no chance of a double cross from the buyer . . . for a generous percentage, of course." Her dry smile said the percentage was more than generous.

"But what does that have to do with meeting him at fourteen?"

Her smile vanished like the moon behind a cloud.

"Brokers tend to have very specific currencies. Some deal in gold, others in jewels. Kiril deals in lives. He buys and sells them, takes or ruins them, according to his own code of justice and what the highest bidder is willing to pay. My captain at the time thought he could get a better price for the duke Kiril had him kidnap if he instead ransomed the duke back to his family. My captain met his end with Maro's garrote around his windpipe."

"Maro?" I asked.

"They were Kiril's assassin when I met them. Sent to tidy up when Kiril's deals went awry. They killed my captain in the open, up on the quarterdeck. They seemed like a vengeful angel, and I begged them to take me with them. They brought me to Kiril, and . . ." She shook her head. "I don't know. Kiril's perverse. He recognized potential in me. I was angry at the world. I saw the fear and respect that the brokers commanded, and I wanted that. The chance to control my own destiny, rather than being afraid of every man on my ship."

As she spoke, her fingers drummed an agitated rhythm on my arm. I didn't know if she even realized she was doing it. The longer she spoke, the rougher her voice became. I had no idea what she saw in her mind's eye, but it wasn't an easy memory. "It took six months for me to realize my mistake. The brokers are merciless, and if they send you to kill someone, you have no option but to say yes. If they want you to torture his family and burn his house to the ground while he watches and then kill him, then that's what you do. Any deviation forfeits your life and the life of your crew. So you kill and you torture because someone's paid the broker's fee, and if you hesitate, your life is over."

The grief of those years was written clearly on her face. If she was trying to break my heart with her honesty, she might finally succeed.

"But you got away," I insisted.

"Still looking for the happy ending." She smiled at me. The arch from her throat to her jaw was long and beautiful. I wanted to trace it with my fingers and memorize the line.

Instead, I nudged her like I had when we were children and I needed her to finish telling her story of brave adventurers.

Lou sighed. "The brokers are only interested in two things: money and power. Kiril, in particular, is only interested in power. He has more money than most kingdoms, but even he can be paid if the price is right."

"I gather it was a lot for you."

"And Maro. I couldn't have borne this life without them. But if anyone knows what a life is worth, it's Kiril. The price he set for our freedom was so high, I think many others would have given up and continued in his service or thrown themselves into the deep. Raising the money took us years, and we earned it the only way we knew how. We ran down ships and sent their crews to the bottom of the ocean. We ruined a number of wealthy men and even a few countries. It was selfish but necessary for our survival. We built a reputation."

Eat your dinner or we'll sell you to Captain Cinder.

But if what she was saying was true, she hadn't lived that life in at least a few years. Where had the lost ships gone?

She was still speaking, unaware of my question. "I hated myself by the time it was over. I'm doing my best to atone, but Georgie . . ." The sadness in her face was bottomless. "It'll take a lifetime to cleanse me of the people I've killed and all the others I've hurt, and that's if no one kills me first."

"But you saved people too. People like Davi. Like me." I slid the rest of the way toward her until our knees and legs tangled together and I could wrap my fingers around her hair. "That must count for something."

"Maybe. But Kiril broke something in me. I may never get the blood off my hands."

She'd been a warrior the first time I'd seen her, with dirt on her face and suspicion in her eyes. To see her now, humbled and ashamed, with her shields of bravado completely down—I knew I had to bring her back to me.

"Come with me," I said. "You can do good in Redmere. Rosie and I . . . well, Rosie mostly. She knows people. You can—"

She shook her head, and what hurt the most was the way she wouldn't meet my eyes. "No. I can't."

"Then I'll stay with you." These were the options, and if she rejected one, then she would have no choice but to accept the other.

She brushed her nose against mine. Our lips were nearly touching. I wanted to feel that again so badly, the soft pressure of her kiss, the demanding entrance of her tongue.

"As long as you're on the *Siren*, the prince will never stop coming for you. He couldn't stand the defeat. The *Perseverance* won't be the last time. I can't risk my crew, and you can never be truly safe here. You need to go and live your life with your big heart and your kind soul. That is the best gift you can give to me."

She was wrong. But now that I knew the truth, I'd let her believe she'd won for now.

21

My instincts were to surround Lou and make her see that she couldn't give me up but pressing that too quickly wouldn't serve my purpose. I left the cabin, because if I couldn't win her over just yet, then there were other people I needed to speak with.

"Princess!" Maro's voice brought my head up.

"Maro," I said as I joined them on the quarterdeck.

We watched the ocean in silence for several minutes. On days like today, when the wind was up and the sun was out, it was easy to understand why some people were drawn to the sea. The openness of it, the freedom—so different from the looming gray of crowded buildings that I'd known in Redmere City, where it felt like someone was always watching.

"I asked the captain to come with me when we reach the brokers."

They laughed softly. "I thought you would. She said no?"

I nodded.

"You offered to stay with her then?" Maro said. I nodded at that too. "She's stubborn. She has your sense of Redmerian shame in her blood. I don't think she knows that no number of rescues will make up for our pasts."

"She wants forgiveness," I said.

"The only person who can forgive the captain is herself."

"You've probably killed more people than she has. Are you looking for forgiveness too?"

"No." Their reply was short and certain. "Where I come from, we don't believe in some cosmic tally, a final weighing of good and evil. I've made my peace with who I've been, and I'm trying to do better now to see what that's like. But the captain . . . Your people believe so strongly in right and wrong and hiding their shame away where others can't see. I don't know if she'll ever overcome it."

The *Siren* rolled under our feet. I squinted to the horizon. I had no idea how long it would take to reach Kiril, and the more I thought about it, the longer I wanted it to be.

"Will you help me convince her to come with me?"

Maro sighed. "I won't fight you."

From Maro, that small concession was as good as a victory.

I excused myself from the quarterdeck as my stomach growled. After the wrecking of the *Perseverance*, I'd eaten very little. I made my way down to the mess, which was mostly empty. Petru was asleep on a stool near the wall, and Rosie was stirring a pot of something that smelled heavenly.

"What's in there?" I sniffed the air.

Rosie smiled when she saw me. "Petru sneaked ashore while we were at Davi's and went to the market. It's salt beef stew! Try it."

The stew was brown and greasy, with thick chunks of what could have been turnips and potatoes. It was the best thing I'd eaten in ages.

"Rosie," I said between mouthfuls. "This is incredible."

She ladled another portion into my bowl with a smug smile. "Eat up."

I did. Without hesitation and without speaking another word. It truly was the most delicious thing, rich and meaty and—

"You didn't come back to the cabin last night," Rosie said, earning her a glare for interrupting the end of my meal.

"I spent the night with Lou. I got myself into some trouble up the mast, and she . . ."

I didn't know what was between us and didn't feel ready to share. Lou had entrusted me with so much truth. I shook my head and kept eating.

"I heard she found you half-drowned and a hundred feet above the ocean."

My eyes dropped to my empty bowl. "I'm sorry if I worried you."

"By the time I heard about it, you were already safe." Her cheeks went pink. "I might have had some company."

Her candor eased some of my embarrassment. "Just as well for both of us then. I have no desire to be assaulted by Ender's nudity again."

"He's very nice when he's naked." She grinned, swaying her hips as she stirred her pot. "He likes to—"

"Stop!" I laughed and leaned back on my stool. "I'm happy you appreciate those aspects of a man's form, but I am not interested."

She grinned impishly, but then her smile stilled. "Not at all?"

I wiped the last bit of gravy from the corner of my mouth and licked it off my finger. On the open ocean, was there any reason to hide? "Not at all."

"Never?"

Old fear, as much a part of me as the color of my eyes, fluttered in my chest as I watched her carefully. I'd never said it aloud before, not to another single living human being.

"No. I've never met a man who's stirred any sort of interest in me. It's always been women."

She nodded. "That would have made being queen difficult."

"I could have held the title well enough. Being married to the prince, though." I tapped my spoon on the side of the bowl. "He wouldn't have needed to manufacture a reason to kill me in the end."

"Don't say such things! They don't kill people for that anymore! The worst that could have happened is they would have sent you to prison."

As if that had ever been relief to the people Beverly had locked away over the years. "I think, as the spouse of the monarch, prison wouldn't have been enough. Hard to legitimize future children if the old queen and her proclivities are still alive."

Rosie shook her head and growled. It was adorable. I would always appreciate the ferocious way she protected me.

Petru started on his seat, coughing and snorting. We both jumped at the sound, but then he settled down again.

"You should stay here," I said.

She laughed. "Me? Here?"

"Your family would want you to be safe and happy. You have Ender now. If you wanted to stay with him, I would understand, and so would they."

"No. I promised you I—"

"I'm not a princess anymore, and I never had a maid until I was one. You should stay." The *Crimson Siren* wasn't the place I'd thought it was. She'd found a place here. Maro and Ender and the others would look after her. If she stayed, she would make a difference to people like Davi and me, who were trapped and in need of rescue. Rosie had rescued me before Lou had ever blown a hole in the courtyard wall.

"I admit I'm enjoying myself. Not just because of Ender," she said when I arched an eyebrow. "Saving the crew from Petru's cooking is its own kind of humanitarianism."

"You're the salvation they've been looking for."

"Would you stay too?" she asked.

The question struck a pang in my chest, but I wouldn't lie to Rosie. "I'll go where Lou goes," I said. But if we left, I would miss Rosie desperately.

Rosie wrapped herself around me in a fierce hug. We could be so physically close in our ship's clothes, our heads uncovered.

The restriction of our cloaks and veils felt like a long time ago. A different life, even.

"I love you," I said.

"I know. I told you I'd be the best friend you'd ever had." She sniffled. "Well, one of the best. I didn't realize at the time that Lou would come back from the grave and give me a run for my money."

"I don't know if Lou is my friend." I didn't know what we were to each other. Everything. Nothing. A reminder of who we'd been. A wish for a future together. I ran a hand over Rosie's hair. "But you are so much more than a friend. A sister. I never had one, but I think you could be my sister."

She squeezed me tighter. "You would have been the best queen Redmere had ever had. They don't deserve you."

I would have failed as a queen, overwhelmed by the prince and his plans. I would have soon been out of touch with the very people I thought I was helping as he kept me locked away to be used for his purposes only.

I wished we could all stay together. Rosie. Lou. Even Maro and Ender and the rest of the crew. I wished my presence didn't mean we'd be a target of Redmere.

Still looking for that happy ending.

I wasn't sure there were happy endings anymore. Just a choice of the pain I could live with.

THERE WAS A SAYING in Redmere that famine could make a crumb feel like a feast. If I was going to make Lou realize we couldn't be separated, I would have to starve her of my presence long before I was off the *Siren*.

But making myself scarce on a pirate ship was no simple matter. The farther we got from Redmere, and even from Beldridge Landing, the warmer it became. The interior of my cabin was stifling during the day and could only be made bearable at night by leaving the door open at all hours to help what little air was below decks circulate.

If I couldn't shut myself away, I had to make myself otherwise unavailable.

"Princess," Maro said. "The captain wants to see you."

I'd just appeared on the deck and reached for my bucket. "After I'm done with the scrubbing. We wouldn't want the wood to become slippery, would we?"

They raised an eyebrow. "Highness."

"You said"—I smiled sweetly at them—"you wouldn't fight me."

They paused for a moment, perhaps the first time I'd ever seen them lost for words. But finally, with a twist of their mouth and a jerky nod, they spun on their heel. "As you say, Highness."

When I was finishing the final pass, Ender appeared. "Lady, the captain has asked if you'd come to her cabin."

I glanced up at him, wiping my brow with a cloth-wrapped hand. "Don't you think the fittings are looking rather dull?"

He must have spoken to Maro or possibly Rosie, because he didn't disagree at all. His shoulders shook with suppressed glee, and he tipped me a salute before he carried on his way.

My hands were nearly green, my cheeks had burned in the sun, and I'd pinched one fingertip so many times in the hinges of the lantern I was holding that a dark red blister had raised up beneath the skin, when a long shadow fell over me. I squinted up, and it was like seeing Lou for the first time all over again. She was silhouetted against the sun, and a brimmed hat cast a wide shadow over much of her face, but her hands on her hips and the thin pinch of her mouth were unmistakable.

"George," she said. "I believe I asked—"

"I'm so sorry," I said with a casual laugh. "The day got away from me. A ship like this is a very busy place, you know."

She quirked an amused eyebrow. "Is it?"

"Oh, yes." I scrubbed my lantern with excessive vigor.

"Are you nearly finished?"

"Nearly." Truthfully, my fingers were numb.

"Then after, would you mind—"

"I'm sorry, Captain, but Rosie has asked if I could come down to the mess and help with supper."

Lou fell silent.

"Was there something you needed?" I asked, taking my eyes off the lantern long enough for it to exact its revenge on my fingertip once more. Cursing, I sucked the injured digit in my mouth and glanced up at Lou again. Her nostrils flared, and she stumbled back as if she'd been struck, then quickly marched away from me.

I watched her go. She muttered something to Maro, who was halfway up the deck. The first mate looked baffled for a moment before they smothered laughter behind their hand. Lou huffed in exaggerated offense and stormed off to her cabin, where she remained for the rest of the afternoon.

I was in the mess, eating with Ender and Rosie. Even Maro, lured by the second round of Rosie's excellent salt beef stew, had joined us, when Lou appeared at the bottom of the steps from the upper deck.

The mess grew silent, and the sailors around us all knocked their thumbs to their brows in reflexive salute. Lou looked distinctly uncomfortable as she made her way through the crew, eyes on our table at the back.

My pulse quickened as her gaze settled on me. I also threw her a short salute before I returned to my meal.

"Captain," Ender said, pleased. "Have you come to join us?"

"You're just in time," Rosie added. "The stew is nearly gone."

"No, I . . ." Lou glanced from me to Maro, to the people watching us, then back to me. "Princess. I was going to ask if you'd like to have dinner in my cabin, but I see I'm too late."

I hoped she was starving as I dragged my spoon around the edge of the bowl. "I did say Rosie needed my help in the mess this evening."

"Yes. Yes, you did. I . . ." She rocked up on her toes, a motion which one might have attributed to the motion of the ship, but her hands were on her hips again, and her eyes continued to dart around uncomfortably. "Well, if it's too late for supper, perhaps you'll join me for a drink? I have some Vestrian wine that is . . ." She cleared her throat. "I thought you might enjoy it, princess."

I could have insisted she use my name, but my goal was to humble her a little, not humiliate. So I smiled politely and said, "I would love to. After I've finished helping Rosie with the washing up."

Lou wrinkled her nose. "But—"

"Oh, that's all right." Rosie stood hastily, making the table swing from its ropes overhead until Ender steadied it. "We can manage."

"But you said—"

Rosie waved me off. "No, you've been more than enough help today. Petru's hardly done anything today."

The old cook coughed a protest from where he sat at the next table, but Rosie sent him a cutting glare and he subsided.

She gave me the same blithely oblivious smile I'd just gifted Lou and said, "Go on. The captain clearly has something she wants to discuss."

Lou scowled at her, but Rosie was invincible when it came to sweet-talking her way through anything. The next thing I knew, I was following Lou out of the mess and toward her cabin.

Not for the first time, as soon as the door was closed, I was pushed and stumbled, only saving myself from disaster by staggering to the small, upholstered couch. This time, however, instead of a lecture, what followed was Lou's body on mine, her lips mashed against mine as she groaned.

"What are you doing?" she asked between kisses.

I laughed softly, tipping my head off the sofa's arm so I had an upside-down view of the ocean that spread endlessly behind the *Siren*. "What do you mean?"

Lou trailed her mouth down my throat. "Busy bee today, weren't you?"

"I have no idea what you're talking about."

"We'll see about that." Her fingers skated over my ribs, and I squealed involuntarily, wriggling underneath her and settling farther into the cushions. This was perfect. Exactly what I wanted. Lou so incandescently in love with me that she would never let me go.

She stilled as she placed a palm to my cheek. I turned my face to kiss it, and the scarf I'd wrapped around my hair pulled loose. Lou tugged the scrap of black fabric free. Maro had provided it earlier that morning, when the wind blew my hair in my face while I scrubbed the deck. It had the weight and texture of the dress they'd worn in Beldridge, and I couldn't help but wonder if they'd cut it up expressly to ensure they'd never have to wear it again.

"You know you don't have to wear this," Lou said, holding the material between two fingers like something rotten. "Not here. Not anymore."

I reached for it, tucking it into my belt. I'd lost two already, and spare fabric on the *Siren* was in short supply unless we continued to eviscerate Maro's wardrobe.

"It's practical."

"It's oppressive."

"It's a piece of fabric that keeps my hair from becoming an impossible snarl of knots while I scrub the deck."

She tsked, running her fingers through my untangled hair. "Well, we can't have that."

Her words unsettled me. "Do you hate everything about Redmere that much?"

She brought my wrist to her lips, kissing the blue veins there and making me tremble. "Not everything."

This was what I wanted. I needed Lou to be so consumed with me that she wouldn't dream of being separated, and I was running out of time to convince her.

"I'm going back," I said. "To Redmere."

She sat up, dropping my hand. "What?"

"You said Kiril could send me anywhere. I want to go home."

"They'll kill you."

"The prince will kill me. But there are so many more people there, and they need all the help they can get to overthrow him."

"Georgie." She cupped my cheek. "You can go somewhere else. Live your life. One person can't make that much of a difference."

"You do," I said.

"I have a crew. I have Maro, and—"

"You could have me." I shifted beneath her, finding the places where our bodies fit together.

"You can't stay here," she said, but she dragged her nose along my jaw as she spoke, inhaling deeply.

"Then come with me. Bring the others if you want, but come with me. If you won't go back to Redmere, we can make a place like Davi's."

Lou snorted. "You want to run a brothel?"

"I want to help. I know what it's like to feel trapped."

"George, it's not—"

In a flash, I pulled the scrap of fabric from my belt and wrapped it around her throat. She froze as I pulled at the ends, overlapping the octopus's waving tentacles.

"If you say it's not safe for me when it's somehow perfectly safe for you, I will strangle you right now and get Maro to help me hide your body."

She froze, tension vibrating through every muscle. It wouldn't take much for her to pull free of my hold. I expected her to push me off, to tell me to go back to my cabin and stop asking for things I couldn't have.

Instead, her mouth came down on mine again, the intensity of her kiss hot enough to set the whole ship on fire.

"I love you," she said.

My heart surged at the words I'd been desperate to hear. "Always."

"You won't see reason, will you?"

I shook my head. "Not when it comes to you."

She pressed a thigh between my legs, making my whole body warm. This and so many other things were what I wanted, no matter the risk.

"George." She pressed her forehead to my collarbone. For once, I was glad for these clothes that never completely covered my body.

"I can live with the pain of pursuit. Of the prince coming for me, or of some merciless pirate hunter who wants the *Siren*'s figurehead as a trophy."

She jerked her head up and her expression darkened. "They would never—"

I cupped her face, stroking her hard cheekbones with my thumbs. "I cannot live with the pain of knowing you're out here and I can't see you every day."

She nuzzled into my hand, sighing long and slow. Her eyes were closed, and like this, I could see the girl I'd known.

Finally, as she began to work open my belt, she said, "You win, George."

"I do?" My smile made my sunburned cheeks sting and I didn't care.

"I've never been able to deny you. Ever. However long we have, we'll spend it together."

The only reply I could manage was another scorching kiss, but it was enough.

Forever. That was how long we had.

———

Two days later, as I was about to scrub my last length of deck, Lou appeared at my side. Her mouth was set in a thin line, and her hands fidgeted, as if she wasn't quite sure what to do with them.

"Will you come with me?" she asked, and I quickly scrambled to my feet, following after her to her cabin. She'd done this a few times the day before, always looking for my advice or a moment of my time. Behind closed doors, she needed something very different from me, and I was only too happy to give it.

This time though, a dress that swirled and shimmered in a dozen shades of blue was laid out on the sofa.

"We'll be arriving at Kiril's this afternoon. I want you to wear this when we see him," she said, shaking it out. Its cut and design were even more elegant than the dress she'd worn in Beldridge Landing.

"Another one of Maro's angry ex-lovers?" I asked.

She grinned, and the openness of it, the good humor made me heat up. "No. An Oarian noblewoman whose husband was trying to trade her for a new horse."

"Trade her?"

"He told her it was a very fine horse. She tied him to a chair and ran away, eventually making her way to me."

"She paid you in dresses?" I ran my hand over the blue fabric. It was light and cool to the touch, like it had been spun from the ocean underneath us.

"She paid me in jewelry. Quite a lot of it. We had it melted down, but she also left us that dress." She pressed it to her chest, and then glanced up at me through her lashes. "Will you wear it today?"

I wrinkled my nose. "It doesn't look very practical."

"We'll take other things too. But Kiril will respect you more if you're dressed this way."

I sighed. Not too long ago, I would have been fascinated and scandalized in equal parts by a dress like this. Now, though . . . "I'm so tired of dressing according to the rules and expectations of men."

Lou kissed my cheek. "I know. But if you go dressing the way you normally do, he'll see a ship's girl when I need him to see a queen. The scale of the request has to match what's on offer, otherwise he'll refuse it for not being worth his time."

She wouldn't force me if I said no. We were past that now, but there was a fine tremor in the way her fingers held onto the material. The outcome of this meeting with Kiril wasn't a sure thing, and if she needed me to play a part to facilitate our success, I wouldn't refuse.

I played with the fabric, my fingers twitching nervously.

"George?" she said.

"This doesn't feel right."

She sighed. "You don't have to wear it for long."

"No." I took her hand. "Kiril. You shouldn't have to give up your ship and your crew for me."

She pulled me to her, fingers sliding in the leather of my belt. "I would give up everything for you."

"But this is your life. This. The *Siren*." We'd had this conversation nearly hourly. While I was confident Lou and I would spend our days together, I couldn't understand why she was so willing to walk away from the ship that was her home and the crew who was more of a family to her than her own family might ever have been.

"Maro knows what to do. There are always sacrifices for freedom."

It still didn't sit right with me. She'd already given up so much. But there was no way for me to win this argument. She wouldn't let me stay on the ship and risk the crew, and I wouldn't leave without her. I would have to make peace with one pain or the other.

Lou helped me dress. The neck and shoulders of the dress were covered in heavy gold embroidery and bright beads and stones that trailed down flowing sleeves. I lifted it, and the front floated away from the back. A line of ribbons dangled from the separated halves on each side.

"Let me do that for you," she said.

I would be the first to admit I wasn't very worldly. I'd spent the better part of my life trying not to be noticed in a very small country with little access to what lay beyond its borders.

But even I could tell I was being seduced while being dressed at the same time.

The collar weighed heavily on my neck and shoulders, but beyond that, I might as well have been naked. Lou said there were no undergarments to be worn underneath it, but there were enough layers of fabric that the essentials would be covered, even if there was nothing to hide the shape of my body.

Her fingers brushed softly over my skin as she tied each of the tiny ribbons, starting at the top nearest my arm and ribs and slowly working her way down, fixing each one with care. The sensation scrambled my mind.

When she finished, I caught her hands as she stood up and pressed the small, silver circle between our palms.

"Take this," I said.

She stared at the bracelet, which I'd taken to wearing strung around my neck, and pinched it between her fingers. "How do you still have it?"

"Because you gave it to me. I couldn't leave it behind. It was all I had left of you."

Lou slid the bracelet over her wrist, and her expression as she watched it turn was unreadable. "Our years together have always been the best part of my life. You've always been the best part of me."

We were the moon and the tide, the push and the pull. We'd never been apart, and now we'd be together until the end.

22

When we arrived, it was hard to tell we were anywhere. Maro gave the command to lower the anchor and furl the sails, but all I could see were mountains covered in green and great pillars of rock that stood straight from the surf, towering over the *Siren*'s tallest mast.

"Someone lives here?" Rosie asked. We stood at the rail, watching waves roll up to the shore.

"Kiril likes his privacy," Maro said as they joined us. They looked up and down at my dress, and I pulled my shoulders back, waiting for their verdict. "You've come a long way, princess."

I bit my lip. "I'm sorry if I've been inconvenient."

They gave me a half smile, and the sun might as well have risen across their face. "It's been good having you here." They glanced toward Lou, who was coming toward us. "She's been better for it."

"Who has?" Lou's hand was on the small of my back, warm through the thin layers of material, and she glanced around us. "Where's Ender?"

"Here, Captain!"

Lou said that Kiril's lair was inland and unreachable by the *Siren*. The crew lowered a boat to row us ashore. It took some work to get me down the ladder in the filmy dress, but I'd done more difficult things in very recent memory.

Ender rowed. Rosie and I sat together, with Lou facing us at the stern and Maro at the bow. I'd told Rosie we could say our farewells on the ship, but she'd insisted on coming with us as far as she was allowed, and Maro had relented.

The *Siren* sat silent beyond us, rolling gently as we bobbed away. A surprising pang swelled to life in my chest. Even if I hadn't always been happy there, the ship had been integral to my escape. Once I'd grown used to the dead fish and tar smell, it really hadn't been bad.

I thought Ender would take us onto one of the beaches where the waves crashed, but instead, he steered the longboat at an inlet that led to a swiftly flowing river.

The surf and the wind died away as we went upstream. Skinny, gray trees with long roots that dangled into the water like fingers lined the banks and crisscrossed overhead. I did my best not to be alarmed when slithery, scaled animals poked their heads out of the murky water to watch us pass or dangled from branches and blinked their flat eyes at us.

The farther upriver we went, the quieter the world became, until the only sounds were the steady splash of the oars as Ender and Maro rowed and the periodic shriek of unseen birds above us.

"This is very ominous," Rosie said.

"Well, of course," I said. "He's not a very secret member of a very secret pirate organization if he has a sprawling estate on the coast, is he?"

Maro snorted. "Estate."

Lou was smiling with a particular gleam in her eye.

"What?" I asked.

"You'll see. Easy on the oars." She glanced at Ender, who lifted his oars out of the water.

The longboat drifted around a bend in the river, and the air opened up above us again, the trees stretching to the sky. We were in a pool so big, it might have fit the entire palace in Redmere City within it. At the far side was a waterfall that cascaded down from a cliff so high, I could barely see the top of it.

I thought the thing in the middle of the pool might have been a wrecked ship at first, some poor vessel that hadn't escaped the edge of the waterfall and the punishing impact of the water as it fell. But on second glance, it revealed itself as several boats piled on top of each other, like they'd been dropped there from the sky. They weren't moving; they didn't even appear to be floating, as though the pile descended all the way to the bottom of the pool and had attached itself there.

"Kiril's estate," Lou said.

The tower was an amalgamation of railings and decks, with long posts that looked like columns but were undoubtedly repurposed masts. It was five or six floors high, although the top few leaned so precariously, I hoped no one ever ventured up there.

"Where did it come from?"

"Myrtle," Lou said ominously.

"Who?"

"Kiril's pet sea monster."

I laughed. "Very funny."

Lou's face was utterly serious. "She guards the opening of the pool. When I said we couldn't bring the *Siren* upriver, I didn't mean it was impassable, only that it would draw too much attention. A boat like ours is too small for her to notice unless we make a great deal of noise with the oars, but the bigger ships that come up here, she'll tear them apart."

Wordlessly, Maro picked up a large trunk that I suspected Lou had packed full of useless dresses and heaved it over the side of the longboat with a splash.

"What did—" My question was cut off by a great churning of water, before the trunk was enveloped by tentacles the size of tree trunks and pulled beneath.

Rosie gasped. "A cephyr."

"Told you they were real, little miss." Ender said.

I watched, shocked. The long, swirling limbs broke the water a few more times, as if searching for any more tasty morsels, before the surface finally subsided.

"She's not very friendly, but she does have an insatiable appetite," Lou said flatly. "The wood that makes up Kiril's fortress is what remains of the ships that tried to breach the island and found Myrtle instead."

"Is this the only way in?" I asked.

"There's a back way beyond the waterfall, but it's treacherous. Besides, we want Kiril to know we're coming. He doesn't like to be surprised."

Ender nudged the boat alongside a small jetty, barely more than a jumble of rocks that stuck out from one side of the structure, using his oar to brace.

"Well," he said. I glanced over my shoulder. His smile disappeared under his beard and pushed his cheeks up so high, his eyes vanished under his bushy eyebrows.

My stomach knotted. This was it.

It was difficult to hug someone in a wobbling boat while they held on to an oar that was the only thing keeping you from floating underneath a waterfall, but I did my best.

His big hand gently patted my back. "Take care, lady."

I hugged him harder. "I will. Thank you. Look after Rosie."

He laughed. "I will so long as she doesn't have a knife in her hand."

Lou and Maro had already exited the boat, and they helped me navigate my way out with my skirts trailing behind me. Rosie followed after me, and everyone turned their heads discreetly away as we cried for a moment and whispered our goodbyes.

"You'll always be queen in my mind," Rosie said.

"You'll always be the best friend and sister I've ever had."

Eventually, Ender helped Rosie back in, enfolding her in his big arms and giving me a reassuring smile.

Lou and Maro were speaking in hushed tones. Maro looked

unhappier than usual, but Lou put a reassuring hand on their arm, and they stilled. There were no hugs between the two of them, only a quick clasp of hands before Maro was climbing back into the longboat and Ender pushed it away into the pool. I expected Lou to wait until it disappeared around the bend, but once they were no more than ten or eleven oar strokes from the jetty, she strode toward me, chin raised, eyes clear.

"Let's go, then."

Two guards waited at the point where the pile of rocks became more uniform. Both were dressed in a ragged variety of shirts and vests, trousers that had been mended too many times to hold their shape, and boots that were more scuff than leather. Both had their hands on their swords. One smiled widely at Lou as we approached. The other eyed me in a way that would have made me nervous a few weeks ago but today only made me tired.

"Cinder!" the smiling man said. "We knew you'd be back."

"You shouldn't be so happy to see me," she said. "I told you I'd cut your lying tongue out if I ever saw you again."

His smile vanished, but his friend did not seem to be so easily dissuaded. He jutted his chin at me and said, "Did you bring Kiril a peace offering?" When I curled my lip at him, he laughed and took a step forward, but suddenly Lou was in front of me.

"If you touch a hair on her head or a thread on her dress, you'll wish I'd stopped at cutting out your tongue."

He puffed up his chest and squared his shoulders. His sword hissed as he pulled it partway out of his scabbard. Tension coiled in Lou's spine, but the other man, now unsmiling, put a hand on his fellow guard's shoulder and said, "We'll tell Kiril you're here."

"He already knows I'm here."

"Do you have any weapons?" the first one asked.

Lou sneered at him. "Do you think I'm that arrogant?"

Weapons had been discussed before we'd left the *Siren*. Specifically, Lou had said we wouldn't be bringing any. "There can be no suspicion that we're here for any purpose other than what I say," she'd said. "Armies have tried to kill Kiril and failed. We can't disrespect him by implying we think we can do better."

"If you don't have weapons, how are you going to cut out our tongues?" the younger guard taunted. Lou stared at him wearily.

"You should see what she can do with a tarnished bell and a length of rope," I said.

His eyes lit on me, sneer growing, but before he could say anything, his colleague rounded on him. When the older man's fist connected squarely with his jaw, he yelped and fell to the ground.

"I'm sorry, Cinder. My lady." The older guard knocked me a salute the way the crew had on the *Siren*. "He's young and keen to prove himself."

Lou snorted. "He won't last."

The young man clutched his face and whimpered beneath us.

"No, likely not. They never do." The old man stepped aside to let us pass. "On your way."

Kiril's tower was as confusing on the inside as it had been from the outside. We walked through narrow halls, climbed through gangways that led to new decks, and went back down again. Sometimes, I was sure a doorway would open into empty air and instead discovered another passageway. The whole structure groaned endlessly as we walked.

Occasionally we passed other people, mostly men. Some had the bearing of soldiers like the men at the door had. Others were stooped and cowering, as if they hadn't been outside in years. Every single one of them stared at Lou with terrified eyes. The word "Cinder" was an endless whisper on the stale air. A few got too close, but a sidelong glance or a clearing of her throat had them slinking away once more.

It was a surprise when we emerged into sunlight again. I held my hand to my eyes, squinting.

"Almost there," Lou said. It was hard to tell given the jumbled construction, but it seemed we were on the third or fourth floor. I followed her along an open deck not entirely unlike the *Siren*'s and up a winding staircase that might have at one time led to a quarterdeck.

Lou paused with her foot on the first step. "When we see him, I'll do all the talking. No matter what I say, you must not react."

I nodded impatiently. "Yes, yes, we've been over all of this."

"Georgie," she said. "No reaction. Trust that I've known him a long time and I know the best way to ensure your safety."

I pressed a palm to my heart. "Whatever you say, Captain."

Away from the muffling sound of waves and wind as we were, our feet echoed oddly. Instead of a quarterdeck, at the top of the stairs were two wooden doors engraved with wolves and bears and inlaid with flecks of gold that said once the wood had been painted or even gilded. Maybe they'd sat at the end of some conquered king's throne room. Now, they announced our arrival to the monster's lair.

The room inside was larger and airier than I'd expected. Looking up, it became apparent that the upper two levels were in fact one, with high ceilings and wrought chandeliers that trailed congealed drips of wax from hundreds of evenings of celebration. This had once been a fighting ship, and the gun ports were open on each side, letting in light and a soft breath of wind. The floor was covered in a variety of ornate rugs and furs, leading to a raised dais where—

"Cinder."

My shoe scuffed on a carpet, and I nearly tripped as it rolled up under my foot. Lou was three paces ahead of me with all the bearing of a queen. Head up, shoulders square, she walked down the long room to the creature who sat on the throne.

"Hello, Kiril."

Kiril was hunched in his chair, looking like a vulture waiting for its prey to die. He was monstrous without being overly tall. Stooped, with wrinkled, gray skin, and bony fingers that looked more like claws. "Have you come back after all?"

"It's good to see you again," Lou said.

His laughter rattled like crumpled paper. "You traitorous

bitch. Don't think your lies fool me." He grinned, and what teeth of his weren't missing were a sickening yellowish brown. But his eyes were sharp. A hunter's gaze. Eyes like those missed nothing.

A scream like a dying animal's or an injured child's sounded behind us, followed by a whooshing as a great bird flew over our heads, close enough that I ducked instinctively. Lou remained unmoved. The bird, a huge green and red thing with a tail as long as my arm, settled on the head of Kiril's chair.

"Liar!" it shrieked. My heart beat so loud, I was surprised it didn't join the echo of Kiril's hands as he clapped and gargled out another round of laughter.

"You remember my pet, don't you?" he asked Lou.

"Liar!"

"She's always been an excellent judge of character."

The bird took a hopping step onto his shoulder and nuzzled at one of his cheeks. He made wet kissing noises, and she returned them. They cuddled like lovers might, and for a minute it was as if we disappeared, left to be unwilling spectators.

"We're here for passage." Lou motioned to me to come forward. "This woman has escaped a terrible man."

Kiril rolled his eyes and clucked his tongue. "I'd heard that was what you were doing now. Seems an awful waste of talent, though I'm sure the market for your services is nearly endless. A terrible man. Is that true?" His eyes landed on mine.

Silence fell. Lou had said I shouldn't speak, but no one answered for me, and Kiril waited.

Finally, I cleared my throat. "Yes."

"Did he beat you?"

I risked a glance at Lou, but her face was impassive.

"No."

"Burn you?'

"No."

"Mark you in any way?"

Only because I hadn't stayed long enough. "He would have killed me."

"Would have?" Kiril waved his gnarled hand, and the bird squawked and hopped, flapping its wings before settling again on his shoulder. "Cinder, what is this? I don't deal in hypotheticals. You can't bring me someone whose husband *would* have killed her. Especially when her husband is clearly someone important. Look at her. I like to keep a low profile, and requests like this don't help."

"You'd prefer she waited until I was dead?" I didn't mean to say it, but fear and nervous energy radiated from me, and the words squeezed their way out.

A moment of stunned silence filled the room, only interrupted by slow, dry laughter rasping over the air, growing slowly in pitch and volume. Only as the bird began to bob its head did I realize she was the one laughing, but soon enough, Kiril joined her.

Lou said nothing, but she rested a hand on the small of my back. A silent warning not to speak again.

My cheeks flamed, and my heart pounded in my chest, but I bit my lip and cast my eyes down again.

"Passage," Lou said, "and assurances of safety."

"This seems like quite a lot of work when this woman's husband sounds no worse than many others," Kiril grumbled in his chair. "What are you offering me in return?"

"Andel's death." She pulled something out of her pocket and tossed it at Kiril's feet. The red ruby clattered to the floor.

The bird croaked. Kiril belched. "Was that your doing? Very messy. A bell? Yes, I'd heard about that. I'm sure Maro didn't approve at all. He was an annoyance, but he died too easily under your hand to be worth the favor you're asking in return."

"You've had a price on his head for years. He's taken more of your crews and sunk more of your ships than anyone else."

Kiril waved dismissively. "I can always find more men for crews."

"You offered a fortune for his death. Don't pretend you didn't. I don't want money," Lou snarled. "I want passage in exchange."

After a silence, Kiril patted the wide arm of the chair, knocking a small, brass bell to the ground with a gentle tinkling sound. The bird shrieked and launched into the air. It swooped a wide circle around before diving down to grab it and drop it into Kiril's lap. Kiril chuckled and shook the bell.

A door opened behind him, and a thin man clad only in ragged maroon pants ran in, dropping his head in a subservient bow as he rounded the chair. I could count every single one of his ribs under his skin.

"Bring me something to eat," Kiril said. "None of that foul quail thing from last week. It made me sick for days."

The servant retreated. Kiril tickled the bird's chin. It chuckled softly as the feathers on its neck arched, then settled into place again.

"No."

Kiril uttered the single word, and the room dropped into creaking silence again.

"No?" Tension rippled down Lou's spine.

Kiril's eyes narrowed, and I had the thought that this was a man who was rarely questioned. "It's not enough. Look at her." He pointed at me. "She's clearly a woman of consequence. One dead man who was motivated by glory? It's not enough. What else can you give me, Cinder?"

"I'm not—" Damn Prince Beverly. Damn him. How many times would I have to explain that I wasn't anyone? I buried my hands in my skirts, wanting to rip the dress off. This wasn't who I was, any more than I hadn't been the princess in rabbit-trimmed splendor.

"We aren't here to play games," Lou said. "How many others would have—"

"You!" Kiril said abruptly. He pointed at me, and I flinched, but when I glanced at Lou, she gave me the barest of nods.

"Yes," I said.

"Come here."

I might have been standing there my entire life for all my legs were willing to take the first step. Kiril loomed, a breathing husk straight out of a child's nightmares, and I did my best to hold myself upright. Lou had said I needed Kiril to respect me for him to understand the value of what we were offering. But with every step, the breeze floated through my dress and tugged at the ribbons that Lou had so carefully tied earlier, and I was left feeling exposed.

I stepped up on the dais, and Kiril leaned forward, motioning me to come closer. An overwhelming smell of perfume wafted toward me—and underneath it, something sour and rotten, like a decaying carcass left out in the sun.

He grabbed my chin suddenly, his grip bruising. Kiril turned my chin side to side, squinting at me. "Is your husband very rich?"

"Yes," I said between clenched teeth.

"Powerful?"

"Yes."

"Are you afraid of him?"

I didn't want to be. It seemed like a million years ago that I'd stood by his side. Yet the prince was the reason I couldn't stay on the *Siren* with Rosie, so his reach remained undeniable.

"Yes."

Kiril grinned and then let go of me so suddenly that I stumbled, nearly tripping over the trailing hem of the dress.

The door opened again, and the servant returned, carrying a tray full of strong-smelling cheeses and salted meats. Kiril picked through the tray and squeezed a strip of some sort of preserved fish between his lips. He chewed, eyes closed, mouth working quickly like a rodent's, while his gray skin hung from his bones. The cowering servant scurried away, closing the door behind him. I stayed where I was, not daring to check behind me for a signal from Lou.

Kiril swallowed and glanced up, leaning back as if surprised I was still there. He split a piece of cheese between his fingers and waved at me in dismissal. I didn't bow. Instead, I swept my skirts free and descended to the carpeted floor. When I reached Lou again, I turned so we stood shoulder to shoulder. Whatever happened next, we would face it together.

"It's not enough," Kiril said around his meal.

"Not enough!" Lou's voice was sharp, and I could sense the tremor that went through her as she fought for control. "Andel was—"

"He was a drop in the bucket. Look at her, Cinder. A face like that? Do you know how much you'd have to pay me to keep her safe on a ship?" His smile was thin and malicious. "You know exactly how much a woman's safety is worth among men. No. It's impossible."

"But—"

"No." Kiril leveled a fearsome stare at her. "It's not enough, Cinder. This lady is worth ten times what you're offering. If you want to bring her to safety, you'll have to offer me something else. What do you have?"

I should have come in my ship clothes. The dress shifted over my skin, reminding me how naked I was under only a few sheer layers of fabric.

Look at her. A face like hers.

I had nothing else to offer. Once upon a time, I would have lain with the prince to survive, no matter how much I didn't want it. Now, I had Lou, the memories of her hands on me, her mouth on mine. If I held on to that, surely I could bear someone else touching me if it meant a chance at the future.

Davi had said it wasn't so bad. It would be my choice. As unpleasant as it was, I would be the one making it.

"Well?" Kiril's fingers flexed on the arms of his chair, and the bird at his shoulder laughed its dry, menacing laugh.

"I'll give you myself."

I blinked, my skin going hot with the dawning horror that the words hadn't been mine.

They were Lou's.

Like the man at the gate, through my own stupidity and self-assurance, I never saw it coming. The blow of what she said rocked me off my feet, and I stumbled back.

"You can't!"

The bird screamed and took to the air, circling around us. "Liar! Liar!"

Kiril clapped his hand and cackled.

"Lou, you can't!" My voice rose until it mingled with the bird's. A lie. She had to be lying.

"Now that's something worth bargaining for!" Kiril lurched down the stairs to stand in front of Lou, a vicious lizard looking for a meal.

"The lady," Lou said in a rush. "Safe passage anywhere she asks. No one will touch her."

"Well, I can't swear that no harm will come to her once she's out of my care." He licked his fingers. "The lady here doesn't seem very steady on her feet."

"Promise me, Kiril!"

His tongue swept over his bottom lip like one of the slimy creatures that inhabited the swampy river outside.

"Twenty years."

"Twenty years of what?" I said.

"Service." He grinned at me. "You want safety and security? I need trustworthy people in my service, and Cinder here is as diligent as they come."

"No!" I clung to Lou's arm. Twenty years of murder. She couldn't do that for me. "Lou, you can't."

Lou's spine was taut. "Ten years."

"Lou!"

"Eighteen. Don't test me, Cinder. Your friend is very pretty, and my men have been lonely as of late."

"Fifteen."

He sneered. "Seventeen."

I flinched when she spat in her hand and held it out to him. The tears flowed freely down my face when he shook it firmly.

"Welcome back, Cinder." He slithered back to his chair. "Say your goodbyes." He rang the bell again. Another servant, just as hunched and trembling as the previous one, reappeared almost immediately. "Send someone to collect the lady."

No. No, no, no. Lou, Lou, Lou. It was an endless babble repeating in my head. She—she'd left me. She'd traded herself for me.

She'd *lied* to me.

"You promised!" I wanted to launch myself at her. Claw her eyes out. She would be of no use to Kiril if she couldn't see.

"Georgie. For the time we have." Her face was beautiful and stoic as she came to me. "It's the only way."

"You knew!" I spat. "You knew it was going to come to this, and you lied to me!"

"I have never lied to you."

"You did! Maybe not in your words, but you knew what I thought! You knew what I wanted, and you want it too! We would have gotten there, Lou." But not after seventeen years. She'd said he'd broken her already. She wouldn't survive, not with her soul still intact.

"George," she said, and her kind smile broke my heart.

"You can't lie to me. Your heart, your body. Those things can't lie!" When I went for her, she took me, wrapping me close before I could inflict any harm.

"I know," she said into my hair, kissing it. "I know."

On the day she leaves, we stand in front of my father's house—she in her smart uniform, her hair cut short to look like a boy's, and me in my new dress, with its itchy high collar and boots that pinch my toes.

"Come with me," I beg.

"I'll come back," she says.

"No. Come now!" Fat tears of a heartbroken child roll down my cheeks.

She scuffs a polished boot in the dirt. "I'll write to you every day."

"That's not good enough!"

Lou gives me a guilty smile. "I know."

The sob that broke out of my chest was eight years old, grown sharp and jagged where it had lived in my chest. I sagged under the weight of it.

"Shh. Georgie." She petted my hair. "It's the only way. I always knew it would be this way."

"No." I pushed back, stumbling toward Kiril. "Take it back. We'll leave. I don't need anything from you."

Kiril grinned. "But I need Cinder, and she has given her word now."

"Then take me." I wasn't above begging. "Use me." Whatever he wanted, I would do it. Lou had already survived too much at his hands. I would take her place if it meant saving her like I hadn't been able to eight years ago.

But Kiril only laughed, and I knew what I looked like to him: a spoiled princess in a fancy dress with nothing to offer.

"Please," I said, but Lou took my wrist and gently tugged me back. "No. No. This isn't right. It's not fair. You can't—" I shook my head against her chest, smearing snot and tears, but I didn't care about the mess.

"Yes." She pulled my face up between her palms, holding it so we could gaze at each other. "I told you. You are the best part of me. Kiril can't take anything else."

"Seventeen years." I hiccuped over the words.

"It's only time. We've waited this long. What are more years?" She smoothed her thumbs over my cheeks before kissing them.

"I love you," I said, but the fight in me was dying. She had never been mine to keep.

"I know," she said, then kissed my lips quickly. "I love you too, Georgina Elizabeth Millicent Cressida. All your names, all your smiles. The little indent that forms between your eyes when you frown, and the dimple that hides except when you laugh." She traced my skin as she spoke. "I love that you never gave up on me and that we found each other again. When seventeen years are over, whatever is left of me will come for you."

Her hands were in my hair and she kissed me passionately,

like we could breathe and find a way to live again in each other's mouths.

The hall filled with a clattering as men, dressed in the same patchwork as the guards at the end of the jetty, swarmed the room. There were thirty or more, and they carried an array of wicked-looking knives and swords. I buried my face in Lou's neck, not wanting to see them, not ready for our time to be over.

"Come, Lady Georgina, let's bring you home. Your people are waiting."

Dread turned my insides to stone at the sound of that voice. The title.

Lou moved first, instincts honed in a way mine would never be. She placed herself between me and the new arrival, a protective hand on my arm, but I knew it would do no good.

Standing next to Kiril was Prince Beverly of Redmere.

23

"Dearest," my former future husband preened, "it is so good to see you're all right."

"What is he doing here?" Lou asked Kiril. Her fingers dug into my wrist hard enough to bruise.

Kiril was feeding a lump of cheese to his bird, and he glanced at Lou like he'd forgotten we were still in the room. "Who? The prince? He and I have known each other for years."

"Years?" I asked.

Kiril's smile was sickening. "The prince is an astute businessman. I've been providing guards to him for years."

"Guards?" My stomach heaved. "The City Guard?"

The prince shrugged. "Rebellions are very expensive to end. I prefer to think of the Guard as an investment to save significant costs in the future."

And in the process, they'd enforced his vision of modesty and morality, made neighbor suspect neighbor, and terrorized us.

"But how do you pay them? Redmere has no money—"

But we had men. Hungry men who would do anything to feed their families. We had ships, so many lost at sea, never to be heard from again. Kiril was a man who could get you anything for a price.

There were too many pieces to fit together. Kiril. Beverly. Women at the gates of the naval yard waiting for news of husbands and brothers. Ships that had disappeared even though Captain Cinder was no longer prowling the seas.

"What happens to them?" I asked.

"My crews need replenishing, and good servants are hard to find. And the weakest ones . . . well . . . Myrtle is always hungry." Kiril shrugged.

I swayed in stunned horror.

Hundreds and hundreds of men lost and families destroyed, for what? For the prince's greed? For a sea monster's appetite?

Lou only had one question. "Why is the prince here now?"

Kiril waved an indulgent hand. "He arrived yesterday. Had the most astonishing story about a princess kidnapped by pirates in broad daylight." He bowed courteously to me. "I can only assume he meant you."

I scowled at him.

"Georgina." Beverly held out a hand. "It's time to go."

I tucked my hand in Lou's and glared at him. "I won't go anywhere with you."

"Kiril," Lou said. "This was not our arrangement."

He leered at her. "Wasn't it though? Safe passage." He pursed his lips. "I can't think of anywhere safer for this lady than with a husband who is so clearly concerned for her welfare that he would come all this way to ask for my help in finding her. You delivered her into my lap without my having to lift a finger."

"You never do any of your own dirty work anyway," Lou sneered.

"He's not my husband!" I shouted. "We were never married. He has no claim on me."

Kiril's eyes widened, but his astonishment was insincere. "Prince. Is this true?"

Beverly smirked. "A technicality."

"He's going to kill her," Lou said. "Would you break our agreement? You promised her safety."

"Kill her?" The prince's expression was all innocence. "Would I have gone to all this trouble if I meant to hurt her? My country needs a queen, and the people are already in love with Georgina."

"You said you wanted a martyr. I heard you!"

Kiril sighed. "Prince, your pretty bride is growing shrill. You'll have to deal with that when you return home."

"Oh, I plan to." He smiled, and I bristled against Lou.

"Kiril," Lou said. "Stop with these games. He has no claim on her. Let her go, as we agreed."

The broker shook his head and strode toward us. "Not married, you say?"

"No," I said through clenched teeth.

He studied me with murky green eyes before he pursed his lips with a tsk. "Cinder!"

"What?"

His narrowed gaze swung to her. "Now is not the time for impoliteness. You are barely in my service again. It's not too late for me to kill you."

The seconds before she spoke felt endless. "Yes. How can I be of *service*?" She leaned on the last word, and it made Kiril chuckle darkly.

"I need you to perform a very simple service for me as a captain."

"I left the *Siren* to my crew. I'm not a captain anymore."

He waved an annoyed hand. "I have ships aplenty for you. You could never be anything but a captain, and now, I need you to do a captain's duty."

She sighed. All I could think was that there was no way she would survive seventeen years of being subservient to this man.

"What would that be?"

"Marry this couple."

I snorted. "Don't be absurd."

The prince clapped his hands. "A splendid idea."

Kiril said, "Well, Cinder?"

Lou stared at him with so much hatred on her face that a

weaker man might have fallen over dead. Kiril simply stared back with bland amusement.

The prince crossed to me. He looped his hand around my elbow and led me away, as he'd led me everywhere in Redmere.

"This is perfect! Romantic, even. I found you in the clutches of pirates and married you to save you! The people will be beside themselves when they hear the story."

"Let go of me!"

He pulled me closer and hissed in my ear. "Would you rather they hear that I saw you in the arms of a woman? Kissing her? Saying you loved her? Would you rather be a queen or a pariah?"

"You don't want someone like me beside you. On your throne. In your bed."

His grin was calculating and wicked, so much at odds with all the charm and consideration he'd poured on me in Redmere. "Yes, but the people are expecting your return. They ache for it. I worked very hard to spread the story of your terrible abduction, and they are outraged on our behalf. Besides, the alternative is that I kill you and Kiril kills your whore this very minute. Would you rather that?"

"Get your hands off me! You're the one who's disgusting!"

"George."

I stiffened at the sound of my name, so flat and defeated on Lou's tongue. If I didn't turn around, I wouldn't have to see the blank look on her face. But if I didn't turn around, I would have fewer and fewer opportunities to see her face at all, and I wanted to take every one of them.

Her smile was soft, but she slumped her shoulders. "Do as he says."

Kiril sneered. "I knew you'd see reason."

I started to shake my head, but Lou's lips thinned. My heart picked up. She had a plan. She must have one. Maybe this had been the plan all along? Maybe she'd known the prince would be here and this would be her only chance to kill him and set us free, once and for all.

Kiril strode back to his great chair. The bird squawked and shrieked. He flicked an impatient hand. "Get on with it."

I'd never stopped to consider what my wedding would be like. I'd spent so many years terrified someone would find out about my attraction to women. When a marriage had finally been on the horizon, the time after I'd gone to the palace and before Lou had taken me had been such a whirlwind, there hadn't been time to think about what a royal wedding would actually entail.

Now, as the prince pulled me into the space at the foot of Kiril's throne, I didn't think this situation would have ever occurred to me: marrying the Prince Beaverly of Redmere, in a secretive and villainous pirate leader's den, while my supposedly-dead-best-friend-turned-pirate-turned-lover stood between us, grim-faced but determined as she prepared to officiate the ceremony.

The prince took my hands, his expression solemn. It probably cut at him and his Redmerian sensibilities to have Lou as the one to marry us. Regardless of whatever pomp and circumstance he might have planned in celebration of our marriage, the actual wedding ceremony in Redmere City would have been a very grave thing performed by an ancient and serious priest. Here, the solemnity was shattered by the pirate captain with barely suppressed murder in her eyes and a shrieking bird who could only be silenced with more food.

"Marriage . . .," Lou said slowly. I shivered at the word. The Redmerian ceremony spoke about commitment and duty, about a wife's responsibilities toward her husband. If Lou planned to speak about the same, the odds were equal that I would start laughing or crying on the spot.

The prince squeezed down on my knuckles until they popped. "Behave," he said through clenched teeth.

Lou took a big breath, and her words tumbled out in a rush. "Marriage is an antiquated tradition invented by men more concerned with protecting power and heredity than happiness and partnership. Women have been subjugated into it because it provides security and, depending on if her husband is a prince or a pig farmer"—she gave Beverly a pointed glare, and two spots of pink formed on his cheeks, but his mouth was pressed shut—"a measure of power, always at the indulgence of her husband."

Kiril barked out an amused laugh, and his bird joined him. "Liar! Liar!"

"However." Lou inhaled. "Since the alternative to this particular marriage is death, and none of us are willing to accept that alternative, *today*"—another glance at the prince—"we are gathered to unite this man and this woman in a union neither of them especially want."

"Cinder..." Kiril growled.

She sighed. "Prince Beverly of Redmere. It's clear you want to marry this woman, but for the purposes of the official record which—" She glanced around. "Is anyone writing this down?"

"Get on with it!" Beverly said through clenched teeth. I couldn't stop the tremble of delirious laughter forming in my chest.

"Beverly of Redmere. You wish to be honored by marrying this woman, Lady Georgina Elizabeth Cressida Millicent—"

"It's Georgina Elizabeth Millicent Cressida," I said while my shoulders shook.

"It is!" Lou put a hand to her mouth in mock embarrassment. "I'm so sorry, lady. Prince Beverly. Do you—"

"Yes. I do."

Lou scuffed a boot on the wooden floor. "You didn't let me finish."

"Kiril." Beverly glanced over his shoulder.

"Yes, prince?"

"Does your captain here need all her fingers to work for you?"

Kiril wrinkled his nose. "I don't think so."

He turned back to Lou. "For every minute more of my time that you waste, I will have a guard cut off a finger. Am I clear?"

Lou rolled her eyes. "You didn't answer my question."

"What?"

"Do you understand the honor you are asking for in marrying George?"

He blinked rapidly at her, then at me, before he finally said, "Yes, I do."

"Excellent! George!" She clapped her hands and turned to me. "I won't repeat all of that. He's a swine, and a hateful swine at that. Are you sure you want to marry him?"

I cleared my throat. "Can you repeat the question in a way that doesn't make me a liar or cost you any fingers?"

She waggled her brows at me. "Given everything I've said, are you willing to marry him anyway?"

I waited. For what, I wasn't sure. Respite. A punchline. The bird to magically transform into a long-forgotten sea goddess who protected women lost at sea.

Nothing came.

I said, "I am."

Her smile was kind.

Seventeen years. We would be thirty-seven. Hardly ancient. Assuming I could survive a life with Beverly or—better yet— escape again. Maybe I'd find a way to get a message to Maro and Ender. Niall was dead, but the dressmaker was still there, although I had no doubt Beverly's intentions no longer included showering me with dresses.

"Traditionally, this would be the part where you kiss," Lou said. "But it's not—"

Beverly lunged forward. His kiss was rough, wet and demanding. I struggled against him to turn my cheek. My lips were for Lou only.

Still, his smile was satisfied when I opened my eyes again. "It's done. Kiril, I will be taking my wife and leaving now."

"Of course, prince. Pleasure to see you."

The prince's hand around my wrist was secure as he walked toward the door through which he'd entered earlier, but I dug my heels in. He glanced back to snarl, but I ignored him, already reaching for Lou.

"I love you."

She knocked a thumb to her forehead. "Stay alive, princess. I'll find—"

The building rocked so hard that the prince released my hand as we stumbled apart. I hit the ground awkwardly.

"What is—" Kiril started, but a second explosion caused the whole room around us to shudder again. Wood splintered, followed by a great groaning sound.

"George!" Lou scrambled toward me.

The building settled, and the grinding and cracking sounds faded, only to be replaced by the roar of people and heavy footsteps coming toward us. I barely had time to register it before the door we'd first come through at the far end of the room burst open again, and Maro and Ender pushed through. Their swords were raised high, and they screamed as they charged in, followed by what appeared to be the rest of the *Siren*'s crew.

"Guards!" Kiril shouted the single command, and his men approached, swords drawn.

"Captain!" Maro had a sword in each of their hands, and they tossed one to Lou.

She never saw the prince. Neither did I. Not until it was too late. In one perfect movement, her hand clasped the hilt of the flying sword, and she turned to meet whatever would come at her.

But the prince was already there. He plunged a knife into her body in a vicious motion. Lou's eyes bulged, and her mouth dropped open.

"No!" My scream was so loud that my throat hurt, my horror so complete that the room went silent and spun. The prince stepped away, and Lou staggered, one hand on her stomach as blood poured through her fingers.

I stumbled, reaching for the sword Lou dropped—though I didn't know what I'd do with it once I had it—when Beverly sank vicious fingers into my hair and pulled, dragging me to the door. Lou fell toward me, her face blank astonishment. A man rushed up behind her, sword raised, and she didn't hear him.

I grasped for every piece of furniture and corner I could to slow our progress. My scalp was on fire, and I struggled, ignoring the sensation of clumps of hair being ripped from my head.

Finally, Beverly slapped me, hand heavy on my cheek. "Enough of that."

Lou. I waited, fought him every step, but she didn't come.

I howled. Screamed. I only stopped when the tip of his blade pressed to my throat. The hilt was still slick with Lou's blood. Beverly's eyes were dark and furious.

"You will be quiet, and you will do as I say," he said through clenched teeth. "Or I will open you up from ear to ear right here."

Tears poured down my face. She wasn't coming. The building shuddered under us, and smoke rose up the sides and between the boards under my feet, but no one appeared on the winding path we'd come.

If she wasn't coming, then I would have to save myself. To do that, I would have to stay alive. I couldn't overpower him. Nothing had changed. I might as well be back in Redmere. The prince had outsmarted us all, and I would have to wait for him to slip.

But everything had changed. Lou. I'd found her. Loved her. I would hold those memories forever.

A small longboat with two sailors dressed in their painfully familiar Redmerian uniforms was tied off at the base of the stairs, on the far side of the tower from where we'd arrived. It would have been impossible to see from the river mouth.

The prince pushed me into it and I fell, banging my shins painfully against hard wooden planks. The murky water at the bottom seeped into my dress.

"Let's go," the prince said impatiently, stepping into the boat. The two sailors stared at me with wide, frightened eyes. Their fear was palpable. I knew their desperation, and now, I knew the cause of it.

I lunged for the side of the boat, but I wasn't fast enough. Once again the prince caught hold of my hair, wrenching me back until I hit my head on the opposite gunwale. Was this why he insisted we keep our hair covered? So it couldn't be used against us? If I survived this, I'd have to remember to cut it short. Maybe find a razor and shave it off entirely. I wouldn't let him have a scrap of power over me.

I shivered uncontrollably as the longboat pushed off. Behind us, Kiril's fortress was on fire. The bottom three floors were slowly consumed. People were visible on the uppermost levels. Some were still fighting, others running. It was impossible to see if they were the *Siren's* crew or Kiril's men.

Just as a few threw themselves over the railing, the whole building shuddered violently, and I watched in horror as it leaned to one side. Flaming bits plummeted, and as it tilted farther, men fell too, tangled with the burning wood. Great tentacles emerged from the water, dragging bodies and falling wreckage to the water below.

The structure collapsed. I watched it all for a moment, dispassionate. I would be sorry later for Maro and Ender if they'd been trapped inside. For Rosie, who I hoped had been left on the longboat or even sent back to the ship. Would she even know what had happened to me?

But right now, I could only grieve for Lou.

The waterfall's roar grew louder. We weren't rowing toward the river. Sheets of water plummeted down, but Beverly's men rowed around it expertly, finding the narrow passage that led to a darkened chamber beyond. Water splashed down next to us in a deafening cascade. The force of it would drive a person's bones to the very bottom.

The old dream where Lou stood on the bow of her sunken ship, reaching toward me, came back. Except now, it was the adult Lou, the broken one who tried so hard to be whole, who loved me with all her fractured heart. Her arms stretched out to me, welcoming.

Home. She would always be my home.

As we moved deeper into the cavern, the waterfall obscured the view of Kiril's ruined fortress and any sign of what might have happened to the *Siren*'s crew. The prince shouted orders, and we went on, into the darkness.

24

The sun was most of the way down when we reached the other side. Behind us, the island stretched up in a gray and green mountain that went on forever. Offshore, a two-masted ship flying Redmerian colors was anchored.

I was freezing. The tunnel had been damp and cold, and my dress was now fully soaked to my knees. The blow to my head had caused the skin to split open above my eyebrow, and it bled profusely for a while before congealing into something sticky along the side of my face. I couldn't stop my teeth from chattering, no matter how I tried.

We arrived at the side of the ship, and the prince climbed up first. I stared back at the island, imagining where the *Crimson Siren* lay. Had any of the crew returned? Did the others know that something had gone horribly wrong?

A nervous throat-clearing dragged my attention back to my surroundings. The two sailors were watching me anxiously, and when I glanced up, the prince and what must have been the entire crew were leaning over the rail, waiting. The prince's expression was pinched annoyance, and I wondered what plan I'd ruined. No doubt he'd meant for me to trail behind him to the deck so he could present me as the lost princess, finally returned.

I wasn't his toy anymore. But I also couldn't stay in this longboat forever. I hitched up my skirts, and one of the sailors gasped. Several of the ribbons that Lou had so painstakingly tied had come undone. My ankles and calves were exposed.

I made my way to the ladder hung along the ship's side. It was narrow, with wooden slats hung between stout ropes. In my ship's clothes, I would have been able to scramble up in no time. In this ridiculous Oarian dress, I had my work cut out for me, but if the sailors were aghast at the sight of my ankles, imagine their paralyzing terror if I stripped out of the dress entirely.

None of the soldiers dared to touch me, and I lifted my chin high as I came over the rail. The prince held out his hand for me to take like I'd once done at a party in a winding garden labyrinth, but I kept my hands firmly at my sides.

Beverly smiled to the assembled crew as if everything was going according to his plans. "Gentlemen. We have been successful. The princess has been returned to us, and in an effort to ensure her safety, not only have I rescued her, I have married her!"

A few muttered gasps came from the crowd. I stared them all down. They were all guilty in this. They'd brought the prince here and, as a result, were complicit in Lou's murder. I would never forgive any of them.

The prince's smile faltered, but he raised his hands and pressed on. "Please join me in celebrating the return of our beloved Princess Georgina!"

The cheer that went up was half-hearted, but Beverly seemed satisfied. He nodded to a man in an officer's uniform who began shouting orders to the sailors. They were quick to hop to their posts, but the atmosphere on the ship was not as confidently easy as it had always seemed on the *Siren*.

The prince held an arm out to me. "This way, my dear. I'm sure you'll want to put on something"—his gaze traveled up and down my body with barely concealed disgust—"appropriate for your station."

"This dress seems appropriate enough."

I ignored the curious gasps of the sailors at my insolence. Their fault. This was all their fault. I once thought I might save these people. What was there to save?

But that wasn't fair. They were prisoners as much as I was, forced out onto the ocean through poverty and starvation. Every single man who joined Redmere's navy knew the risks, the chance that they would be lost and never heard from again. But none of these poor souls knew the reason so many had been lost wasn't because of some vicious storybook monster—though it did turn out there was a literal monster at the end of their story —but the villain who ruled over all of them. They'd forfeited their lives so Beverly could keep their families crushed under his thumb.

The prince's solicitation turned cold, and he jerked my arm so hard I tripped, falling to the deck. When I didn't rise fast enough, he yanked me again, and small slivers of wood jammed themselves into my knees and palms. His decks needed scrubbing. I took some small joy in the imagined humiliation on his face if his new wife offered to scrub them.

The prince's cabin was at the stern of the ship, and was not nearly as large or as well appointed as Lou's. Everything smelled of mold and mice, and half the windows had been boarded over.

"Make yourself presentable," the prince snarled. "You're an abomination like that. Look at you. A ship full of men, and you parade yourself around like some dockside whore."

I laughed, because if he knew about my afternoon at Davi's, the shock might kill him right there. I was not the woman he'd plucked from obscurity.

He slapped me once more. "Cover your hair. Surely your corruption hasn't robbed you of the most basic modesty. You can't be seen with your head uncovered like that."

"You think I'll go back out there? So you can show off your prize?"

His eyes flashed. "I can't promise your life will be a long one, but every word of insolence that comes out of your mouth will make it shorter. Now do as you're told." Before I could say anything else, he marched out of the cabin, slamming the door shut. A few seconds later, a lock scraped into place.

I ran to the windows. Kiril's island was already disappearing into the distance, a black curl of smoke still rising from the trees. Too far to swim.

Lou had said drowning wasn't so bad.

But despite everything, I still wanted to live.

I found an officer's coat in a trunk beneath the narrow bed. It was moth-eaten and too large, but it was made of heavy wool, which warmed me. I slid into it and set about my next task.

Weapons.

Not that I expected the prince to leave a knife handy, or that I had real skill with any weapon, but if Lou—my heart stuttered over her name—could smash a man's face in with a bell, surely I could improvise something. Unfortunately, the room was decidedly sparse. Not even a curtain sash to try to strangle him with. The best I could do would be to pull a button from my coat, somehow force him to swallow it, and hoped he choked.

The sun went down. My shivering stopped. The bottomless well of grief still called my name, but I wouldn't let it win. Not today. Lou had been trying so hard to overcome her own grief and self-loathing. I couldn't succumb to mine. The best thing I could do for her was live to help the people she hadn't been able to save.

My stomach growled. I missed Rosie. I even missed Petru's foul fish stew. The prince did not return.

The remaining windows at the back of the cabin didn't open and were too narrow for me to escape through if I broke them. Instead, I pulled the chair up beside them and stared out at the stars.

We are lying at the top of a hill. It is my eleventh birthday. Lou and her mother baked me a pie made from fresh apples from the abandoned orchard at the edge of the property. We had eaten it all until our stomachs hurt, and then we had gone outside to watch the stars.

"Do you know the stars are different in different parts of the world?" Lou asks.

"No they aren't," I say, because how can they be? The stars are so high up and so far away. How can there be even more of them that I cannot see?

"They are. My brother sent us a letter. He wrote it six months ago, but it took forever to get home. He said the constellations are completely different where he is."

I lie there, considering, before I snort, even though my tutor says ladies don't snort. "That's impossible. They can't possibly change."

What if the stars did change?

How far would I have to go to see new ones? The thought filled me with a flighty panic, because the stars here were the ones that Lou knew when we were together. If they were different at home, that was suddenly one more part of her I could lose.

I couldn't stop my tears then. Couldn't stop the memories of my time on the *Siren*. Lou's flat eyes and the way they crinkled softly when she smiled. Her excitement with Maro as they'd planned how to defeat the *Perseverance*, and the gentle pull of her fingers in my hair after she'd brought me down from the mast.

What am I going to do with you?

What would I do without her?

He finally came long after the sun had set. He carried an oil lamp and a bottle of wine, and made a show of leaving his dagger with a soldier at the door. I sat in utter darkness, and he had to swing his lamp to find me, huddled in the corner. When his eyes met mine, he gave a short laugh. "Well, it's just the two of us for the night. How cozy." He shut the door and locked it, pointedly sliding the key into his coat pocket as if he thought I would dare rush him for it.

Instead, I turned my head back to the window. He loomed

behind me, the lantern flickering wild shadows off the walls around us and glaring off the windowpanes, blocking my view of the stars.

"I told you to make yourself presentable." His voice was dark and angry.

I ran my fingers through the tangled strands, peeling the hair away where it was stuck to my face with blood, pulling at the knots like he hadn't spoken.

"Did you hear what I said?"

"If you wanted me to make myself presentable, you should have brought me better clothes to wear." I poked my fingers through the holes in the coat. "This one's had other tenants."

His lip curled as he considered me, eyes darting all over my face and body. "Crawford will be so disappointed. He said you were such a beauty, and now look at you."

I couldn't help myself. I made sure he saw my smile before I said, "The count is at the bottom of the ocean, along with the rest of the *Perseverance*'s crew. He'll never see anyone again."

I thought he might strike me a third time. He tensed like he was considering it, but finally, he gave another short laugh and stood up, going to the table where he'd set the wine and pouring himself a glass. He toasted me, and then drank half of it in one go.

"You've changed, Georgina."

"Because I know what you are?"

He swallowed the rest of his wine, wiping his mouth with the back of his hand. He refilled the glass before he slunk toward me. I held still, but couldn't help my inhale when he dragged an index finger along my jaw, stopping with the tip of it pressed below my chin. He forced my face up toward his.

"Do I disgust you?" he asked. "Do you think I'm sort of monster? Do you know how much it costs to run a country? How much work it is when your military is incompetent and your people are too poor to do anything useful?"

"It's your fault they're poor," I said.

"They're poor because they're lazy," he hissed. "They're worth more to me sent off to Kiril than they are working five years in the fields."

"So he can feed them to his pet?"

His teeth were stained faintly purple as he smiled. "Still with that saintly heart. You truly were a find, Georgina. But you must know by now. Redmere and its people, they're all mine. I can do whatever I want with any person under my rule, including you." His finger flicked off the tip of my chin, the nail scraping my skin.

He stalked the cabin like a caged animal, circling long passes through the small space. He refilled his wine glass from time to time. I turned my gaze back outside. The stars were harder to see now, obscured partially from the glow of his light, but they were still out there. Still free.

"It's my father's fault, you know," he said, sometime later. I didn't reply. I didn't care how they'd come to their arrangement. "He knew, even years ago, that we were running out of options. He'd led a number of costly wars long before either you or I were born. Then, the rebellion came. The country never recovered."

Lou would never recover. Even if she'd somehow survived the prince's blade, she would never be the child I'd known again. The families who had lost their fathers and husbands, the surviving women that had almost no ways to earn a living, would never be the same.

"It must be very difficult for you." I shook my head scornfully.

His eyes were soft, a little glassy, as he said, "It is. But now that I have you—have you back, I mean—the people will love you. They'll love me for bringing you home. No one will question me after that."

"You don't still intend to make me queen?" I asked, suddenly horrified at the idea of a great ceremony in the city where he expected me to once again play the role of the blushing bride.

"Under any other circumstances, no, but given the ordeal

you've put me through and the period of mourning that's ending, you'll do." He took another drink and grimaced. "Not for long, of course. They'll want an heir. And since I know *what*"—his smile was deranged—"you are, I think we can agree that you're hardly appropriate to be the mother of a future king."

He'd talked about killing me three times since I'd come onboard this ship with him. Something had changed since the city. Whether it was the discovery of my sexuality or the trouble I'd caused, I'd never know, but the truth was clear. He was done being the charming prince. Done pretending he was in love. He would use me for as long as he needed, and then I would meet a quick end from a long drop off a palace tower.

"It's about power," he said. "If you have it, people respect you. Or they fear you, which is a kind of respect. Fear becomes respect once they know they're helpless."

He wasn't speaking to me, not directly. I happened to be in the room, but he was mostly indifferent to my presence.

He was drunk. His gaze was unfocused. I'd thought his swaying was from the motion of the ship, but as I took the time to really watch him, it became apparent he was moving to his own internal rhythm that had nothing to do with the waves rolling beneath us.

I straightened in my chair, and he blinked, giving me a half smile. "You hate me, don't you?"

I didn't know what to say. Of course I hated him. We both knew that. Admitting it would get me nothing.

But perhaps that was the point.

I dropped my eyes. "Yes, sir."

"Do you hate all men? Someone like you—with your . . . tastes . . . Did you think I wouldn't find out?"

I clasped my hands between my knees. He thought women were weak, subservient, and easily led. Anyone who escaped that vision was an aberration. Something to be hunted down and removed from proper society.

Like a pirate.

"It was Cinder." I made my eyes wide, as if I was just as horrified at my behavior. "She—I don't know. She's . . . not normal. She said things. Did things." I bit my lip, but when I glanced up through my lashes, he was watching me intently.

"Did she seduce you?" Something like fascination glimmered in his eyes.

I couldn't force myself to blush, so I settled for wringing my hands and nodding as though I were ashamed of anything Lou and I had done. In truth, I was only ashamed we'd waited so long to be honest with each other. The delay was Lou's fault. If by any miracle she'd survived, I might kill her for that.

The prince weaved back to the table to refill his glass. He swallowed and topped it up again before he held his hand out to me. I tightened against the instinctive flinch and forced myself to take it. His skin was as cool and smooth as that first day in the garden. Then, he'd been all kind words and sparkling gifts. Now, there was something dangerous curled just under his skin. He was more like Lou had been during those early days on the *Siren* than the man I'd first met.

"Power," he said slowly, "can be very seductive. I suppose Cinder had her own power. She certainly caused me enough problems. But"—Beverly gave a satisfied smile—"in the end, she was no match for me."

I tried not to picture the surprise on her face as his blade sank into her body. The pain mixed with regret as our eyes had met.

Beverly's hand came up to the side of my face. He traced where the blood had matted my hair to my forehead.

"That was unfortunate. You know I didn't mean to be so rough, don't you, Georgina?"

He had. He did everything with intention. Knew exactly how to exploit weakness. I had no doubt he'd only allowed himself so much wine because he was absolutely confident in his ability to control and overpower me.

I was done trying to show him the error of his ways.

He kept talking to me. He told me he was sorry for hurting me and threatening me. That he'd been angry and frustrated with how far he'd had to travel to win me back, as if I'd been a nervous bride who only needed some coaxing and sweet words to realize her intended was a good man after all.

The wine in the bottle disappeared, and he called for another. He told me more things. How he'd first heard of Kiril when he'd been searching for a way to end the rebellion. How close Redmere was to bankruptcy because the City Guard's salaries took every penny he could earn in taxes and trade. How, when he couldn't pay, he sent sailors to Kiril to meet their fate instead. How he sent others out in futile attempts to sell what goods we had to other nations, knowing full well they were as likely to be taken by pirates.

"But what loss is that? They're like mice, the people," he said. "They breed and multiply, and how are we supposed to take care of them? There are too many of you. Too many mouths, too many voices begging for help. Help yourself, I say. And that foul siren Cinder sitting just off our shores, waiting. If I blamed her for more than her share of the ships lost, what's the harm in that? Women like her don't deserve to exist."

He spoke to me like an equal and a toy at the same time. I poured the last two glasses for him, and he thanked me.

"Your brother said you could be a bit wild," he said as he toasted me. He was no longer able to hold himself upright, instead slumped against the headboard. "But I think we could still come to an understanding, you and I."

"Of course, Your Highness," I said.

"Don't think about trying to escape." He pointed a finger at me, smiling like we were sharing a good joke. "We're too far from land to swim, and I have loyal guards on the longboats."

More like terrified guards. But fear and respect were only two heartbeats apart.

"You would have made a spectacular queen, Georgina," he

said, stretching out along the bed. His voice thickened with every word. "It's a shame I'll have to kill you."

The fearsome Prince of Redmere snored.

For a while, I watched the stars. Hope whispered that Lou was somewhere, watching them too. Grief said I was truly alone now.

Neither hope nor grief would save me from the prince.

I waited until he was so deeply asleep that he didn't respond except to snore deeper when I pinched the soft skin between his thumb and forefinger. He lay on his side, the pocket I'd seen him put the cabin key into trapped between his body and the mattress. I rolled him slowly, waiting for any sign that he was about to waken, but the wine had him deep in its grasp.

I slipped my hand into his pocket, ignoring the warmth of his thigh through the fabric, and held my breath as I slowly withdrew the key.

He said he had loyal men guarding the longboats, and certainly, neither of the guards who had rowed us away from Kiril's had done anything to help me. But would they do the same if he weren't there? If he were locked away in this cabin where he couldn't hurt them, maybe I could convince one of them to let me by. I would figure out the longboat on my own and head back the way we'd come. I had no idea if the *Siren* would still be there or if any of her crew had survived, but I would be away from here.

The lock clicked under the key. I glanced once over my shoulder. The prince lay on his back with a contented half smile on his face, as if he were dreaming of something pleasant, although I shuddered to think what that might be.

My hand froze on the latch.

If he woke up and I was gone, what would happen? If a longboat was missing and the whole watch had let me slip by, they'd never see Redmere again. At best, he'd kill them. At worst, he'd ship them to Kiril. He'd dispose of the entire crew, even those currently asleep in hammocks below the decks, oblivious to my escape until the morning.

I couldn't condemn them like that.

Lou had asked me if I thought rebellions were as bloodless as passing notes in school. Perhaps I had. It had been easy enough to imagine the people, moved by Niall's pamphlets and their own desperation, rising up and storming the castle once more without placing myself among the crowd. But Lou's way was never bloodless, and even the prince had been forced to acknowledge her power.

Perhaps it only had to be bloody in name, not in the action itself.

He snorted and started, but settled quickly again as I turned the lock back in place. My heart squeezed in my chest, and I pressed a palm to the door to steady myself. I was making the right choice, but it was a hard one. I might not have the strength, but I couldn't leave him here to hurt others.

As I walked back to the bed, the cabin was so quiet that it pressed in on my ears. The static of waves and oceans swallowed everything until the prince and I were the only two people in the world.

His features were slack, mouth open slightly. I'd once thought him handsome, and he still was, so different from the rodent-like drawings on Niall's pamphlets. In sleep, you could believe he was a beautiful and kind ruler, the sort who loved his people and was delighted to be among them.

But in life, he was a monster, and always would be. Nothing would change that.

I hesitated a few steps away from the bed, envisioning how this would go. He was bigger than I was. Stronger, but maybe not after so much to drink.

All my nerves prickled, terrified that he might wake up at any moment. Slowly, lifting my skirts out of the way, I knelt on the mattress, watching where his body shifted as the bed sagged under my weight. His snoring continued as if nothing had changed.

I was on my knees next to him, one hand under his head to lift. He gave the same half smile again. Maybe he dreamed of a lover. A soft, pliable woman who was impressed with his might, who didn't know the difference between power and terror.

His head sank down again, lower than before, and his snoring stopped. I froze, gripping the pillow so tightly between my fingers, my knuckles had gone white. He brought a hand to his face like he might scratch his nose, but he missed and dragged his nails over his lips before his hand settled at his side once more.

He was snoring again as I pressed the pillow over his face. Every instinct said to rush, to push it down and put all my weight on it. But I forced myself to move slow, hoping to keep him relaxed until he was the frog in the pot, too late to save his own life.

My angle was wrong. I was kneeling to one side of him, and if he did wake up, it would be no effort to throw me off. Moving until I knelt over him with a leg on either side of his body and pinning his arms took a trick. I was too afraid to lift the pillow, but he didn't give any indication that my change in position had disturbed him.

I pushed down.

The snoring stopped.

I don't know if he woke up or if his body reacted on reflex. I only had a second of warning where his body tensed before he started to struggle. His legs thrashed behind me, and his arms pulled. I tightened my grip on the pillow, pressing it against his face, and squeezed against him with my knees. For a moment, it was like riding a wild horse. One of his hands managed to get halfway free, clawing at the inside of my thigh, but he couldn't untangle himself from my skirt.

He gasped beneath me, his whole body desperately trying to find the air it needed. I leaned into him until my cheek was nearly pressed against the pillow. I closed my eyes and held on.

Finally, his desperate attempts for breath stopped, more suddenly than I'd expected. The tension and struggle in his limbs peaked and subsided, flowing away like water. I stayed where I was, lying on top of him, waiting, my whole body tight and ready if this was all a ruse and he was waiting for his opportunity to fight.

It didn't come.

I unclenched my thighs first. His trapped hand fell to the bed, limp, leaving hot trails in my skin where his nails had bitten in, trying to dig their way free. When he still didn't move, I sat up, careful to keep the pillow over his face. I slumped back on my heels, watching his motionless chest.

Slowly, I unwound myself from his body, crawling until my feet slid to the floor, leaving my torso awkwardly arched so my arms still held him down.

He didn't rise.

I let the pillow fall to the ground.

In death, he was just a man. His features were frozen, eyes closed and mouth open, without any of the tension that would have spoken of his desperate last seconds.

Lou had told me she didn't regret killing any of the men who had terrorized her those first few years at sea. Looking down at the prince, I couldn't find any of the sucking grief that had consumed me when I watched the *Perseverance* go down while her crew shouted and screamed.

There was no pain to live with. Only relief. I would lose no sleep over killing this man.

In fact, I was suddenly very tired.

It might have been smarter to leave the cabin and continue with my earlier plan. I would beg the crew to let me go, maybe leverage my new status as their liberator. I would promise them nearly anything if only they would give me a longboat.

But suddenly, I could barely make my limbs—the ones that had confidently suffocated the tyrant of Redmere—work. The steps it would take to get to the door were too many for me to manage.

I sank to the ground and pulled myself to the wall, putting what little room I could between myself and the corpse on the bed. I pressed my head against the window frame and stared at the stars.

Maybe Lou was watching them too. Maybe she wasn't. Maybe Rosie and Ender were. Rosie would be hatching a plan to rescue me from Redmere again, even if it meant blowing up the harbor a second time.

I rolled my head to face the unmoving corpse on the bed.

Maybe I didn't need rescuing anymore.

25

I didn't intend to sleep, but the silence pressed down on me like I had pressed the pillow over Beverly's face. The next thing I knew, a glow on the horizon greeted me through the grimy window as I opened my eyes. I was still hunched against the wall, and my whole body protested as I slowly uncoiled myself. My joints popped and crackled as I stretched.

He was still there. His face and hands had lost their living flush, but he was still recognizably himself, and I felt only muted satisfaction as I gazed at his face.

A shout sounded through the door, followed by another, and I realized a similar one had woken me. Feet sounded on the wooden decks, and more orders were shouted.

I recognized one word.

"Cinder!"

My hands shook as I fumbled for the key, still in the lock from the night before. I squinted into the growing daylight as I pulled the door open. Around me, men moved with worried efficiency, climbing the rigging and rolling heavy cannons into place.

"Look sharp!" a voice called over my shoulder. I spun, but the speaker was obscured, too high on the quarterdeck for me to see. I hurried up the stairs, gathering my skirts around me. More of the ribbons had come undone in the night, so the dress was open to my knees. My feet were bare, I was still wearing the moth-eaten coat, and my hair was streaked with grime and blood. I must have looked like a creature rising from the deeps, if the startled look the officer at the wheel gave me was anything to go by.

"You—my—Your Highness. What—"

"What's going on?" I said, using the voice I hadn't needed since I'd thought I was a spy, staring down checkpoint soldiers in the city.

"The pirate—the—" He shook a jerky thumb over his shoulder. His face was nearly as white as the prince's. "It's the *Crimson Siren*, my lady."

I followed the direction he'd pointed. My heart skipped. The *Siren* bore down on us like an avenging angel, her sails spread out like great wings.

"Take your positions!" the officer called. Below, shouts of acknowledgment came from the crew as they gathered at the guns.

"Tell them to stand down," I said.

"What?" The officer was shocked, his eyes wide with fear.

"We will not fight. Tell them to stand down. Send someone up the mast to run up a white flag. We will surrender."

"Your Highness." The officer gaped. "Captain Cinder. She will —the prince—"

"Prince Beverly is dead."

His mouth was open so wide, a small family of swallows could have moved in and built a very cozy house inside.

"M-my lady," he stuttered.

"The prince is dead. I am his wife, and so, by rights, I am in command of this ship. Do you question that?"

His mouth snapped shut. He gave me a startled look, eyes moving up and down. He was no doubt wondering how the prince was dead and I was alive without a scratch on me, and weighing what that meant about me versus his fear of Captain

Cinder. Four vicious welts in the shape of fingernails had formed on my thigh, but he didn't need to know that.

I glanced at the ship behind us. She was closing the distance quickly. My whole body tingled with the knowledge that Lou was coming. I may not need rescuing, but the minute the *Siren* was close enough, I would fling myself around her and make her promise to never leave me again.

The officer pulled himself together, knocking me a formal salute. "Your Highness. We will do as you say." His white knuckles on the hilt of his sword said he didn't trust me. Still, he shouted the orders. Men stepped away from the cannons, and one sailor scrambled up the rigging with a long, white pennant tucked into his belt. Others brought in sails so that we slowed.

I stood at the stern as the *Siren* drew closer, watching for friendly faces. She came alongside us, and I saw the familiar dark hat at the wheel.

"Captain," I said to the officer.

"I'm only a lieutenant," he said, a bit shyly. His eyes were fixed on the other ship as the woman in the black coat and hat, the one who was said to have killed hundreds of his countrymen, climbed down into the longboat that would carry her to us.

"Lieutenant. Call your men to order. We are Redmerian. We will not cower."

He seemed to take strength from that and nodded, shouting more orders. The crew gathered on the deck, standing in neat rows. Their uniforms were faded, but they still looked very sharp, even if more than one of them carried terror on his face.

I stood in front of them, the lieutenant behind my shoulder like my chaperones had once done.

The black hat came first up the ladder, then the dark hair, then the sharp eyes and unsmiling face.

My heart dropped, and my throat grew tight, but I held myself in place and said, "Captain Cinder, we surrender."

Maro's mouth twisted as they said, "Your Highness. It's good to see you unharmed."

I nodded as if we'd rehearsed this, as if every part of my brain wasn't screaming to ask where Lou was. Why wasn't she here? Was she alive? With Kiril? On the *Siren*?

"We surrender," I said, my voice a little unsteady. "But please, let these men live and return to their families."

Maro strode along the deck as if they were considering my offer. "You seem to be short a man. Where is the prince?"

"He is dead," I said, ignoring the shocked murmurs behind me. "I killed him myself."

The murmurs grew, but Maro's gaze was sharp and approving. "That sounds like a bloody business."

"It wasn't," I said, a bit softly, and Maro's lips twisted into a wicked grin.

"So you surrender?" they asked.

I nodded, collecting myself, still ignoring the desperate impulse to ask about Lou. "Provided you let my men return home."

"I'll consider it. Please accept my hospitality. Come to the *Siren*. We can discuss the terms of your surrender and what it will cost you to keep these men safe."

My face screwed up. I went to protest before I realized what they were offering. *Come to the* Siren. Their stare was hard and intent, as though they were trying to tell me something. They'd had the same wordless conversations with Lou so many times.

Lou.

"Thank you, Captain. I would be pleased to accept your hospitality."

"Good. I'll leave a few of my men here to keep your crew in order."

They didn't need to do that. I didn't care what this crew did. My hope was, as soon as I was in the longboat, these poor souls would set sail and head straight home, where they could tell everyone they'd barely escaped the clutches of Captain Cinder. Perhaps they'd also talk of the princess who murdered the prince and exchanged herself for their safety, but that tale would be false. They would only ever know half the story.

Maro went to the rail, and I hurried after. They helped me down until my feet found the ladder.

"George, are you all right?" they asked, voice low.

"Fine." I was sure I looked anything but fine to her. "Where's—"

"Where's the prince?"

I nearly bit my tongue as they cut my question off, but I remembered that acknowledging they weren't the real Captain Cinder might not be the best course of action.

"He's in his cabin."

"Dead? Truly?"

I met their gaze. "Dead."

Their smile was wicked, and I glowed under their approval.

The trip on the longboat was a matter of a few oar strokes, and we were there. I climbed the ladder with trembling arms and legs, only to be dragged up the last few feet by hands the size of dinner plates and crushed into Ender's chest with a massive hug.

"Hello, Princess," he said, voice rumbling in my ear.

"I'm not a princess," I said as best I could with my mouth crushed into his shirt. But I might be a princess after all. Was a forced wedding in a hidden pirate fortress enough for me to take the title?

"George!" I was pulled from Ender so forcefully I could only expect another giant, but instead it was Rosie, who hugged me even tighter than Ender had. My bones creaked, but I only pulled her in harder, gasping and laughing.

"You came for me," I said.

"Of course we did." She lifted her head so we could see each other, and her eyes widened. "Oh, George! What happened to you? Did he hurt you? Where's the prince?"

It had seemed relatively easy. Kneeling over him, listening as his body had struggled to stay alive, even sleeping in the same room with him, had hardly made a mark on my conscience. But looking into my best friend's eyes and telling her the truth...

"I killed him."

Rosie's mouth fell open, but before I could say anything else, she threw herself onto me again. "Of course you did. You've always been so brave. Of course you killed him."

"Princess!" Maro snapped. Rosie and I leaped apart, and Maro looked between us, clearly annoyed. "Your men are watching."

Onboard the other ship, several sailors stood on the rail, faces turned to the *Siren*. No doubt me falling into a joyful reunion with the pirates who walked their nightmares wouldn't earn me much credibility in their eyes.

"Apologies," I said, bouncing with a curtsy.

"You're such a mess," Rosie said, plucking at my skirt. "We need to clean you up. Is your head all right? Is that your blood?"

"Perhaps we could take this inside? To the captain's cabin?" Maro glanced at us meaningfully.

"The captain's cabin," I said softly, as if the Redmerian sailors were able to hear me as well as see me. "Is the captain . . . there?"

Maro stepped aside, holding one arm out to the *Siren*'s stern. "After you, Your Highness."

I did my best not to run.

She wasn't in the main cabin, and for a minute, my heart sank. But the door to the small rear cabin was open, and a light flickered inside, like someone had lit a lantern. I rushed through the small door.

"Lou?"

She seemed so small lying in the bed we'd shared two nights earlier. Her face was pale, and the old quilt was pulled to her shoulders, while the doctor sat at her side.

"Lou?" I dropped to my knees beside her, finding her hand under the blankets. Her skin was cool, but her fingers wrapped around mine as I squeezed them.

"She's alive," the doctor said in his croaky voice. "I've given her something to sleep. She had a rough go of it yesterday but wouldn't settle long enough for us to stitch her up."

I grinned through my tears. I didn't know how they'd all come back on the ship, but I could only imagine Lou barking orders, driving her crew after the prince with a knife wound slowly seeping away her guts.

"Will she be all right?" I asked.

"Georgie?" Her voice was thin, so at odds with the clipped assurance she'd always carried before. Her eyes were half-open. I gasped and cried, kissing her knuckles.

"Yes. Yes, I'm here."

Her smile was drowsy. "I told you we'd be together."

Her features relaxed again. I watched the quilt a long time, marking the steady rise and fall of her breath to reassure myself that she was alive.

The doctor's shaky hand fell on my shoulder. "Let's take you down to the infirmary and look at that wound on your head."

I wanted to tell him I was fine, that I would stay with Lou, but I was dirty and quite smelly at best, and the cut on my head throbbed forcefully.

"You won't be putting any of that foul paste on it," I said as I followed him. "It'll heal fine on its own."

Once the wound had been cleaned, he had Maro stitch me up, sparing me from his shaking hands. The stitching was almost as painful as the cut itself, but the doctor said a pretty face like mine shouldn't be ruined with the scar the wound would leave if it wasn't closed properly.

"What should we do with your sailors?" Maro asked as they worked.

"Send them home. They won't cause you any trouble."

They laughed. "They won't. They're boys, all of them. Even the one in charge can't be more than nineteen. What sort of navy is your prince running?"

I was already still under their needle, but at the mention of the prince, I might as well have turned to marble.

Maro's hands stayed steady and their voice turned conversational as they sewed me back together. "I sent a man to his cabin." They tsked. "Suffocation is risky. It takes time, and when the opponent is larger than you, you have every chance of failure."

"He drank himself to sleep first. I thought that worked to my advantage."

They snorted. "Did he think that little of you?"

"I think he assumed because he'd left me no knife and I was on a ship full of men, I had no hope of doing anything but what he said."

They nodded, setting the needle and thread aside. "What do you want done with the body? We can send it back to Redmere."

I shook my head. "Toss him overboard. He doesn't deserve any sort of recognition or funeral. The sailors will tell everyone what happened. They don't need to see the body."

Maro arched an eyebrow. "They might say he was murdered by pirates."

"Does it matter to you if they did?"

"I suspect Lou's plan was to storm the ship once we caught up, chop off his head, and feed him to the sharks in tiny pieces. So only your efficiency stopped 'death by pirate' from being the truth."

I laughed. "But you're not really pirates anymore."

"And are you a princess? We are both what the world sees and what we know ourselves to be. It's rare those two things are the same."

They brought clean clothes—simple trousers, a shirt that fit for once, a belt to hold it all together, and a scarf for my hair—and shipped me down to the mess. Rosie was waiting with a bowl of fish stew, and she hovered anxiously as I shoveled it into my mouth. I hadn't eaten since the day before and, faced with food—even fish stew—I was ravenous.

While I ate, Rosie told me about how, as she and Ender and Maro had rowed back up the river, they'd met with the *Siren's* other longboats—one full of crew members, the other loaded down with a cannon. She told about how they'd rowed the cannon right up to Kiril's fortress and opened fire.

"Maro said they'd always known Kiril was looking for a way to double-cross us, but they hadn't been able to convince Lou there was any other way to save you."

The longboat had sunk under the force of the blast, but the cannon had done its work, slowly crumbling the precarious structure's foundation.

"I saw you for a minute when we burst into the room," Rosie said, "but then the captain was stabbed and everything was chaos. When I looked up again, you were gone."

She told me about how Maro had slit Kiril's throat and how they'd barely managed to get Lou out, injured as she was, before the building collapsed.

"So, are you staying?" Rosie asked. She'd stopped pacing and was sitting across from me at the narrow table. I'd long since finished my meal, dragging my spoon around the bottom of the bowl.

"I think so," I said. "I could have returned to Redmere on the prince's ship. With him gone, I don't know what'll happen there. I could help. But . . ." I trailed off. With Lou injured and her self-sacrificing streak laid bare, I couldn't leave her. I would never lose sleep over what I'd done to the prince. But if I thought for one moment that Lou was in harm's way and I had no means of protecting her, I would never sleep again, and I'd been tired for a very long time.

―――

THE SUN WAS low on the horizon. I was coming down from my watch on the mast when I found Lou leaning against the rail. Someone must have helped her out from the cabin, but the sight of her, upright and alive, was enough to make me burst.

She scowled at the stitches on my forehead. When she

touched it, she winced and let her arm drop, wrapping her other hand around her middle.

"You should be in bed," I said.

"You sound like Maro," she said, gaze turning to the ocean.

"They're a very sensible person."

"I'll make you a deal," Lou said.

"What's that?"

"If you don't berate me for getting myself stabbed, then I won't tell everyone about the time you named your pony Sir Chester Ponington and promptly got thrown into a mud puddle the first time you rode him."

That seemed like a fair trade. Chester had not been one of my finer childhood moments. "What will you give me if I don't berate you for trying to trade yourself to a murderer for my freedom?"

She was silent for a moment, then eased herself slowly around so she could face me. Lou reached for my fingers, tangling them with hers. "What do you want?"

"You," I said, without hesitation. "Wherever I go, you come with me. It's the only way I can keep you alive."

Her thumb brushed over my knuckles. Her eyes were like the ocean around us as she looked up at me. "I will never be parted from you again."

"Good."

I had to be gentle as I approached her, conscious of her healing wound. Still, our kiss lasted so long that a laughing whistle and a few hoots sounded from somewhere above us—and then I kissed her a little longer, because I didn't care. Let them watch.

"You heard about the prince?" I asked eventually.

Lou nodded. "Maro told me. Suffocation is—"

"Not the most direct approach, I know."

The sun sank lower. Above us, the first stars appeared.

"You could be queen now," Lou said. "You were married to the prince."

"For six hours." I laughed. "Then I murdered him."

She shrugged, a little lopsidedly. "You wouldn't be the first monarch to ascend the throne that way. But what matters is what you would do after your ascension."

"I'm not—" I bit my lip. We could go home. Both of us. But I would be a queen now, not a spy. If the prince was dead, what would the resistance look like? I didn't know what place there was for me. "I'm not sure."

"Or," Lou said, grimacing as she stepped closer so our shoulders touched, "you could stay on the *Siren*. I can't promise the glamour and jewels of a crown, but we do good work here. You could help a lot of people."

The horizon went from orange and purple to endless, inky black, studded with a million tiny diamonds.

"You'll stay with me? Regardless of what I choose?" I asked.

Lou's body may have been weakened, but her voice was all warm strength as we scanned the sky for possibilities.

"To the end of the world."

ACKNOWLEDGMENTS

When I set out in these uncharted waters, I had no idea what a voyage I was undertaking. So many people have heard me talk about "the pirates," and this book would be incomplete without thanking at least a few of them.

Britt Smith and the 2018 Rising Tides crew were the first to hear bits of this story, and they were excited for George and Lou's adventure even before I fully knew where that adventure would take them.

Beta readers often see the rough cut, and this was one of the roughest. Tanya, Sam, and Lisa, thanks for soldiering through. Kelly, thanks for telling me even the grizzly bits were awesome.

And finally, to the professionals who make me look like a professional too. Cate Ashwood's amazing cover brought tears to my eyes. Manuela Velasco, Adam Mongaya, D. Ann Williams, I'm convinced editors and proofreaders are wizards, and you are doing an amazing job of supporting my case.

ABOUT THE AUTHOR

Whether she knew it then or not, Alli Temple has been a writer since the second grade, when she wrote a short story about a girl and her horse. Her grandmother typed it out for her and said she'd never seen so many quotation marks from a seven-year-old before. Alli took that as a challenge and has tried to break that record in all the stories she's taken on since then. It's good to have goals, right?

Alli lives in Toronto with her very patient husband and a growing pack of rescue pets. She tries to split her time between writing, community theatre stage management, and traveling anywhere that has good wine. Tragically, this leaves no time to clean the house.

CONTEMPORARY ROMANCES BY ALLISON TEMPLE

Out & About

Work-Love Balance

Honeymoon Sweet

The Seacroft Series

Top Shelf

Cold Pressed

Hot Potato

Shared Series

Puppuccino (part of Bold Brew)

Destination Bedding (part of Summit Springs)

Standalone

The Neighbourly Thing

Up North

Boyfriend With Benefits

The Pick Up

LGBTQ+ FANTASY BY ALLI TEMPLE

The Pirate & Her Princess
>Uncharted
>Unbroken
>Unleashed

Milton Keynes UK
Ingram Content Group UK Ltd.
UKHW040728241124
3085UKWH00040B/261